"I never pegged you for an easy kill," I told him. Which was true. The reports of his death two years ago had actually surprised me more than his reappearance just now.

"It wasn't planned to fool anyone with a modicum of intelligence. But tell me the news of my passing pained you, and I'll do my best to assuage your fears."

Patches of light and shadow moved over his face. Sullivan's profile had always been strong, aristocratic, dominating the Imperial police bulletins and Fleet patrol advisories. But he'd aged since I last saw him, about six months before his highly publicized demise. The thick, short-cropped black hair was sprinkled with silver. The dark eyes had more lines at the corners. The mouth still claimed its share of arrogance, though—as if he knew he'd always be one handsome bastard.

All the more reason to ignore his attempt at taunting me. "What do you want, Sully?"

"You, my lovely angel—and no, don't look so skeptical. Though I may be a veritable walking list of negative personality traits, the one thing I am not, and never have been, is a liar. So if I say you're lovely—" He reached for my chin with his fingertips. I jerked back and almost fell off my log.

"Don't tumble for me yet, darlin'." He laughed. "We have business to attend to first. Death has afforded me a new perspective. A new maturity, if you will. While my goals haven't changed, my methodology has. That's where you come in."

"A mere captain of a peashooter squadron?"

"That's Fleet's appraisal of your talents. Not mine."

"No, you always called me an interfering bitch."

"If you must quote me, please be accurate. A beautiful, interfering bitch. And now that I find I'm in need of one particular beautiful interfering bitch, I can't think of one better. So tell me, my angel, are you ready to leave this veritable paradise and make a pact with the ghost from Hell?"

ALSO BY LINNEA SINCLAIR

Finders Keepers

GABRIEL'S GHOST

LINNEA SINCLAIR

BANTAM BOOKS

GABRIEL'S GHOST
A Bantam Spectra Book / November 2005

Published by
Bantam Dell
A Division of Random House, Inc.
New York, New York

All rights reserved
Copyright © 2005 by Linnea Sinclair
Cover illustration copyright © 2005 by Dave Seeley
Cover design by Jamie S. Warren Youll

Bantam Books, the rooster colophon, Spectra, and the portrayal
of a boxed "s" are trademarks of Random House, Inc.

ISBN 0-553-58797-8

Printed in the United States of America
Published simultaneously in Canada

www.bantamdell.com

OPM 10 9 8 7 6 5 4

WITH THANKS TO:

To Rob Bernadino, husband of infinite patience who believes in me;

To Kristin Nelson, agent extraordinaire and her wonder dog, Chutney;

To Anne Groell, my editor, for being sharp-eyed and soft-hearted;

To my wonderful crit partners: Nancy Gramm, Darlene Palenik, and "Commander" Carla Arpin, who threatened me with bodily harm should anything happen to a certain secondary character in this book;

To the Neopia Avenue Elite—the best adult guild in Neopets—and especially to Karen (Tamlara) James, for keeping me sane (hah!) through edits; and

To my feline duo: Daiquiri and Miss Doozer, thanks FUR all your help.

GABRIEL'S GHOST

Only fools boast they have no fears. I thought of that as I pulled the blade of my dagger from the Takan guard's throat, my hand shaking, my heart pounding in my ears, my skin cold from more than just the chill in the air. The last rays of light from the setting sun filtered through the tall trees around me. It flickered briefly on the dark gold blood that bubbled from the wound, staining the Taka's coarse fur. I felt a sliminess between my fingers and saw that same ochre stain on my skin.

"Shit!" I jerked my hand back. My dagger tumbled to the rock-strewn ground. A stupid reaction for someone with my training. It wasn't as if I'd never killed another sentient being before, but it had been more than five years. And then, at least, it had carried the respectable label of military action.

This time it was pure survival.

It took me a few minutes to find my blade wedged in between the moss-covered rocks. After more than a decade on interstellar patrol ships, my eyes had problems adjusting to variations in natural light. Shades of grays and greens, muddied by Moabar's twilight sky, merged into seamless shadows. I'd never have found my only weapon if I hadn't pricked my fingers on the point. Red human blood mingled with Takan gold. I wiped the blade against my pants before letting it mold itself back around my wrist. It flowed into the form of a simple silver bracelet.

"A Grizni dagger, is it?"

I spun into a half crouch, my right hand grasping the bracelet. Quickly it uncoiled again—almost as quickly as I'd sucked in a harsh, rasping breath. The distinctly masculine voice had come from the thick stand of trees in front of me. But in the few seconds it took me to straighten, he could be anywhere. It looked like tonight's agenda held a second attempt at rape and murder. Or completion of the first. That would make more sense. Takan violence against humans was rare enough that the guard's aggression had taken me—almost—by surprise. But if a human prison official had ordered him . . . that, given Moabar's reputation, would fit only too well.

I tuned out my own breathing. Instead, I listened to the hushed rustle of the thick forest around me and, farther away, the guttural roar of a shuttle departing the prison's spaceport. I watched for movement. Murky shadows, black-edged yet ill defined, taunted me. I'd have sold my soul then and there for a nightscope and a fully charged laser pistol.

But I had neither of those. Just a sloppily manipulated court martial and a life sentence without parole. And, of course, a smuggled Grizni dagger that the Takan guard had discovered a bit too late to report.

My newest assailant, unfortunately, was already forewarned.

"Let's not cause any more trouble, okay?" My voice

sounded thin in the encroaching darkness. I wondered what had happened to that "tone of command" Fleet regs had insisted we adopt. It had obviously taken one look at the harsh prison world of Moabar and decided it preferred to reside elsewhere. I didn't blame it. I only wished I had the same choice.

I drew a deep breath. "If I'm on your grid, I'm leaving. Wasn't my intention to be here," I added, feeling that was probably the understatement of the century. "And if he," I said with a nod to the large body sprawled to my right, "was your partner, then I'm sorry. But I wasn't in the mood."

A brittle snap started my heart pounding again. My hand felt as slick against the smooth metal of the dagger as if the Taka's blood still ran down its surface. The sound was on my right, beyond where the Taka lay. Only a fool would try to take me over the lifeless barrier at my feet.

The first of Moabar's three moons had risen in the hazy night sky. I glimpsed a flicker of movement, then saw him step out of the shadows just as the clouds cleared away from the moon. His face was hidden, distorted. But I clearly saw the distinct shape of a short-barreled rifle propped against his shoulder. That, and the fact that he appeared humanoid, told me he wasn't a prison guard. Energy weapons were banned on Moabar. Most of the eight-foot-tall Takas didn't need them, anyway.

The man before me was tall, but not eight feet. Nor did his dark jacket glisten with official prison insignia. Another con, then. Possession of the rifle meant he had off-world sources.

I took a step back as he approached. His pace was casual, as if he were just taking his gun out for a moon-lit stroll. He prodded the dead guard with the tip of the rifle, then squatted down and ran one hand over the guard's work vest as if checking for a weapon, or perhaps life signs. I could have told him the guard had neither. "Perhaps I should've warned him about you," he said, rising. "Captain Chasidah Bergren. Pride of the Sixth Fleet. One dangerous woman. But, oh, I forgot. You're not a captain anymore."

With a chill I recognized the mocking tone, the cultured voice. And suddenly the dead guard and the rifle were the least of my problems. I breathed a name in disbelief. "Sullivan! This is impossible. You're dead—"

"Well, if I'm dead, then so are you." His mirthless laugh was as soft as footsteps on a grave. "Welcome to Hell, Captain. Welcome to Hell."

We found two fallen trees, hunkered down, and stared at each other, each waiting for the other to make a move. It was just like old times. Except there was the harsh glow of his lightbar between us, not the blackness of space.

"I never pegged you for an easy kill," I told him. Which was true. The reports of his death two years ago had actually surprised me more than his reappearance just now. I balanced the dagger in my hand, not yet content to let it wrap itself around my wrist. "When I heard what happened at Garno, I didn't buy it." I shrugged and pushed aside what else I'd thought, and felt, when I'd heard the news. My feelings about the death of a known mercenary and smuggler mattered little anymore.

He seemed to hear my unspoken comment. "It wasn't planned to fool anyone with a modicum of intelligence. Only the government. And, of course, their newshounds. But tell me the news of my passing pained you," he continued, dropping his voice to a well-remembered low rumble, "and I'll do my best to assuage your fears."

A muted boom sounded in the distance, rattling through the forest. Another shuttle arriving, breaking the sound barrier on descent. He turned toward it, so I was spared answering what I knew to be a jibe. Regardless, I had no intention of telling him about my pain.

Patches of light and shadow moved over his face. Sullivan's profile had always been strong, aristocratic, dominating the Imperial police bulletins and Fleet patrol advisories. He had his father's lean jawline, his mother's thick dark hair. Both were more than famous in their own right, but not for the same reasons as Sully. They'd been members of the Empire's elite; he was simply elusive.

The lightbar reached full power. It was almost like shiplight, crisp and clear. He turned back to me, his lips curved in a wry smile, as if he knew I'd been studying him.

He'd aged since I last saw him, about six months before his highly publicized demise. The thick, short-cropped black hair was sprinkled with silver. The dark eyes had more lines at the corners. The mouth still claimed its share of arrogance, though—as if he knew he'd always be one handsome bastard.

All the more reason to ignore his attempt at taunting me. His existence had been far more troublesome to me than his purported passing. "What went down on Garno? You cut a deal?" Moabar or death had been offered to a lot of people, but not to me. Most chose death. I hadn't had that luxury.

He snorted and raised the rifle almost to my nose. "What's this look like? How long have you been here, three weeks?"

I knew what it was. Illegal. Damn difficult to come

by. A rifle didn't wrap around your wrist like my dagger, or fit in the sole of a boot.

A thought chilled me. Maybe the Taka weren't the only guards the prison authorities used.

"Yeah, three weeks, two days, and seventeen hours. Time flies, you know." I held his gaze evenly. His eyes were dark, like pieces of obsidian, unreadable. "That's a Norlack 473 rifle. Sniper model. Modified, it appears, to handle illegal wide-load slash charges."

He laughed. "On point as ever, Bergren. Dedicated captain of a peashooter squad out in no-man's land. Keeping those freighters safe from dangerous pirates like me. And even when they damn you and ship you here, every inch of you still belongs to Fleet Ops." He shook his head. "Your mama wore army boots, and so do you."

"What do you want, Sully?" I jerked my chin toward the dead Taka. "You cleaning up after him? Or finishing what he didn't?"

He turned the rifle in his hands. "This isn't prison stock. This is contraband, wasn't that how your orders phrased it? Stolen. Modified." He paused and pinned me intently with his obsidian gaze. "Mine."

We'd had conversations like this before—me, on the bridge of my small patrol ship. He'd be on the bridge of the *Boru Karn,* his pilot and bridge crew flickering in and out of the shadows behind him. He rarely answered anything directly. He threw words at you, phrases, like hints to a puzzle he'd taunt you to solve. Or like free-form poetry, the kind that always sounded better after a few beers. He loved to play with words.

I didn't. "Okay. So no deal was cut and you're not working for the Ministry of Corrections. Don't tell me you've added Moabar to your vacation plans?"

He laughed again, more easily this time. But not easily enough for me to put my dagger back around my wrist.

"A resort for the suicidal but faint of heart? Don't bother to slit your own throat, we'll do it for you." He gestured theatrically. "If I couldn't market it, hell, no one could."

"Not a lot of repeat business."

"Ah, but that is the operative word. Business."

"Is it? What are you funding here, prison breaks?" If he wasn't with the MOC, then he had to be working against them. But I'd never heard of any successful escapes from Moabar. There was no formal prison, per se. Just an inhospitable, barely habitable world of long frigid winters that brought airborne viruses, and bleak, chilled summers. Like now. I was lucky my sentence started when it did. I'd have time to acclimate. Others, dumped dirtside in the midst of a blizzard, often died within hours.

"If I'm funding anything, it's freedom for a cause. I've found, since my untimely but useful demise, that this place can provide me with a source of cheap, willing labor."

"*Willing* being the operative word, I take it?"

"*Willing* being the operative word, yes."

"Doing what?" I knew many of Sully's operations before Garno: stolen cargo, weapons, illegal drugs, ships, and everything that fell in between. I just couldn't see why he'd chosen to seek me out. Unless he'd lost his pilot, needed someone to captain a ship for him. But why come to me? He could have his pick from those who lined the barstools in any spaceport pub.

But then, I'd ignored his all-important earlier comment: my mother wore army boots.

"You know the system," he told me. "You were raised in it. As were your parents, and your parents' parents.

Captain Chasidah 'Chaz' Bergren. Daughter of Engineering Specialist Amaris Deirdre Bergren and Lieutenant Commander Lars Bergren. Sister of Commander Thaddeus Bergren, currently second in command at the Marker Shipyards. Granddaughter of Lieutenant—"

"I know who I am."

"So do I."

"Good. Then you know my mother's been dead for almost twenty years. I haven't spoken to my father in over ten. And my brother, since the trial, won't permit my name to be mentioned within earshot. What's the point?"

"The point, my lovely angel—and no, don't look so skeptical. Though I may be a veritable walking list of negative personality traits, the one thing I am not, and never have been, is a liar. It's my great downfall, Chaz. So if I say you're lovely—" He reached for my chin with his fingertips. I jerked back, almost fell off my log, and had to drag my boot heel in the dirt to keep my balance.

"Don't tumble for me yet, darlin'." He laughed. "We have business to attend to first. As I was saying, death has afforded me a new perspective. A new maturity, if you will. While my goals haven't changed, my methodology has. That's where you come in."

"A mere captain of a peashooter squadron?"

"That's Fleet's appraisal of your talents. Not mine."

"No, you always called me an interfering bitch."

"If you must quote me, please be accurate. A beautiful, interfering bitch. And now that I find I'm in need of one particular beautiful, interfering bitch, I can't think of one better. So tell me, my angel, are you ready to leave this veritable paradise and make a pact with the ghost from Hell?"

I turned the dagger in my hand, watched the light play over the blade. I'd been willing to sell my soul earlier for a nightscope and a laser pistol. On Moabar, that would guarantee survival. But Sully was offering me more. He was offering me a way off Moabar. Freedom. On Hell's terms, but freedom nonetheless.

I nodded, stuck my hand out. "Officers' agreement."

He clasped my hand firmly, then went down on one knee and brought it to his lips.

I pulled my fingers away from his mouth, angry at the invisible firemoths that seemed to dance across my skin at his touch. "This is a business deal, Sullivan."

He sat back on his heel, grinning. "Whatever you say."

"Damn straight." I pushed myself to my feet, transferred the dagger to my right hand, and started to let it wrap around my left wrist. Then stopped. He'd retrieved the rifle and now stood towering over me, his dark eyes glinting brightly from the lightbar in his hand.

I let my fingers close around the hilt of the dagger, kept it between us as I followed him into the forest. Maybe I'd hold on to it this way for a while. Just in case my ghost's good humor dissolved like mist from the moons.

Sully tabbed the lightbar down to half power, just enough to guide us over fallen logs and rock-filled ditches. He held it low, our bodies blocking its telltale glow. I lengthened my strides to match his.

The only sounds were our footsteps crunching against the carpet of brittle twigs, the occasional slap of a branch against our dark jackets.

We slipped like shadows between the shaggy trees. It was as if I were twenty-two years old again, back in basic training, on a dirtside recon exercise. Sully moved that way too, with a cautious grace. A bright patch of moonlight cascaded through an opening in the forest canopy. As one, we edged around it.

I caught a wry half smile on his face. He angled his mouth down to my ear, echoing my thoughts. "Feels like boot camp."

I couldn't remember any stint in the military on his dossier. I was about to ask where he'd trained when something glinted ahead of us, far off to the right.

Instinctively I flattened against a tree. My fingers tightened on the dagger. The lightbar blinked out as my heart rate picked up. Then my face was in Sully's chest. I flinched back, surprised not only by his action but by a rush of heat. Then it was gone and I tagged it as nothing more than adrenaline fighting against a severe lack of sleep. He pushed me to my knees, crouched down with me. He flicked the safety off the rifle, angled it up.

His left hand cupped the back of my head, drew my face against his shoulder again. "Damned redhead," he whispered. "You glow like a jumpgate beacon. Now, hush. Be still for a moment."

A rush of wind rattled the leaves around us. I ducked my head further down, even though I knew my hair wasn't that red. It was dark auburn and, after three weeks on Moabar, far from glowing. I doubted the color was Sully's real reason, anyway. I didn't know if there was something out there he didn't want me to see, or if he was simply feeding his ego by playing hero. Either way, I wasn't about to argue. My strange light-headedness had returned. I needed a moment to steady myself, find focus.

His breathing was deep and even. He turned away from me, his gaze locked on something on the right. As I was hunkered down between him and the large tree, I could only see the outline of his hand on the rifle and the dark, skewed shadows of the forest floor.

"What is it?" I asked as quietly as I could. His fingers threaded into my braid as if he wanted to unravel it. Or, I realized with a blinding flash of stupidity, as if he searched for a way to get a strong and painful grip on me.

I remembered what had been on that Takan guard's agenda and tried to jerk my head back. Then I heard it.

A wheezing noise. A crackling. The sound that tissue paper would make if it were composed of glass. And another rush of wind, air pushing past me.

My mouth suddenly went dry.

Sully shifted his weight, brought the rifle up to eye level. The faint greenish glow of the nightscope reflected back on his face.

The crackling stopped.

I smelled something foul. My stomach clenched in response. A jukor. A vicious, fanged mutant beast with the distinctive scent of rotting garbage. A breeding experiment by the MOC, jukors were a distorted, hideous version of the imaginary soul-stealers. They'd been bred to combat the very real telepathic Stolorth *Ragkirils*. The government halted the jukor experiment ten years ago, when it had become apparent the creatures couldn't be controlled. Not like Takas.

I knew the smell because I'd had escort duty with a ship hauling a pack of jukors to be destroyed. It was a smell I'd never forget.

It was one I knew I shouldn't be remembering now.

A long wheeze, closer. My heart thudded at the sound. It was scenting for something. Us, most likely. Or its mate. If it chose us as prey, its powerful hind legs and winged upper arms would make it damned near impossible to evade.

If it was scenting for a mate, it would kill any other creature in its path in its lust.

A frightening thought. If it *was* scenting for a mate, that meant jukors were alive, breeding again, for MOC purposes. Perhaps even new and improved—jukors now resistant to the virus that condemned them to eight-month life spans?

Either way, we were dead unless Sully killed it first. My dagger would barely be able to pierce its hide.

Fingers tugged at my scalp. He *was* unraveling my braid. I mentally questioned my ghost's sanity and jerked my head away, frowning.

He yanked it back. His breath was hot against my ear. "Your hair wrap. I need it. Now."

I swore silently, slapped the dagger back around my wrist, then unraveled the leather and fabric laces. My hair fell almost to my waist, drifting over my arms as I shoved the cords into his outstretched hand. My mind still questioned his sanity.

He thrust the rifle at me. "Keep a lock on it."

As I brought the nightscope to my eye, I caught a glimpse of Sully grabbing a stout, broken tree limb from the ground.

Two moons dotted the night sky, adding their light. The jagged form of the jukor almost jumped through the eyepiece at me. It was twenty-five feet from us. Upwind. Its long snout moved slowly side to side. I heard the crackling again as it flexed one wing. Barbed tips, like tiny razors, glinted sharp and cruel.

Its lower arms and legs were furred. A hide formed of rock-hard scales covered its chest and back. Only the base of its throat was vulnerable. A soft spot, unprotected.

Damned small.

I moved the rifle slightly as it moved its head.

Sully's hand covered mine, traded rifle for a leather-and-fabric-wrapped tree branch.

"It will see it, scent it." He put the eyepiece to his eye again, the greenish glow like a small alien moon on his face.

I understood. The leather and fabric held my scent.

"Beer toss," he said.

I understood that too. Wasn't a station brat in civilized space who didn't. Old pub game.

"On three." He adjusted his balance slightly. He'd have to move the moment the jukor sprang.

"One." The word was a soft rustle of leaves.

I rose slowly, becoming part of the tree on my left.

"Two."

I started my windup.

"Three."

I hurled the branch high, arcing it upward in the clear moonlight. The dark form lunged. Powerful wings shot out, pushed downward. An unbearable stench rolled toward me just as three flashes of light erupted on my right.

Sully: springing, moving, firing.

The dagger snapped into my hand. If he missed, or only wounded it, it would be here in seconds.

A roaring sound. An enormous blot of darkness descending from the air at an unbelievable rate of speed. Wings beating, fingered forelimbs yanking itself through the trees at us.

Sully, firing. "Run!"

He hadn't hit the jukor's throat.

I bolted sideways, headed for the thickest brush, hoping it would snag a wing, entangle an arm.

Branches whipped at my face, but the only pounding footsteps I heard were mine.

I stopped, spun about. Saw Sully drop to the ground, roll, come up firing again as the jukor's barbed wing slashed inches from his body.

Shit! I plunged back through the trees just as the jukor roared and slammed Sully to the ground.

The hideous body of the jukor reared back, then flailed sideways. It landed almost at my feet, a tangle of wings and limbs. Its long head lolled to one side. In the bright light of the moons I could see a sizable hole in the charred flesh of its soft throat.

I heard Sully cough, gag. "Hell's ass! That thing stinks!"

I jumped over the beast's hindquarters, fell to my knees on the hard ground beside him. "You okay?"

He grasped my arm. I helped him into a sitting position. He was breathing hard. He wiped one hand over his face, then grimaced. No doubt the jukor's oily scent was on his skin as well.

"Hell's ass," he said again. The poet, never at a loss for words, repeating himself.

"You missed the first time."

He nodded, still gasping for air. "You noticed."

"I've never bagged one. Not even in the old sims." There were no jukors in the new training sims since there were, we were told, no living jukors. And why learn to kill something that no longer exists? We had to be content to hone our hand-to-hand combat skills on simmed mind-sucking Stolorths and giant Takas. Plus the usual crazed human scenarios.

Sully struggled to his feet. I grabbed his elbow, stood up with him. He leaned one hand on my shoulder for a moment. "This is not," he said, looking down at me, "a fortuitous turn of events."

"Maybe it's time you tell me what in hell is going on."

"I will. But I think it best we keep moving." He stepped back toward the barely discernible path we'd followed. Turned, probably because he didn't hear my footsteps.

I was wrestling to rebraid my thick, now totally disheveled hair. I hurried up to him, arms angled awkwardly behind my neck.

"I prefer it down." He reached to smooth the wild strands from my forehead. "I've told you that before. Remember?"

"Too bad." I ducked away. Yes, I remembered. Even though it'd been almost three years. I was glad he couldn't see the flush of color on my cheeks. I brought the braid over my shoulder, fished in my pants pocket for a small tie.

We picked up our pace. The moonlight was bright, the lightbar no longer needed. I kept a vigilant watch ahead, and to the left. Sully did the same, to the right. From behind we were vulnerable.

Nobody's perfect.

But that night, nearly three years ago, almost could have been. If Sully hadn't been perpetually on the wrong side of the law, if I hadn't been shaken back to my senses by my ship badge pinging an incoming transmit advisory that had interrupted kisses far more passionate than I'd ever experienced. It had left a lot of questions unanswered. But it had soothed a deep ache in my heart, if only for a little while.

It had been strictly a physical attraction, aided by one too many pitchers of the Empire's finest ale. But that night I'd desperately needed to know that I was attractive.

He'd confirmed that, in a dark little bar in Port Chalo where Fleet captains and known smugglers could leave their reputations and vocations outside the doors for a while. Then my ship badge had pinged, saving me from making a fool of myself. Doing yet another thing that would have shocked my ever-righteous brother.

Though not quite as much as the appearance of the jukor shocked me now. I shoved the troublesome memory away and returned to my habit of analyzing my situation, gathering facts. Sully hadn't been surprised by the creature's appearance. Had he heard that the Empire was resurrecting the project? That was one of the many questions plaguing my mind as we walked. Questions that had been stilled by a need for silence, for stealth.

But after Sully's firing of his rifle, any pretense of a silent approach on our part was just that: pretense. Plus, my need for answers was growing. "Where're we going?"

He pointed over the treetops, past the higher moon, into the star-filled sky. "Second star to the right—"

"—and straight on till morning? Yeah, I've heard that before. Lit of the Ancient Homeworlds 101. Where are we going, Sully?"

"Most immediately, to a secure dwelling within a fifteen-minute walk from the spaceport. Eventually, to the spaceport itself."

I threw him a questioning glance. "You are suicidal." The spaceport was MOC controlled. More Takas to

the square inch than anywhere else on Moabar, save perhaps for the temple on Solstice Day.

"Most definitely not. I assure you I have a lusty"—he
leered down at me—"interest in life."

The path curved, narrowing. We were shoulder to
shoulder, or rather, my shoulder to his arm. He smelled
more than faintly of jukor. "I hope this secure dwelling
of yours has a bathtub."

"That bad?"

"Unique."

"It has. As well as a change of clothing. Which is required for us to access the spaceport. Our shuttle leaves
in about two hours."

It occurred to me, not for the first time, that this
might be a setup. Sully could be an Imperial agent for
the MOC or any of the numerous ministries. They were
trapping me, testing me, baiting me. I couldn't figure a
reason, but then, I'd never known a government to require reasons.

On the other hand, there were far more politically important and dangerous prisoners on Moabar. I was a
mere pebble in the asteroid field of personalities on the
prison world.

It also occurred to me that my brother could've hired
Sully to kill me. Or to put me in a position where the
MOC would. That would nicely clear up the stain I'd
placed on the family name, a stain that rankled Thaddeus, though not Willym, my half brother. He was only
nine, still innocent of what it meant to be part of a military family.

Sully increased his pace. He seemed disinclined to
further conversation. That gave me time to think. When
we approached the edge of the forest, twenty minutes
later, my dagger was back in my hand. He kept just inside the line of trees, paralleling a narrow, graveled

road. Behind me, it went to the spaceport. Every few minutes, lights from the tower beacons strafed our path.

At a curve in the road, he took my arm, hesitating when he saw the dagger. "Still don't trust me, Chaz?"

"You noticed."

"Wait for the tower lights to pass again. We'll cross the road, pick up the path over there." He pointed to the thick trees. "I wish our nocturnal luminaries weren't so enthusiastic this evening. But then again, it is definitely romantic." He let his voice drop to a sexy drawl.

"Your fragrance, Sully. I can't tell you how it makes me feel."

He chuckled. The lights approached, flared. We ran just behind them.

The woods closed around us again. He resumed his dogged pace. I quickened my stride. "How are we getting on a shuttle? Without the MOC noticing us, that is."

"With MOC permission, of course."

And MOC rifles pointed at me as I tried to board? I grabbed a handful of his jacket with my left hand, yanked. "Damn it, Sullivan!"

He stumbled, stopped, and glared at me with obsidian eyes.

I glared back. "How much did Thad pay you?"

"Thad?"

"Thaddeus. Commander Thaddeus Bergren. Second in command at Marker. Firstborn of the Bergrens. What did he pay you to set me up?"

His gaze flicked down to the dagger I held between us. His rifle was slung over his back. Foolish move on his part. If he'd studied my dossier as he'd claimed, he knew I ranked consistently high in my division in small-weapon, hand-to-hand combat. And not just in sims. I didn't care that he was at least ten inches taller than me, outweighed me by probably eighty or more pounds. He'd have to swing the rifle around to flick off the safety, and then turn it on me. I'd have the dagger in his chest, or his throat, by then.

"Problems with sibling rivalry, Chaz?"

"Sullivan!" My warning tone was clear.

"Think, Chasidah Bergren. Who am I? Who is your esteemed brother? Spit-and-polish company man, all the way. I'm the antithesis. Even in the abstract we could not coexist. In the flesh, he resents my family's wealth where yours had none. I'm the wastrel. He finds that appalling." He shook his head. "I don't know which pains me more, my angel. That you think so little of me that you believe I'd accept employment as a common assassin, or that you see me not only to be a vulgar cad but one who'd work for your supercilious ass of a brother as well."

He'd obviously met Thad at some point. The description was accurate.

But he was right. Thad might wish me dead, daily, but there were light-years between him and Sully—in more ways than one. And I was on Moabar. That was the same as being dead. For Thad to have me killed would only be redundant.

I let go of his jacket. "I don't like walking into things blind. What you've told me so far sounds too easy. If getting off Moabar is as simple as a change of clothes and boarding the shuttle, why isn't everyone doing it?"

He grinned and, in spite of his pungent odor, still managed to exude a rakish charm. "Because they don't have me to help them. Come on. Drogue's waiting for us. And I've got to evict Ren from the bathtub."

Moabar hadn't always been a prison world. It was the only human-habitable world in Quadrant E-5—a region so remote it didn't even warrant a name, like the inner quadrants of Aldan or Baris. A region otherwise worthless to an Empire thriving on galactic trade and the conquest of neighboring systems.

History vids said Moabar had been acquired as the result of the spoils of victory. Reality said Moabar was part of the Empire because no one else wanted it.

The Empire tried colonizing it, farming it. But the soils that produced lush, thick forests in abandon were caustic to edible plants. They withered, died. Colonists fled.

A scientific research team moved in next. But the atmosphere corroded their equipment. And the winters brought a strange plague-virus. Most died. Those who could make it to the shuttles fled.

So the Empire decreed it a penal colony. Well-being of lifers was not their concern. Survival of one winter's frigid temperatures and plague-filled storms was luck. Survival of two was a miracle. Three guaranteed an immunity to the virus, but never the cold.

Yet Takas thrived on it. I thought of all this as I stared at the "secure dwelling." Sully's secret.

A Takan monastery.

The low, sprawling stone structure appeared suddenly as the forest thinned. Lights from the spaceport stroked its mottled surface, flared in its tall windows. We were closer to the port here than we were on the graveled road.

Englarian religious symbols were carved into the wood-planked gate, the arch-and-stave chiseled over the doorway. The Taka had had no religion until Jared Eng had preached to them, some three centuries past. We had vids on that too, in the academy's required Non-Human Cultures class.

I followed Sully through a back door that opened at

his code and stepped cautiously into a large communal room: a kitchen, replete with the aroma of a meal recently finished. Something tangy hung in the air. Three long wooden tables were on my left, with benches. One round table on my right, with six high-backed wooden chairs. Behind that, a long cooktop and the matte metallic doors that fronted most refrigeration units. A thick clear coating covered the flagstone floor. Our footsteps echoed to the high ceiling and left smudgy marks behind.

"Brother Sudral? That you?" A voice called out from a hallway adjacent to the kitchen.

"Aye," said Sully.

Brother Sudral? I shot him a glance. He winked.

A squat man, human, bustled through the arched doorway. Englarian monks were usually human, though I'd heard they recently accepted Takas to their ranks.

The man wore the traditional monk's garb of widelegged pants and high-necked overtunic in a coarse, grayish-tan fabric. Thick-soled brown boots explained his otherwise silent approach.

"Blessings of the hour, Guardian Drogue."

"Blessings of the hour upon you, Brother Sudral." Drogue steepled his hands in front of his face and bowed.

I'd seen Drogue before, once or twice. The rank of Guardian granted him access to all MOC buildings on Moabar, just as it would in any Imperial station or port. I remembered seeing his round, almost cherubic face when I'd picked up my allotted supplies—two blankets, a folder of ration chips, and the ubiquitous and useless pamphlet of MOC Rules and Regulations—when I'd arrived dirtside, and perhaps another time after that. But Englarian monks were the least of my concerns. Sanctioned by the Empire, they were in no position to make a difference in the life of a disgraced Fleet captain, wrongly convicted or not.

Drogue's bright-eyed gaze ran up and down my length, or lack thereof. "Captain Chasidah Bergren. Yes." He stuck out his hand.

I accepted it.

"You are well?" he asked.

I tried to place his accent. South system, Dafir. "All things considered, yes." Some of my wariness returned. The Englarians were invariably cooperative with the government. I still had visions of a firing squad as a reception committee, Sully's protestations notwithstanding.

"Considering we had an intimate encounter with a jukor." Sully clapped Drogue on the back, then held his arm near the man's nose.

Drogue's head jerked backward. "Praise the stars! Yet you live."

"I'm a stubborn son of a bitch. Where's Ren? Soaking?"

The bathtub. I remembered Sully's earlier comments. Could water immersion be a little-known Englarian ritual?

"He left the hydro not ten minutes ago. He should be down shortly. He knows time is a factor tonight."

Sully pushed up the sleeve of his black jacket, glanced at his wrist. "Hour forty-five. You'll be ready? I need to soak this stench off me first. Feed her some tea, will you?" He jerked his thumb at me.

His abrupt dismissal rankled. Especially as I'd been thinking so kindly of his kisses earlier. "Sullivan—"

If was as if he'd heard my thoughts. The fingers that moments ago pointed at me grabbed my hand. He planted a long kiss against the inside of my wrist before I could jerk back. "I won't be long, my angel. Every second we're apart pains me. I promise I'll return to your side with all due speed."

"You stink. Go wash."

"Come bathe me. The touch of your hands could restore my weakened form."

My hands wanted to smack him a good right cross on the side of his jaw. He appeared anything but weak. His wide shoulders filled out his jacket only too well. There were any number of derogatory appraisals of Gabriel Ross Sullivan over the years, but none of them ever suggested he was anything less than extremely pleasant to look at.

Why were all the handsome ones always such bastards?

I smiled at Drogue. "I'd love a cup of hot tea."

The short man grinned affably, motioned to the round table. "Sit, please! I will make a cup. I'm sure Ren will join us momentarily. You too, Brother Sudral, when you have finished your ablutions."

"Tea's about all we'll have time for." He strode for the arched doorway, turned. "She'll need more time than you think to get changed, Drogue. Likes to fuss with her hair. So get her moving, as soon as possible." His footsteps echoed down the hallway.

Kettle in hand, Drogue watched Sully's retreating form. I caught his eye before he turned back to the cooktop. "Would you please explain to me what's going on?"

He put the kettle on the thermal grid, tabbed it on. "Brother Sudral's said little?"

"Brother Sudral talks in circles."

"For security purposes, I'm sure. Should we be captured prior to departure, none of us would be able to place the mission at risk."

Mission? Involving Englarian monks and the ghost of

a poet turned mercenary? "You don't seem surprised we ran into a jukor."

He placed a steaming cup of fragrant tea in front of me. His smile was still pleasant, but something flickered in his eyes, something tense laced his words. "Little surprises me at my age, Captain."

He wasn't, in spite of his bald head, that old. Fifties at most. My father was older. "It's Chasidah. Or Chaz. And jukors were banned. Exterminated."

"I'm a theologian, not a scientist."

He was also frequently at the spaceport.

"You saw them off-load a shipment, didn't you?" Live cargo, other than prisoners, didn't come into Moabar. Someone would have noticed. It wasn't unlikely that it would be Drogue.

"Do you not like your tea?"

I hadn't sipped it. It didn't interest me as much as things I couldn't explain. Things that hinted of something gone more awry than my travesty of a court-martial for dereliction of duty in the face of a direct order. A dereliction that resulted in the deaths of fourteen officers and crew in the Imperial Sixth Fleet.

An order the court said I'd acknowledged, then ignored.

An order I swore on all I held holy I'd never received. My ship's logs showed otherwise. Forgery, the court said, was impossible.

As impossible as jukors prowling the forests of Moabar.

I sipped my tea, listened to my brain engage in a familiar litany. This was Moabar. Why should I give a damn what happened here? Jukors or Takas. Illegal or legal. If the Empire needed more devils for its Hell, this was the place to grow them. It wasn't my concern. I was neither scientist nor theologian. I was alive—praise the stars—and an hour from freedom.

"The tea's fine," I told Drogue. I meant it. Time to focus on what's now, not what should be. What could have been.

At a soft sound in the archway, I turned, expecting Sully.

For two seconds I froze in my seat. It was as if one of the old training sims had come, horribly, to life. The dagger snapped flat into my hand. My chair fell backward, crashed to the floor. I was almost to the door when Drogue's voice stopped me. "Leave now, Captain, and you will surely die."

"Chaz! He won't hurt you."

This time I did see Sully, freshly scrubbed, his hair still damp and glistening. And in a monk's uniform, its pale sandlike colors contrasting sharply with his dark hair and eyes.

His humanness contrasted sharply with the Stolorth filling the archway. Sully squeezed by the tall, humanoid form and strode toward me, hand outstretched.

I backed up a step. If he thought I'd give him my dagger he was wrong. Dead wrong. But I did take my hand off the door leading outside. I did lower the dagger. "Explain."

He stopped, two dagger lengths away, and glanced over his shoulder. The Stolorth hadn't moved, save to lean a little to its left on a cane it held in its six-fingered left hand.

His hand. The Stolorth was definitely male. Like Sully, he wore the pale sand-gray pants and tunic of a monk. But his biceps and thighs strained the fabric. He topped Sully's height by four, five inches.

He could almost pass for human, if you didn't see the gill slits on his neck. Could almost pass, if you didn't notice the thick silvery-blue hair plaited in a braid not unlike my own. Could almost pass, if you didn't see the webbing between the fingers.

Now I understood the role of the bathtub.

"I'm sorry." The Stolorth spoke. His voice was deep, surprisingly soft. In it, I heard waves echoing on a shore I'd never visited. "I thought she knew."

Sully had the good grace to look sheepish. "I was going to tell her. Then I fell asleep in the tub."

The Stolorth angled his face toward me. "Captain Bergren, it wasn't my intention to startle you."

Startle me? No, when a Stolorth *Ragkiril* was finished with a human mind, there was nothing left to startle. Nothing left at all.

Sully took a half step closer. I could smell the soap on his skin. A small drop of water lost its grasp on his tousled hair, made a rivulet around the edge of a thick eyebrow, and trickled down the right side of his face. "It's okay, Chaz. Trust me."

I could think of a dozen reasons not to. But reality dictated I had no choice, and nothing to go back to. If I died on Moabar, death would be slow and painful. At least with a Stolorth, he could plant pleasant memories as he ripped my mind to shreds.

"He's blind, Chaz. He can't hurt you."

Blind? "That's impossible. They kill their—" But even from across the kitchen I could see the film over his silver eyes, dulling them.

By all that was holy. A blind Stolorth in an Englarian monastery? And a full-grown male at that? We were told Stolorths killed defective young and weak elders. Blindness was especially heinous to them. Their telepathy—their *Ragkiril* mind talents—depended on eye contact with their victims. With their own kind, it was their primary means of communication.

I saw the cane, grasped by six fingers. And let the dagger wrap itself around my wrist. He couldn't hurt me. His own kind wanted him dead. Oddly, I felt a small pang of kinship with him. I knew what it was like to be rejected by people who were supposed to love you.

"We were just having a nice cup of tea." Drogue sounded immensely relieved. "Please, sit and join us?"

I noticed, not for the first time, the spotlessness of his kitchen. The blood bath I could have created would have been hell to clean up.

His name was Frayne Ackravaro Ren Elt. Sully performed the introduction. Ren was his birth name, Elt the name of his grandmother, Frayne, his mother, and Ackravaro, his clan-of-region.

He answered to Ren.

In spite of his size, and his blindness, he moved gracefully to the round table, selected a chair, and sat. Drogue handed out fresh cups of tea.

I sat across from him, with Sully on my left, and tried to make sense of this. I'd never known Englarians to associate with Stolorths. They were even more fanatically opposed to telepaths than the Empire was.

"Again, I apologize, Captain Bergren. I sensed no disquiet in your presence—"

"How can you sense if you're blind?" My caution resurfaced. My Non-Human Cultures class had been known to be wrong.

"My blindness negates those aspects you fear—my mind-speech with my people, as well as any threat you may feel I present to yours. But my empathic abilities remain."

"And are put to use through prayer and meditation,

as taught by Abbot Eng," Drogue added. "Brother Ren is a fine example of the results of studying the purity of thought. His blindness, through the grace of the abbot, has become a gift."

My academy class was very wrong. Englarians didn't view all Stolorths as soul-stealers. And blind Stolorths did survive to adulthood.

"So you sensed my presence? As what?"

"Human female, inquisitive variety." Sully raised his cup as if in mock salute. "Drink up. We have a shuttle to catch."

"We?" I wasn't questioning Sully's participation. I realized for the first time there were to be two more: Drogue and Ren. The latter still worried me, but I understood the pressures of a flight schedule.

"We." Sully laid a stack of ID cards on the table, spread them with the flair of a dealer in a casino.

Apt, I thought. We were placing bets with our lives.

Four cards, all bearing the crossed-arch symbol of the Englarian clergy. Drogue picked them up, one by one, and examined them.

I finished my tea and stood, damning Sully for not telling me of his plans.

Drogue ushered me to a back room, complete with a lavatory and a wide couch. A wooden-fronted closet was half open. Tan-gray tunics and robes filled it. I had a feeling I was to be Brother Chaz.

"We have you logged as Sister Berri." Drogue rifled through the closet, pulled out a cowled robe and shift-like gown, and held them up against me. If I had to run for it, I'd fall on my face. But other than that, it was fine.

"Your boots are fine," Drogue said as he left. "Leave your clothing on the couch and it will be sent with our luggage to the shuttle."

I found a wide-toothed comb on a dresser, ran it

briskly through my hair while I stood in front of a large mirror. The room stared back at me in reverse. The arched doorway was directly behind me. On one wall, there was a wooden replica of the arch-and-stave. On the other was an artist's rendering of Abbot Eng, stave raised, about to kill a soul-stealer. Eng had preached that soul-stealers encased their victims in a mind-numbing "unholy light." Only the Pure, trained in his church, could defeat them. The large painting was one of the more common depictions, showing the imaginary demon, half-human male, half beast. Its scaly skin was overlaid with a silvery glow; its wings were splayed wide. The winged man's mouth was open in a scream. Lovely decor.

The lavatory was small. I splashed water on my face, longing for a bath, but there was neither time nor inclination. I was traveling with a Stolorth, an aquatic humanoid that could gut a mind as easily as my dagger could gut a fish, with or without any unholy light. Things deep and watery were best avoided, for now.

I donned the shift, then the robe, and was securing the wide fabric belt when a knock sounded on the door.

"Come." It took me a moment to remember certain technologies couldn't exist on Moabar. I had to walk to the door and manually open it.

Sully was on the other side, grinning disarmingly. And no doubt was also impatient. I hadn't been ten minutes. "I'm ready."

He grabbed my shoulders, turned me around. I glimpsed something in his right hand. He waddle-marched me toward the long mirror on the wall.

"Not yet." He snatched the comb from the dresser on his right.

"What do you think you're—"

"Hush."

He sunk his hands into the long mass of hair I'd half-braided and tucked down the back of my robe. He began unraveling my braid. In the mirror I saw a length of corded leather, dotted with shiny silver beads, dangling from his fingers.

"We don't have time—"

"Hush!" His grin faded, his brows slanting down. Concentrating. Braiding my hair, weaving in the beads and leather.

Making amends for the hair wrap I'd tossed to the jukor? Or remembering that night in Port Chalo? I'm sure it had meant nothing to him. Or maybe he thought a few kisses had earned him the right to taunt me now.

I wasn't in the mood to be teased. "I can do that a lot faster than you."

"Hush, hush, hush." Softly. His voice was not much more than a deep rumble in his throat. His hands were firm, yet more gentle than I would have thought he could be. And warm. A whisper of soft heat played down my neck where his fingers brushed against my skin. I didn't pull away when they stroked my hair, my scalp, the back of my neck. Instead, I let myself sink into the sensations, bargaining with myself as I did so. What harm was there in letting him braid my hair for me?

My eyes wanted to close. I'd fought exhaustion for hours now. He was so warm. His knuckles brushed my jaw. Fingers traced my lips...

His intimate caress jolted my brain awake. I lurched forward, my hands splaying against the rough-hewn mirror frame. I caught a glimpse of his face, his obsidian eyes half-hooded, molten.

I felt my own face flame with heat. I didn't look in the mirror for fear of confronting a fool I knew only too well. I turned, my braid swinging heavily against my back. The beads on the leather cord tinkled lightly against the glass.

"Business deal, Sully. Strictly business." I sounded far more breathy than I wanted to.

He still watched me through hooded eyes, though the sensual curve on his lips was gone. We were almost toe-to-toe. But my hand already encircled the bracelet on my wrist, fingers on its spring points.

He let out a long, slow sigh. "Chasid—"

"Brother Sudral? Sister Berri?" Drogue rapped on the door and walked in, seeming totally oblivious to what was going on. Or else, with Sully, he was used to it. "We must be going."

Sully spun around, reached for the short, stocky man, and clapped him on the shoulder. "I was ready an hour ago. It's this one." He jerked his hand back in my direction, but didn't turn. "Has to fuss with her hair."

Why are all the handsome ones always such bastards?

We walked down the graveled road toward the spaceport, four robed figures of divergent sizes. An antigrav pallet with our meager luggage trailed behind.

Antigravs and thermal grids worked on Moabar. Autodoors, medistats, and a long list of other technological necessities didn't.

Humans fared only marginally better. Winter was approaching, with its recurring plague. Abbot Eng's followers were devoted, but not stupid.

"Our replacements will be already on station," Drogue told me as we walked in the bright moonlight. No need to hide, to dart though the trees. "They've shown an immunity to the plagues. They'll run the monastery, sit devotions with the Takas, lead the festivals until spring. I'll return then."

Sully had said we were going to Moabar Station to intercept an outgoing freighter, bound in-system. Step Two in freedom for Chasidah Bergren. But I had to live through Step One first.

"You're not coming in-system with us?"

"Oh, no, Sister. We have a very active temple on station. And it's Peyhar's Week, don't you know?" His round face poked out from under his hood. "Oh, perhaps not. We haven't quite made the inroads in our missionary work with the military as we have in other arenas."

As far as I knew, the Takas were the only ones they'd made inroads with. But I wasn't going to deflate his attempt at proselytizing.

"The MOC isn't going to question my presence in the group? Or Ren's?"

Another negative from Drogue. "Brother Ren Ackravaro has visited Moabar Monastery several times on retreat."

"But I haven't."

"Neither has the real Sister Berri. But her reputation will serve you well. She's a much-lauded missionary, known for her tireless works in the rim worlds. There's still much to be done there." If by "much to be done" he meant widespread poverty, he was correct. The Empire's rim had a long history of neglect. "Her ID—yours now—bears the arch-and-stave. As Guardian, I vouch for your veracity."

Why? What had caused this gentle man to align himself with the ghost from Hell? Was there a financial gain? "You're taking quite a risk."

He sighed. "More is at risk if I do not, Sister."

The mission. And Sullivan, a different kind of missionary.

"Brother Sudral is still being vague about that."

Sully fell into step with us. He'd lagged behind, talking to Ren, who walked with one hand on the pallet, the other on his cane. "For good reason. Curiosity tends to be an overrated trait. I'm sure the Empire taught you that at some point. At the moment, your overwhelming gratitude toward me is best expressed through silence. There's nothing you can contribute at this point, but there's much to be lost by being premature."

His sudden formal phrasing irked me. Sully the mercenary. Sully the poet. And now, Sully the pedant. "I'm glad to know you think so highly of me."

He slanted me a glance. "Highly enough to risk my life to save yours. I was outvoted, you know. Fortunately I rarely listen to my advisers."

"Really? I'd never have guessed." Nor could I picture him having advisers. In all the years I'd known him, he'd always been the one in command, pilots and techs following his orders.

Sully dropped back, picked up his conversation with the Stolorth.

Drogue and I walked on in silence. We were close enough to the spaceport that I could hear the distant clank and clatter from the cargo hangars, the occasional shout of human voices, the rougher call of the Takan guards. It was a chilly night when we started, but now my body felt warm under the robes. I could feel small wisps of hair starting to curl around my face.

Thoughts, equally as annoying, coiled and uncoiled in my mind. *You know the system,* Sully had said, sitting across from me in the clearing, lightbar between us and a dead Taka at his back. Therefore he needed access to military information, military procedures. He'd recited my pedigree.

Access to military personnel.

Why? My simplistic early assumptions revolved

around money, even a heist of a Fleet payroll ship. That would be a way to divert funds to the rim worlds, and the church could be the perfect cover for getting it there. Then I saw Ren.

During the Boundary Wars, twenty years ago, Stolorth *Ragkirils* had excelled at interrogating prisoners. Torturing them, before the Baris Human Rights Accord had made such methods illegal. I'd seen vids on the results of their handiwork. Or mind work, actually. That's why seeing one on Moabar so frightened me. Perhaps the Empire had finally realized that more than inmates died on this prison world. Their secrets, coconspirators, sources, died with them as well. A Stolorth *Ragkiril,* well placed, could extract information that would elude even the best detectives. And on Moabar, there were no prisoners' rights offices with which to file a complaint.

Reason, and a Non-Human Cultures class I was beginning to doubt, told me a Stolorth wouldn't adapt well to Moabar's climate. And the ponds here were all poisonous. At least, poisonous to humans.

Ren might not belong here, but the jukor fit only too well. The Stolorth would best survive on Moabar Station, providing there were no others of his kind. Because a Stolorth *Ragkiril,* sensing Ren's handicap, would be duty-bound to kill him. That much I did believe, Non-Human Cultures class and all.

We were near the main gate. Drogue touched my arm, passed me the slim ID card. I tucked it into the slit in the front of my belt.

"And your name, Sister?" he prompted.

"Berri Solaria, Sister of Mercy in the Order of Abbot Eng the Merciful." I rattled off my ID number, my home convent, and the date of my fictitious arrival at the Moabar Monastery. It was nothing compared to what

Fleet had me memorize over the years just to requisition a med-kit. But the consequences of an error in this recitation were vastly more serious. I tried not to think about that, nor about the nervous flutterings in my stomach.

I ended the recitation with the ritual "Praise the stars."

Drogue's face relaxed into a smile.

We climbed a steep rampway. I glanced back. Sully flanked Ren, the ramp not wide enough to accommodate the Stolorth and the pallet. I remember how he'd shielded me in the forest, when we'd first seen the jukor.

No, he'd seen it. And put himself between the creature and me.

Had it been about to spring then?

With his back to it, Sully would have been killed, immediately.

But his rifle would have fallen into my hands. And in the time it would have taken the jukor to rip Sully apart, I could've killed it. I would've survived because of Sully's sacrifice.

The thought chilled me. I almost bumped into a Takan guard who stepped in my path.

"Restricted. Present ID." The Taka's voice was harsh and choppy, like most of his kind. I kept my head bowed, folded my hands at my waist. My fingers drifted lightly over the Grizni bracelet under my sleeve.

"Blessings of the hour upon you, my friend." Drogue beamed a smile that was completely genuine. "Truvgrol, isn't it?"

The guard's small eyes darted rapidly as he assessed our group. "Guardian! Blessings. Travel up?"

"It's time for me to assist with temple matters on station. We have a wonderful Peyhar's Week festival planned. One in the temple here as well. Brother Frannard will be leading you."

"Frannard, yes!" The Taka's shaggy head nodded. Evidently Frannard was a popular figure.

"Will you require our ID passes? You know Brother Sudral, Brother Ren Ackravaro. Sister Berri Solaria . . . I do apologize. Have you not met Sister Berri?"

I could almost feel the Taka's gaze on me. My heart pounded in my ears. I steepled my hands in front of my face, bowed low. To a Taka. A few hours ago, I'd killed one.

Truvgrol mimicked my gesture. "Blessings," he growled.

"Praise to the stars in the abbot's holy name. May fortune smile upon you this week, Brother Truvgrol." I raised my head slightly, handed him my card. He passed it through the scanner, barely looking at it.

"Good journey, good journey." He waved us on.

I quietly let out a small sigh of relief.

We were similarly waved through three more checkpoints before we were admitted to the spaceport itself.

I pulled the hood of my robe closer. Even Drogue's presence wasn't completely reassuring now that I was in a closed building, with MOC personnel hurrying back and forth through the gray-walled main terminal. Drogue nodded at faces I would only glimpse at, nodding as well.

"Praise the stars. Blessings of the hour." I kept my voice bland, uninteresting.

Sully had booked passage on one of the Chalford fleet supply ships, a squat short-hauler contracted to MOC service. The ship had come in a few hours before, might even be the one that had punctuated my first conversation with Sully with its booming entry. The ship was berthed at Cargo Dock One.

Moabar Prison Spaceport had three docks: one passenger, two cargo. Dock One was down a short corridor that jutted off to the right. A solitary window just before the rampway afforded me my first view of the ship.

Chalford's *Lucky Seven* was a B10-Class "load-up-and-go"—or "lugger," as they were called in the freighter trade. Compact ships with dirtside capabilities, which the larger starfreighters lacked. What weren't cargo holds were engines: heavy-air and sublight. Luggers had no jumpdrives.

And no passenger cabins. A ruddy-faced crew member escorted us to the lounge. His suit patch said *Chalford Cargo Services—Wilard, P.—Navigation.*

"Bulkhead seats got harnesses." He pointed to three pairs of fold-downs. "Don't unstrap till you hear the all-clear from the bridge."

I watched him leave. *This is too easy. Much too easy.* Pull a robe over my head, flash an ID card with a religious symbol, walk off Moabar and into freedom.

I chose a seat from the pair nearest the exit out of habit, folded down the armrests. My throat suddenly seemed dry, my hands cold.

This is too easy. I tried to think about what P. Wilard was doing on the bridge at nav. The captain would be running through his or her preflight, doing a last-minute systems check. I knew the routine well.

But that little voice in the back of my mind wouldn't shut up.

Sully unfolded the seat next to mine. "You're frowning, Sister. Don't tell me flying makes you nervous."

I was about to remind him of all the hours I'd logged at the helm when I realized our conversations might well be heard on the bridge. I answered as I hoped Sister

Berri would. "I was trying to decide which of the Twelve Blessings I'd recite for our departure." I snapped the harness across my chest. "Perhaps you have a suggestion, Brother Sudral?"

Sully glanced at Drogue and Ren on his right. Bright orange straps crisscrossed the front of their pale robes.

"I'm fine," Ren said.

Sully hadn't asked. Ren must be used to Sully's almost protective attitude by now, anticipated it. He stared straight ahead, one hand resting lightly on his cane tucked through the straps.

"I always enjoy the Blessing for Good Fortune through Purity of Effort," Drogue said. "Permit me to lead."

"That was about to be my suggestion as well." Sully turned back to me, dropped his voice to a low rasp. "However, perhaps later we could perform the lesser-known Invocation for the Convergence of the Male and Female Physical Essences—"

Intraship chimed twice. It was followed by a man's voice, sounding bored. "This is Captain Newlin. We've got clearance. Push-back coming up."

I closed my eyes, leaned my head back against the padding of the seat, waited for the jerk-and-thump as we were towed to the taxiway.

All hatches were sealed. Ship was secure. I was either headed for freedom or into a trap. Either way, there wasn't a damned thing I could do about it right now.

I listened to Drogue recite the blessing. Purity of Effort. I guess the road to—and from—Hell was paved with good intentions.

The tow disengaged from us at the taxiway with a final shimmy. The heavy-airs, which had been idling, were thrown to full. A muted roaring rumbled through the ship.

Then we were moving, rising, my back flattening into the seat.

I was free. Or I was dead.

Artificial gravity kicked on with a thud. Something, somewhere, hadn't been strapped down. I only hoped someone hadn't been underneath it when it fell.

Captain Newlin sounded the all-clear. I was already unhooking my straps. Habit. My body knew the routine, knew the feel of a ship as her heavy-airs kicked off and sublights switched on. I wriggled the stiffness out of my shoulders. The lights on the commissary panels on the opposite wall beckoned. Tea, hot, with plenty of sugar. My mouth felt chalky.

Sully's eyes opened when I stood. Whether he'd been sleeping, daydreaming, praying, or plotting through most of our ascent I didn't know. I was just thankful he'd been quiet. He had a marked tendency to try to bait me. I was too tired, and too wary, to want to play his games right now.

"Two hours to station," he told me.

I remembered my trip down, three and a half weeks ago. Seven of us had started our sentences together that trip. We were all quiet, fear and anger hanging heavily in the silence on the small transport ship. None of us was a fool; we knew what awaited us on Moabar.

I was still afraid. I had no idea what awaited me on station, or beyond that. Fear sharpened the senses. Mine had to match my dagger if I were to survive.

Sully followed me to the commissary panels, leaned one shoulder on the bulkhead as I tabbed in my request for tea. His lazy smile reminded me of our encounter on Port Chalo and made me force my mind back to the business at hand.

"Who's running us in-system?" The unit's hum provided a nice, bland background noise to my quiet question, in case someone had the lounge rigged for listening.

Sully arched an eyebrow. "You sound very sexy when you whisper."

I shot him a warning glance. "Brother Sudral—"

"Drogue's known Newlin for a long time." He glanced back at Drogue, seated at a far table. He was focused on a microscreen slatted out of the tabletop in front of him. "And Newlin knows better than to ask questions. Or be concerned with what happens in the lounge. He's not going to risk losing his glory-seed connection."

"Newlin's Takan?" His voice had sounded human. Which he was, I realized as my brain caught up with Sully's words. *Glory-seed connection.* Takas wouldn't need a connection or a source for a narcotic that was legal for them. They could grow them, chew them, or distill them into honeylace: a nectar they used to reach a meditative state during their religious festivals.

Festivals run by Englarian Guardians.

Sully watched me with a bemused smile as if he knew I'd answered my own question. "Newlin's always glad to assist the followers of Abbot Eng whenever he can. And Chalford likes to keep Newlin happy because it's hard to find crew willing to work the Moabar run."

I cupped my tea in both hands and headed for one of the small tables. "He better not be doing shots of honey-lace on the bridge." Or he wouldn't know which of the six stations spinning in front of him was the real one.

"Not quite regulation?" Sully leaned his forearms on the back of the chair next to mine, then reached over and, with a brush of his hand, pushed my hood back. I didn't jerk away this time. I finally caught on. Just as he baited me with his words, he liked to see my reaction to his touch. It was a game with him: let's see just how nervous we can make this very proper, respectable, military-born-and-bred female. Whose mother wore army boots.

I'd promised myself I wasn't going to play his games anymore. I regarded him coolly.

He chuckled. "Don't fret. Newlin's been flying this bucket for years."

A typical Sullivan nonanswer, which in no way reassured me the captain wasn't in some drug-induced fog. The only thing I did know now was that I didn't have to be cautious with my questions. "In-system, Sully. How we're getting there?"

Ren's cane lightly clacked against the chair on the other side of me. He sat down, threaded the cane through a small loop on his belt. It took a moment for my stomach to unclench. He was blind, harmless. I focused on Sully.

"There's a tri-hauler waiting for us. *Diligent Keeper*. She's a regular, but engine troubles have her momentarily delayed. Her troubles will be fixed just shortly after we arrive. She'll head back in-system."

"And then?" I prompted.

Sully knotted his hands together, glancing briefly at Ren before answering. "Then I put you to work on this small project of mine."

The one that needed a good, interfering bitch. The one that had made him go against his advisers' recommendations, search me out on Moabar. Kill a jukor. The one that could yet get me killed. Moabar Station was an MOC facility. Just because my boots weren't touching Moabar soil didn't mean I was free. "Tell me."

He was still leaning over the back of the chair, his posture casual. His eyes narrowed. "I need you to get me into the Marker Shipyards."

"Why?"

He hesitated only a second. "We're going to destroy them."

"What?" It was a good thing I'd just put my tea down.

"Ren and I've spent the better part of the past year following the trail of some interesting rumors. Involving Marker. And gen-labs." He watched me very closely.

"That jukor you killed."

Ren turned as if he could see me. "I learned of a breeding pair. Sully and I were tracking them. Moabar was one possible destination."

I turned back to Sully. "Then you knew—"

He shook his head. "One possible destination. Confirmed now, of course."

Ren made a small gesture with his wide hand. "Because we've learned of one pair doesn't mean there aren't others."

One pair was far too many for me. Though it was half a pair now. "If this is coming out of Marker, then it's an Imperially sanctioned project."

"We've considered that," Sully said.

The definitive tone of his answer spoke volumes. This

wasn't Gabriel Ross Sullivan, the poet. This was Sully, the mercenary.

And if the gen-labs were an Imperial project at Marker, my brother Thad might have knowledge.

I leaned my mouth against my fist. Maybe if I didn't say it, it wouldn't be true. Thad might well be, as Sully had said, a supercilious ass. But could he condone a project that created mutants whose sole purpose was death of any living thing they saw? Two hundred and seven men, women, and children were brutally, horribly massacred on Corsau Station ten years ago when a shipment of jukors escaped from a transport ship. It was then the Empire realized the beasts they'd bred to replace border-patrol security dogs had evolved into something far, far from that.

The only positive was that the jukors had escaped onto a station—a closed environment. Had they been dirtside their recapture would've been almost impossible. Their short life spans notwithstanding, their genetically enhanced rapid breeding rate ensured they could easily decimate the population of a small city in months, perhaps weeks.

I pulled my hand away from my mouth. "How many labs do they have? What's their date for project completion?"

"Those are exactly the kinds of things that I need a beautiful, interfering bitch to find out." Sully smiled grimly at me. "Would you happen to know of one, Captain Bergren?"

I did. And she knew the shipyards very well.

"You might want to look at this, Brother Sudral." Drogue leaned back in the chair, swiveled toward our table.

Sully turned. "You have a schedule?"

"Partial. Brother Verno regrets he could not get more."

Sully swung back to me. "Marker's made some interesting requisitions as of late. Items one wouldn't expect they'd need for the two new Arrow-Class destroyers under contract." *

"What office is issuing the requisitions?" Marker was a big shipyard and sometimes served as a way station for supplies going outbound to small repair facilities. Sully's mention of schedules told me he'd tapped incoming cargo. But if that same cargo was outbound again, he might be way off in his theory about gen-labs. Though the appearance of the jukor told me at least part of his theories were valid.

"The shipping manifests, best we can tell, are just tagged for Marker."

"Wouldn't be." I drummed my fingers against my mouth. I'd sat in my mother's office at the shipyards for too many hours as a child. Helped her sort and code incoming and outgoing requisitions for Marker's Quartermaster's Office, Sublight Division. Once in a while something tagged for enviro or nav-pack would come in, erroneously linked to her files by a junior data tech who hadn't had a second cup of coffee that shift. She'd clean up the file, send it back along with a reprimand.

Details, Chaz. Efficiency and security are built on details.

"Wouldn't be," I repeated. He straightened as I stood and motioned toward Drogue's screen.

Drogue started to rise.

"No, sit." I leaned over the back of Drogue's chair much as Sully had moments before at my table. The slice of data had been taken from an Imperial transit beacon, recording starfreighter movement in Baris. Overlying that was a ship's manifest from its departure point at Port January.

The beacon data logged the ship's heading, speed, and cargo category. Biohazards and any other potentially dangerous cargo were always routed through the outer lanes, away from populated stations and worlds. Away from commercial passenger traffic.

A freighter squawking a hazard code would activate an immediate security breach when passing an inner beacon. Patrol ships, like the one I commanded up until six months ago, would pursue.

A captain could deny what he carried was hazardous. He could claim the wrong code had been logged in his ship's systems. But he couldn't deny me and my boarding party access to his ship or his systems.

I was well used to unraveling altered manifests, tweaking out hidden shipping codes. Breaking into cargo holds, if I had to. I'd built a career on it.

I studied the data before me. Drogue was right; it was only a partial. A preshipment manifest, not verified and lock-signed. "This isn't a final. Container codes haven't even been entered completely in column three."

"Brother Verno is working on a source for the final manifests," Drogue said. "For the moment, this is the best data we've been able to get."

Brother Verno. At some point I wanted to know why the Englarians were involved, other than the similarity in appearance between Abbot Eng's soul-stealers and the jukors. But at the moment, the data held my attention. "This comes from Core Central Medical Designers. Their shipping codes always carry an M-432 prefix. Sometimes they ship as Core Em-Ex, but you'll pick them up from the M-432." The truncated data told me little more other than pickup and estimated delivery dates. But I knew Sully knew how to read that.

"How about those four containers that are coded?" Sully leaned one hip on the edge of Drogue's table.

"The only thing you need to look for is this section right here: M-432-NH1. All that tells me is nonhazardous, class one. Which means no special care required. Exposure to heat, light, cold permitted. I'd say nonbreakables, hard goods. But you might," I continued, reaching around Drogue to scroll the data to the left, "look at the container classes themselves. See, they're not duro-hards. So we've got lightweight nonbreakables. You could have four gross of bedpans."

"Does Core Central manufacture bedpans?" Sully sounded disappointed.

"Core Central contracts with a lot of small factories for just about everything. If you're looking for supplies that would build a gen-lab, though, I'd be watching for shipments from Core Em-Ex. That's their high-ticket research division."

Drogue turned his broad face up to mine. "You have a remarkable memory, Captain Bergren."

I shook my head. "Repetitive. I've seen this stuff almost every day of my adult life." And much of my childhood, as long as my mother had been alive.

Sully folded his arms across his chest. "Now you understand why we need you."

A good interfering bitch with a working knowledge of Marker and Imperial shipping? I was far from unique. Every other patrol captain in the Imperial Fleet had my knowledge of cargo codes. And last I knew, over five hundred and fifty people worked at Marker. Many of them possibly had knowledge of Marker's routines and those same codes I did. But I was the only one sitting on Moabar.

Some of my unease about my pact with the ghost from Hell subsided. "All right. Count me in," I told

Sully. "But let's make sure of your information first." Those five hundred and fifty Marker workers included my brother. I wasn't going to convict them on partial evidence, or misinterpreted data. I knew only too well what that felt like.

Newlin came back on the intraship when we were cleared for docking. "Strap down and secure. I mean it, this time." Evidently he'd heard that ominous thump two and a half hours before. We were a little behind schedule. Newlin said only that the station was having a problem with their escort tugs.

Ten minutes later a long shimmy rattled through the ship as she was gated to one of the station's extended docking ramps. Two hard jolts. Clamps secure. We were probably lower level. Luggers usually didn't rate the better berths. A tri-hauler like *Diligent* should be somewhat higher, closer to the MOC command center, stationmaster's office, rec facilities.

I made a mental appraisal of how much longer I'd be in the MOC's company. Another five, ten minutes until we were cleared to disembark. If I ran the station, there'd be another ID check. But then, I tried to run my life, and my ship, the way my mother had taught me. Details. Ask questions. Get facts.

If they did recheck ID, that would delay us another five. Then we had to find the lifts, find the *Diligent*. Fifteen minutes. Sully had said they'd file for departure as soon as we were on board.

Half hour. Forty-five if they were having a problem with the tugs. I'd be generous. An hour. An hour to wait and then I'd be heading in-system. Free.

It's still too easy.

Sully unsnapped his harness as I did. "You stay with Drogue." He stepped away from me, headed for Ren. A light touch of his hand on the Stolorth's elbow preceded his quip. "Showtime."

Hazy silver eyes turned toward Sully. "I'm ready."

Wilard arrived to escort us off ship. All conversation ceased as we filed after him toward the airlock. Drogue touched the wide belt at his waist, signaling I should have my ID ready.

Okay, five minutes, Chaz. This is the toughest part. You can do this.

Drogue didn't know the Taka waiting at the bottom of the ramp. We went through the ritual greetings but without the easy familiarity of the spaceport.

"Blessings of the hour to you, Brother."

"Blessings of the hour. Guardian?" The Taka spent much more time on our ID cards than his kin dirtside. When he tapped his vest's comm badge and growled in a request, my heart stopped for a few beats.

An MOC officer in a dark brown uniform appeared quickly. Female, mid-fifties. Short dark hair with one wide streak of silver on the left. Her almond-shaped eyes showed only boredom as our cards processed through a second time.

Then her right hand rose. "Sister Solaria?"

I'd taken perhaps two steps past her. A slight chill of fear rippled through me. I forced myself not to flinch, turned slowly, plastered what I hoped was a holy—and wholly innocent—look on my face. "Praise the stars, Sister. How may I assist you?"

Her name tag said *Tran, D.* "Your immunizations aren't up to date."

Minor problem. Go to Medical, get a hypospray. Not a minor problem. My bioprints wouldn't match the real Berri Solaria's. But they would match Chasidah Bergren's in the MOC's central files.

Drogue spoke up quickly. "An error, I am sure,

Officer Tran. Sister Solaria is one of our most active missionaries. She would not be permitted to carry on her work unless she had full medical clearance."

"I'm aware of that, Guardian, but her card file shows—"

"Perhaps I can assist." Ren's soft tones flowed over Drogue and Tran, standing almost nose-to-nose.

I waited to see her reaction to the Stolorth's presence. Most people would have backed up a step. Or five.

Tran peered up at the silver-tinged face under the hood. "Brother Ren Ackravaro. Back again?"

I didn't know if her recognition of Ren was a good or bad sign. Things were starting to look slightly less easy.

"Final trip for a while, I'm afraid. Moabar's winters and I do not get along." Ren motioned toward me, knowing where I stood, I guessed, by the sound of my voice. "Sister Solaria's medical files were appended at the convent. Perhaps they were entered incorrectly?" Ren held his card toward Tran. "Ours came through the Guardianship in Dafir. Perhaps if you compare them?"

"It might just be a difference in origination code." Sully lightly touched Tran's shoulder as he offered her his card. "Could we trouble you to make sure this is not the case before we must experience a delay at Medical?"

Tran stared at Sully for a moment. Then, obviously taken in, as most women were, by that slow, sexy smile of his, she shrugged and slid the three cards through again. Sighed. "Someone logged them with the wrong parameters. They're fine. Jalvert?"

The Taka stepped over. I caught a brief flash of irritation in the small eyes. Didn't like an MOC officer correcting his mistakes, most likely.

"She's clear. Just a skewed entry."

Drogue bowed. "Our apologies. We often have our

young novices do the clerical work. I appreciate your diligence, Officer Tran."

The woman nodded, waved us on. "Praise the stars."

"Praise the stars," I called back to her. For the first time, I meant it.

No one said a word until the four of us were alone in the lift.

"I thought we cleared up that glitch in the program." Sully glanced over at Ren.

"I believed we had as well."

How could Ren see to program if he was blind?

Sully flashed me a wry smile. "Sorry, my angel. I guess I'm not perfect after all."

My first inclination was to reply with some biting comment in agreement. But two could play at this flirtation game. I went with my second. "Pity. Wedding's off, then."

I was rewarded with a moment of surprised silence, then a deep chuckle. "Perhaps two weeks on the *Diligent* with me will convince you to change your mind."

I wasn't even thinking about the next two weeks. I still needed to get through the next two hours.

The lift doors opened on Corridor Level Seven-Blue. Brown MOC uniforms wove past freighter blues, greens, and grays, and past security's darker gray with the telltale white stripe up the pant legs. The hulking, furred presence of the Takas towered over all.

I was just shaking off the chill of fear from Tran's questions. I wanted to run, board the ship, seal the airlock. We walked instead at a leisurely pace.

"We'll part company at your ship," Drogue said. "We'll meet again, praise the stars, under more pleasant circumstances."

"I hope so." Pleasant circumstances sounded wonderful. "I appreciate your help."

"No, Sister. We appreciate yours." Drogue held my gaze for a moment. Clearly, Sully's mission was personal to him. I had two weeks with Sully and Ren to find out why. Not that it mattered, overall. If someone in the Empire was breeding jukors again, that was sufficient reason for me.

"What berth are we looking for?"

"Seven-Blue Nineteen, I believe." Drogue glanced back at Sully, who nodded.

We were at Berth Twelve. Then Fourteen. At Sixteen I fought to keep from quickening my pace, played my little time game in my mind. Ten minutes to board. Half hour, maybe forty-five minutes to get clearance to undock.

At Eighteen I stopped dead in my tracks. A thin chill raced up my spine. Bright yellow security 'bots ringed the next airlock, lights flashing. Sully's hand splayed against my back. His voice growled in my ear. "Stay here."

I had no intention of getting anywhere near the security 'bots, or the half dozen MOC guards and security stripers standing in a tight knot under the illuminated *19* on the overhead. Illuminated in orange: ship under security seal or quarantine.

"Face me," Sully ordered.

I did, turning away from the scene that sent my heart into my throat. Drogue and Ren kept moving. Their credentials weren't forged like mine. Or Sully's. "What's going on?"

"I don't know. And I don't like it when I don't know."

"They're under a Code Orange."

"I can't imagine Milo doing anything to elicit that. He excels at being cautious."

"An accident? Crew problem?"

"Milo'd never let anything on ship get to the docks. He knows better." Sully frowned, his gaze over my shoulder.

"You're sure it's the *Diligent*?" Ships switched berths for any number of legitimate reasons.

He answered my question with a squinting of obsidian eyes, then, "Still reads so."

Shit. Easy was disappearing fast. "Options?"

"Let's cross that— Ren. Talk to us."

The Stolorth stepped next to me, bowed to Sully, fingers steepled. "Brother Sudral. Sister Berri. I feel a need to meditate. I suggest we return to the temple and pray."

Oh, shit! So much for easy. I bowed my head as Ren and Sully flanked me. "Where's Drogue?" I asked quietly.

Berth Seventeen. Sixteen. "He will meet us at the temple," Ren said.

Fourteen. Twelve. "The MOC stripers received information a certain ship was to assist in a prison break." Ren's voice was as calm as if he were commenting on the color of the decking below our boots. My heart pounded. Berth Ten. "That information pointed to a ship called the *Diligent Keeper*," Ren continued.

Sully was silent. A cluster of blue-uniformed freighter crew strolled by, laughing.

As we passed Berth Nine, Ren added, "An attempt was made to take the ship, two hours past. The *Diligent* broke dock. However, I regret that her captain, Nathaniel Milo, is dead."

"Bastards." Sully's voice was harsh, bitter. My downcast gaze saw his fists clench.

Moabar Station suddenly felt very small.

Seven. I noticed Ren's cane now tucked through his sash, as if it were no longer needed. "Authorities believe a ship, with the escapees, is due in at seventeen-hundred, station time. Manned by supporters of Sheldon Blaine and possibly with Blaine himself on board."

That was four hours from now. I wasn't Blaine—I had no royal blood in my family—and I was already here. That was no guarantee they wouldn't look at all ships making station within a much larger time window, triple check all IDs. Especially if they were watching for Farosians: a small but pervasive band of terrorists based on Tos Faros, who upheld Blaine's claim to the throne. They maintained that their research showed the emperor's paternal grandmother—the much lauded Dowager Empress—to be an impostor, an infant substituted for one stillborn ninety years ago. That put the succession of Prewitt II and Prewitt III in question. A shuttle accident credited to the Farosians killed Prew's father, Emperor Prewitt II. Prew surrounded himself with impenetrable security and, as his father had, ignored the Farosians' requests for genetic verification testing.

We passed Berth Five. "There will be much security activity until they determine whether or not Captain Milo warned the other ship in time to abort the escape."

Or whether it had come in earlier than anticipated.

The temple was two levels up. We stepped into the lift with an MOC officer on my right, two Takas behind us.

"Praise the stars. Blessings of the hour." I tried not to listen as my voice shook. Fear and anger, again. Just like the shuttle trip dirtside. Fear at being discovered, interrogated, tortured.

Anger, to come so close. To be stopped—and not just in my attempt at freedom. But to be stopped from unmasking the gen-labs, the jukors. Somewhere during that trip on the *Lucky Seven* my reasons to leave Moabar had shifted. The picture had become larger, encompassing more than just Chasidah Bergren's personal survival. It brought in Drogue's and Ren's and Sully's as well.

Sullivan. I had no idea what the Empire would do when they found out he was still alive.

No, I knew what they'd do. And that's what really frightened me. There wouldn't be enough left of him to ship down to Moabar.

He should've listened to his advisers.

The doors to the Temple of Abbot Eng the Merciful, Moabar Guardianship, looked like all other commercial-establishment doors on station: auto double-wides in green, the color designating this level. They were flanked on the left by a wide window. But these doors were stenciled with the arch-and-stave. Through the large window, rows of benches facing a long raised platform were visible. The wall behind it was backlit. An outline of the Englarian symbol filled most of it. No one sat on the benches at this hour, but as we walked by, I caught a glimpse of a robed figure moving past the platform.

The entrance to the temple offices was through a single green autodoor a few feet farther down the corridor. It slid open as Ren approached. That meant the temple doors weren't locked. Locked right now would be preferable. It wouldn't stop the MOC or the stripers, but it might slow them down.

We entered a short gray-walled corridor with bright overheads and three doors. The one to my left I assumed went into the rear of the temple. Another, directly ahead, was marked *Temple Office*. The last door was just to the right of that.

I thought we were going to the office, but Ren stopped and held out one hand in Sully's direction, halting him. Perhaps they were having second thoughts about coming here?

"My quarters, for now," Ren said. "I'll wait in the office, in case anyone else comes in."

Anyone else, I knew, meant stripers. Ren's presence here was official. Ours wasn't.

I followed Sully through the doorway on the right. Another hallway, longer, with five doors this time. Three left, two right. The first on the left was open. I glimpsed a round table and a commissary panel. The others must be sleeping rooms. Ren's quarters were the last door on the right.

I let out the breath I was holding when the door cycled behind me. "How much did Milo know?" I was in damage-control mode now. *Don't accept that you're boxed in. Gather the facts. Look for loopholes, options.* There had to be options.

Sully pulled back his hood, ran his hand over his short, dark hair. His mouth was a thin line, but I didn't know if he was angry at himself, or Milo, or the whole damned universe.

"Waste of a damned good man." He spat out the words.

Angry at the universe, then. Milo must have been a friend. I waited, giving him time to compose himself, and took in the sparse room. An arch-and-stave hung on the far wall, over a long, narrow bed half shielded by a privacy curtain. Kitchen panels on the left. Foldout desk on the right with a door beside it that was probably a lavatory. Ren's quarters had to have a bath. Stolorths could survive without water for forty-eight hours before their gills dried permanently shut.

In the middle of the room was a long, padded bench, not unlike the ones in the temple. I pushed my hood back, eased down on one end. The stiffness in the set of Sully's shoulders spoke volumes. And made me want to let him know he wasn't alone. "I'm sorry."

Sully slanted a glance at me, then thrust both hands through his hair this time. "Damn it!"

He plopped down next to me, the bench wobbling slightly under his weight. He leaned his elbows on his knees, rested his eyes against the heels of his hands. I knew he was concerned over the abrupt change of plans, at the new risks we now faced. But I also felt that Captain Milo's death pained him on a very personal level. It was an unexpected glimpse at a side of him I didn't know well.

This wasn't Gabriel Ross Sullivan, the poet. Or Sully, the mercenary. This was almost someone else. Someone closer to the man who'd met me in that bar in Port Chalo, who'd seemed to intuitively know I was hurting that night. I had an urge to put an arm around him, say something comforting. But I wasn't sure who I'd be comforting, or if it would even be welcomed. So I waited.

He raised his face, steepling his fingers in front of his mouth. "Waste of a good man," he said again, finally. "And no, Milo wouldn't talk. He didn't know who I went down to Moabar to retrieve. You learn not to ask questions in this business."

"His crew?"

"Six. Ship was mostly automated. But she'd been running legit for two years now. He was doing me one last favor because I did him one, years ago. The stripers should never have tagged him." He turned to me. "I don't make mistakes like this, Chaz. I can't afford to."

I almost pointed out to him that my forged ID card wasn't perfect either. But now wasn't the time. "Ren said someone tipped off the stripers."

He nodded, calmer. More thoughtful. "That's of deep concern. If there's a leak within my crew, I can't risk bringing you on board. Anyone with half a brain, and a few of those still exist in the government, would eventually discern the value of your particular area of knowledge. Your family's connections."

"My mother's choice of footwear?" I gave him a half smile.

He caught it, though the one he gave back was tinged with sadness. "She taught you well."

I had a feeling he knew far more about me than I was comfortable with—especially as I had no idea of his source. If we lived long enough to get off Moabar Station, I just might ask him. But inherent in that *we* was part of the danger. "Maybe Newlin should take me back dirtside. They might not think—"

"No!" Strong fingers grasped my forearm. "You're not going back there. We still have options. They'll take a bit more time, but we have them." He seemed conscious of his sudden intensity. His grip relaxed, his hand draped over my arm.

"This is only a setback. It seems worse because of Milo. Well, it seems worse to me. You didn't know him." He talked more to himself than to me. "He knew the risks, and that death was one of them. One he would accept only because there was no other choice."

Was the breeding of jukors something a man would give his life to stop? Evidently Captain Milo believed so. And it was enough for Drogue, a gentle monk. And for Ren, who was everything I'd been taught Stolorths couldn't be. If caught, Drogue would most likely face Moabar, as I had. But Ren could well be turned over to his own people. His death, the Empire could honestly say, wouldn't be on their soul's slate.

Sully was, purportedly, already dead. The Empire was large. Add to that the few outlying systems that lived peacefully nearby and there were hundreds of worlds on which Sully could've taken a new identity. A new life. Yet, after a two-year absence, he was back, moving again through dark and dangerous shadows. I couldn't understand why. But then, Sully had always been an enigma to me.

I almost put my question into words, but his hand had slipped down my forearm and now encircled my wrist. My pulse fluttered under his fingers. His dark gaze held my own, then flicked down to my mouth. I felt a very real heat start in the pit of my stomach, flare up through my chest, singe my cheeks.

"*Chasidah.*" I heard my name whispered so softly that for a moment I thought I'd heard it in my mind. But it was Sully's voice I'd heard, and it was Sully's face now so very close to mine.

I don't know what frightened me more. The very real hunger I saw in his eyes when his gaze flicked back up, or the fact that the hunger wasn't only his.

I bolted up from the bench. *You're losing your mind. It's the stress. Lack of sleep.* And an overabundance of one extremely enigmatic, very sexy male.

I buried my unbidden emotions and forced myself to refocus on the real problem: the MOC, the stripers, the reappearance of the jukors.

"Time's not on our side right now, Sullivan." I adopted my official Fleet-issue-the-captain-is-speaking-now tone. "Station can put us all in a lockdown, peel back ID by ID. This is what they do every time it's even hinted the Farosians are involved. I know the routine."

His only response was a slightly surprised expression. Did he think I didn't understand the problems we faced?

"Staying together," I told him, "is the biggest risk. You, me, Ren, Drogue. You might as well hand them your whole operation in a duro-hard."

I hoped his silence meant he was considering my words. But there was that slight puzzlement in his expression. Something in his heated gaze again sent a little flare-up inside me. Finally, he shook his head. "I'm not sending you back down."

"Why not?"

"I have my reasons."

"Which are?"

He studied me for a long moment. "Valid ones."

I wanted to call him an idiot. I wanted him angry, not offering me this odd mixture of patience and something I couldn't define. I wanted him to see what I saw, the lives he risked, including his own. I didn't want his to be one of them. I wasn't worth it.

I was on Moabar for a valid reason. Whether or not I believed the Empire's evidence against me, fourteen people were dead because of a decision I'd made while in command.

And now Nathaniel Milo. Make that fifteen. I didn't want to count the Takan guard. He'd attacked me first—an action that still puzzled me. But I had bigger problems at the moment than one Taka's bizarre behavior.

"Reach Newlin. Or anyone. Send me back while you still can."

His chin lifted. "I never pegged you for a coward."

"I'm not," I snapped. "I'm an Imperial Fleet officer,

trained to assess a situation and make decisions, based on facts. There's no shame in pulling back, regrouping."

He rose. "Martyr doesn't suit you either, my angel."

His flippant use of the affectionate term grated. "Damn you, Gabriel Sullivan, listen to me!"

He grabbed my shoulders so quickly I didn't have time to step back. His eyes were dark yet empty—his touch almost searing. When he spoke, bitterness, pain, and frustration mixed in his deep, harsh tone. "I'm already damned, consigned to a Hell I can never escape. It haunts me, consumes me. Until all that's left are things that make me feel a pain I hope to God you never have to feel. Anger and pain are very valid reasons for what I do. Remember that."

He released me and turned abruptly away.

I hugged my arms tightly around my middle. In all the years, in all the situations I'd faced Gabriel Ross Sullivan, I'd never seen him as deeply angry, as deeply hurt, as I had just now.

The sound of the door sliding open startled me. Ren followed Drogue in. The Guardian's round face showed clear signs of tension. "This is most disturbing," he was saying.

I slanted a glance toward Sully and caught his gaze fixed on Ren. Ren's face tilted questioningly and out of the corner of my eye I saw the slightest shake of Sully's head. A dismissive shrug of his shoulders.

A sharp chill crept up my spine.

I'd seen a vid in training years ago. Two Stolorth telepaths having a conversation. To the listener, the questions and answers were disjointed. Until the teacher pointed out to watch for movement. All humans and most humanoids unconsciously tilt their heads when listening. All humans and most humanoids nod, even in response to their own silent thoughts. Stolorth *Ragkirils* were no different. Certain gestures stubbornly remained, even if the words were silent.

I started adding up the gestures, the answers to questions unspoken. Something I sensed but couldn't before define. Ren might be more than an empath. In spite of Sully's protestations, in spite of what Fleet had us believe, Ren might have the ability to communicate telepathically. Link his mind to another's. To Sully's, I was beginning to suspect.

Ren stated he couldn't link with his own people. He never said whether he could link minds with a human.

He was obviously blind. I still believe that negated his ability to rip a mind apart. So why not admit to a limited telepathy? I didn't have answers. And didn't like when I didn't have answers.

"We must sit, discuss things," Drogue said.

I sat, somewhat more cautious, on the end of the bench. I didn't like being lied to. But there was nothing I could do about it right now. I recognized it could all just be conjecture, an overreaction on my part.

However, the first chance I had, I was going to ask some serious questions. And not of Sully; we had a shared past that raised other issues, dragging us off topic. I had to talk to Ren.

I took a deep breath, settled myself down. Calm, professional.

Sully leaned back against the desk, his arms folded much as mine had been a few minutes ago. Classic defensive posture. Ren sat on his bed, drew the curtain back to the wall. Drogue stood in the middle of us.

"We have lost Brother Nathaniel. This saddens me, as I know it saddens both of you. But we have greater concerns."

"What's the status on the *Diligent*?" Sully asked.

"She has eluded pursuit to this point, I am told. At

least, her capture has not been announced. The Fleet has been alerted."

"What did the MOC learn?" Ren asked. "And from whom?"

Drogue shook his head. "The stars, in their wisdom, have not yet convinced the authorities on station to share that with me. I only know the temple is not under suspicion. They stated we were free to continue with the festivities and rituals for Peyhar's Week. I strongly suggest we do so."

Peyhar's Week. Non-Human Cultures 101 again. An Englarian holiday of celebration and renewal. Glory seeds and honeylace would be shared. A station full of mellow, happy, eight-foot-tall guards wasn't a bad idea at all.

Still, I wanted off Moabar Station. "Can we get another ship in that time?"

"Of course." A Sully-like smirk accompanied his words.

"Is there somewhere I can stay until then?" I asked Drogue. "I don't think my ID will pass a second scan. I'd prefer it if the stripers could forget they ever saw Sister Berri here."

"The wisdom of the stars blessed me with a different idea. If you'll permit me?" Drogue motioned to Sully, who nodded, obviously curious. Ren sat forward on the bed.

"The stripers, as you call our security force, would find it odd that Sister Berri Solaria not participate in Peyhar's. You have been seen on station, as has Brother Ren Ackravaro. Your absence would cause remarkings. Your person would not."

"Best place to hide is in full view," Sully quipped.

"Wait a minute. I can talk the basic lingo. Praise the stars. Blessings of the hour. But I've never been to a

Peyhar's celebration and my Non-Human Cultures class was a long time ago. I'll sweep out the temple, fold prayer rugs, whatever. But I'm an obvious amateur—"

"Virgin," Sully put in.

"And not a sacrificial one," I snapped back. Damn him! He was baiting me again.

"She has a point," Ren said. I thought I began to see a pattern. Sully gets me riled and then Ren empathically reads me like a datascreen on max download. Wonderful.

I didn't care that Ren knew I was afraid. I was hardly a virgin, but my ignorance of the Englarians was wide and vast. I hated going into something without the facts, unprepared. No details.

Sully was disagreeing. "She'll be functioning as an acolyte. Most of the focus will be on Drogue and Clement. She just has to put in a few appearances. If a ship gets here that we can use, we'll just say we had the call to meditation." He shrugged, shot a glance at Ren, who turned, almost as if he could feel Sully's gaze on him.

"Brother Sudral sees well." Drogue turned to me. "Formal festivities start tomorrow. I suggest we all get some rest. I can assure you the temple is secure. I'll provide you with some basic descriptives of the ceremonies, if you like, Captain Bergren."

"Please."

Ren stood. "You may have my quarters. The office has room for a cot, which will serve me well."

"No, I can't put you out." My answer was automatic. Yet even as I declined his offer, I knew it was more than that. Of all of us, Ren was the least adapted to a human environment, the most in need of special accommodations. In spite of my suspicions, I had no desire to see him inconvenienced. I doubted the office had a bathtub.

The Stolorth offered me a small smile. "The temple has a baptismal pool, if that's your concern."

Was my concern that apparent? Or was it something else? My suspicions over his minor mind talents surfaced again. Maybe they weren't so minor. "None of us can afford to be less than optimum right now."

"Then know that I would do nothing to jeopardize your safety, or my own."

Or Sully's?

It hit me then. They didn't trust me. That's why Ren was here, to see if Chaz Bergren, former Imperial Fleet officer, would cooperate. As if I'd say no, let me stay on Moabar. It was just starting to get cozy down there.

I had to get Ren alone. Surprisingly, that thought didn't discomfort me as much as it should have. Amazing how three weeks on Moabar can suddenly make one more receptive to a wide range of ideas and experiences.

"I'll compromise," I told him. "Bring the cot in here. I'll use it. It's probably more my size, anyway. Then you can have your own bed and bath. It shouldn't be for more than a day or two, at best. Unless you'd feel uncomfortable with me here?"

I felt and heard, more than saw, Sully straighten and push away from the desk. He hadn't counted on my offer. Good. Nothing works better than divide and conquer.

Ren's reaction surprised me. His mouth softened, some of the lines disappeared from around his clouded eyes. His face tilted slightly, as if he weren't sure if he should be amused by my offer or even believe it at all.

Several hours ago I'd run from him in fear. Now I was telling him that I, a human female, trusted him, a

Stolorth male. Or rather, I knew I had to convince him to trust me.

I had a feeling he knew that as well.

We ate a small meal in the temple common room at about the time those on station would be having dinner. It was a way to force our bodies into the station's rhythm.

Another man in monk's garb, who Drogue introduced as Brother Clement, came in just as we were dishing out the stew. He greeted me with a reassuring pat on my shoulder and a promise that the stars would keep me safe. But he called Sully "Brother Sudral," so I was unsure of exactly what Clement knew, or didn't. But, like Sully said, the less everyone knew, the safer we all were.

Thick slices of bread—baked, not replicator issue—were stacked in the center of a round table not unlike the one at the monastery dirtside. Clement led the Prayer of Thanksgiving. He was about Drogue's age, mid-fifties, with skin the color of my favorite Imperial ale and glossy silver curls. He had a wiry build, a rumbling laugh, and a demeanor that was much less serious than Drogue's. He ate a bowl of stew, then wrapped some bread in a napkin and left, pleading a file full of unread theological treatises in his quarters.

"He's quite the scholar," Ren told me. He'd relaxed noticeably since our pact to be roommates. Sully alternated between unconcern and dropping into long, serious conversations with Drogue. I heard ship names mentioned. None was familiar to me, and I knew a fair amount of the freighters that worked the Empire's rim worlds.

We finished the stew, the bread, and a bottle of dry wine. I helped Drogue stack the dishes in the scrub unit, swiped down the table with a handvac. Sully and Ren were by the door, talking. By all appearances it was a friendly discussion. Then Drogue headed for the temple. Last-minute preparations for the festival to be checked one more time. He declined any offer of help. "You know where the cot is in the storage room, Brother Sudral? Good. Blessings of the hour, my friends. Morning meditations at six. Listen for the chimes at quarter of."

I followed Ren to his quarters. "You don't use a cane on station?" I remember he'd left it in his quarters.

Ren seemed slightly puzzled. "You thought it was for guidance. No, Moabar's climate disagrees with my body. I find my legs and my back much weakened by the cold."

"Makes me do all the work," Sully intoned, but his voice was light. The anger and darkness I'd sensed in him earlier were gone. He flipped the latch on a narrow closet door next to his quarters. "I'll get the cot while you rest your aching bones."

Ren chuckled as we stepped inside, then tabbed off the autodoor so it would stay open. "You're tired," he said as I sat on the bench.

"Slightly frazzled, yes," I agreed. "But I probably won't fall asleep for a while. My mind is still sorting through too many things." Did he know what they were? I wanted to open the door to that discussion. "Will that bother you, keep you awake?"

Ren eased down on the edge of his bed, shook his head. "Do you mean do I watch your thoughts like a vidcast? No. I'm not a telepath. But even if I were, we're taught selectivity. Control. Or else everyone's emotions would overwhelm us, drive us close to insanity. Of course, as an empath, if someone is experiencing intense emotions I'd be aware of that. But in most cases, I rarely read people's emotions. I only do if I feel I could be of some help. Perhaps to pray with them."

I caught that he denied, again, being a telepath. But I also heard his "even if I were."

The muted thud of a door closing in the hallway and the heavy sound of footsteps halted any further questions on my part. Sully appeared, grinning, in the open doorway, cot and folded blanket tucked under one arm. "Someone here order a cot?"

I played to his jovial mood. "Should have been here an hour ago. Hope you're not expecting a tip."

He dropped the cot on the floor behind me, dumped the blanket over my head. "Hope you're not expecting a pillow."

"Sully!" Ren sounded honestly horrified.

I flipped the blanket over my head and laughed. And wondered again what Ren "saw." Or did he just sense a playfulness?

"Chaz needs someone to tease her." Sully pulled the blanket off my shoulders, tossed it onto the cot. "After all those years of being called Captain, she takes herself far too seriously. What do you say, Ren, shall we teach her how to play with the big boys?"

I was about to protest when he suddenly leaned over and scooped me into his arms. His body felt hot and hard, very male. Something glinted in his eyes that I thought I recognized, and it wasn't playfulness. I yelped, my arms flailing behind him as I squirmed, wanting to reach for my dagger. His arms tightened around me with a strength that seemed almost nonhuman. Fear flashed through me. I had no intention of finding out what his version of playing with the big boys meant. I had no intention—

—of landing flat on my back in the middle of Ren's narrow bed, my dagger still around my wrist, Sully grinning down at me like the Devil's own kin. I scrambled backward, almost kicking Ren in the process. "Sullivan, you—"

"Play cards? Of course I do, my angel. Scoot over now, will you?" He plopped down next to me and threw a deck of cards in my lap.

Ren, who was reaching for Sully, stopped.

For a few seconds the entire scene froze in my mind. Sully's wicked, sensual smile. Ren's face, tight with fury, right arm lashing out, stopping only inches from Sully's throat.

Ren had clearly felt my fear at what I thought was going to be an attack, a possible gang rape. And Ren had reacted, defending me, from...

...Sully. Whose joviality masked something much deeper. Anger. Pain. Which Ren had to have felt as well.

But not an intention to hurt me. Once Sully had dropped me on the bed, I saw that. There was nothing threatening in his posture, nothing but childish mischief on his face. I'd misjudged him. Mistaken his continuing game of "bait Chaz" so Ren could empathically read my emotions.

Well, if they wanted to know what fear and anger felt like, they'd just seen it.

I was breathing hard. So, I noticed, was Sully. Only Ren had pulled back within himself, calmly, his hand resting peacefully against his knee. But his voice had an odd timbre to it when he spoke. I had the feeling he didn't approve of Sully's actions just then.

"Sully. Hand me the cards. I will deal."

The cards had fallen from my lap when I'd tucked my legs underneath. Sully picked up the deck and held it out to the blind Stolorth. The six-fingered hand closed around his with a surety, a firmness. Quite possibly a message.

Sully laughed and pulled his hand away. "Keep an eye on him, Chaz," he said as Ren shook the deck from the box, feathered the cards with a professional air. "He cheats."

I learned several things that night.

I learned the blind could play cards if the cards have raised areas they can distinguish through touch. "There are other words for it, in other cultures," Ren told me. "We call the system *vaytar*."

I learned that other blind Stolorths do exist, but predominantly in a small Englarian community on Calfedar. One more bit of information that ran opposite to what I'd been taught in Non-Human Cultures. We were taught the Englarians viewed a Stolorth's *Ragkiril* mind talents as soul-stealing, something far more heinous in their view than the violation of privacy as defined by the Baris Human Rights Accord. But the blind ones—their blindness a "gift" from the abbot, as Drogue had said—were considered acceptable.

Which made me question, again, the extent of Ren's talents. Drogue seemed so sure he was nothing more than an empath. Or was a limited telepathy acceptable to the Englarians as well?

Ren had lost his sight gradually, had been brought to

the compound when he was seven, fully blind by then. He still remembered being able to see.

"What do I miss seeing the most? My ocean. It's a brilliant blue-green. And there's a flower we call a *mai-isar* that grows along the shore. Quite lovely. A deep reddish-brown in color but streaked with gold. It glistens. It's very soft, with a marvelous scent."

I was watching Ren describe his memories and didn't know Sully had reached for me until his hand ran down my braid.

"Like Chasidah's hair," Sully said.

Could empaths receive a sense of color?

I learned that Ren had spent very little time with humans. The Englarian compound was staffed by Takan families devoted to the church. Humans he saw only at church services or in upper-level classes at school, and then mostly males.

I was the third human female he'd ever spoken to at any length. He admitted he'd never met the real Sister Berri, only listened to reports of her work. I was one of two human females he'd ever shared a meal with, played cards with. Obviously, the only female roommate he'd ever had.

I learned he was thirty years old, five years younger than myself. But that was in human terms. Stolorths had longer life spans. If his own kind didn't kill him, he could expect to live at least one hundred fifty years.

It was almost 2330 hours, station time, before I could dislodge Sully from the game and the bed. No MOC or stripers came calling. Save for several outbursts of colorful epithets related to the sequence of the cards, it was blissfully quiet. The earlier tensions between Sully and myself had dissolved. And I accepted that much of what I'd thought was about to happen had been due strictly to misinterpretation.

It didn't take much self-analysis to note I was over-wrought and exhausted.

Sully left, grumbling. He owed Ren four thousand two hundred twenty-one credits. Add that to the one million, seven hundred thousand credits he already owed the Stolorth, and someday Ren would be very wealthy. If Sully ever paid.

I broke even and was tired enough to almost trip on my robe on the way into the shower. I fell gratefully into the cot, which now held a pillow as well, while Ren went to soak in the tub.

I read Drogue's pamphlet on Englarian rituals for a little while, but couldn't keep my eyes open. Any questions I'd wanted to pose to Ren slipped from my mind. I don't remember hearing Ren finish his bath or climb into his own bed. But he must have, because when I awoke, disoriented for a moment, I could see the outline of his form. The clock on the wall read 0420.

Morning meditation was at 0600. I rolled onto my back. I'd had only about five hours' sleep, but it was more than I'd had in one stretch since I'd been taken to Moabar. I could make it to morning meditations. But I didn't know if I was expected to attend.

I'd ask Ren when he woke. Maybe ask him about other things as well. I found I looked forward to that—not so much because I could get some questions answered, but because he was truly pleasant to talk to. It felt odd to feel a friendship toward an adult male Stolorth, yet not. He wasn't a *Ragkiril* capable of intruding into my thoughts and manipulating them. And he might be a thirty-year-old male, but he was in many ways the most innocent thirty-year-old male I'd ever known. There was an eagerness in him, an honest desire to please that reminded me of Willym, my nine-year-old half brother.

I'd seen Willym a few times last year when my orders had brought me through Marker. That's when Thad and I still, marginally, got along. And my stepmother, Suzette, was in a mood to irritate my father.

I was sure they'd told Willym I was dead. I hoped they had. He was a good kid. He didn't need to grow up with any shadows. Or ghosts.

"Sadness, Chasidah?" Ren's voice was as soft as the pale glow of light filtering under the door.

He was reading my emotions. Given the early hour, I felt guilty for awakening him. "Sorry. My mind was wandering."

"I've been reciting my meditations. It was no disturbance. And please, I didn't mean to intrude." His covers rustled as he turned on his side.

"You're not." I knew he was doing what Sully had asked him. But he was also, I suspected, genuinely concerned.

"Your sadness is so very singular. This is normal for all human females, yes?"

"Singular?" That struck me first as an odd comment, and then terribly true. We did suffer quietly, within ourselves. "Humans can't share emotions like you can."

"And when you're sad, you...think about it? You hold it within yourself until it goes away?"

That was an accurate description. "Usually. Some people cry a lot. Some drink. Or just talk to a friend."

"This dispels it?"

"For a while. What do you do, Ren, when you're sad?"

"I rarely am."

This from a blind Stolorth cut off from his own people by a death sentence. Like I'd been. "Stolorths just don't get unhappy, or you don't?"

"My people are always linked to the Great Sea. To

the stars. Through the wisdom of Abbot Eng, I reconnect with that."

"But not as a telepath?" This was my key question.

"This still concerns you. I lost the High Link when I lost my sight."

I accepted his answer for the moment. There were times to press, times to pull back. "And your family?"

"Was that the source of your sad thoughts, Chasidah? My family were the Takas who raised me, and all my brothers and sisters in the church. And now I have more family with Sully, Marsh, Dorsie, and Gregor. And you."

I recognized two of the names. Gregor was Sully's pilot, Marsh his second in command before his well-publicized demise two years ago on Garno. I'd often wondered what happened to them.

I also had a feeling they were the "advisers" who'd voted against my rescue. I'd never made their lives particularly pleasant.

I sat up in the darkness, now wide awake. 0435. "Join me for some tea? Coffee?"

"That's always needed at this hour, yes."

I'd slept in the long shift. It was probably wrinkled, but my robe would cover it. I splashed water on my face, and when I came out of the bath Ren was dressed.

I was sitting on the cot, combing the knots out of my hair when he came out of the bath, his long hair also unbound. Something else we had in common.

I held up the comb and then belatedly realized he couldn't see it. "I'll do yours if you'll do mine."

He tilted his face.

"Hair," I told him. "I'll do your braid, if you like. Unless your arms bend backward more easily than mine do."

He chuckled. "There are some times that I miss what families do for each other."

He sat on the edge of the bench. I straddled it behind him, combed out his hair. It was a beautiful shade of blue; its texture thick, silky, magnificent. In the room's lighting, his damp skin was silvery. He closed his eyes as I worked his braid, his lashes dark against his cheeks.

I leaned slightly sideways to study Ren's profile as the braid flowed through my fingers. His nose was straight, his mouth generous, the lines of his jaw and cheekbones almost regal. He had a handsomeness defined by elegance. Which was reflected in the fluid way he moved. In the gentleness—and genuineness—I heard in his voice.

He handed me a short leather tie as I finished off the braid. "Thank you. My *marala* used to do that for me."

"*Marala?*"

"It is a Takan term of affection for *mother*."

"My mother used to braid mine too." I switched places with him, pressed the comb into his hand. It was webbed and six-fingered. It didn't bother me as it would have a week ago.

He pulled my hair back through both hands. "Your hair's very long." He sounded surprised.

Empaths couldn't see images, then.

"It's thick, though, so it braids up shorter," I told him. His fingers moved in an unfamiliar pattern. I reached back, felt his work. Intricate. I'd have to look in a mirror later. Though from what my fingers could feel, I doubted I could replicate it.

"It's all right?"

"Different pattern. I like it."

"The color's beautiful. Like a *maiisar* blossom."

"You can sense the color?"

A moment of silence. "Sully told me."

I remembered that. I handed him a short hair tie, let

him wrap the end. Ran my hand down it one more time. Good braid. It would stay nicely in place.

"It's ten after five," I told him as he stood and reached unerringly for the desk to put the comb on top. The red numbers glowed on the wall. "I want to get coffee." I hesitated, remembered I was talking to an empath, plunged ahead. "But first I need—"

"Something disconcerts you. How I can help?"

His responses were an admission that he was sensing me, reading me. "Did Sully ask you to read my emotions because he thinks my allegiance is still to the Fleet?"

He thought for a moment. Or perhaps read some more of my emotions. "Sully is very worried about you. But I'm his friend, not his spy. He knows what you've been through. His respect, and faith toward you, is greater than you realize."

"I don't think he trusts me."

"He trusts you, Chasidah. He fears you do not trust him."

"I believe in what he's trying to do. Shut down an illegal gen-lab."

"So do I, or I'd not be here." He ran his hand across the row of hooks on the wall by the bed. Both our robes hung there. He fingered the small tag at the neckline, correctly chose his own. Touch-labeled, like the playing cards Sully carried.

He draped the robe over his arm. "Chasidah..."

When my name hung in the air without anything further, I nodded, then remembered again he couldn't see that. "Hmm?" The universal noncommittal.

"May I ask...may I request a small favor as well?"

"Sure." After all, he'd just answered my prying question.

"May I see you?"

"See me?" I didn't quite understand.

"Yes, see you. I'd like to see your face. I've not . . . I'd like to believe, in spite of our beginnings dirtside, we are friends. Am I presuming too much?"

"No, you're not." I thought I understood his request. Blindness was an infirmity unknown in humans in the Empire. I'd read accounts, in Ancient History classes in the academy, of times when blind humans could "see" a face through touch. "If you touch my face, you'll know what I look like, is that it?"

He nodded. "If this is too intrusive, tell me. I just . . . it's just that I've not known anyone like you before."

"Don't know many court-martialed Fleet captains turned prison escapees, is that it?" I grinned wryly.

A small laugh. "You are unique, Chasidah Bergren."

"I'm not the one with blue hair and six fingers," I quipped.

I sat on the bench. Ren dropped his robe to the floor and sat facing me, his back to the door. He raised both hands, cupped my face. His touch was soft yet firm. His clouded silver eyes watched me, unmoving.

Both thumbs moved up my jaw, fingers traced my ears, moved across my cheekbones, down my nose. Ren's explorations reminded me of a sculptor examining the details of a carving. I was very aware he was male, but there was nothing intrusive, nothing erotic, in his touch.

"I have freckles," I told him. "But you can't feel those."

"Freckles?"

"Tiny darker spots of pigment, across my cheeks and nose. I was always told they were cute. Once I passed the age of twelve, I hated them." I hated being cute, though I long ago resigned myself to the fact that the description probably fit.

"Ah, freckles. Kisses from the sun on the face." His

fingers brushed across my brows. I closed my eyes. He softly touched my lids, my lashes.

"What color are your eyes?"

"Like my hair. Brown and gold."

His hands cupped my jaw again. "Sully told the truth, then. You're a beautiful woman."

I laughed off the compliment. "I have a feeling Sully thinks all women are beautiful."

"That's not what he tells me."

I didn't have an answer to that one. But I remembered the fool I saw in the mirror in the monastery, and the obsidian eyes watching her. And I remembered a mouth brushing mine in that dark bar in Port Chalo. Gabriel Ross Sullivan was a dangerous man, who played dangerous games. I didn't even know the rules.

Ren held my face a moment longer. "Thank you." He leaned his forehead against mine. I felt a strange calmness, a warmth flutter through me.

Then a sound, a hushed whoosh. And a sharp intake of breath.

"Lovely. What do we have here?" The voice was harsh, deep, very male. Very Sully.

I jerked back. He stood in the doorway in his monk's sand-gray robe. His dark brows were slanted into a frown.

Ren turned toward the door. His hand drifted down, casually clasped my wrist. A slight pressure, a squeeze. Reassuring warmth traveled up my arm from his touch. "Sully. Blessings of the hour. We were going to get a light breakfast."

"Really?" One word, heavily laced with sarcasm.

"Sully." Ren's voice was a combination of gentleness and firmness. I didn't know how he did that. He should give classes at the academy.

A long pause. "You said she was beautiful. She is."

Sully snorted. "It's a requirement for Fleet patrol captains. Disarms the enemy." He stepped back into the hallway, one hand on the door to keep it from closing. "You want something before service, you'd better move it."

He pulled his hand away. The door slid closed on his retreating footsteps.

Morning meditations, I learned, consisted of two parts: primary or essentials, then, after a short break, secondary or supplications. I sat quietly between Ren and Sully through the essentials, listened to the tinkling of the bells as Brother Clement played them on the raised platform. I mimicked Ren's and Sully's posture, head bowed under my hood, steepled fingers touching my forehead. But I had no idea what words went through their minds.

My own raced over too many things. My strange and unexpected sense of kinship with Ren, a Stolorth. The constant threat of the MOC officers and stripers just outside the temple doors. The Takas I no longer feared—at least, not here on station. Too many of them were Englarian; the temple was half full this morning. Almost all of them would, at some point today, begin Peyhar's celebrations. Sully confirmed my earlier theory. A station full of mellow Takas was a good thing.

His anger over Ren's "seeing" my face—if that's what it was—had dissipated when Ren and I entered the common room. He talked animatedly about the celebration, complained to Brother Clement about his ever-mounting financial debt to Ren. He was still in a light-hearted mood when we walked down the short corridor and in through the temple's back door. When the bells chimed again, his right boot snaked around my left. Playing "footsie," like a mischievous child in church.

I tilted my face just far enough to catch a glimpse of his. He peered around his fingertips at me, winked.

Three deep chimes. Brother Clement rose from the short bench in the center of the platform, spread out his arms. "May peace and wisdom fill your hearts today, brothers and sisters. Supplications for the devout will follow shortly."

The Takas around me shifted, sighing deeply rumbling sighs. Heads lifted. Some stood, others stayed seated.

Sully's hand cupped my elbow. "Come on," he said softly.

I glanced at Ren. He nodded, but he didn't rise as we did.

I followed Sully to the common room. He pushed back his hood as the doors closed behind us. I did the same, knowing this meant we were safe here. Only in the public area of the temple did we keep our heads and faces covered as much as possible.

He pulled out a chair. "Sit." He took the one next to mine.

I folded my hands on the tabletop. "When do we have to go back?"

"As long as we were seen at the essentials, that's good enough for a few hours." His expression held that familiar arrogance, chin slightly tilted up. "I found us a ship. All you have to do is fly it for us."

I straightened. *Praise the stars!* ran through my head. Shit. I was turning into an Englarian. "Here?"

"Scheduled to make station tomorrow. I don't have an ETA yet. But she's listed on incoming, slated for a berth on Level Six-Green."

The temple was Nine-Green. Three levels below us. Not lugger territory. Another tri-hauler, like the *Diligent*? "How large a freighter?"

"She's not a freighter. She's a Lancer-Class P40."

I sat, stunned. My last command had been a

Lancer-Class P40. A little peashooter, as Sully had called it. "How in hell are you going to convince an Imperial patrol ship to get us off station?"

He grinned. "I'm not. You are. I told you, you're going to fly it for us."

"There's no way—"

"It's our best chance, Chaz. You know those ships, their security systems and overrides."

"You're talking about commandeering an Imperial P40!"

"They can't court-martial you twice."

"That's the least of my worries. You're putting the three of us against ten, fifteen officers and crew. Armed officers and crew. Berthed at a military station." And one of us was blind.

"Yeah, I know. Sounds like fun to me too."

"Sullivan!"

"It's the last thing they'll expect. Surely you appreciate that. I spent a couple of hours last night roaming through the stripers' reports. They can't confirm whether Milo sent a warning message, but they suspect he did. There were some scrambled transmits that went through the MOC filters dirtside yesterday. I sent two more last night and back-transed them, just to keep them busy. So they're watching ships coming up from dirtside. Watching short-haulers and luggers."

I had to be crazy. He was starting to make sense.

"Plus, there were some antigovernment demonstrations on Tos Faros last week. Now the stripers are sure that's what the *Diligent* was doing here. Looking to spring Sheldon Blaine."

Blaine's trial had been about two years ago. He was a flamboyant figure, and I was never quite sure what fueled him: his passion for the throne or his love of newshounds' vidcams. It was the latter that tripped him up, though. He was caught on camera negotiating the funding for an assassination attempt on Prew so that he could take his rightful place on the throne. He was sent to Moabar for that. I'd been in rather elite company down there.

"They're concentrating on anything coming from or through Tos Faros," I guessed. "Or any crew with Farosian ties." And not, I hoped, on a ghost and a court-martialed patrol captain who could run a P40 in her sleep. "She's due in tomorrow?"

"Updates should be in ops by 1300. I'll have more then."

"Do we know which ship? The captain?"

"That I do, my angel. Captain's listed as Kingswell. Ship's the *Meritorious*."

My mouth hung open for a moment before the words exploded out of it. "*Meritorious*? God damn you, Sullivan! You know that's my ship!"

He was grinning widely, dangerous lights dancing in his dark eyes. "Told you this would be fun."

I sat back in the chair and stared at him. The *Meritorious*. Coming here. With that pompous son of a bitch Lew Kingswell sitting in the captain's sling. My captain's sling.

Sully was right. This was definitely going to be fun. I didn't even pull my hand away when he reached for it and planted a kiss on my wrist. It just seemed right, somehow.

Peyhar's Week celebrations officially began at 1930 hours station time. Our celebrations started a little earlier.

Sully accessed his link to station ops shortly after 1300 hours. He confirmed the *Meritorious,* under Kingswell's command, would arrive at 1100 hours tomorrow, completing her duties as special escort for the new assistant stationmaster. Commander Hilary Burnell was retiring. Commander Izak Chaves got her post.

Lucky Izak. I wondered whom he'd pissed off to warrant a five-year stint on Moabar Station.

I'd handled special escort service before; all patrol ships did from time to time, when something small and fast was required. Especially when the dignitary was someone as minor as an assistant stationmaster. So I knew the routine. I spelled it out to Ren and Sully as we lunched privately in Ren's cabin, the long bench an impromptu table, the floor, our chairs. We sat in various cross-legged or angled positions and enjoyed our celebratory lunch. Sully had even cadged another bottle of wine.

"It's going to be by no means easy." I pointed my fork at Sully, who was still gloating. "If I can get on board, yes, I can take her systems. Then we have to get the crew off. As quietly and quickly as possible."

I didn't like Lew Kingswell. Never had. But I had no grudge against him and whoever his crew was now. I only knew his crew wasn't mine. My exec and second had stood in my defense. They were demoted, busted down to supply-barge duty somewhere, last I heard. "Sparks," my engineer, had put in for early retirement, and had sent me a long transmit when I was still in star-port lockup. He'd lost faith in the Fleet, he said. And in the Empire.

His sentiments were echoed, in one form or another, by the eight others serving under me on that fateful tour of duty. None stayed with the *Meritorious,* though I doubt they'd been offered the chance.

So we would face an unknown crew, anywhere from ten to fifteen counting Kingswell—a pompous, loud braggart who took great pleasure in bullying junior offi-cers and crew.

I didn't like him, but I didn't wish him dead.

Ren dunked the hard crust of his bread in his soup. "Could we stow away, take the ship when she heads back in-system?"

"Ten or more of them against the three of us? Not great odds," I told him.

Sully shook his head. "Workable, if we take them out one, two at a time."

"You might be able to take out two, trank and stow them somewhere. But by the time you grabbed crew member three, the other eight or so would notice. You're talking a P40. This is a small ship. Three decks. Bridge backs up to the captain's cabin, which abuts common room, crew's quarters. Whole lower deck's engines and cargo, or troop space, depending on your orders that tour. Sick bay, weapons, repair, and enviro on second. That's it."

He wasn't easily dissuaded. "Let's leave it as an option."

"We can leave it as an option, but not a top choice. Keep in mind that an action taken in the lanes could result in a mayday. Could result in a response from Fleet, in the form of a cruiser or, worse, destroyer. Then you're facing down the big guns. No, we need to take the ship here, on the rim, slip somewhere out-system for a while. Keep them wondering."

Sully's lips curved in a teasing smile. "Is that what I used to do to you?"

I laughed. "I never wondered about you, Sully. You were consistent in your inconsistencies. I never had any trouble finding you in the midst of some wild escapade."

He leaned his elbow on the bench. "Did it ever occur to you that's because I wanted you to find me?"

I shot him a disbelieving look. "Did it ever occur to you that you have a difficult time admitting you're not infallible?"

"Why," he drawled, "would I admit to something that's not true?"

I touched Ren's arm. "No more wine for him. He's delusional."

A deep, soft laugh, like water tumbling over stones.

"Gentlemen," I said, "we still have a problem to solve. And less than four hours in which to do it." Our presence would be required at the temple ceremonies this evening. Drogue had insisted on that.

Sully poured another round of wine. "We could invite them to Peyhar's. Get them all furry on honeylace."

"Kingswell doesn't get furry. He swaggers around,

finds something he thinks is small and weak, then beats on it and claims victory."

"Delightful. Introduce us, will you?"

"You don't fit the requirements." He wasn't remotely small or weak. He'd picked me up last night without a struggle.

"Won't his crew take some liberty here?" Ren asked. "There are several pubs popular with off-duty station security and MOC personnel."

And it was a long run from in-system. "Depends on their tour. More than likely they didn't come from Aldan or Baris Prime, but ran an intercept to a cruiser that had Chaves on board."

"Even if they intercepted at Dafir," Sully said, "it's still a good week at top speeds to Moabar."

"True." I sipped my wine, played with some scenarios. The Empire was gridded on an ancient linguistic–numeric character set. The inner quadrants were Aldan and Baris, Prime through Four. Further out were Calth and Dafir, Prime through Six, with Six being rim. Moabar was in No-Name Quadrant E-5. A good seven-day run for a P40 from Dafir Six. My own trip from the Imperial prison on a starport in Baris Three took three weeks and two jumpgates just to get to Dafir Six and the waiting MOC transport ship.

So it was a week back to Dafir for Kingswell and his crew. "They just might take liberty." Ren's idea began to have some possibilities. "In shifts, of course."

Ren splayed his six-fingered hand against the bench. "Working on the most negative scenario. Captain plus crew of fourteen. How would liberty be structured?"

"On an unsecured port, small shifts, minimal exposure. But this is a secure port. Very little commercial traffic. Mostly military, government. No civilians."

"Except us," Ren said.

"You're clergy. The government loves you because you keep the Takas happy." That was true. We had standing no-interference orders on Englarians.

"So if they take liberty, or can be encouraged to take liberty," Ren continued, "we will then have a much smaller onboard situation to deal with."

Sully made a dismissive gesture with his hand. "Then all we have to do is break docking clamps, drop into the lanes, and offer prayers, of course, that no one in ops or departure control notices our slight transgression. Or the alarms blaring on their consoles." He leaned toward me. "That's the risk, Chaz, of pulling anything right here."

He was opting for the stowaway scenario. But he was wrong. "We're not going to have to blow the clamps. Ops will gladly withdraw them. And we'll get clearance to undock as well."

Station might figure out something was wrong when we hit the lanes, but we'd have at least ten minutes on any pursuit ships at that point. And my little P40 could do a lot with ten minutes if she were up to speed.

Ren smiled. "I believe the captain has a plan."

I smiled back, knowing he couldn't see it but hoping he could feel it. "Yes. I do."

Sully arched a dark eyebrow.

"Tugs." My gaze switched from Sully to Ren, then back to Sully again. A second eyebrow slowly rose. "When we came in on Chalford's ship, we were delayed because the tugs were busy moving a couple of luggers off dock due to interface malfunctions. What if we can duplicate those problems at Six-Green Three? Kingswell's not going to have his ship sit with no fresh water and only intermittent power. And no trans link. He'll have to move to another berth and won't call back a full crew on liberty to do so. Engineer probably, and helm. Plus, he won't need a tug. P40s are designed for close maneuvering."

"And we'll just happen to be on board," Sully said. A slow, wicked smile spread across his face.

"Fancy that," I told him.

Ren, beside me, let out a quiet sigh. "Praise the stars."

"No. Praise Chaz. The best interfering bitch in the quadrant. Maybe," Sully added, reaching for my hand, "even in the entire damned universe."

He planted a soft kiss on my wrist, winking at me from over my own fingers.

Brazenly, with a newfound confidence, I winked back. It had begun to feel as if I had a chance at winning this game.

Showtime. Not the more dangerous one, taking the *Meritorious*. We were still a few hours from that. But the beginning of Peyhar's, with me in a silver gown and gauzy, hooded robe, standing on the raised platform of the temple. Sully, in a deeper gray robe, stood next to me. We were both to the right of Drogue and Clement in the center, wearing bright gold robes trimmed with wide bands of silver.

All eyes were on them. Yet I felt exposed and tried to keep my face shadowed. Which wasn't easy with the lights shining on the large arch-and-stave behind me on the platform.

Clement struck the chimes, Drogue's voice lilted into a songlike prayer. Ren, in dark gray like Sully, moved down the center aisle with two other acolytes, swinging incense lanterns left and right.

The temple smelled smoky-sweet. A very mild mixture of glory seeds and some harmless herbs, Drogue had told me shortly before the ceremony. Relaxing, but far from intoxicating.

The Takas and a few humans on the bench seats breathed deeply, almost as if one. I fought the urge to sneeze, focused instead on the mural on the back wall: Abbot Eng again, red cape billowing, with a glowing soul-stealer kneeling before him. No, not kneeling—collapsing, the abbot's stave sticking out of its spine. Long black hair, matted with blood, fell almost to the ground, hiding the demon's face. It was naked from the waist up, wings unfurling from a muscled back. Its silvery glow was muted, fading. Wonderful image to hold in your mind while you breathed glory-seed fumes.

Yet an oddly appropriate one. According to legend, a few thousand years ago Eng had fought the soul-stealers. Now his followers would be taking up the same fight against jukors, the distorted lab-bred version of their mythical cousins.

The chimes tinkled again. Sully touched my arm, indicating we should step back to the wall.

My sole function, and Sully's, was to hand Drogue and Clement the sacred objects from the low table behind us. All I could think about was taking back the *Meritorious*. The slow, languid movements of the ceremony felt like torture.

I caught a slight nod of Drogue's head, the first signal. I turned to the table, reaching for a metal flask. Sully's warm hand covered mine for a moment. I looked at him in surprise.

"Relax." His voice was just above a whisper, his small smile just the slightest curve of his mouth.

My heart pounded. Every time I thought of my ship, adrenaline raced through me. I gave him a short nod as I handed him the flask. "Okay," I whispered back.

I picked up the metal plate with four squat goblets, held on to the plate with both hands.

"Breathe," he told me as we walked to the center of the platform.

I didn't want to breathe. The incense tickled my throat. I inhaled deeply anyway. Fleet had taught me long ago how to stay focused. This was far from my first mission.

Clement took the plate from me; Drogue took the flask. A short invocation, then Drogue and Clement drank the liquid in one swallow.

Honeylace, I realized belatedly. Good thing those goblets were small.

Drogue smiled at me, took the remaining two goblets from the plate, held them out to Sully and myself.

They expected me to drink this stuff? Tomorrow would be tough enough without a hangover.

Drogue must have caught my frown. "Sip and put it back," he said softly.

I tilted the goblet, let a drop fall on my tongue. Sweet, cloyingly sweet. I placed it, full, on the tray.

Sully's went back empty.

Oh, great. I hoped he didn't share Newlin's predilection. I needed him sober and functioning tomorrow. It would be difficult enough taking the *Meritorious* with a blind Stolorth. A blind drunk would make it damned near impossible.

More singing, more chanting, more incense, more honeylace. Three more times we refilled the goblets. Three more times Sully finished not only his but, when we turned back to the table, mine.

"Sullivan!" I hissed when he put down my empty goblet.

"Relax." Obsidian eyes, half-hooded, glinted.

Oh, great.

But he moved easily, without faltering. Maybe the stuff wasn't as strong as the honeylace the Takas used. Logically, it shouldn't be. Drogue and Clement wouldn't be able to conduct a ceremony totally furred.

Ren and the other acolytes brought the incense lanterns to the platform, positioning them in the center. Gray smoke spiraled upward. One of the acolytes drew a larger flask from a side alcove, while Ren retrieved a basket of small goblets. The Takas and humans filed out of the benches, lined up, hands open expectantly.

Clement filled goblets, Drogue bestowed them along with blessings of the stars, of the hour, for wisdom, for peace . . .

I suddenly realized I stood alone by the small table. Sully was missing. Then I spotted him at the end of the line, Ren beside him. They took their goblets, drank. I noticed Sully held a third.

The temple emptied out. Sully strode up the short steps, his robe rippling over his body, outlining his wide shoulders, narrow hips. His gaze, shadowed by his hood, was directly on me; his mouth curved slightly in a smile, as if he wanted to grin but knew this wasn't the time or the place for it.

"Chazzy-girl. Peace, wisdom, and, most of all, love." He offered me the goblet. "You did fine."

I took the goblet, but only to put it on the table behind me. "I didn't sneeze or trip over my robe. I consider that a rousing success."

His gaze went over my shoulder to the table. "Sacrilege to waste that."

"I can live with that sin."

"You're much too beautiful to be consigned to Hell." He took the goblet back, drained it. "That makes twice now I've saved you from perdition."

He put the empty goblet on the table, hooked his arm

through mine as he moved back. "We're not needed here any longer."

Ren, who'd been talking to Drogue, turned as we passed him. Sully put his free hand on Ren's arm, held his sightless gaze. "All of life's a risk, isn't it?" His voice was wistful.

Drogue bowed slightly. "Our prayers and the guidance from the stars go with you. All of you."

It dawned on me that Sully and Ren were probably as nervous as I was about the *Meritorious*. About getting off station alive. About evading any pursuit the MOC or the Imperial Fleet might send after us.

That was easy to forget around Sully because he seemed to show only two emotions: confidence, or anger and confidence. Yet he had to know the odds weren't overwhelmingly in our favor. He'd been in the business, as he called it, a long time.

I let him lead me through the temple's back doors, past Abbot Eng and his demon, and forgave him his slight indulgence in honeylace.

His fingers slipped through mine as we stepped through the second doorway. The wall clock in the common room glowed 2115. But we didn't stop there.

We came to the end of the hallway. He turned me away from Ren's doorway, touched the palm pad for his own, across the way. He held my hand tightly, and for the first time I saw something hesitant in his obsidian gaze, something in the way his lashes lowered quickly, then flicked up. Something in the way he started to speak, his mouth parting, then quickly closing.

Oh, God. The *Meritorious* wasn't coming in. It was the only thing I could think of that would make him appear so dismayed, so unsure. He knew what it meant to me. The infallible Sullivan hated failure.

"All of life's a risk," he said softly. "I'm about to take a big one."

He pulled me against him, his arms locking around me. His mouth covered mine, taking in my gasp of surprise. He answered with a kiss I remembered well, a kiss of intense passion, his tongue stroking, probing. His hands splayed on my back, pushing me against the hard planes of his body.

Heat seared, flared through my senses as if I were absorbing it from his touch. For a moment I was lost, breathless, dizzy, as if I'd downed a bottle of honeylace ...

Honeylace.

Fool.

I twisted my face away. His lips brushed my neck. "Sullivan. Stop it." My voice rasped into the folds of his robe.

He stopped, though his arms still held me tightly. I could feel him breathing hard, his chest rising and falling rapidly against my face. I could smell the clean, soapy scent coming off the heat of his skin. I could taste the tingling sweetness of the honeylace from his mouth.

I could ignore the warning sirens screaming in my mind, tell my self-respect to hit a jumpgate, and could very, very easily rip his robe off. With my teeth.

I wanted to. Praise the stars I wanted to. I wanted him. But I couldn't. I pulled my face out of his chest. And tried not to see the desperate hunger in the depths of his obsidian eyes. A hunger that matched my own. But, I suspected, for different reasons.

"Not this way, Sully," I told him.

"Why?" His voice was as raspy as mine.

I curled my hands into small fists, drew a deep breath. "Because you're seriously furred. And I'm"—I let the breath out—"confused."

Strong fingers stroked my spine. "Maybe I like my women confused."

His women. There probably was a lengthy list.

I pushed away from him, a wry smile on my lips. "Maybe I just don't want to be another one of your confused women."

"Chaz?" He reached for my hand, but I'd already stepped toward Ren's door.

I hit the palm pad. "Get some sleep, Sullivan. The real show starts tomorrow. Common room, 0600."

I was still sitting on the edge of my cot, turning my dagger over and over in my hands, when Ren came in an hour later. He tilted his face up in a gesture I recognized as his sensing for a presence. The door closed behind him.

"Hello, Ren."

He shook his head. "Sully," he said softly, in a voice that rippled of breezes over a long-forgotten pond, "is very angry with himself."

I didn't doubt that. He wasn't used to failure. Or, I suspected, to a woman turning down a chance—my second chance—to snag a coveted place on the list of his women. Probably very few had.

But all I had left was my self-respect. The Imperial military court had stripped me of everything else. And I'd be damned, just because they'd fucked me over, if that gave everyone else the right to do the same.

I let the dagger wrap around my wrist as I stood. "I'm going to take a shower." I didn't want to hear him make excuses for Sully. I didn't want to hear anything about Sully at all.

He only nodded, began to undo the sash around his robe. "I'll have tea for you when you come out."

The kindness, and acceptance, behind Ren's simple

offer made a lump form in my throat. I wondered how I'd ever thought he was innocent. He had a wisdom deeper than those oceans he so treasured, and so missed.

I'd have to find him one. Hell, I was Chasidah Bergren, Court-Martialed Captain. The Best Interfering Bitch in the Universe. If I could hijack a P40 and sabotage the Marker shipyards, I should be able to commandeer an ocean.

And maybe even drown Gabriel Ross Sullivan in it when I got the chance.

In the morning I pulled on my fatigue pants and black jacket. Later, I'd add the robe. It would feel bulky but I wouldn't have to walk far. Just to the lift, then down three levels to Six-Green.

Ren was in the bath when I slipped from his quarters. I headed for the common room, intending to return his gesture of the night before and bring back tea. I knew it was possible I'd run into Sully. Better to get it over with, face the ghost in his own lair. We had too much to accomplish to let inebriation and hormones become an issue right now. Because that's all it could be. I'd thought about it all night. Twice he'd kissed me, twice he'd been drunk. Sober, the flamboyant, charming Sullivan wouldn't even notice someone like me.

Which was probably one reason why I found him so damnably attractive.

He was seated at the table, a steaming mug cupped between his hands. He raised his face when I walked in. He looked like a man who'd done some serious drinking. His dark eyes were shadowed. He'd not shaved. His short, thick hair was tousled.

"Chaz."

"Sullivan." I headed for the commissary panel, tabbed in two orders of tea. Leaned against the wall while the unit hummed softly.

Sully had turned in his seat, and watched me. He had on a black jacket, spacer-plain like mine, dark pants. His jacket was open to reveal a black, high-necked shirt underneath.

I damned the fact that he could look so good while looking so bad. "You pick up a confirm on Kingswell's ETA?" Business, let's stick to business. It was 0545. Fleet regs would have required the *Meritorious* to relay her position and speed to ops forty-five minutes ago.

If they were going to be early—or late—we needed to know.

"On schedule." He propped one arm on the back of his chair.

I took the first mug of tea as it appeared, hit the tab to okay the second. "Kingswell will be early. He doesn't like the big wide darkness." There was a lot of nothing between Moabar and the closest station in Dafir.

I grabbed the second tea, walked past his chair.

"Chaz."

I closed my eyes briefly, then half-turned. The pungent aroma wafting up from the mugs set my stomach to growling. The trepidation in his voice when he said my name shot a small pain through my heart. I knew what was coming. The apology, the disclaimer. Sober, I wasn't his type. Even though I expected it, it would still hurt to hear it. I opted for the quick and painless route. "I've got to get this to Ren while it's still hot."

His gaze zigzagged for a moment, as if he were reading lines of data in the air between us. "About last night. I'm sorry."

I shrugged, careful not to spill the tea. Careful to keep my expression impassive. "You were furred. It makes people do stupid things."

He stared at me, didn't say anything.

I was giving him a legitimate out, damn it! Why didn't he take it? Make it easy, less embarrassing for both of us. The hot mugs began to burn my fingers. I drew a deep breath. "It's not important." I held up one mug. "Let me get this to Ren, okay? Then I need an absolute confirm on berth allocation so we can start skewing their dock interfaces." I backed up toward the door. "And we need to know if a Taka's assigned to ramp security."

I was almost into the hallway before he nodded. "Ren will handle that."

"Fine," I called out over my shoulder. I juggled both mugs in one hand, hit the palm pad with the other.

Ren was by his bed, straightening the long sleeves of his black thermal shirt. He smiled in recognition when I walked in.

"Got us tea," I said.

"I can smell it. Many thanks."

I set his mug down on the small bed table behind him. He wasn't wearing the light-colored wide-legged pants of an Englarian monk but dark fatigues, similar to my own. I'd never seen him in civilian garb before. His muscular form was even more striking in the tight-fitting shirt and straight pants. Another admittedly handsome male specimen. But he didn't affect me the way Sully did.

"How'd you know it was me?"

A slight frown. "I know your voice."

"No. When I walked in. You smiled before I even

spoke." Imperial Fleet ships all had ID scanners over cabin doorways. But even if the temple's quarters had them, Ren couldn't see them.

"I know your resonance."

"You mean, you scan, or read, someone who walks in?"

"No. Reading you empathically is different than seeing your resonance."

"Explain."

"An empath sees or senses individuals by the vibrational colors their bodies resonate. Each one is unique. All I need to do is see your pattern, attach your name to it in my mind, and it, to me, is you."

"A walking rainbow?"

He sighed. "It's been many years since I've seen a rainbow, but yes. Something like that."

For a moment, the story of Abbott Eng's soul-stealers flashed into my mind, accompanied by a trickle of unease in my gut. But no, that was wrong. Ren wasn't sending light or colors to me. He was reading *my* light, my energy field. It wasn't at all the same thing. "Can I change my colors? Disguise them, so you wouldn't know me?"

"Your pattern is your pattern. But it does vary slightly depending on many things, like illness. Or moods."

"Sadness?" I remembered his questions from the other morning. "Fear?"

"Yes. But your pattern does not tell me your thoughts. Or the reasons for your moods. So it is not intrusive. It still retains the holiness and purity of your mind." He reached for his tea, unerringly.

"Thermals. You sense or see heat. That's how you know where the tea is."

He smiled. "Very good."

"Then you're not completely blind. You don't move around in total blackness. You can see..."

"Indistinct images or forms outlined in colors." He took another sip.

"Living things and inanimate objects?" Not all objects emitted heat, though most everything contained some form of energy.

"Yes."

I began to understand. And saw how I'd misinterpreted that for telepathy. He could "see" someone walk in and would nod in greeting just as a sighted person would. "So you can tell how tall I am, for example, compared to—" I waved my hand in the air, not wanting to name the first name that came to my mind.

He did. "Sully. Compared to Sully, I know you are smaller."

"He was in the common room, when I got the tea."

"Was he?"

It was a question that wasn't a question, and that told me Ren knew Sully was there. I wondered if different colors tumbled through my rainbow when I thought about him.

A dangerous man. Dangerous to even think about. I had other problems. "He said you might be able to find out if a striper or a Taka was set for ramp duty for Six-Green Three."

"Probably a Taka. With Peyhar's this week, they all reschedule to early duties in order to be able to attend the services at night."

I finished my tea, tossed the empty mug in the recyc. "I don't want anyone hurt, if we can help it. Any chance we could get a Taka to look the other way for a while?"

He felt on the bed for his jacket, found it on the second try. I guess jackets didn't have strong rainbows.

"Possible. If not, we could set off some kind of diversion."

"Good. Let's run this by Sully. Then I need to get to work on those docking interface programs."

Sully was coming down the hallway toward us and motioned toward his door. "Clement and Drogue will be in the common room after services this morning. Let's talk in here."

Ren touched the glowing palm pad, guided, I understood now, by the unit's energy. I followed him through, Sully behind me.

"Lights," Sully said. The room—about half the size of Ren's quarters—brightened. Sully's short-barreled Norlack Sniper was on his bed. So were two small laser pistols in shoulder holsters. I took one out, tested its weight in my hand. It fit comfortably in my palm. Fleet-issue Stinger. Modified for slash, like the Norlack. Nice work.

Sully took the laser pistol from my hand and thumbed off the power panel. "Still has a short-range safety setting. I thought you'd prefer to work that way, on station."

I could feel the heat of his body where he leaned against my arm. His face was tilted toward mine, his breath ruffling my hair. I couldn't look at him. Every time I did I felt things I didn't want to feel. I tried to keep all of them out of my voice when I answered.

"Yeah, I do. I think we all do." Short-range safety reduced the risk of bystander injuries. Fatalities. Our purpose was to get off station, not massacre people.

I picked up the other laser pistol. It was slightly larger than the Stinger. It took me a moment to place it. With Sully so close to me, my brain and my body didn't seem to want to think about weapons right now.

"A Carver-12," I said, when my brain finally kicked

in. "Damn." Very accurate. Very expensive. The elite of high-energy hand weapons. Prew's personal bodyguards all carried them.

Sully's hand slid over mine, locking it against the small curved grip. A burst of sweet fire surged unexpectedly through me, made my heart skip a beat, made me catch my breath. Made me realize that Ren had to be seeing fireworks right about now and there wasn't a damn thing I could do about it.

Except to damn Sullivan, the handsome bastard.

And to damn Chasidah, the fool denying her fears.

"Mine," he said softly.

Somehow, I knew he meant more than just the laser pistol.

I raised my face, met his obsidian gaze. Chose my words carefully. "An expensive play toy. It's different, so people want it. Then they get bored, look for something newer, better. I don't work that way."

A slow nod of a face badly in need of a shave. "I don't either."

I slipped my hand from under his, picked up the Stinger again. "There's much to be said for dependability. Reliability. Consistency." I held it up, as if in inspection. It was plain and functional compared to the sleek Carver. "It's not fancy. No frills. But it will never, ever let me down."

He brushed the back of my hand with his fingers. "Neither will I," he said softly, but without hesitation. "If you believe nothing else, Chasidah, believe that."

I damned myself for wanting to believe him, for needing to believe him. For even wondering if maybe those kisses in Port Chalo, and the one last night, meant more than just inebriation and hormones.

But this wasn't the time to think of such things. I grabbed the shoulder holster, then turned and caught a wide grin on Ren's face. And wondered what colors I could send through my body that would tell him, *Oh, shut up*.

I peeled off my jacket. Sully tabbed up the microscreen from the desk. He leaned over it, keying in programs while I adjusted the shoulder holster over my T-shirt. Ren sat on the prayer bench, the Norlack resting on his knees. I had a feeling he was a better shot than I would've given him credit for earlier.

I peered around Sully's shoulder. "You've something to keep them from tracing you?"

His smile was warm and confident. "Don't need it right now. The temple has legitimate access to a number of areas." He touched the screen, opened a databox. "Because the Takas are tied so closely with the church, no one thinks twice when we look at work schedules. Or a particular individual's current location. The church serves as a liaison to their homeworld. If Grandfather dies, it's Clement's job to find Grandson and tell him."

"So who's on duty at Six-Green Three around 1100?"

"Grevarg." He turned toward Ren. "Know him?"

"He's saddened when Guardian Drogue returns dirt-side. He doesn't think Brother Clement can sing."

"Will he help us?" I asked.

"I don't think he will hinder us, or ask too many questions, if we appear to have a legitimate reason to be at Six-Green Three."

"We'll have to accept that, for now." Sully tabbed through a few more screens. "Let's check ops again. See if Kingswell has anything new to report."

He touched his thumb to a databox on the lower part of the screen, brought up a filter I'd not seen before. He segued into ops smoothly. The *Meritorious,* on schedule, still set to berth at Six-Green Three.

Getting into station schematics took him a little longer. Sully pulled down the attached desk chair, sat, and frowned. Ren excused himself, came back with a plate of fruitbread.

I handed Sully half a thick slice in a napkin. "Pull up the old work order from when the *Lucky Seven* came in. See what the dock malfunctions were, pick up their axis and sequence. The system might let you in as a maintenance verification, or follow-up. Then—"

"Got it, got it." His fingers flew over the screen. Data tumbled, merged, dropped into a pattern. "Got it!"

Two hours passed quickly. I went in search of a pitcher of ice water and saw Drogue in the common room. Morning meditations were finished.

"Sister?" His round face bore signs of worry.

"Things are coming together." I gave him what I hoped was a reassuring smile.

"But in other ways they are falling apart." He shook his head. "I was just on my way to Ren's quarters to tell you."

My stomach tensed. As Sully had so well pointed out, the church was tied in to the Takas and, through them, the MOC. If there were questions about the *Diligent* or her supposedly illicit purpose, Drogue would hear of them eventually.

"We're in Sully's quarters. You want to come back with me?"

Drogue followed, his footsteps heavy.

Sully was seated at the desk, Ren leaning over his shoulder. Both turned as we stepped inside. Drogue's presence seemed to surprise Ren. But I knew now how he knew who was with me. Rainbows, not illegal and invasive telepathy. "Guardian. Blessings. Is there a problem?"

"An unfortunate incident. I've just learned of it, and I apologize for not coming immediately. But I needed a moment to settle my thoughts."

Sully stood, dark brows slanting. He motioned to the prayer bench. "Sit, please."

Drogue's shoulders slumped slightly under his pale robe. "One of our Takan brothers, Jalvert, has been taken into custody by station security."

Jalvert. The name sounded familiar. Then I remembered the narrowed eyes of the Taka who'd cleared my ID card yesterday.

"Charges?" Ren asked.

"Rape. And murder."

My mind flashed to a wooded clearing, a muddy twilight, and a large Takan guard who'd tracked me, silently, until he thought we were far enough from anyone that my screams wouldn't be heard.

Yet, even with my recent experience, I knew a Taka attacking a human was rare. I'd concluded my confrontation was not only unusual but due most likely to the mentality of the Taka recruited for dirtside service. Certainly the ones on station, and the ones who worked the spaceport, were cleaner, more professional.

Jalvert had none of the stench, none of the slurred speech my attacker had.

"Against one of their own?" I followed my thoughts to what I felt was a logical conclusion.

"No. This is the concern. Jalvert is charged with the rape and murder of a human female. An MOC officer."

"Stars protect us," Ren said softly. "May her soul find peace."

"Security has been tightened," Drogue continued. "There's talk of suspending Peyhar's until more is known. I don't know how much this will hamper you. But it is clear. You must get off station as soon as possible. You must act on what we know is happening at the shipyards. Or this incident may well herald the start of something far more serious, far more bloody."

I understood the security considerations. But I didn't see what an isolated incident, though violent, had to do with the gen-labs or Marker. "Do you know who Jalvert's charged with killing?"

"Delia Tran. The officer who questioned your medical records when we made station."

"I thought Jalvert looked upset over that. Could that be why he attacked her? Was she an overbearing superior officer—"

"She was human, Chaz." Sully stepped toward me, rested his hand lightly on my shoulder. "He attacked her because she was human and she was female. He did to her what the Empire's doing to his people."

"Yeah, they fucked me over too, but—"

"This is about the gen-labs. The jukors. The Empire's using Takan females as surrogates to breed stronger, viral-resistant jukors." There was a hardness, an anger in the obsidian eyes. "The newborn jukor literally rips the Takan female apart as it's born."

The horror of his words was almost beyond my comprehension.

"This is what we have to stop." His hand tightened on my shoulder. "Or the Empire will face an enemy, a war from within, far more dangerous, and bloody, than it can ever imagine. And the enemy will deserve to win."

Takan females forced to breed against their will. Mutilated, murdered by the very creatures they gave life to. And all this under the auspices of the Imperial government.

"Did Jalvert know about this?" I stared up at Sully, my voice sounding thin. Horror strangled my words. "How long has this been going on?"

"The breeding project? A year, perhaps a little more." His grip loosened, his thumb moving over my shoulder in a brief caress, a small apology, perhaps for his angry grasp a moment ago. "As for Jalvert, I don't know. But I suspect he did. Word has spread in the Takan community." He glanced back at Ren, standing by the desk.

Ren. A Stolorth. Raised by a Takan woman he called his mother.

Ren made a small, aimless motion with one hand. "We do not have all the facts. Only small pieces. Much may be conjecture."

I spun on Sully, anger welling up inside me. "Why didn't you tell me all this before?" Like when he found me standing behind the dead Taka.

He seemed to expect my reaction. "Because we're still trying to put the information together. I—*We* were following rumors of the gen-labs. We kept hearing stories of Takan females taken by force. It didn't seem related until a Taka showed us a holo of a female's body, bloodied. And a bit of a jukor wing stuck in her chest."

His face turned toward Ren again, as if he were worried about the effect of his words. No emotion showed in Ren's hazed, silvered eyes, but he must have seen the colors in Sully's rainbow change. He nodded.

Sully turned back to me. "That was about a month ago. When I started searching for you."

"You've been—how long were you on Moabar?" I added up days and tried to put everything in a time line.

"Almost as long as you. Three weeks."

"Trying to find me?"

He nodded.

"Because of this?"

"That was one reason."

My ties to Marker, my Fleet training no doubt were others. That and my court-martial. It increased the probability I'd be a willing accomplice.

Sully's words spun through my mind. I tried to analyze the information as I'd been taught. Details. "You said a Taka showed you a holo. Genuine? Not altered?"

"Best I could determine, genuine. I wasn't the first to see it. It's known in the Takan community."

"I heard rumors weeks before Sullivan approached me," Drogue said. It was the first time I heard him call Sully anything but Brother Sudral. "I've never seen this holo, nor any documentation. But things are very tense with the Takas right now. Sullivan told me you were attacked on Moabar?"

"I thought the guard was drunk, crazy. And he . . . well, he didn't know I had a knife."

I glanced at Ren, saw his soft smile of acceptance. "You had to defend yourself. Killing human females at random will not solve this problem."

"And Jalvert?" I asked Drogue. "You think his attack on Tran was motivated by stories of Takan females being used to breed jukors?"

"We know of three other similar attacks in the past six months," Drogue said. Sully nodded. "Two in Dafir. One in Baris. The reports came to me through our missions. The Takas accused all carried a small disk carved with a slogan: *the circle of life breeds death.* Jalvert had one of these."

"So did the guard who attacked you on Moabar, Chaz." Sully's voice was soft. He dug in his pants pocket, pulled out a small disk. "I found this in his vest."

Drogue breathed a small, anguished sound.

I remembered Sully hunkering down by the dead Taka, checking, I'd thought, for life signs. I plucked the disk from Sully's open palm, stared at it, trying to see it as something evil. But it was just a round metal circle engraved with unfamiliar, angular symbols. *The circle of life breeds death.* The clock on Sully's wall glowed 0900. The *Meritorious* was due to arrive at 1100. I would take her back, completing another circle.

I opened my mouth to rail at Sully again for keeping this information from me, but he swiveled the chair around and faced Drogue. "What's the mood on station now?"

"The Takan community knows. Security has tried to keep the incident quiet, but not successfully."

"Perhaps you should check ops again." Ren touched Sully's arm. "Grevarg may not be scheduled at the ramp. Security might not want to risk an incident with a new stationmaster."

I made a mental note to lecture Sully later about the dangers of withholding information and focused on the immediate problem at hand. "We could still gain access," I said. It would be a little more difficult, but it could be done through the same diversion we'd planned. It was as easy to draw away a human security guard as a Takan.

"If not this ship, you must find another one." Drogue's expression was insistent, almost pleading. "The church will help in any way it can. Not openly yet. We'd be shut down. But anything else we can do, be assured we will."

I understood. At the moment, the Englarians were the only sane voice in this matter. Whoever was behind this breeding of jukors clearly was not.

Sully confirmed Grevarg was still on the duty roster. The *Meritorious* was still slotted to Six-Green Three.

I touched the dagger wrapped around my wrist for reassurance, like a talisman. "We have work to do. And not much time left to do it."

Drogue stood. "Tell me how I can help."

I thought of all I knew about ships on liberty. Ten years' worth. More than that. I'd grown up on Marker-2. "Do you have a connection with any of the pubs on station?"

"Tamlara's Tavern. Mistress Kizzy is a friend."

"Human?"

Drogue nodded.

"We need some quiet, untraceable invitations issued to the officers and crew of the *Meritorious*. She's due in around 1100, Six-Green Three. I need as many of her crew off-ship as possible. Shouldn't be any more than fifteen. Captain is Lew Kingswell. I need them well-fed and well-furred."

"I will make sure word of Tamlara's superior ale and hearty portions reaches the proper ears."

I had a newfound respect for the round-faced, gentle monk. "Thank you."

"Praise the stars." He grasped Ren's hand, held it, then let his other rest on Sully's shoulder for a moment. "Blessings, blessings." I reached out my own in a parting gesture. He clasped it tightly, then stepped for the door. His footsteps, muffled by the fabric of his robe, receded softly.

As I'd told Sully, Kingswell had no love of the big wide darkness. The *Meritorious* arrived early. Her berth confirmation and clearance flashed on Sully's deskscreen. I swiveled the chair around just as Ren dealt a new hand onto the middle of Sully's bed.

"Put the cards away, boys. It's time."

There were two others in the lift when Sully, Ren, and I stepped through the parting doors. Both human, one in a brown MOC uniform. The other wore utilitarian gray coveralls with no ship's patch. I figured the woman for a tech or dockworker. The MOC officer was male, portly, his belly straining the seams of his shirt. He glanced at us, his lip curling slightly as we offered blessings of the hour. We were just a bunch of crazy people who chanted to the stars and waved incense.

The hooded robe covered our dark clothes, our weapons, and Ren's blue hair as well. His hands he kept folded in the wide sleeves. It wasn't a precaution he normally took on station. But it was a precaution we needed now. No one should remember anything particular about a trio of Englarians on this particular day.

It was 1205. The *Meritorious* had been in for over an hour. Chaves had already been greeted by a small contingent of MOC officers at the ramp, bearing, no doubt, the latest news. A rape and murder on station. On Chaves's first day.

Welcome to Hell, Izak. Welcome to Hell.

Level Six-Green. We left behind the officer and the techie heading to different destinations. Maybe even Tamlara's. There was talk of a challenge having been issued. The crew of a Chalford lugger was betting meals for all at Tamlara's that the crew of an Imperial patrol ship couldn't drink as much ale as they could.

Everyone knew that Tamlara's had the best Imperial ale on station. Everyone knew that Tamlara's had the best food. Real food, not from commissary panels.

Six-Green Three. A lone Taka ambled between Berth Three's ramp and Two's. The laser pistol strapped to his hip was visible just below the edge of his brown vest.

"Grevarg." Ren said the name softly, confirming the Taka's identity for us through his rainbow image. Shortly, the guard would be called away to answer a message Sully had arranged from an untraceable source, and wouldn't be there when we returned.

We walked past, by all appearances a trio of monks handing out blessings of the hour to the stationers traversing the corridor.

Six-Green Five. Eight. Ten. Three gray-suited maintenance techs trotted by. One spoke rapidly into the comm badge clipped to his shirt. "Interfaces are down again?"

I could see the small, slow, wicked smile on Sully's lips.

"Praise the stars," I told him.

Eleven. We stopped, looked toward the rampway. Another Taka, his back to us, stared out the viewport. The curved bow of a freighter was visible. An unfamiliar ship's name glowed on the overhead. I couldn't make out the company markings on the hull. But the blackness of the starfield beyond beckoned.

We turned.

Eight. Sully drifted toward a row of seats in a small waiting area. I kept pace with Ren. Moments later, he caught up with us.

Seven. "Just a little fire," Sully said modestly. "More smoke than damage."

Five. A maintenance worker hurried by, tool kit wagging behind on an antigrav pallet. "Sorry, coming through. Sorry."

"Blessings. May your work be fruitful."

Three. The *Meritorious*'s hatch lock was open at the top of the ramp. Grevarg was nowhere in sight. A maintenance worker at the base of the ramp was leaning over the control podium, shouting, "Tell ops the captain wants her moved. No, don't need no tug. This is one of them Imperial boats. Fifteen still open?"

The answer was softer, but I clearly heard it. "Fifteen's cleared. Request approved. Slotting them to departure now."

Sully stepped up to the worker. "Pardon, Brother. We seek a Takan brother with urgent family news."

The man barely glanced at Sully as he ran his hand through his thinning hair in an exasperated motion. Chatter still came from the podium speaker.

"What's that? Hang on, I got some religious guy here needs to find a furry."

Sully half-turned toward the hatch lock, as if looking for someone. He raised one hand to adjust his hood, shielding his face.

I walked toward him, hands curved over my mouth and nose, my breath catching in a squeak as if I were crying. Such urgent, sad family news.

"Shit, what now?" The worker waved us on. "Yeah,

go ahead. He might be in there, trying to get the damn clamps unlocked. If not, check Berth Five."

Ren hurried behind me, ducking his head through the *Meritorious*'s hatch lock just as the fire alarms wailed far down the corridor.

Sully stepped quickly aside to let me lead. This was my ship. I knew every inch of her.

We were on main level, amidship, just aft of the bridge. I opened the seal seam of my robe with a quick thrust of my hand, drew the Stinger from its holster. We needed somewhere to stay, unnoticed, for the five minutes it took the ship to undock. The ready room, across from us, was too risky. Sick bay was the most likely.

We soft-footed down the narrow access stairs in a blur of sand-gray robes. Sully had the Carver drawn and primed. Ren had the Norlack's strap resting on one shoulder. The sublights already hummed noisily beneath my feet.

I knew all the sounds of my ship and it sounded empty, in spite of the noise of the engines. Intraship was quiet. But there had to be someone else on board, maybe two. Someone was on the bridge, handling the short ride to Berth Fifteen.

We'd take the bridge as soon as she was moving.

I stopped at the hatchway to Deck Two, threw back my hood, listened. My heart pounded. I could feel Sully's breath on my hair.

"Okay," I breathed. I stepped out, laser pistol in both hands, and swept the corridor quickly left and right. "This way."

The autodoor to sick bay, sensing my presence, opened. Sick bay was one large room, containing three small automated regen beds. Behind a movable panel was a hydrotherapy tub. All was quiet, empty.

A long half wall shielded a workstation. "There." In four steps I was behind it. Sully and Ren followed.

I sat and stared for a moment at the microscreen. It was active. I touched a databox, brought up ship's status. Sully leaned over my shoulder, his hand lightly on my arm. Ren stood close behind him.

We spoke in whispers. "Docking clamps should unlatch...now."

The ship jerked slightly, shimmied. Thrusters fired. More shimmies. Then a lurch as we dropped away.

Whoever was at the helm had pie plates for hands.

I waited a few more seconds just to be sure. "We've got ten minutes, boys. Let's do it in less."

I peeled off my robe, then started for the door. Sully and Ren followed, now all in black, like me. Ren held the rifle with an obvious familiarity and ease. It was not, I figured, a skill he'd learned at the monastery.

Back to the hatch at the stairs, up again. We faced only two possible scenarios. Two crew or officers on the bridge. Or crew and officer split, one on the bridge and one in engineering, on Deck Three. Given what was going on at Tamlara's I figured the chance of finding three sober crew was rare. Therefore, we'd take the bridge first. If anyone was in engineering, we'd deal with him or her later.

I eased the hatch door to Deck One open, listened again. This time, I could hear voices on the bridge. One lower-pitched, male. One higher, female. I wished for the hundredth time I knew more about Kingswell's crew.

I nodded to Sully. My job was to take the captain's sling. Sully's was to secure engineering. Ren had to prevent anyone from accessing communications or interfering with us.

It was that simple.

It was far from easy.

I nodded once more. "Now."

We moved quickly, weapons raised, our backs skimming the bulkhead. Like hard shadows we flowed past the single door to the captain's quarters, then the ready room, past a narrow maintenance panel and, across from that, the airlock to the emergency escape pod. Listening, watching. Ren reading thermals and rainbows.

The hatch to the bridge was open—sloppy, sloppy. Voices filtered out. A man's drawl: "Yeah, well, what do you expect. Out here. Bunch of assholes with no brains." His voice was slurred, drunk.

We stopped just short of the hatch. Ren hunkered down almost in the middle of the corridor, his face tilted up, sightless eyes reading thermals and rainbows fifteen, eighteen feet away. He moved back in a fluid movement. "Male in the center. Female on the right."

Someone in the captain's sling. Someone at engineering.

"Go," I whispered.

Sully and I moved first. Ren was immediately behind. I focused on the man in my chair. Brown hair slicked back, right arm outstretched, fingers grasping a lightpen, wiggling it. A nervous habit.

I recognized it just as I thrust the barrel of the Stinger against the base of his skull. A sick feeling rose in my throat.

Captain Lew Kingswell.

I knew him. He knew me.

I was going to have to kill him.

"Down, Captain! Now! On your knees! On the floor!" I shouted the orders, knowing Kingswell might recognize my voice. Praying he didn't. Prayed that the man stumbling out of the chair, falling forward, wouldn't turn around and see me. His identification would be absolute. Anyone else's would be conjecture.

I kept my laser pistol in his back as he hunched over, watched his hands, making sure he couldn't yank my feet out from under me.

"Facedown! Hands behind your back!"

He flattened himself with a grunt. Ren moved beside me, grabbing Kingswell's hands, locking them in a sonicuff.

"What do you want?" Kingswell bellowed, his face against the decking.

I ignored him and glanced at Sully. A young woman with short, curly blond hair lay cuffed and trembling at his feet. Her face was half hidden by his boots. He caught my glance, jerked his head toward the floor. Mouthed Kingswell's name.

I nodded.

He mouthed another word: *shit*.

There were still a few brains left in the government. And they might eventually figure out what Chaz Bergren knew.

He motioned to the woman, moved his feet slightly. I could see her a lot better than she could see me. She had a short nose, her blond hair the color of honeylace. I shook my head. Didn't know her. I'd caught a glimpse of her ID on her uniform when we barged in. Lieutenant.

And that was all we had time for. We were expected to redock in five minutes.

Sully holstered the Carver, stepped quickly away from the woman, touched Ren's arm. They lifted Kingswell away from me.

My job was to fly the ship. I left Kingswell and the lieutenant to Sully and Ren and took the sling, angling thrusters, pulling us away from the station.

I could hear Kingswell struggling behind me as he was carried to the rear of the bridge. His anguished demands echoed. "Who are you, damn it! You can't do this!"

"*Meritorious,* this is Moabar Departure. You're heading off course. Repeat, you're heading off course. Acknowledge."

I hit the red alert. Sirens wailed through the bridge. Sully grabbed a headset at the comm panel, keyed it open, well knowing how the game was to be played. "Having slight problems here. Will advise."

He keyed if off. I killed the sirens.

Kingswell's boot hammered the bulkhead in front of him. "You Chalford's people? This some kind of game, assholes?"

Don't damage my ship, you bastard.

Then there was a muffled cry of anguish, as if

someone tried to shout through material. I looked back quickly, saw Sully, grinning, tucking a roll of gauze back into a med-kit.

I pointed to engineering. He tossed the kit into the nearest chair and stepped over the woman on the floor. He slid into the seat, made a few adjustments to the board before him.

"Move her," he said to Ren.

Ren was more gentle with her than they had been with Kingswell. But I caught the look of pure fear on her face when she saw the webbed hands on her arms. She was Fleet—had worked the same training vids I had. I knew what she was thinking. *Ragkiril.* A creature who could rip apart her mind.

Ren placed her along the base of the opposite wall, on the other side of the hatchway from Kingswell. She lay on her side, her head angled crookedly. Soft sobbing filtered past the beeping chatter of the screens and scanners.

Moabar Departure tried to contact us again. Did we have an emergency? Did we require assistance? So far, no one was in pursuit. That's just the way I wanted it.

I hit the red alert again. Sully keyed the comm mike on the engineering console. "Got a fuel leak. Advise traffic to stay clear. Repeat. Hazardous fuel leak."

Red alert fell silent. I knew that would keep them away from us for a while.

At least until we hit the lanes at full bore. Then they might just suspect something else was going on.

But by then it wouldn't matter. As long as I stayed at max speeds, they wouldn't catch me. And once I got to the jumpgate, they'd never find me.

A series of three tones sounded on my right. Moabar's outer beacon. I sent back an acknowledgement from the list on my screen. Nice of Kingswell to have the ship fully functioning, all systems open and on-line. I'd change his passwords later.

The beacon chimed back. We were clear. My fingers played over the keypads as if it'd been only six hours, not six months, since I'd sat in this chair.

My entry flashed on Sully's board. "Full power, active now."

The *Meritorious* shot away from Moabar at top speed, her sublights blazing like the brightest fires in Hell.

"Captain. May I get something from below?" Ren's voice was soft as he stood next to my chair, rifle slung over his shoulder.

I took a quick glance at the boards. Everything was secure. No threat from Moabar yet. I nodded.

I heard his footsteps recede, then, minutes later, return. I glanced over my shoulder. He had his robe over his arm. He lifted the young woman's head. She tried to jerk from his touch. He tucked the robe underneath, eased her head against it. She stopped struggling and lay there motionless, except for the rapid rise and fall of her shoulders.

Ren went back to his seat, but his hands didn't touch the comm controls, though I knew he could see their outlines. But no way for him to identify their different functions, and this wasn't the time for me to train him.

Twenty minutes out and we had no pursuit. Nothing to do but wait an hour to reach the jumpgate Sully wanted to take. He had a ship positioned on the border of Aldan and Baris. The *Diligent* would have taken us there directly. Now we were forced to take the long way around, through no-man's-land. Running the rim in a stolen ship. While jukors were born and Takas died, somewhere in the Marker shipyards.

Sully stood, no better at this waiting game than I was,

I thought. He leaned his hands on the armrest of my chair and stared at me for a long hard moment. He still needed a shave, but the shadows were gone from his eyes.

The questions weren't. I didn't know quite what had happened between that passionate but unexpected kiss in the temple hallway and his none-to-subtle message when I inspected the Carver laser pistol, but something had. He might have been slightly furred when he'd kissed me, but he'd known exactly what he was doing when he'd clasped my hand.

Mine, he'd said. *Trust me* seemed to be just a breath behind that. And hours before that, something about taking risks.

Hell, why couldn't we have met again in a nice little spaceport pub, like the last time? It all would've been so much simpler. This wasn't. This was a tangle of fears and desires and anger and faith. Lives hung precariously on our actions, including my own. Yet there was an intensity in his gaze that told me that, in spite of all the turmoil swirling around us, this unanswered question mattered as much. Or more.

Could I risk that again? He was a man I'd known for years, yet didn't know. Our interactions had often been colored with flirtatious innuendoes. But they'd just as often hinted at something deeper. It was something I'd always felt, even when he was my constant adversary. And I was his beautiful, interfering bitch.

"You okay?" he asked softly.

Kingswell kicked the bulkhead again, but at least he'd stopped grunting.

"Yeah," I said. And took a risk. I brushed my fingers across his mouth. Watched surprise flash across his features, watched obsidian turn molten.

His hand curled around mine, his lips warm against

the pulse on my wrist. Then another few inches and his lips were against my mouth, hesitantly, not like last night's demanding kiss. But tasting, testing. Exploring.

I explored back. Heat fluttered on velvet wings around my heart.

Thump-thump-THUD-thump. Not my heart, but Kingswell's boots.

"Damn him," he said, but he was grinning a Sully grin, full of confidence, like the true handsome bastard he was. "You're distracting enough."

"So are you." Heat rose to my face. I touched his mouth again. A surprising warmth tumbled through my fingers, down my arm. God, how the man affected me! But I couldn't afford further distractions.

"And we've still got work to do." I pulled my hand away, keyed in a slight course change toward the jump-gate. Risked one more heated glance.

"We make a good team," he said softly.

I returned my focus to the data on my screens. We had one last item to attend to before we hit the gate. Kingswell and the lieutenant had to be placed in the escape pod. They'd be rescued within twenty-four hours. The pods were rigged to last a week.

Of course, twenty-four hours in a small pod with Kingswell might feel like a week.

Sully straightened a bit, surveying the bridge in a proprietary fashion, but kept his voice soft. "Nice ship. Always liked it."

I cuffed him lightly on the arm. "Gee, thanks."

"I always liked her captain more." He caught my hand, folded it in his own.

I was about to comment that hijacking freighters in my sector was a strange way of showing that when Ren came over and leaned on the other armrest. I felt as if two tall trees flanked me.

"The robe was a kind gesture," I told him.

"She's very afraid. She believes we mean to kill her."

"You have my permission to tell her we won't. Will that help?" I realized Ren was on a small bridge with two people whose fearful emotions probably churned out of control. And two more who had adrenaline and hormones pumping. It was probably like having four nonstop red-alert sirens blaring. *Thump-thud-thump* still resounded behind me.

"I will convey that. Thank you."

I swiveled halfway around to watch him as he knelt behind the young woman, careful not to touch her. His head angled down as he spoke to her, his words inaudible.

A few hesitant nods of the curly-haired head. Then Ren sat, silently.

An abrupt movement behind Sully caught my attention. Kingswell. No longer wedged against the bulkhead. Somehow in his squirming and kicking, he'd turned. He was flat on his back and glaring at me. He grunted two sharp syllables through the gauze stuffed in his mouth. But I heard them as clearly as if he'd said them on intraship.

"Berg. Gren."

The identification was absolute.

Sully clenched his fist. "Now we've got problems."

Twenty-two minutes to the jumpgate's outer beacon. We had to get Kingswell and the lieutenant strapped in the pod and jettison them before we went through. But Kingswell had recognized me, would tell Fleet that Chasidah Bergren was no longer on Moabar but had possession of an Imperial P40. And that she had help in the form of two males, one human, one Stolorth.

If Kingswell had recognized Sully he didn't say—or

rather, grunt confirmation—when Ren and Sully hoisted him into the open corridor just behind the bridge. I didn't think he would. Sully had always been my territory. Kingswell, a few years behind me in the academy, had never worked patrol. He'd flown a desk on Starport 6 in Baris, the *Meritorious*'s home port. Sucking up to the brass and pushing around thin-shouldered ensigns had taken up most of his time. Patrol duties would've interfered with that. And just might get his impeccable uniform dirty.

Besides, Kingswell was too busy staring at Ren to pay much attention to Sully when they laid him on the floor of the corridor, in front of the escape-pod hatch. Every training vid Fleet had on Stolorth *Ragkirils* was no doubt replaying through his mind.

My own was snagged, looping like a fractured computer program on a decision I didn't want to make. I couldn't let Kingswell tell what he'd seen. But I couldn't kill him without destroying a part of myself.

I stood at the apex of the bridge, arms folded across my chest. Kingswell glared at me from the corridor, but he was still cuffed and gagged. Ren propped the young woman into a sitting position across from Kingswell, then came back to where Sully and I stood. We talked softly, but not to hide my identity anymore.

"The news will hit Marker before we will." Sully's hand on my arm was meant to be reassuring. "You know that. You know we have no choice."

"Fifteen people, fifteen innocent people, have already died because of me. Sixteen if you count the Taka. I don't want one more."

"You had to kill the Taka in defense. This isn't anything different—"

"Damn it, it is! The Taka attacked me. Kingswell's here by happenstance. And what about the lieutenant? She doesn't know me, but she'll know he does. Do we put two dead bodies in the pod?" I swung away from Sully, abruptly dislodging his hand, and stared out the forward viewports at a starfield that I'd always found comforting before. Now it looked cold, threatening.

I felt the heat of his body as he moved up behind me. "A trank overdose would be painless." He ran his hands down my arms, threaded the fingers of his right hand through mine and squeezed lightly.

I shook my head. "I'm not a wanton murderer. Neither are you. I don't want us to be like them. Like the ones at Marker."

There was a moment of silence where all I felt was Sully, breathing against my hair. My own heart pounding, angry, confused.

"There is an option," Ren said softly.

I turned. Sully did the same. The gentleness on Sully's face hardened, brows slanting. He drew in a sharp breath and pulled his hand out of mine. "No."

Something that felt like fear prickled at my skin where his hand had held my own.

Ren's face tilted slightly. "Are you not asking Chasidah to make a worse sacrifice? To be something she's not?"

"It's not remotely the same." Sully's answer was clipped, harsh.

"No. Her risk is greater. The option you're giving her violates what she truly is. The option I'm suggesting does not."

"What?" I glanced rapidly from Ren to Sully. "What option?"

"It's not an option."

"It is."

"Damn you, not now!" A viciousness filled Sully's voice. It was directed at Ren.

"What not now?" Something felt very wrong. I

touched Sully's arm but he didn't look at me, wouldn't take his gaze from Ren's clouded one.

"She will eventually know." Ren's soft, calm voice was the complete opposite of Sully's.

"Shut the fuck up." Sully jerked away from me. He tried to push past Ren. But the Stolorth gripped Sully's forearm, hard. The skin on Ren's knuckles whitened. The muscles of Sully's arm bulged under the black fabric as he twisted back around, brought his fist up, clenched. Cold, angry fear hardened obsidian eyes into two chips of black ice.

"Risks," Ren said softly.

Sully was breathing hard, his mouth a taut line. My heart pounded, my hands suddenly clammy. Rainbows—very dark, ugly, storm-filled rainbows—hung between the three of us. I couldn't see them, but I could feel them.

Sully lowered his arm, flexed his fingers. His gaze locked on Ren's.

I glanced at the console on my left. Fifteen minutes to outer beacon. "What option?" My voice shook.

Ren released his grip.

Sully shot a quick glance toward the corridor where Kingswell glared at us and the curly-haired lieutenant leaned wearily against the bulkhead, an Englarian monk's robe wrapped around her shoulders, her face pale.

He shoved his hands in the pockets of his pants, stared down at his boots for a moment. When he brought his gaze up, his eyes were shadowed again. "Mind-wipe," he said. "Their memories of all this can be altered."

Fear slammed through me like a ship hitting a jump-gate cold. They'd lied. Even blind, the Stolorth could rip minds apart. Shred them, destroy them. Ren wasn't a harmless empath. He was a *Ragkiril*. I closed my eyes, willed my heart to stop hammering in my chest, ignored the nauseous feeling in my stomach.

Grabbed for facts.

I knew Ren. Granted, only for a few days, but even in that short time he'd been nothing but gentle. Calm. Controlled. Logically, I had more reason to fear Sully. Known terrorist, smuggler, mercenary. A passionate, volatile man. Angry, for valid reasons, he'd said. Gabriel Ross Sullivan. Poet. Warrior. Lover.

But it would be Ren doing the mind-wipe. He would be considerate, if such a thing even existed in tandem with the destruction of a mind. The thought sickened me, but Ren was right. It was the only option. It left them both alive. Murder sickened me worse.

I opened my eyes, took a steadying breath. "I need to know two things. First, is it painful?" I was concerned for the young lieutenant. She was the most innocent. Kingswell could do with a little discomfort. "Second, how much damage will it do? Turning them into vegetables is not an acceptable option."

Sully glanced at Ren, then answered. "It doesn't have to be painful, no. It won't be. It's *zral,* a memory-wipe. Not *zragkor.*"

I remembered the Stolorth words from my training. *Zragkor.* Mind-death. At its worst, hideous. Painful. Terrifying. Complete. At its best, still terrifying. Still a complete negation. But one done under the guise of a false ecstasy so that the victim would be totally unaware of the hideous process. It took a *Ragkiril*'s telepathic link to perform a *zragkor.*

But not for a *zral.* It was easy to forget the distinction between the two. It had been twenty years since the war, and even then *zral* and *zragkor* had not been common terms. A whole generation had been born since, one that no longer heard daily reports of atrocities committed by *Ragkirils*. Ren, blind, couldn't do a *zragkor*. But he could perform a *zral*. Still, an invasion of the only thing we humans feel is totally our own: our minds, our thoughts. But it wasn't a total negation of the person. Something would remain.

I hated the words even as I said them. "You've got ten minutes, Ren. Twelve max."

"I cannot do a *zral*, Chasidah."

"But you just said..."

But he hadn't. Sully had.

An abysmal, foul cold wave gripped me. I forced myself to look at the man I knew, but didn't know at all. Gabriel Ross Sullivan.

Obsidian eyes like ice. Hands jammed in pockets. And a mind that could alter another's with a touch and a thought.

"Ten's all I need." His voice was hoarse.

He spun around and strode toward the corridor.

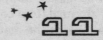

11

I sat hunched over in the command chair, elbows on my knees, my chin resting on my hands. My fingers were steepled over my mouth as if holding back words I couldn't bear to say. Words that stabbed my mind as if they were carved out of ice.

Sully. Mind-wipe.

"He will need my help getting them into the pod." Ren touched my shoulder.

I nodded.

"Chasidah."

I shook my head. Chasidah wasn't here right now. She was on a little trip, looking for someplace warm and safe and quiet. Someplace no one would ever find her. Someplace with no ghosts, no handsome bastards. Someplace with no mirrors reflecting back the face of a fool.

Ren left, closing the hatchway of the bridge behind him.

I breathed a shuddering breath against my hands, straightened. Mechanically, I checked all screens and monitors. We were on course for the jumpgate. All systems optimal.

Good ship, a P40.

A light flashed, a soft double chime. Two minutes to jumpgate outer beacon. Where had the time gone? Must be having fun.

Three chimes. The quintessential beacon calling card. I keyed back my answer. *Hello out there. Nice to meet you. Have any minds you need destroyed? We're having a sale.*

My hands shook as I moved them from the keypad. I clutched them to my midsection, doubled over. Took long, deep breaths. I can deal with this. Just as I accepted Ren as an empath. I can deal with this. We are, after all, on the same side, aren't we? A team? Friends? Not lovers—no, not that. It'd been only a kiss or two. Nothing serious. A few overly emotional moments resulting in some playful behavior.

I straightened. Sully wasn't doing a *zragkor*. Just a blanking of a small part of memory. He wasn't a *Ragkiril*. He must be an empath. Like Ren, only human. *And Ren's okay.*

I can deal with this. I can.

The hatchway cycled open, admitting the sound of footsteps. I didn't turn around.

Ren's voice sounded gentle, like raindrops pattering against a placid stream. "They're in the pod. Secure. Comfortable."

I tapped the screen, brought engine controls to my keypad, decreased power. Engines cycled down past one-quarter sublight. I angled thrusters, arcing us around the beacon.

I tabbed on intraship, spoke to my invisible crew. My ghosts. "Stand clear. Pod clamps releasing—"

The lights on my short-range scanner suddenly flared.

Sirens wailed through the ship, red alerts engaging automatically. I stared at the screen in disbelief. Incoming. Two armed Imperial cruisers, running hard and fast. And heading directly for us.

I slammed my hand on the keypad. "Releasing pod. We got bogies, two. Coming in hot!"

I lunged for engineering, threw the sublights into emergency overdrive. The *Meritorious* surged forward with a wrenching jolt. I careened back toward my chair. The ship lurched. I stumbled against Sully, heading for his seat.

For three long seconds his hands grasped my wrists. His gaze, wary, tired, locked on mine before I wrenched away, pulled myself into my seat. I raked the straps across my chest, dragged the armrest controls in front of me.

I heard Ren's straps click to my left, at communications. Then another click, from engineering on my right. I checked status, swore. We were fifteen minutes out from the working edge of the gate. At top speed, the cruisers would never catch us. But we were under one-quarter sublight moments ago. We might as well have been standing still.

I disconnected safety overrides with three quick taps. "Bring hyperdrive online, now!"

I hated hitting a jumpgate cold, but I had no choice.

Sully worked the board quickly, his movements sharp, precise. No hesitation in his fingers, no second thoughts.

No time.

I called out shield status, distance to jumpgate, time to intercept with the cruisers streaking toward us.

"Got it." Sully's voice was sharp. "Got it."

"I need those hypers!"

"Working on it."

A shimmy racked through the ship. The hypers were cold, and angry at being awakened. Another alarm blared. Pressure warning. An unhappy sound.

Then a third. Weapons. "Cruisers in range. They're targeting us." I segued power to defense. "Aft shields at max."

Movement on my screen flickered in a deadly staccato. Incoming from the cruisers. Small. Lethal. "Birds incoming. Taking evasive action."

I banked my ship, hard. It skewed us off the course to the jumpgate, sent us away from our only chance at freedom. But the plasma torpedoes heading for us gave me no choice.

I released a scatterfield from the ship's underbelly, hoping to confuse the torpedoes' guidance systems. Two followed the debris, veering. The other kept coming straight on.

I slapped the alarms into silence. I needed to outrun the bogey, get back to that jumpgate. I needed the hypers, pulsing, online.

"Sulliv—"

"Returning fire."

"Damn it! We don't have time. Hard edge in two minutes, ten seconds!"

Hard edge, no hypers, and a torpedo, hot, with my name on it.

The shimmying quieted, the pulsing began.

"Hypers online. Twenty percent."

Smirking. Damn him, he was smirking. I could hear it. Bastard. It felt good to feel angry at him. I didn't want to think about why.

"Two minutes." I flattened vanes, scanner dishes. Torpedo still closing but losing speed, the looming gatefield muddling its tracking sensor.

"Thirty-five percent."

"Minute forty. I need sixty percent at crossover."
God. Sublights were still online. They had to be disengaged before hypers hit fifty percent or the ship would rip apart. Like a mind undergoing a *zragkor*.

"Forty-seven percent."

"Edge at thirty seconds. Cut sublights!"

"No can do, Chazzy-girl. Fifty-three percent."

I felt the gate grab us, felt the ship skew, slide. "Damn it, Sully!"

Ren's voice answered, soft, serene. "Merciful Abbot Eng, grant us now your everlasting protection—"

We slammed through the jumpgate, screens erupting, sparking. Drives pulsing, sublights grinding up the neverwhen, the nowhere–everywhere of jump.

My body jerked forward. The straps cut into my chest, branding my shoulder. I couldn't breathe. Bridge lights flashed off, flickered on, died.

Someone groaned, grunted in the blackness.

Then a piercing sound, like metal screaming, torquing.

I was whipped to my left, the armrest impaling my ribs. I clawed at my straps, tried to pull myself upright, away from the pain coursing through my body. Something slammed me back, lifting my feet off the decking, my arm off the control pad, my body—

—ached. Must've been one hell of a party. My head throbbed. My arms and legs felt as if they weren't a part of me yet.

My eyes wouldn't open. Then something warm surrounded me. Something gray and fuzzy and soft. For a moment, I felt as if I knew it, recognized it. But no, how could I? Still, I let it surround me, let it draw me back together, piece by piece.

I opened my eyes. The world was dimly lit, red-tinged

on the edges. Lights twinkled in the distance. Nice colors, red, green, yellow. I was in the middle of a room. No. A ship's bridge. A chair, my chair, the captain's sling, was in front of me.

Interesting. If I wasn't sitting in it, where was I? Something soft and warm was behind me. I tried to turn but my shoulders protested. I glanced down. Decking, under my legs. Another pair of legs, longer, angled against mine. Black-sleeved arms crossed over my midsection. Large hands covering mine.

Mine.

I forced myself to be very, very still.

"Chaz." A deep voice, soft, rumbling. "Back with us?"

Sullivan.

A shadowy movement on my left edged my vision. Ren, kneeling down, a few inches away, cloudy eyes studying me. His braid had partly unraveled and his lips were pinched. He looked worried, or in pain.

I drew a deep breath, struggled to sit up away from the enveloping warmth. Away from a man who could perform a mind-wipe. But one who needed my help with Marker, I argued mentally. Needed my help because of the Takas. The jukors. Needed my help with this ship. I was still alive and thinking, wasn't I? He needed me that way. I was the only captain he had. Sully wasn't trained as a pilot. He needed me alive and my mind intact. Time to remember that.

"Status?" My voice cracked.

Sully answered. "We're fifteen minutes into transit. Hypers working at seventy-two percent efficiency. Sublights took some damage but we've got them operative."

By all that was holy. I'd been unconscious for fifteen minutes? Then I remembered slamming into jump, cold, sublights grinding. I wrenched around, my concern for my ship overriding all else, even my fear of the man sitting next to me. "What in hell did you think you were doing?"

A half smile quirked on his lips but didn't reach his eyes. His mouth, like Ren's, was taut. "What I've done before, when I had to. Used the torque of the sublights to slough off the resistance coming into a jump cold."

I stared at him. Why did all the handsome ones always have to be such brilliant bastards? And why did they have to have minds that could—

I halted the thought, threw that into my mental durohard container in cold storage with all the others. "You could've warned me."

He could've warned me about a lot of things. Jukors. Disks with strange symbols. Mind talents.

"We were all busy with other matters."

Understatement of the century.

I drew my knees up and rested my elbows on them. My fingers found the release points on the Grizni bracelet on my wrist. It tingled reassuringly. I took another deep breath.

Fifteen minutes into jump. Probably an hour forty yet to go. I'd know more when I read the data at my console. Good old, consistent, reliable data. "No one followed us in, I take it?" That should've been one of my first questions, if I'd been thinking like a captain. But I hadn't finished putting Chasidah back together yet.

"They saw us go in pretty cold. Probably figured we wouldn't make it."

The torpedo wouldn't have been able to cross the gatefield. So we were safe, for the time being. I pushed my hands flat against the deck, struggled to stand. Sully grabbed me easily under the armpits, lifted me, turned me to face him when I wobbled on my feet.

"I suggest you sit for a while, Captain."
Good idea.

Bridge lights were back on. I adjusted the straps locked across my chest. They were half torn. Just as well, because they didn't chafe the bruises I knew were blooming on my skin. Bruises that matched, no doubt, the one on Sully's right cheek. Even Ren moved stiffly, probably wishing he'd remembered to bring his cane.

We all looked like we'd been through one hell of a good pub fight.

It took me fifteen minutes to run a thorough systems check from the controls at my armrest pad. I knew Sully had already done one, but I needed to see for myself that we were alive and slicing through the neverwhen without any more than the usual problems. I needed to keep my mind busy with ship operations, ship data. I didn't need it wandering, asking questions, until I'd calmed down and could face answers I might not want to hear.

I couldn't even face Sully right now. Because that started the questions surfacing.

I finished the check, shoved the arm pad away. My body ached for reasons I didn't care to explore. I leaned my head back against the cushion and stared at the ceiling, listening to the ship's noises. Sensors beeped softly every five minutes, signaling the completion of a sweep and initiation of a new one, like wings reaching outward from the skin of my ship, brushing through the neverwhen. Other data clicked, trilled. The sound of the hypers was a soft but familiar hum. I glanced down at my armrest controls. I had systems to coordinate, but my body was reluctant to cooperate. A few minutes later I forced myself back to work. When the aching resurrected itself we were thirty-eight minutes to exit. I rested my head against the cushion, tried to will the ache into a far galaxy. Footsteps sounded on my left. Ren's face came into my field of vision. His braid was almost completely unraveled, blue strands tangling around his shoulders.

If he were reading rainbows, he had to know I was unraveling too.

"Commissary panels are off-line. But I can get some water. Would you like some?"

"Thanks. Big mug."

He brought back one for Sully, one for myself. Mine was in a mug marked with the captain's insignia. It was standard issue, but Kingswell had probably been the last to use it. I thought it was just coincidence until I realized the insignia was raised. Ren could feel it with his fingers.

"I washed it clean first." His webbed hand rested lightly on the armrest on my right.

I tried to make my voice light, not reflect the strange numbness I felt in my soul. "I'll put a commendation in your file." I took a sip, my fingers tracing the same raised areas his had. My thoughts rested for a moment on the other captain. I wondered if he'd know me if we ever met again. Would he thank me for sparing his life? Did he even know he had one, or was the Lew Kingswell placed in the rescue pod more than an hour ago someone else now?

"Ren?" I hesitated, anxiety clashing with fear. I forced myself to ask. I had to gather my facts. It was the only thing I knew how to do, the only thing that had never failed me. "Kingswell. And the woman. They'll be okay?"

Out of the corner of my eye, I saw Sully turn at his station.

Ren answered. "No worries, Chasidah."

Oh, yeah. My rainbow. I wondered what color worry was. "They'll remember nothing?"

Sully's chair squeaked as he leaned forward. "They know who they are. Where they're from. Things in their past."

I took another sip. "How far past?" I asked the hazed, starless jump darkness through the viewport. Not Sully. I couldn't look at Sully. "Childhood? Academy? Current Fleet posting?"

A long silence. "It depends. I . . . I did what I could. There wasn't a lot of time."

So it had been an imprecise cut. Jagged. Memories torn away like the fabric of a sleeve caught in a doorway, ripping, unraveling. Events trailing like broken threads. Hopes, dreams, shredding.

I felt sick.

"I did Kingswell last. I took more time with Tessa because I know you—"

"Damn you, Sullivan!" I wrenched around to face him, anger, shame rising in me. "Don't tell me her name." I didn't need to make her real and personal. Didn't need to add her to the list of the other sixteen.

I knew all their names. And except for Nathaniel Milo and the Taka, their histories. The husbands and wives they left behind. The children. The parents.

I knew them all. And now I had Tessa. An innocent, her mind gutted.

A stranger stared back at me through Sully's eyes. Then suddenly he ripped off his straps, thrust himself to his feet. For one long terrifying moment I thought he was coming at me, his expression hard and bleak. But he charged by me, past Ren reaching toward him. He stepped over the hatchlock. His arm lashed out. His fist slammed against the corridor wall.

Two more steps, another slam. And another. And another. Echoes of anger. Echoes of pain, fading when he reached crew's quarters.

"Chasidah." A harsh, disapproving tone came from somewhere I never expected it. Ren.

I swiveled around. His face was pinched, his lips thin. His voice shook slightly when he spoke, like ice-crusted waves crashing against a frozen shore. "I do not know how to explain this—it is not my part to do so—but I must. I cannot let you destroy him."

"I didn't—"

"You are. He feels your rejection, just as I do. Your fear. You know this now."

I nodded, numbly. Ren wasn't the only one who could read rainbows.

"I will tell you what you do not know. He offered his life to save yours. On Moabar. He knew the risks. He was alone in this, searching for you. I couldn't help. The planet drains me, physically. He did this alone. To find you."

I splayed my hand. "I know the shipyards. I know—"

"Nothing, Chasidah Bergren! You do not understand. He couldn't live with the knowledge that you were on Moabar. That you would be harmed. That you would be alone, afraid."

He was right. I didn't understand. We were talking about Gabriel Ross Sullivan. About six years of tag-you're-it out on the rim. About hijackings I'd interrupted and illegal escapades I'd appeared in the middle of, like an unwanted guest at a party. Our brief chance encounter at Port Chalo didn't seem to be sufficient motivation to pull me off Moabar.

"Final day of your trial, the starport experienced a major power loss," Ren said. "He tried to free you. Damned himself because he failed."

I froze, memories washing over me. I was back sitting in lockup, deep in the starport's brig. Judgment against me had just come down. Sentencing would follow, but my options were clear. Moabar or Moabar. They'd never offer me death.

Then darkness. The corridors rang with hard-booted guards, rifles glinting as the red-tinged emergency lights flickered on.

They'd flanked my cell. Belatedly I realized the force field was down. I could've run. Don't know how far I would've gotten. But I could've tried.

Two hours passed before the power came back on.

A prank, a guard told me nervously. Bored station brats.

Not a prank. Gabriel Ross Sullivan had tried to rescue me, because he didn't want me to be alone and afraid.

I turned to Ren, but had no words. I didn't need them. Ren could read rainbows.

His voice softened, the waves still coming, but no longer to an ice-covered shore. "He knew you couldn't live with yourself if Kingswell died. But he also knew you'd hate him when he gave you the only option that would let Kingswell and the lieutenant live. This is what he risks for you. To feel your hatred, because he cannot do otherwise, being what he is. And he offers this so that you won't have to feel the pain."

Suddenly, my fears seemed foolish, stupid. "I didn't know." It was a weak, horrible excuse. But it was all I had.

A small smile met my trembling voice. "I've often told him to give you those poems he's written to you. But he's been afraid. Until you showed you could be friends with me. Showed you didn't mind someone reading what you call rainbows. He reads, has been reading yours for a long time. Hoping. Waiting."

"Hijacking cargo to get my attention? Getting himself killed, hoping I'd come to his funeral?" I wasn't disbelieving his words. But I needed to put all the facts together.

"The first I'll let him explain to you. The truth may surprise you. But the second, I will tell you, because you know more of the truth than you realize. You know who he is, the wealth and power his father held in the Empire when he was alive. You know also his family disowned him. Two years ago, shortly before his mother died in a shuttle accident, he believed she was open to reconciliation. But that meant the mercenary, the smuggler known as Sullivan, had to die. He agreed to that, faked his own death, not because he had any interest in his inheritance, but because he wanted respectability. So the next time he met you in a bar, you wouldn't run away."

Port Chalo. Ren knew about Port Chalo. I started to say something but he held up his hand.

"His mother died before he could reconcile with her. Her unexpected death put the estates in the hands of a cousin. So he has nothing to offer you now, except what he is. Someone you can trust with your life. Someone who will never let you down."

I closed my eyes, felt as if my heart had been ripped in half. Then I opened them, quickly. Because I knew where that other half of my heart was: at the end of the corridor behind me, in the *Meritorious*'s crew's quarters.

12

He was leaning against the bulkhead at the end of the corridor, arms spread wide. A figure in black outlined against the light gray wall. His back was to me, his head was angled down. I could see the rapid rise and fall of his shoulders. His palms were flat, fingers splayed. He looked like a man trying to push his way through the wall.

Or like a man who awaited crucifixion. Damned by an Empire that labeled mind talents as filthy, cursed. Damned by a woman whose life he'd saved.

I couldn't change the former. Only the latter.

I wrapped my arms around his waist and lay the side of my face against the hard planes of his back. I could feel him trembling, his breath shuddering against me. A frigid chill raced through me, met up against a rushing heat. The heat mushroomed, flowed outward as if through my hands. Then it cascaded back into me, tingling, intense, passionate.

I said nothing, didn't have to. I sent rainbows. And accepted the ones he sent back to me.

It took a few minutes for the trembling to stop, for his arms to relax, for the warmth to settle to a steady glow that I realized had nothing to do with his body's heat, or mine. He straightened away from the wall, his hands covering mine.

I threaded my fingers through his and said the one word I thought he might want to hear. "Mine."

He squeezed my hands. Heat surged, spiraled, settled. Then he turned, drawing me into his arms, pulling us both back against the wall. He pressed me tightly against his body, his face in my hair, his fingers stroking, kneading.

Needing.

I ran my hands up the front of his shirt, across his shoulders, responding in kind. The muscles in his biceps were taut, powerful. My hands circled back to his shoulders, stayed there as I clung to him, sending rainbows.

He tucked my face at the hollow of his throat. His breathing had slowed, but it was still ragged. I could feel his heart pounding.

"Sully? I'm sorry. I shouldn't have—"

"Shhh. Hush, hush." A hoarse request.

His fingers wriggled into my hair, wound through the braid but didn't undo it. Just stroked, caressed. I leaned my head back into his hand. His eyes were closed. Then his lashes lifted slightly.

I ran my fingers over his lips, searching for a hint of that Sully smile. His lips parted. My fingers met the tip of his tongue, and I heard a soft intake of breath. His lips closed against my fingers, sucked.

Heat fluttered, spiraled through me. I stood on tiptoe, pulled my hands down to his shoulders, and let my lips brush his, softly. Let the tip of my tongue touch his, softly.

He groaned, pulled me into his chest, held my mouth

in a long, deep kiss while fireworks arced just beneath my skin. I wrapped my arms around his neck, raked my fingers through his hair. His hands lost their gentleness, traveled boldly, insistently.

I tilted my face away from his, breathless, and ran my thumb across his mouth. Kissed him again. And this time I heard bells, chimes.

Then Ren's voice. "Excuse me, Captain. But I think we're about to exit the jumpgate."

"Shit." We said it at the same time. He pushed away from the wall. I turned, almost stumbling over my own feet. So much for the captain in control. He grabbed my elbow, propelled me forward. "Go, Chaz!"

We raced around Ren, hopped over the hatch tread, and tumbled into our chairs just as the last set of triple chimes sounded.

I swung the armrest controls around with one hand and tapped in commands with the other. "Initiating exit sequence." I hooked on my tattered straps and was back in command mode.

"Bringing sublights online," Sully answered.

I heard Ren's footsteps, the squeak of the chair at the comm station as the rumbling noise started beneath my boots. Nice, friendly sublights, ready to go after a short nap.

I picked up the exit beacon, verified coordinates, locked them in. "Three minutes to hard edge."

"Got it."

We traded more chatter, all of it intense and technical. Personal lives, all the joys and the conflicts, disappear during a jumpgate transit. I ran over the data for mass, velocity, and inertia, checked for dump points. Sully monitored weapons. We didn't know what might be waiting out there when we came through. We still squawked an Imperial ID. There wasn't time to alter the *Meritorious*'s codes now.

"Thirty seconds to hard edge."

"Got it. Preparing to disengage hypers."

"On my mark. Twenty seconds." I watched the screens and monitors, felt the first shimmy as the jump-gate's hold on us began to recede.

"Ten seconds. Eight seconds. Four. Mark. Now!"

We dropped out swiftly, the black starfield suddenly glistening through the forward viewports.

My fingers flew over a series of touchpads. "Max sensors, full sweep. Bogey check, bogey check."

"Weapons active." Sully was reaching, tabbing, watching monitors just as I was. "Clear, clear."

I let out a short sigh of relief. Either those cruisers following us had no idea which exit we would take out of the jumpgate, or they believed our cold entry had been fatal. Or we were just plain lucky.

I didn't know how long our luck would hold out.

"I need to delete all the Imperial codes. Take the helm for me; get us on course." I yanked off my safety straps, pushed out of my chair. I glanced over my shoulder just as Sully turned in his seat. And damned the heat rising to my face as his gaze followed me. Then realized that the color on my checks was probably nothing compared to what else I radiated. Which only made my cheeks heat up more.

"Need my help?" he asked.

"Take the helm," I repeated. "I won't be long." We had unfinished business, lots of it. Lots of questions, explanations. But if I didn't get those codes changed, those explanations might not matter.

He seemed to catch that. "I'll be waiting for you." He added a slow grin to his words.

"Just don't get us lost."

Ren's smile was wide as I tripped over the hatch tread. I sent him my *oh, shut up* rainbow and didn't look back. I strode toward the captain's cabin. This, at least, was familiar territory.

Lew Kingswell had kept his command-code file exactly where Fleet regs said we should. I'd never kept mine there. I'd kept a partial, just in case during a surprise inspection someone wanted to see if Chasidah Bergren knew the rules.

I did. I also knew that most of civilized space did as well.

I'd kept the full command codes in a buried file, surrounded by trip alarms. It took me about fifteen minutes to create another. Then I reset all commands and passwords. But not the *Meritorious*'s ID. I had to be on the bridge to do that.

I made copies of everything on a small datapad I found on a shelf next to the desk. This was slow work. The ship was under full power, with the hypers the only cold system. I couldn't shut down the sublights, couldn't shut down enviro, recode, and bring them up again. So I inserted patches that would hamper any attempt by intruders to take the ship. I'd make the permanent changes when we met up with Sully's ship on the border.

A noise from the open doorway made me raise my head. Sully cleared his throat and leaned against the doorjamb, arms folded over his chest. Unshaven, dark hair tousled, clothed all in black, he exuded an undeniable sensuality.

He arched an eyebrow. "Ten minutes I've stood here, and you've yet to notice. Demoralizing to be so quickly forgotten."

My brain seized, fogged, and overheated. It was rare for me not to have a rejoinder for one of Sully's quips, yet I couldn't think of one. A slight twinge of apprehension mixed in with the sensations from the past two days. The heat of his body, his kisses, his hands caressing my skin all flooded through my memory. At the same time, I remembered another heat, surging, spiraling through me when we touched. I knew empaths read emotions, some could even transmit them. But I didn't understand it. That made me nervous.

And there had been that unsettling coldness in him when he'd agreed to handle Kingswell. As if he weren't comfortable with what he could do. Why? Part of me longed for answers, for the facts. But part of me feared the answers more than the questions. Maybe that's why the routine of changing ship's codes had seemed so preferable once we'd cleared the jumpgate.

I gestured toward the deskscreen on my right, stuck to that safe topic. "It takes longer to do this when we're under way."

He stepped inside. "We've time. Two and a half weeks yet."

"The Aldan–Baris border's at least three and a half—"

"I take risks." He pushed the datapad to the center of the desk and sat, angled on the edge. "The *Boru Karn* will meet us in Calth."

"Not at the A–B?" The Aldan–Baris border contained a number of asteroid belts and abandoned miners' rafts. They provided excellent places to hide, especially for a ship the size of the *Boru Karn*. It was one of the few places Sully had ever managed to lose me when I was on his trail. Calth was more open, more heavily trafficked by Imperial ships. "Is that wise?"

He responded with the quiet, gentle stare I suddenly tagged as Sully's way of reading me, like Ren's barely perceptible head tilt.

"Wisdom's only proven in hindsight, my angel. Without application, it's but theory." He spread one hand in an almost elegant gesture. "True wisdom is theory that's been tested through risk."

We'd just kidnapped two Imperial officers, hijacked a patrol ship, almost been incinerated by plasma torpedoes, and could've killed ourselves in a cold jump. And I was listening to a lofty-sounding monologue better suited to the halls of a university than the quarters of a patrol-ship captain. Who'd just found out the man before her was a rogue empath. Maybe I wasn't the only one not quite ready to face the questions and answers.

"Sully—"

"Hush, Chasidah-angel." He put his finger against my mouth. "I have a question." His fingers moved under my chin. "Do you still think it was wise to come down the corridor after me?"

He withdrew his hand and waited.

I thought of his lecture on wisdom. And I'd heard this tone in his voice other times, when he'd played the poet, the pedant. They'd almost always been times of intense emotion. Like Port Chalo. I'd written off his words that night because of the beer. But he was sober now, though no less intense.

I wasn't sure I understood him. I needed, however, for him to understand me. There was too much at risk here, in too many ways.

"Were my actions wise? I'm a Fleet officer, trained to assess situations, act on the facts. You won't find *impetuous* in my service record. Obviously, there's a lot I don't know about you. But there's a lot I do know, after six years. Especially after the past few days. But I'm also not a fool," I added softly. "I have fears."

"Because of risks you don't understand."

"Oh, some I understand very well." I breathed a

small, harsh laugh. "I have had my heart trashed. That's not in my service record either."

His slight frown was encouraging. By all that was holy, I did have some secrets left, even from an empath.

"That's not at risk here."

"I've heard that before too."

"Chasidah—"

I touched my finger to his lips, mimicking his gesture of moments ago. "Hush."

He gave me a small smile, wistful yet oddly warm.

I took my hand away. "So was my coming after you wise? I owed you an apology. It wasn't my intention to say hurtful words. I told you the other night. There are a number of things in my life that I'm not handling well, that confuse me. You're one of them."

"Because of what happened with Kingswell?"

"And because of what happened, or didn't happen, in Port Chalo."

"I never regretted my choice of career until I met you," he said, his wistful smile fading. "I had certain commitments to fulfill. Once they were, I had what I thought was a plan. A reinvention of Gabriel Ross Sullivan, if you will, into someone Chasidah Bergren would meet in an officers' club. Not in one of the disreputable bars in Port Chalo."

"I would've preferred Port Chalo to Moabar."

"So would I. Then Kingswell, and what I had to do, wouldn't be an issue. But with that, my answers are long and complicated. I can't guarantee that clarification is a solution. It hasn't been, for me."

Growing up an empath in a society that condemned mind talents hardly provided any avenues for clarification. I could see why his friendship with Ren was important. I could also see why my acceptance of Ren was equally as important to him.

His gaze flicked down to the desktop, then back to my face. "I have another question."

I nodded.

"Did you come looking for me freely, or because of Ren?"

"Ren didn't ask me to apologize to you. But he did give me facts I didn't have before. They reinforced my feelings."

"For me?"

I thought my subsequent actions in the corridor were self-explanatory. I was sure I broadcasted everything in the appropriate colors. But then, even Ren had questioned the source of my sadness that morning. Identifying an emotional resonance evidently didn't include the source, or motivation behind it, even for an empath. Especially for an empath.

Which also answered an unasked question of mine. If he were a telepath, he'd know what I thought. And why I felt what I did.

"Would it help if I told you what I thought when you kissed me yesterday, after the Peyhar's service? I believe it was something in the order of a desperate desire to take your robe off, with my teeth." I stared hard at him, ignored the heat rising to my cheeks.

A smile played across his lips. "That would be totally acceptable behavior."

"Not when you're furred. And talking about adding me to your list of women."

He opened his mouth, then closed it. Gabriel, the poet, the wordsmith, at a lack. Gabriel, chagrined. "There's no list of women."

"Good."

"But you're still uneasy."

"Why didn't you tell me you're an empath, like Ren?"

He met my question with a long silence. "Fear. I couldn't bear losing you over this darkness that lives deep inside me."

"Is that how you think of yourself?" I asked softly. He'd told me he'd been consigned to Hell. Is that what it felt like, being an empath?

"It's how everyone thinks of me."

"Everyone thinks I murdered the fourteen officers and crew of the *Harmonious*. Do you?"

"No."

I arched an eyebrow. "Well, then."

He closed his eyes briefly, shook his head. "It's not the same. When the truth about you comes out, and it will, you'll be exonerated. The truth about me is only damning."

"That's not—"

His finger pressed against my lips again. "Hush. One last question." He didn't wait for my nod. "Can you accept me as I am, now, on faith? With what you know, and nothing more?" He paused. "I fear that your need for facts, your need for explanations, for things that perhaps can never be explained, will destroy the only chance we have. And I'll lose you."

His fingers brushed against my cheek, then tucked a strand of hair around my ear. His voice was hoarse when he continued. "I promise, I swear, I will never hurt you, could never hurt you. This is no lie." He hesitated, his gaze searching my face. "I do not lie."

A memory surfaced: one of three moons had risen. We sat across from each other as we had a hundred times before, but this time, the blackness of space didn't separate us.

Though I may be a veritable walking list of negative personality traits, the one thing I am not, and never have been, is a liar. It's my great downfall, Chaz.

I reached for him as I stood. My arms wrapped around his neck. His thighs closed around my legs, locking me to him. His hands framed my face.

"Can you accept me as I am, Chasidah?"

I wondered what Kingswell and Tessa had seen haunting the fathomless depths of Sullivan's obsidian eyes. I saw a ghost, locked in his own personal Hell. And a man, badly in need of a shave. And an answer.

I gave him mine. "Yes."

13

Intraship trilled, halting a kiss that could have run away into something we truly didn't have time for right now with only two of us able to run the ship. Something I didn't know if I was quite ready for right now. Just because I'd given Sully my trust didn't mean I was any less confused. But I was very aware of the pain he carried. I didn't want to add to that.

I reached for the touchpad. "Bergren." My voice was distinctly throaty. His arms wrapped around my waist. He rested his face on my shoulder.

"A transmit incoming, I believe," Ren said. I could hear the soft ping from the comm panel over the intraship.

"On our way." I angled back to Sully, brushed my hand up the side of his face, which was rough—through his hair, which was soft, sprinkled lightly at the temples with silver. His eyes half closed, briefly. He was still in the pleasure mode. Heat rippled down my arm when I touched him. I wondered how he did that, but I'd agreed. No questions.

He exhaled a long sigh. "Alterations can be made to convert some of the systems, like communications, to voice response."

Like Ren's clock, or the commissary panels in the temple common room. Ask, it tells you. Tell it, it does. That would help. Reality dictated we were still looking at only two of us who could handle the ship. That most likely meant two twelve-hour shifts, one his, one mine. For the next two weeks.

He said nothing more. But at the doorway, he stopped. He pulled me abruptly against him, his mouth coming down hard on mine, demanding, claiming. Sparks danced through me.

Just as suddenly he drew back and rested his face against my forehead for a moment. "Thank you," he whispered, as breathless as I was. His hands found my shoulders, pushed me back slightly. He grinned, a wry, quirky Sully grin. "Regrettably, we have work to do."

The transmit was from Admiral Weston Rayburn, commander of the Sixth Fleet. My stomach churned for a second. The *Meritorious* was part of the Sixth; Rayburn was my CO. Had Kingswell remembered me?

Rayburn's recorded transmit said otherwise. The Empire wouldn't tolerate such actions from Farosian terrorists looking to force the release of Blaine. If we returned the ship now, we would be granted fair treatment in the Imperial courts.

No mention of Kingswell or his lieutenant.

I deleted the transmit. I'd already been through the Imperial court system. Their version of fair treatment didn't interest me.

I went back to the desk in Kingswell's quarters—my quarters—and retrieved the datapad. Sully checked my patches, verified everything through the command console. Then he altered the *Meritorious*'s ID.

I tackled the comm panel, converted what I could to voice-mode activation and response. But things like weapons, helm, and navigation needed eyes.

That took us almost four hours. Commissary panels still produced nothing but water, tea, and coffee, though now to voice commands. We couldn't get the sublights to crank over seventy-five percent. That would add an extra day or two to our agenda.

Ren looked tired, his shoulders sagging as he sat at the comm station. Almost eight hours had passed since we'd left Moabar Station.

I pushed out of my chair, went over to him, and unraveled his braid full of lake and ocean and river colors. "There's a hydrotub in sick bay. Go soak. I'll rebraid this when you're finished, if you want."

He tilted his head back in my hands, eyes closed. "I should be of more help."

"You're an immeasurable help." I didn't know how to explain to Ren that much of my faith in Sully was because of Ren's trust in him. Ren knew the facts. His acceptance became mine.

"Go play fish, Ackravaro." Sully watched us, leaning one elbow on his armrest, half swiveled in his chair on the other side of the bridge. "It'll be a struggle, but I think we can handle the universe by ourselves for an hour."

Ren straightened, grinning. He moved out of his chair in a graceful, fluid movement. His hand rested briefly on my shoulder as he passed me. Warmth flared.

He stopped at the hatch tread. "One million, seven hundred four thousand, two hundred twenty-one."

It took me a moment to place the figures. The amount Sully owed him for losses at cards.

Sully stood and pointed toward the corridor. "Off my bridge, you swindler!"

Ren's laughter echoed in the corridor.

I put my hands on my hips and faced Sully. "It's my bridge, thank you."

"Is it, now, my angel?" Two long strides and his arm slipped around my waist. He turned me in a half spin, lifting me up. My arms went around his neck and then I was in his lap. And he was in my chair, the captain's chair.

He pulled me against him, his mouth against my ear. A deep voice, incongruously gentle, whispered, "Hush. Just let me hold you."

Heat seeped into me, brushed my senses. I relaxed, lay my head on his shoulder, and closed my eyes. "It's still my bridge, Sully."

Laughter rumbled quietly in his chest. He kissed my cheek. "Mine," he said softly. "Mine."

We were still there, indulgently idle, talking quiet nonsense when Ren returned. He handed me his comb. Sully lifted me off his lap, depositing me on my feet with a sigh. "I can't live on tea until we hit Calth. Where's the base unit for the panels?"

"Deck Two, amidship," I told him as he left.

Ren sat at comm. I combed out his hair, did my basic three-strand braid.

I'd promised Sully no questions, but I didn't think asking Ren about who I'd face when we got to the *Boru Karn* violated that. Or what could be shared with those on Sully's ship about events on the *Meritorious*. And what yet might have to be done. "Who knows, besides you and me?" I hesitated. "About Sully."

A thoughtful silence was my answer.

"Gregor and Marsh?" I prompted, trying to make my question clearer. Obviously they knew Sully. But did they know what Sully could do?

"No."

Ren's answer told me he understood my question. "Drogue?"

"No."

That meant Brother Clement and others at the Moabar temple didn't. Then I wondered about Winthrop Sullivan's unconditional rejection of his son. If he'd known his son was an empath, had mind talents that much of the Empire viewed with condemnation, that might explain his vehemence. But Winthrop had died before he could accomplish it legally. Sullivan was still a Sullivan.

It had been left to Sully's mother to fulfill her husband's wish to clear the family name. I'd occasionally caught her elegant features gracing the society vid clips before she was killed. Sophia Giovanna Rossetti Sullivan, often on the arm of someone like First Barrister Darius Tage or another of the Empire's elite. The Rossettis had money too. I'd seen estimates of the combined wealth. It was staggering—at least, to my Fleet-issue pay-grade way of life. "Did his mother know?"

"His mother preferred to believe he was dead, Chasidah."

Okay, I heard that. No more questions. I wrapped a tie around the end of Ren's hair, then swiveled his chair around. "Sorry."

"Nothing to be sorry for. You don't seek out of curiosity, but out of concern. You must learn to ask him these things, though. He needs to explain—"

"He said he can't. Won't." Ren didn't know what Sully had asked of me. Acceptance on faith. No questions. I made a small, helpless gesture with my hands. "I'm not trying to circumvent that. I just don't want to do something stupid."

"He will tell you what you need to know about Marsh and Gregor," Ren said after a moment. "And the others who come and go. But as for Gabriel Sullivan..." Ren reached out his six-fingered hand toward me. I clasped it. Warmth flooded me. But something else. Certainty. Trust. Compassion. Courage. He pulled his hand back, smiled. "That is all I can tell you." Then he headed down to Deck Two.

I sat in my chair, swung the command controls around, and stared out at the starfield. I thought about wisdom and trust. And faith. And risks. And empaths. And about how very much I had yet to learn.

Not surprisingly, exhaustion set in after we had dinner in the small ready room. It wasn't the best of dinners; selections were limited by a recalcitrant commissary unit. But it was sustenance, filling and reassuring.

I angled the microscreen in the middle of the round table so that it faced me, giving me current status. Everything the bridge knew was there, but in condensed, no-frills form. A P40 could run on autoguidance, but not for very long. And not without someone, somewhere, monitoring the basics.

Sully and Ren were talking about Sheldon Blaine and the Farosians. I tuned them out. I propped my chin in my hand, watched the data, watched distance and time trickle, watched autoguidance keep us on course. If anything large or small tickled long-range sensors, they'd start screaming. Should something get by long range before the bridge could respond, short range would automatically bring shields to max, weapons online. And scream louder.

Good ship, my little P40.

A warm hand on my shoulder jostled me. "You're falling asleep, Chaz."

"Huh?" I was facedown on the table, my cheek

resting on my crossed arms. I lifted my head. Blinked. Sully came into focus.

"I had an hour's rest in the hydro," Ren said. "I can stand watch, four, six hours if you need me to."

I sat up. "We need to work out shifts. We need—"

"Sleep. We need some sleep." Sully pulled me to my feet. "Let Ren take these four hours. I'll take the next eight. We'll work it from there."

"It's my ship," I grumbled as he propelled me toward the door. "I'm responsible—"

"You're exhausted. So am I. Ren's the only one with half a brain left." He turned me to the left, toward my door, hit the palm pad.

"I should shower." But damn, the bed looked really good.

"Shower when you wake. It'll help."

No argument there. I sat on the edge of the bed, undid my boots. The bed sagged next to me. Sully was doing the same.

I stood, undid my belt.

Sully stood, doing the same.

It hit me that I wasn't going to bed alone.

My fingers hesitated. It was only a small lack of movement, a half a breath skipped—but they hesitated.

I felt Sully's quizzical, gentle gaze on me. Goddamned rainbows. *It's not fear,* I wanted to tell him. *I'm not afraid of you.* But I was. I knew that. And I knew he knew that.

I finished unthreading my belt, hung it on the hook on the wall. Stripped off my pants, hung them up too. Thought about faith, about risks. About all that Ren could tell me about Gabriel Sullivan.

I pulled my shirt over my head, realized I didn't have anything to sleep in other than the thin T-shirt and underpants I had on now. The closets were probably full of

Kingswell's things. I wasn't ready to touch them yet. Nor go searching for Tessa's.

Hell. I turned around. Sully stood by the bed, shirtless, bootless, his pants unzipped and angled halfway down his hips.

By all that was holy, he was magnificent. His arms and chest were sculpted with muscles, his shoulders wide. His was a body I could explore for hours, or just as easily curl against, feeling safe and protected. Warmed.

His gaze caught mine again, quizzical, gentle. Reading me. His pants dropped to his ankles. He picked them up and tossed them onto the small chair. Then he held out his hand.

"It's okay. I'm just going to hold you until you fall asleep."

I took his hand.

Warmth.

When I woke, it was 0820. Sully was gone, the bed empty. But the rumpled covers and dented pillow told me I didn't dream falling asleep in his arms. I rolled over. His clothes were absent from the hooks.

I'd slept for a little under six hours. The *Meritorious* had switched to station time when it had docked at Moabar. So the 0822 was accurate for my body as well.

The shower helped. Kingswell's towels. Kingswell's soap. I'd strip the cabin later, when shifts were worked out and I had my off time allocated.

My clothes would go in the laundry as soon as I could scrounge something out of another cabin, from a female crew member left behind at Tamlara's. Not from a lieutenant who wouldn't remember a woman with long auburn hair, a man with six webbed fingers, and another man with hauntingly dark obsidian eyes.

I threaded my belt through the loops of my pants as I stood in front of my desk. Bridge status danced on the microscreen. I tapped on intraship. "Captain's heading for the bridge."

"Bring coffee," came the reply. Sully.

Ren wasn't there. "Soaking," Sully said, sitting comfortably in my chair, legs crossed. He took a mouthful of coffee, closing his eyes in appreciation. And probably, I suspected, to ignore the fact that I stood next to him, waiting for him to vacate my chair.

"How long have you been up?"

"About two hours."

"Why didn't you wake me?"

"Feels rather nice sitting in the captain's chair."

I gave up on dislodging him and sat at engineering, sipping my coffee. We worked on shift schedules. He argued against two twelves. "This isn't the damned Fleet."

We settled for eight on—six on the bridge, two on standby—four off for Sully and myself. Ren would work his schedule to overlap ours, but no more than four on the bridge by himself. There still could be bogies out there, searching for a ghost ship.

In jump it would change. In jump there were no bogies. We were all ghosts. But jump was five days away.

I stayed up for another few hours, tinkering. I coaxed the commissary panels to remember they could make fruit. I also found that the ship had had two other female crew members besides Tessa. I pilfered some clothes. I was looking for shirts for Sully and Ren when Sully found me.

"It's past your bedtime."

"These look like your size. Maybe Ren's too." I shoved three shirts into his arms. All were plain, scoopnecked, long-sleeved. Two were dark blue, one dark gray.

"Bedtime."

"I'm really not tired—"

"You will be if you don't reset your body clock. You go on duty at 1800." He tucked the shirts under one arm, wrapped the other around my shoulders. "I'll read you a bedtime story."

Ren was in the corridor. Sully handed him the shirts. "Chaz's been shopping. Keep what fits. I'll take what's left. I'll be back on the bridge shortly," he added, guiding me into my cabin.

Our cabin.

I pulled off my boots, stripped down. Washed my face, unbraided my hair. I grabbed my pilfered comb and ran it through my hair as I padded back to the bed. Sully sat on the edge, fluffing pillows.

He turned, stopped fluffing. "Stars have mercy," he said softly.

He pulled me to the bed and took over my grooming. I closed my eyes. Fingers and comb laced through my hair, down my arms, my back. "This could become an obsession."

I reminded him he already had a job. And that he was on duty.

He pushed my hair to one side, planted a light kiss on my collarbone. "Get under the covers."

I did. They were cool, pillows nicely fluffed. I lay my hand on his arm. "Sully—"

"Hush, Chasidah." He touched his fingers to my lips. "Close your eyes."

I was about to protest I wasn't sleepy when I felt his fingers on my forehead, then my eyelids, then my mouth again. A soft breeze ruffled over me—

—and my eyes opened. 1605. I couldn't believe I'd fallen asleep that quickly. Or that I'd slept for that long. I wasn't muzzy from it. I knew my body clock hadn't reset yet, but I felt fine.

I splashed more water on my face, then pulled on someone else's clothes. I bound my hair back loosely with a ribbon. "Captain's heading for the bridge."

"Hell's ass. There goes our card game." Sully's lackadaisical drawl made me smile.

They were sitting on the floor of the bridge, to the right of the captain's chair, playing cards. At least I didn't have to fight for possession of the chair.

I leaned on the armrest and watched the game over Sully's shoulder. "Who's winning? No. Delete that. How much does he owe you now, Ren?"

"One million, seven hundred sixteen thousand, four hundred and five."

"That's all?" I teased. "You're slipping."

Sully pointed at Ren. "Thieving chiseler. Swindler."

I chuckled. "Status?"

"He cheats. That's status. It's always been status."

"I don't think that's what she's asking you, Sully."

"She should be. Your lack of integrity is appalling."

I held up one hand. "Gentlemen, I need status."

Sully picked up the stack of cards, arced them into his hand, feathered them back down. "On course, all systems stable. No bogies. No transmits from politically wary admirals." He shuffled the cards again with a skill even the best casino dealer on Garno would envy. Then he angled around to face me, fanned the deck in his hands, and held it up to me. "Pick three. No, four. No, wait. What's your favorite number?"

"Five."

"Perfect. Pick five. Ah! Don't look at them yet. Just hold them. Between your palms, that's right."

I pursed my lips together to keep from laughing.

"Good. What's your favorite card?"

"Favorite card? You mean suit?" I'd seen tricks like this in spaceport pubs, though never with five cards. Two at most, and I'd end up holding two gold-novas, high-nebulas, moon-drops, or heart-stars.

"No, card. Favorite card."

I raised one eyebrow. There were no five cards alike in a deck.

He was grinning his wicked Sully grin.

Hell's ass. "Angel of heart-stars."

"Fitting. Very fitting. Be a good girl, Chasidah; open your hands and look at the cards."

I fanned them out in my hand. Five angels of heart-stars. Five familiar images of slender women, clearly angels because of the halos topping their cascading hair. All identical.

He stood, brushed his hands against his pants. "Tea, anyone?"

"Please," Ren said.

I was still staring at the cards, my mouth open.

"You'd best get Chasidah some too," Ren called as Sully strode through the door.

"How'd he do that?"

"Offer to get tea?" There was the hint of a smile on Ren's lips. He knew I was surprised by something. But unless he touched the cards, he wouldn't know what.

"Five heart-stars. I'm holding five angels of heart-stars. There aren't five angels of heart-stars in one whole deck!" Damn, he was good. I didn't even see him switch decks.

"Gabriel's playing tricks again, is he?"

"Damn good tricks. This could get you more than a few beers on liberty." I closed the cards and shook my head, laughing to myself.

Ren rose, scooping up the remaining deck where Sully had left it on the floor.

I shuffled the ones in my hand, absently, feeling their raised symbols. Then I stopped shuffling and turned them over. Five angels. I felt the raised symbols again.

This wasn't a trick deck.

Gabriel's playing tricks, Ren had said.

I handed the five cards back to Ren. He patted me on the shoulder, gently.

Warmth.

* *⭐
⏻⛛

"Lose this hand and you owe me two million credits, my friend." Ren arched his left cycbrow slightly.

We were an hour from the jumpgate that would take us through most of Dafir and almost to the Calth system. Another four, five days after that and we'd be near the intercept coordinates for the *Boru Karn*. Six days of long shift duty had brought us to this point, safely—though from Sully's viewpoint, not inexpensively.

He stared coolly at Ren, dark eyes narrowed, a hint of a smile on his lips. The quintessential gambler, lounging on the decking, one elbow on a raised knee.

I gave a low whistle. "Two million. What are you going to do now?"

He fanned the cards shut, held them, fanned them open again, never taking his eyes off Ren. "Double or nothing."

"Sully . . ." Ren was clearly giving him a chance to rethink his statement.

"You heard me, Ackravaro. Double or nothing."

Ren stroked his cards. "Agreed. Double or nothing."

"You're witness to this, Chaz."

"I'm witness to this, Sully."

Sully looked at Ren, a triumphant smile on his face. He laid his cards on the deck, one by one, calling them out as he did so. All gold-novas. Sequential. Seven through angel. A good hand. A damned good hand.

Ren sighed and looked distinctly troubled.

Sully's grin widened.

Ren laid out his cards. All high-nebulas. Ten, angel, empress, emperor, galaxy. "Four million. You owe me four million, my friend."

Sully leaned forward. He stared at the cards in front of Ren, then back at his own. "This is a beautiful hand. Then you pull..." He switched his gaze back to Ren again. "You cheated. There can be no other explanation."

"You say that every time, Sully."

"Yes, I know. Ante up?"

"Ante up. Who's dealing?"

"I am. You're obviously not trustworthy."

I laughed. "Make it a quick game, gentlemen. I need you at your stations in fifteen minutes." I pulled my armrest controls around, rechecked our coordinates. A longer jump this time than the one off Moabar. Six hours' jumptime.

We could all use the time off. It was tense, waiting for something to happen. While jukors were born and Takas died.

Two thousand, five hundred twenty-five credits later, Sully was at engineering and Ren sat at comm, monitoring internal systems through voice commands.

Sublights disengaged at forty-eight percent, hypers were on full. The gate grabbed us, drew us in—no twists, no shimmies. The *Meritorious* glided into the neverwhen flawlessly. Just like old times.

I stayed an extra half hour on the bridge, watching the readouts on the hypers, making sure guidance wasn't picking up a skew from the remnant of an old ion trail. I leaned over Sully's shoulder. He pulled me around and into his lap. "You're supposed to be off duty."

"I just like to take my ship through jump."

"And out again, I suppose?"

"Yes, and out again."

"That leaves about five hours with nothing for you to do. Tea sounds good. Can you defend the universe without us for a while, Ren?"

"Most certainly."

"We won't be far." Sully stood, grabbing my elbow. In the common room he coaxed two mugs of hot tea from the panels. I pulled the chairs out from the table, but he shook his head. "Our cabin. Decor's better."

Yes. It had a bed.

Six days. In the past six days, he'd done nothing more than kiss me, tuck me in, let me sleep. But he'd made sure, every hour I spent with him, a little more of Gabriel Ross Sullivan came to the surface.

It was as if he were showing me in small ways what I couldn't ask and what he couldn't tell. But he watched my rainbows, cautiously, waiting for my fears to subside.

And they were subsiding, in equally small ways. That Sully was an empath like Ren was clear. So were a few hundred, or perhaps thousand, other humans in the Empire, from what I'd heard. And I hadn't heard much, other than those who admitted to the rare mind talent often worked as government-sanctioned med-counselors. I could understand their usefulness in that field. Though it had been disconcerting at first to feel the warmth flowing through my body from the touch of

Ren's and Sully's hands, it wasn't intrusive. I didn't fear that. It was a giving, comforting thing.

But I still wondered about the differences between empaths and *Ragkirils*. The Empire called all Stolorth telepaths *Ragkirils*. Knowing Ren as I did now, I knew that wasn't true. Ren was an empath. He didn't have the Higher Link. But what was Sully? Was the ability to do a *zral*, a cleansing of memory, a part of empathic abilities, not *Ragkiril*? I'd never heard of any humans with *Ragkiril* talents, though admittedly, a patrol-ship captain wasn't likely to be informed of such a discovery. Could it be just a stronger version of a reassuring touch, a blurring of a memory rather than the removal? He never said he could do a *zragkor*. That procedure was a mind suddenly inside another's mind, violent, harsh.

I sensed no violence, no harshness in him or Ren anytime their warmth flowed into me. I didn't even know if they were aware they sent the sensation, or that I could feel it.

Sully's card trick with the five angels of heart-stars perplexed me a little more. You can't alter matter by touch, by thought. Even my Grizni dagger was mechanical, a hybrid fluid metal reactive to heat and pressure applied at certain key points, coded only to my fingerprints.

There were only two logical explanations: either Sully did have a second deck, or—why did I have to assume Ren's reference to "Gabriel's tricks" meant something on the extrasensory level?—he sent the emotional resonance of acceptance into me when he handed me the cards. I saw five heart-stars because that's what I wanted to see.

He put the tea on the bedside table, drew me into his lap in the middle of the bed. He took a moment to undo my boots and his own, pulled them off. He wrapped his arms around my waist, nuzzled his face in my neck. "Tea's for later. Though it'll probably be cold by then."

Warmth trickled through me, then a flash of heat, flaring, spiraling. Its unexpected intensity made my eyes open in surprise.

His own sharp intake of breath matched mine. The heat simmered. Gentled. "I want so badly to make love to you, Chazzy-girl. But only if it's what you want. Tell me to wait—"

I closed my hands over his. "I don't want to wait."

Another flare, flames dancing, but I was ready for it this time.

I draped my legs over his thighs, took his face in my hands. Kissed him with small, teasing, nibbling kisses.

He groaned. Tiny explosions rained inside my body.

He kissed me back, hard.

I opened my mouth, tasted him.

His hands found the edge of my shirt, pulled. I broke from the kiss, stripped my shirt off, then the undershirt. He ran his hands lightly over my breasts, his thumbs circling my nipples. His fingers slid down to my waist, stroking, then up again. The heat came in long, coursing flares.

I reached behind my head, unraveled my braid, and shook my hair free. It fell to my waist, tangled and curled.

"Chaz," he said softly. He ran his fingers through my hair, pushing it back from my face, letting it drift down through his hands.

I pulled the edge of his shirt out of his pants. His hand covered mine, impatient. He yanked the shirt over his head, then grabbed me, rolling me onto my back. His hard length covered me. His mouth claimed mine, demanding, insistent. A strong hand cupped my breast. Then his lips burned against my neck, my shoulder, closed around a nipple, sucked with a tenderness that made me ache.

A hot wave rolled over me, soothing the ache, caressing it. Mouth back on mouth now. Breaths shuddered.

I arched my hips against him, felt him throbbing, felt liquid fire racing through my veins. I ran my hands over the sinews of his shoulders, down to his waist, pushed my fingers into the waistband of his pants. "You going to take these off, or do I have to use my teeth?"

His dark eyes glittered with a dangerous passion. "We'll save that method for next time. When we have more than five hours."

My pants and underwear came off too, tossed somewhere over his shoulder. Then there was nothing but heat and hardness, hands stroking, fingers tracing, tongues leaving hot, wet trails.

And fire, searing, cresting, spiraling. I knew it was his emotions I felt, overwhelming me, augmenting and feeding my own.

I found his mouth again, wanting to kiss that wicked, wicked Sully grin. My hands moved up his chest, through the thick mat of dark hair, and clung to his shoulders. His hands slid under my backside, kneading me, lifting me, his hardness stroking against me, slick. I wrapped my legs around his waist, stroked back with my body. He trembled, kissed me with a passion that made me gasp.

"Sully, please!"

I didn't have to ask twice. He plunged into me, sparks surging, cascading, swirling. My body answered with a fervency I didn't know I had, pleasure streaming through me at hyperspace speeds. Everything collided, arcing. He rasped my name, stroking deeper.

And then I swear three suns went nova, half a galaxy

was blown away, and the universe shifted at least a hundred feet from where it had been before.

But it was just Sully, his body hot and damp and heavy against mine, breathing long, ragged breaths against my neck. Sending warm, pulsing waves through me.

I unwrapped my legs, let my feet drift down the back of his thighs in a slow caress. I stroked his hair and, when he moved slightly, bit his shoulder.

He chuckled. "You're a wicked woman, Chazzy-girl."

"You're a wicked man, Sully."

I dozed, curled against him, listening to the rise and fall of his breath. Warmth fluttered through my hand and up my arm when I touched him, traced the line of his jaw.

His eyes slitted open. He grabbed my hand, nibbled kisses on my fingers. "No regrets?"

"None. Well, maybe."

A small flash of concern touched his eyes. His mouth turned into a slight frown.

Wicked woman, Chazzy-girl. "I like my tea hot."

Something between a groan and a grumble vibrated in his throat. He pushed me back, slid on top of me, slid inside me again, hard, throbbing. "Let's talk about heat."

I couldn't. Talk. Passion, hot, molten passion, streamed through me. Then a second wave, but different, almost intoxicating. Then heat again, melting me, melting into me. Then another, floating, rising.

The heat returned, more intense, probing, wrapped around me. Parted, pleasure surged, building, cresting—

"Oh, God, Chaz!" Shuddering, soaring, taking me with him, clinging to each other. Desperate, frenzied kisses.

Then warmth, soft as the breath on my face, enveloping me.

I opened my eyes to find Sully watching me. Reading rainbows?

"You can do that, control what you send? What you make me feel?" Like sensations of intense passion alternating with ones of languid pleasure. Like a sensation of acceptance. Five heart-stars in my hand.

A long wait was filled with the sound of his ragged breathing, finally slowing. He watched me the whole time.

"I'm sorry," I said softly. "I'm not supposed to ask—"

"No. It's okay." His was an equally soft reply. Then Sully's face was next to mine on the pillow, his arm across my chest, hand on my shoulder, pulling me closer against him.

"Yeah," he said in my ear, just a breath of a whisper. A near silent confession. "Yeah, I can."

Fifty minutes to exitgate. The numbers glowing on my bedside clock focused and unfocused in my sleepy vision. Sully's arm was heavy across my chest, his breathing deep, steady. I studied his face. Thick brows, dark lashes, straight nose. No Sully grin on those slightly parted lips. Shame, that. When I'd heard he'd been killed on Garno, it was one of the things I knew I'd miss.

That, and the verbal sparring. Over six years of it. I'd pick up an ID on the border, somewhere in the badlands. Somewhere a ship with that ID shouldn't be. Send out a hail. Get an answer, a flash on the vidscreen. A dark-haired pirate with a wicked smile. His pilot, bridge crew, always moved in the shadows behind him.

"Slumming, Captain Bergren?"

"Weeding my garden, Sullivan. You wouldn't happen

to be waiting for the Osborn Mining long-hauler, now would you?"

"I've no use for synth-emeralds."

"Never said they were hauling synth-emeralds."

A languid shrug, almost aristocratic. "Lucky guess on my part, then."

"You're in a restricted area. You know the rules. Move it, or we're boarding. You know how the Empire feels about forged ownership files."

"I'm in free space, Captain. Well," and there'd be that glance down at the arm pad controls on his left, on the empty pilot's chair, "most of me is."

My own downward glance always mirrored his own. Bastard. Sitting right on the border of the restricted zone, only his bridge and a small portion of the forward section of the ship in violation. "You're playing a dangerous game here."

"It's the only kind worth playing." Then a hand would be offered across the small starfield between us. And a look, dark and suggestive. "Come play with me, Chazzy-girl. I'll let you win."

The memory dissolved as a long intake of breath feathered against my face. A heavy arm moved slightly, and a hand stirred against the side of my neck. His face tilted. Our lips touched.

"Forty minutes to exitgate, Sully."

"Mmm." Another long sigh brushed my mouth. "You're off duty."

"I'm the captain."

His eyes opened slowly. His thumb rubbed across my mouth where his lips had just been. "And I suppose the captain wants her tea hot this time."

I nipped his thumb, then rolled quickly, avoiding his

grasp. "Quick shower. And yes, hot tea. Not coffee. I'll never get back to sleep."

A raised eyebrow and a Sully grin challenged my last statement. There were always his bedtime stories.

When I came out of the shower, tea was waiting, hot. Sully was gone. But a playing card fluttered out of my pants pocket when I picked my clothes off the floor.

Angel of heart-stars.

Thirty minutes to exitgate. "Captain's heading for the bridge."

"Hell's ass. There goes our card game."

We flowed through the gate like honeylace from a crystalline cup. Sweet, sweet little ship, my P40. I thought about that, thought about how good it felt to be at a stellar helm again. And pushed aside those sullen whispers in my mind, those questions about Gabriel Ross Sullivan I didn't want to face. Those fears . . .

We hit the C–D border at Calth early on the fourth day after jump. Ahead of schedule, praise the stars! Sublights were back to specs—better than specs, because I didn't have Fleet safety regs to worry about anymore. That Sully knew ways to coax more power out of the drives came as no surprise to me. I'd figured out long ago that rules existed to a great extent so that Sully could break them.

And that's when he was just Sully. Not pirate, lover, ghost, friend, poet, and mercenary, sitting at my engineering station, weapons silent but active. All ship's sensors on serious watch for Imperial bogies.

Ren had integrated data we'd gleaned, illegally, from the Imperial transit beacon in Dafir. We looked for anything to do with Marker. He'd sorted it by voice parameters, talking softly into his headset.

I reviewed the updated meetpoint coordinates we'd picked up on a blind transmit from the *Karn* last shift. A private yacht turned ghost ship. Sully's home base. It was about twice the size of the *Meritorious* but rigged to run with a minimum crew complement of six. Rigged with other things too. He'd laid them out for me in detail. These were things he wanted me to know. Weapons systems, tracking, sensor-jamming arrays. Sublights, hypers, all with overrides. A comm pack that would make an Imperial techie faint with joy. And a custom, highly illegal ion-trail diffuser. Waves on a beach dissolving the footprints in the sand.

Ren slipped his headset down around his neck and swiveled toward me. "There was an unusual series of shipments inbound to Marker a few weeks ago. You might want to—"

An alarm wailed shrilly, my adrenaline spiking along with it. Red lights flared over my long-distance scanner. I switched screens on my arm pad automatically and saw the configuration of an Imperial cruiser. An hour behind us, but her appearance might not be coincidental.

The *Meritorious*'s old files confirmed her ID: the *Andru Kendrick*. Captain Gemma Junot.

I tapped off the alarm. Sully studied the main screen, which showed the same data as my arm pad. I read off the ship's and captain's names for Ren.

"Know her?" Sully meant Junot, not her ship. He knew what a Maven-Class cruiser signified as well as I did.

"By reputation." Junot was a gruff woman in her late forties. But well liked, fair. Though that was from a fellow officer's point of view. I wasn't one of those anymore. Now I was the enemy. "If she has someone sharp on scan who's spotted us, she'll be looking for reasons why a P40 configuration isn't broadcasting an Imperial ID. She has to know a couple mining corporations use P40s for transport. But she also knows a P40's missing from Moabar—and hasn't been confirmed dead yet."

We had to keep enough distance between us so that the answer to Captain Junot's questions would confirm our cover as a mining transport. If she, or any bogey, came within visual range, the *Meritorious*'s name and Imperial insignia were clearly visible on her hull.

We cruised at max sublight, per spec, not per Sully. I didn't want to attract attention by pushing the ship to a speed a P40 normally couldn't provide, a speed that a mining transport had no need of. I could tell Sully to push her now, ten over spec, put some more distance between us and Junot. But I needed the *Kendrick* to go away, not get suspicious and kick her own engines hot in pursuit.

"Hold speed for now?" Sully echoed my thoughts.

I nodded. "Unless she's got friends coming in from the opposite axis, we should be able to talk our way out of this."

A second alarm wailed.

She had friends.

"Shit." I had no choice. Subtlety was out. I raked down my straps. Sully and Ren did the same. "Change course, ninety degrees. Options, Sullivan. Get me options."

"Changing course. Working on it."

An asteroid field would be nice, somewhere to play duck and hide. Mining rafts even nicer. We'd have a legitimate purpose then. Mining transport working the rafts. But this was Calth, not the A–B border, where such things were possible.

"Bogey two an hour ten ahead. *Kendrick* an hour behind, but closing," Ren said, headset back on.

"ID on bogey two?"

"Not yet," Ren replied.

That was one piece of good news. If I couldn't recognize them, they couldn't recognize me. Yet.

"*Kendrick* changing course." Sully worked the console with a calmness that belied our situation. "Following."

"Damn it, I hate when everyone wants to dance with me at the same time."

"You're just a popular girl, Chaz. Ready to lose them yet?"

"Not until I have somewhere to hide."

"Got to let go of that rule book sometime. All life's a risk."

"I'm at quota for risks this week, thank you. Just keep us moving."

"Bogey two coming in sensor range," Ren said. "Confirm ID. Imperial destroyer *Morgan Loviti*."

I froze, for less than a half a second. I was still a Fleet officer. I was still in red-alert conditions. My mind still focused on data, my fingers moved over the arm pad. But I froze as if ice had been sprayed through my insides.

Philip.

"Captain is Philip Guthrie." Ren announced what I already knew.

"Chaz." Sully's dark gaze moved to me, searching, probing. Ren's too, probably. My rainbow had just turned glacial, cracked, and shattered.

"Know him too," I said. I couldn't find an offhand smile to tag my words. I fell back into Fleet-issue-captain mode. "Hold course and speed."

A duro-hard rattled in my personal cold storage, knocked hard against my mental walls. Or maybe that was my heart. Shit. I didn't know. Couldn't tell. It didn't matter. I had two Imperial bogies on my tail and not a hidey-hole in sight.

And one of the bogies knew me, very, very well.

"Kick us up ten." I was running now, running from more than just bogies.

"Plus ten," Sully replied evenly. "*Loviti* changing course to intercept. *Kendrick* still coming on. Forty-five minutes behind, closing fast."

I tapped at my screen, searching desperately for answers. Running would only bring more ships, more intercepts. They'd box us in, if they didn't start firing first. I had to lose them.

Or I had to negotiate.

"We can take plus twenty." Sully's voice was calm, but I felt an underlying question, a gentle nudge of concern, as if he were asking, *What's wrong? What aren't you telling?*

Lots. A whole duro-hard full. Maybe two. And it wasn't that I didn't want to; there just wasn't time for explanations. "Hold course and speed. No, belay that order, Sullivan. Change course to intercept the *Morgan Loviti*. Hold speed at plus ten."

"Bringing weapons on—"

"Stand down, Mister Sullivan. I need weapons cold, shields on minimum."

"Chaz—"

"Do it!" *God, Sully, don't argue with me. Not now. I'm at quota on risks and still hip-deep in confusion.*

"Changing course. Twenty minutes to intercept." His flat response told me he was complying with my orders. But clearly, he didn't like it at all.

Twenty minutes. Twenty minutes to throw words together that would either save us or damn us. The only thing I knew for sure was that if it came down to the latter, my choice was clear. My life in exchange for Sully's and Ren's. Philip would do that.

He wouldn't even hesitate.

"Fifteen minutes to intercept."

I turned away from Sully's voice. "Ren."

He looked over his shoulder, nodded. His clouded gaze probed me.

"I'll need you off the bridge before intercept. Fleet knows a memory-wipe was done on two officers. They see a Stolorth and nothing I say is going to make a difference."

"I understand, Chasidah."

"Wait in my cabin. Use my deskscreen to follow what happens on the bridge. They will not"—I said firmly, with a glance to Sully on my right. His hard obsidian eyes met my gaze—"they will not take this ship. I will not permit that."

I turned back to Ren. "If I'm removed to the *Loviti*—"

"That's unacceptable!" Sully's voice, angry, rode over mine.

My own rose, correspondingly. "If I am removed to the *Loviti,* understand it's because this is my choice. I'm placing you in command if that happens, Ren Ackravaro."

Behind me, I heard the sharp snap of a safety harness unlatching.

"My orders, if that happens, are this: depart, with all possible speed. No shots are to be fired."

"Chasidah!" Sully grasped my forearm, tried to pull me around.

I yanked back, away from the surge of heat that flared through me at his touch. "Ren. As a friend, you must do this."

Ren's face was impassive. His chest rose and fell rapidly. The emotions on the bridge had to almost suffocate him. And Sully as well, who had my arm in a hard grip, who had to be feeling everything roiling through me. Which is why I had to put Ren in charge. I couldn't trust that Sully would react logically, unemotionally. Not with what I was about to do.

"Do you understand, Ren?"

"The other ship. They will listen to the *Loviti* if we're permitted to leave?"

"Junot will do what Guthrie says, yes. He's got seniority."

Sully wrenched me around to face him. Heat rose, crested. Ice cold came in hard after that. Sharp, biting. Scraping me raw on the inside. He was hurting, afraid. But so was I.

"Take your hands off me, Mister Sullivan, and sit down!" I had to get away from his touch, from the emotions he poured through me. I needed to be thinking clearly to face Philip.

He released my arms but didn't move.

"This ship is under my command as well," he said finally, his voice harsh.

"But I'm her captain. We agreed on that from the beginning. I also know how Fleet thinks, reacts. You don't. So listen to your own wisdom for once. You can't outrun them. You're deep in Fleet territory. You've got two starports in this quadrant of Calth. The only way you'll make it to jumpgate is if they let you."

I took a deep breath. "That's what I'm trying to do. Get their permission. If it means I have to stay behind, so be it. It's a risk I have to take." A wry smile finally found its way to my lips. "I'm guess I'm not at quota after all."

"We're being hailed on all channels, Chasidah."

I turned to Ren. "We'll hold position." I tabbed the sublights down to one-quarter power. "Off the bridge, Ren. I'll open comm from here."

Ren stood, laid his hand briefly on my shoulder, then left. A sad, troubled warmth remained.

I turned back to Sully. "I'm going on visual. It's imperative Guthrie believes I'm in total command of this ship. It's imperative you act in all ways as if I am. Stay in the background, let him see you as little as possible. You've not changed that much in two years. You get recognized and it's over. Now, sit."

A wrenching, gnawing anguish suddenly shot through my mind, my thoughts. Cold and hot at the same time, it was cutting, stark. Probing. It grasped at memories. My breathing stuttered, caught. My hand clenched the arm pad. I stared at obsidian eyes, at a man standing three feet in front of me, not even touching me. And I couldn't breathe.

Then just as quickly it was gone. This was not the warm sensation that had caressed my body. This was not an empath's gentle touch. This was deeper, in my mind, tearing open my thoughts with blatant ownership. I felt violated, naked. And too stunned to face the horror of what he'd just done.

"I will not lose you, Chasidah." His voice was as quiet as the vast emptiness of space, and as dark. He sat.

I clenched my fist to steady my shaking hand, then hit the keypad. The center viewscreen opaqued, locked on the hailing signal from the *Loviti*. It segued through instantly, because this was, after all, Imperial ship to Imperial ship.

An image flickered. I knew it even before it focused. The *Loviti*'s bridge. A much larger, grander bridge than my little P40's. And in the middle, a man in Imperial grays, captain's stars over his breast pocket. He wasn't sitting in the captain's chair. Philip Guthrie liked to stand, reinforce his imposing presence, his slate-gray hair, his piercing blue eyes. His impeccable posture, well-muscled body.

Forty-eight years old and in command of a Galaxy-

Class destroyer. He was a figure and a face that turned heads regularly in bars on liberty. Classic, undeniably masculine. Confident.

I tamped down the shock rolling through me at Sully's intrusion into my mind. Threw it in that duro-hard and somehow dragged out my Fleet-issue confidence. My Fleet-issue resolve. I lounged sideways in my chair as Philip's image solidified, crossed my legs, propped my chin in my hand. I knew Philip would see my image at the same time I saw his. But I, at least, had the element of surprise.

Blue eyes widened and chiseled lips parted, but only slightly. "My God. Chaz."

I arched an eyebrow, mimicking Sully at his best. "Hello, Philip, darling. Miss me?"

A strong, sharp stab of pained confusion cut a second time into my mind. Again, without physical contact with the man sitting off to my right. I shoved it aside, just as I'd shoved aside the questions that had surfaced with Sullivan's last intrusion, the one that had me gasping, clutching the arm pad.

I'd lost my right to ask questions. But I hadn't lost my focus. I knew what I had to do.

I kept smiling, a slow, lazy smile as I waited for Philip to find words. It was almost a pleasure to see him at a loss like this. It'd been a long time.

I could see his crew diligently working the consoles behind him. We weren't in visual range. He knew this was a P40. But not which one. He would have, eventually, if we'd run and they'd blockaded us. Then we'd be looking at a few more destroyers, a good half dozen cruisers and patrol ships. There'd be no bargaining then. But it was only Philip, Junot, and Chaz Bergren right now, out here. And Gabriel Ross Sullivan on my bridge, and a blind Stolorth in my cabin.

Philip gestured sharply toward his comm officer. "Transfer this to my office."

The screen blanked. When it came back on, Philip was still standing. But the background was different. A wide viewport, a high-backed chair. And no one else to overhear what might be said.

"Chaz." Philip repeated my name as if he needed verification of my identity. "There's a report of your—a ship being taken by force. At Moabar." He frowned, looking stern. The venerable Fleet captain, quantifying the facts.

"I'm aware the *Meritorious* was taken. But not by me."

"No. The Farosians. With a Stolorth *Ragkiril*. We know that. How you would get involved with them—how you would get involved with *that*—I cannot understand."

"That" meant a Stolorth. A Fleet-issue sentiment of disgust.

"Kingswell and Lieutenant Paxton were near death when Fleet recovered them," he continued. "Their minds viciously raped, all but destroyed."

Liar! The word speared my mind, blazing with anger. It was as clear as if he'd shouted it in my ear.

I pushed it off; let horror, loathing flicker across my face. The emotions were only partially feigned. "Are you blaming me for this?"

"Are you going to tell me this isn't the *Meritorious*?"

"I am. It's not."

Another moment of shocked silence. Good. I liked when Philip didn't have a ready answer.

"She's a Ninacska Mining Cooperative transport ship, the *Far Rider*. You've been scanning me for five minutes. You know my ID."

"Yes, but—"

"Be logical. Let's assume this was the *Meritorious*. Let's assume I'd taken her from Moabar with your Farosian terrorists and some Stolorth mind-fucker. Do you really think I'd be sitting here with minimum shields and weapons cold? Would I have changed course to meet you?" I shook my head sadly. "By all that's holy, Philip. I thought you knew me better than that."

"You're supposed to be incarcerated on Moabar. Am I supposed to believe you didn't steal this ship?"

I leaned to my left, recrossed my legs, propped my chin in my other hand, shrugged. "You never asked me if I stole this ship. I just said she's not the one you're looking for."

"Then this ship is stolen."

"Not exactly. Let's say I negotiated a trade."

I could tell Philip was having a difficult time putting my facts—my deliberately widely divergent facts—together. He was Fleet, like me. He liked his databoxes all stacked neatly in a row.

I plucked out the first box, opened it for him. "NMC services Dafir and the rim, including Moabar."

"I'm aware of that," Philip snapped.

I opened the next one. It contained a small bomb. "I service the boys at NMC. In exchange, I get work-release duty. It's almost freedom."

This time it was Philip's face that showed disgust. "By all that's holy, I never thought I'd see the day where Chaz Bergren would whore—"

"You have no idea what Moabar is like!" I shot to my feet, fists clenched. "Damn you, Philip. How dare you judge me?"

"I can and I will. I offered you a choice. You rejected it."

"The court would never have believed—"

"They would have. Because I said so." His mouth thinned. "It was your choice. You'd rather have Moabar than me. Or our child."

"That wasn't the problem—"

"No, you married me readily enough."

"Because I loved you! You knew I was career Fleet. We'd agreed children were not in our plans. Five years later, when I'm up for a captaincy, suddenly you want to be a father. You weren't willing to take leave or a desk job and share the responsibility. So that means everything I've worked for stops. It would have been knock up Chaz, leave her on a starport, and see you once a year, my darling!"

I was shaking, shouting at him. God, I thought I'd gotten over this.

From behind me on my right was silence. Total silence. Verbal and mental.

"I told you the child could be raised in a crèche. Then your career—"

"No child of mine would be raised in a damned crèche! With droid nannies, med-techs. And a mother and father who are total strangers." Not like Willym, poor thing.

"You're being archaic. You're just like your mother."

"Goddamned right I am." I glared at him. Amaris Bergren didn't raise a fool for a daughter. I knew my fears. I grew up with them: crèche kids, holos of Lieutenant Daddy and Commander Mommy on expensively furnished dormitory walls. That was the acceptable option in Fleet. Breed and abandon. Check in once a year, pat it on the head, ship out.

"What would your mother say about her virtuous daughter's record now?" Philip's voice softened, but carried a bitter edge. "Convicted criminal. Murderer. Whore."

My hand clasped my Grizni bracelet, felt it tingle, ready, waiting. But Philip was just an image on the screen. I couldn't hurt him. He couldn't hurt me.

Then why did I feel such a pain in my heart?

Philip ran his hand over his face, eyes downcast. "I'm sorry. I didn't mean what I said just now." He sucked in a short breath. "This just throws a wrench in my—I've been working on a way to get you transferred. Something...safer than Moabar. I didn't abandon you, Chaz. You may want to think so. But I didn't."

A ploy to gain my sympathy, cooperation? Philip had never been a game player, but I couldn't discount that the recapture of the *Meritorious* would be a bright spot on his already shining record. Or he could genuinely still care. I couldn't discount that either. But that wasn't what mattered at this point. I took a deep breath. "Do you have an order for the seizure of this vessel, Captain Guthrie?"

"Chaz—"

"Do you?" I demanded. I had to push now. I had to force a resolution. Junot had to be wondering what was going on.

"I loved you. I still love you. It's why I married you."

"Do you have an order for the seizure of an NMC transport vessel!"

A heartbeat. Two. Three. I was presenting him with a legitimate out.

"No."

One down. One to go.

"Philip, listen to me. You offered to lie for me seven months ago. I turned you down. With each lie, we become less and less a person. I am innocent of the charges against me, but I loved you too much to ask you to lie, even knowing that. You're an exemplary officer. A fine man."

"Chaz, we can—"

I held up my hand. "Listen, damn you! I wouldn't have you lie for me then. I'm not asking you to lie for me now. You have no seizure order on this ship. Therefore, by law, you can no longer detain her. You must let her go. The only issue, then, is me." I clasped my hands behind my back, stood in perfect military posture. "If you request that I be removed from the *Far Rider,* I will comply. Because of the nature of my...agreement with NMC, my papers won't stand up to detailed inspection. But you cannot hold this ship. You must let her and this NMC officer here go."

"If I take you into custody," he said quietly, "you know I'm not in a position—right now—to stop them from returning you to Moabar."

"Yes."

Philip shoved his hands in his pockets, stared down at his boots. Then back at me. "Other than your...agreement, NMC is treating you well?"

"I'm at a stellar helm. You know that's the only thing I've ever loved."

He rocked back on his heels. "More than me. Obviously."

I waited. There was no answer to that. And nothing more to say. He had all the facts. He was a Fleet officer, like me. He'd make a decision, based on facts.

His shoulders sagged slightly. Then a small nod. He clasped his hands behind his back, straightened his stance. "You're absolutely correct, Captain. I have no seizure order on an NMC P40. Please accept my apologies for detaining you and your crew. You may resume your previous course and heading. I will put out an advisory that you not be delayed again." He saluted me, crisply.

I returned his salute, my heart pounding, my knees

suddenly weak. "Thank you, Captain." My damned voice cracked.

He reached for the end-transmit tab but hesitated, his blue-eyed gaze searching. But there was nothing left to be said. It had all been over, years ago.

The screen hazed, blanked. The starfield reappeared. I stepped back, shaking, and collapsed into the chair behind me. I jammed my finger at the arm pad, opening intraship. "Ren! Get your ass on the bridge!"

I tabbed it off as I swung to face Sully. His hands were fisted on his knees, his obsidian eyes unreadable, fathomless. "Get us out of here, now," I barked at him. "And while you're at it, stay out of my goddamned mind!"

I turned abruptly away from him, raked my straps over my chest, then grabbed my arm-pad controls. I felt the shimmy of the sublights as they drew power, heard Ren step onto the bridge, and heard the sharp clicks as he fastened his strap. The starfield moved off to my right as we pulled smoothly away from the *Morgan Loviti*.

I was angry, frightened, and couldn't stop shaking as I stared at the viewscreen, then back down to my controls. Five minutes. Ten minutes. No one followed. Not Junot. Not Philip. Ren's voice in the background, talking softly into his headset, was the only noise on the bridge.

Fifteen minutes. My screen showed us at plus twenty. Specs be damned, we were moving.

I still shook. I couldn't stop. But it was only me causing my pain.

Figures danced on my screen, showing coordinates to the meetpoint. Two days yet. Then we'd wait for Sully's ship.

Sully. I crossed my arms at my waist. I couldn't stop shaking.

Sully. What I'd felt. What I'd said. *Stay out of my goddamned mind.* I'd meant it. Stars forgive me, but I'd meant it. And he knew that. When he'd invaded my mind I'd been shocked. It was like everything I'd read; it was like rape. A forced intrusion on my self, my soul.

This wasn't the gentle sensation of a touch empath. This was something else.

Mind-fuckers. We'd always called Stolorth *Ragkirils* mind-fuckers. Now I knew there were human mind-fuckers too.

I heard Philip's voice again. *Kingswell... Lieutenant Paxton... Their minds viciously raped, all but destroyed.*

Then another voice: *Liar!*

I had to get off the bridge. Everything I thought, everything I felt, I was sending. He was reading and, for all I knew, hearing. I pushed the arm pad to my right, unlatched my straps. Stood. "Captain's off the bridge," I announced. Stepped forward, turned left, toward Ren, not Sully. Looked at neither. Kept walking. Legs kept moving. Eyes focused on the corridor.

Stepped over the tread, didn't fall on my face. Found my cabin door, hit the palm pad. Five more steps. Saw the bed. Didn't turn around. Didn't look at Sully's jacket hanging on the hook. Just lowered myself onto the wide softness. Grabbed my pillow, clutched it to my chest, and sat, hugging it.

Breathed. One in. One out. One in. One out.

Thought about faith. Betrayal. Philip. Sully.

Sully was a telepath. Even though I'd never known one before, I knew that's what I'd felt in my mind. A *Ragkiril*. Who'd sensed my fear, my trepidation when I saw the *Loviti* and had to know why. Who'd raked my thoughts, found my private images of Philip and myself. Images he had no right to see. Images that I knew pained and angered him.

And taught him that sometimes you don't always like the answers to your questions.

I knew the feeling.

But did I know Sully? Did I even know what Sully *was*?

Time passed. I knew it did because the clock told me, in little red numbers. I no longer felt totally shattered. Only mediumly wretched. Still confused. Still angry. A little less frightened.

That was an improvement, and in less than two hours. Stars be praised.

I sat up and dropped the pillow behind me. I wiped my hands over my face. *What happened, happened. It's over. There are larger issues here. Marker. The Takas. The—*

My cabin door shooshed open.

My heart froze for a beat. When it restarted, I rested my elbows on my knees, my chin against my clasped hands, and prayed that whoever came through the door was Ren. I was still sorting my thoughts, still examining my anger. I couldn't face someone other than Ren. I couldn't even think his name.

Footsteps came toward the bed. They hesitated, then continued. An arm's length away, maybe two, and the footsteps stopped.

There was the silence of two people breathing. Then, "Chaz." The voice was rasped, raw, but I recognized it.

Not Ren.

I responded quickly. "I'm sorry." I was. I shouldn't have spoken out as I had. Nothing had been gained by hurting him. I should've waited until I was calmer, and not angry at Philip, at myself. At him.

"No. You don't, you shouldn't be ..." He took a deep breath. "Chaz. I'm sorry. It was wrong. What I did, I ..."

His voice seemed to lose its energy. Silence resumed.

I stared at my knees, at the tips of my boots, at the Fleet-issue low-pile carpeting on the floor. I could hear his breathing, harsh and ragged.

I opened my hands as if they might hold answers. But they were empty. I closed them, grasping nothing.

"I was very wrong," he repeated softly.

I brought my gaze up. The pain in his voice was reflected in his face, in his stance. The shadows were back under his eyes. His mouth was tight. One arm was crossed over his chest, his hand cupping his elbow as if part of him was holding back, part of him reaching. "I would never hurt you."

I nodded, listening now. His promise. He would never hurt me. Scare the hell out of me, yes, but never hurt me.

But how would he know what hurt me? When he stopped me from asking questions, he also stopped finding answers for himself. There's a reason to ask questions, to gather data, to look at facts. He could avoid that, if he wanted to. But I couldn't. Not for myself. Not for the Takas.

"We have a lot of work to do yet," I told him. "Ren has data on ships inbound to Marker. I want to go over it."

"You don't have to. You're free to go." He turned his hand, as if he wanted to reach for me but changed his mind. "I mean that. Once we intercept with the *Karn*, you're free. This ship, ID, whatever you need. I won't force you to work with me."

"And jukors are born and Takas die, but it's not

Chaz's problem anymore? Didn't you hear anything I said on the bridge?"

He leaned against the wall as if the force of my words had pushed him back.

"I'm not saying I know what those Takan females are going through. That's an abomination. But I do know what it's like to be told you're going to bear a child or else. I could have had a very nice, comfortable life. With a well-respected, intelligent husband who loved me. Providing I was willing to give up everything that I was, everything I'd worked to become. And then raise a child in the same manner as I would a...a painting I'd loan out to a museum! There'd be my name, on a little thank-you plaque, and I could visit it for free whenever I liked."

I stood abruptly, swept one hand out. "The fact that my child might have needs, the fact that I might have needs, was not to be considered. Others' feelings be damned: Philip Guthrie would have what he wanted or he'd see me in divorce court. Well, guess what? He saw me in divorce court. And the wisdom I learned from that is: be careful when someone says they care about you, *only if.* Only if you do what they want. Only if you ask no questions."

He closed his eyes briefly, shook his head. His lips parted as he started to speak.

I shook my head too, and spoke before he could. "Did you think at all, Gabriel Sullivan, before you ripped into my mind, just what my feelings might be? Did you stop to consider that?" I thrust my finger at him. "Or was your anger, your...I don't know, petulant jealousy, your ego's temper tantrum more important than anything else? More important than Ren's life, your life? Drogue's, Clement's, and all we think is going on at Marker? And if that's just a little too altruistic for you, was it more important than those promises you made, never to hurt me?"

I shoved my way past him. At the bedroom door I turned, threw my hands out in exasperation. "How in hell would you know what hurts me? You never even bothered to ask."

I sent Ren for a soak and a nap. He left the bridge, sensing, no doubt, I was in no mood for a discussion. I sat in my chair and played with the data on the ships flowing into Marker the past few weeks. It kept my mind off Sully's pained expression when I'd stormed out of my cabin.

Our cabin.

We had two days yet to the meetpoint. I had mental duro-hards filled with things I didn't want to think about, and almost all were tagged with Sully's name. Better to busy myself playing with data.

Marker was busy too. Marker was always busy, but ships came and went in the usual illogical patterns of repairs. You can't schedule for when something breaks down. New-ship production was different. That had a definite schedule. But I wasn't looking at outgoing. I was looking at incoming.

I made a grid and stuck my data in. Then integrated the data Drogue had shown us on Chalford's *Lucky Seven* on our way up from Moabar. It took some time, but that was okay, because it kept my mind on a narrow track, kept it away from things I didn't want to think about. Finally, it all came out to a nice fit.

The *Meritorious*'s databanks were crammed with Imperial data. Not as much on Marker as I'd like, but some. I cross-referenced that with the news banks every ship grabbed from the beacons. Months, years of it had been stored in my ship and archived. A captain never knew whom she'd run across on patrol. Never knew what she might need to know about them.

It was standard operating procedure when I'd held command. Kingswell had been more lax. But enough was there. I was sure the *Boru Karn* held more.

I'd need that. One name, sometimes as a source of funding, sometimes as an advisory concept group, kept drifting through my data. It was always an offhand mention, an annotation. Crossley Burke. I couldn't place it, but I kept seeing it. I might not even have noticed it except, years ago, Crossley had been a company that produced virtual vid games, the kinds that every station brat hoarded credits to play in the arcade. They lost the market when holo-hybrid sims came out. I couldn't tie in that Crossley with big-money underwriting or with corporate idea farms.

I needed more data. I tapped a note to myself to that effect, tagged it to the file.

Then I went back to Ren's most recent list of incoming. There was a sequence I'd missed earlier. Not surprising. And not just because it was near end of shift for me.

Sometimes those overfilled mental duro-hards make it tough to keep things straight.

The sequence contained division numericals coded to requisitions. Who, besides the receiving division, would need a list of incomings? It might relate to requisitions

and authorizations, if these were shipments and not repair. But it also might be another office in Marker that
needed, for some mystical reason of its own, to know
who was coming in, and when.

Five of the first eight tandem codes were the same. I
dropped them out of the sequence and was entering
them into my note-to-myself when I realized I knew
them. And knew them well.

God, I *was* mediumly wretched not to recognize
them.

Reports of these incoming were all sent in tandem to
the office of Commander Thaddeus Lars Bergren. My
beloved older brother.

"You're off duty. I'll take over."

"Hmm?" A nervous quiver fluttered in my chest as I
recognized his voice.

Sully waited on my right, hands clasped behind his
back. I'd been preoccupied with the data on my screen
and didn't hear him come onto the bridge. Didn't hear
him come up to my chair.

His eyes were still shadowed. "I said I'll take over.
Ren will relieve me."

"Right." I knew that. I also knew that I always stayed
an extra hour or two, shared tea or a meal with him. I
didn't mention that now. Neither did he.

I unlatched the harness and swung the arm pad back.
Then stopped while my hand was still on it. The fact
that I was sorting out my feelings about him didn't
negate that he needed to know what I'd found in other
matters. "I've been reexamining the data Ren pulled. I
found something that doesn't make sense."

Or maybe I didn't want it to make sense. I pushed out
of the chair. "Five of the ships that came in for repairs

sent a duplicate notice of their arrival to an office that shouldn't be concerned with such things. Thad's office."

He thought for a moment. "He's in the hierarchy. There could be a number of reasons why a confirmation would be sent there."

"Absolutely. But they're not coded for his office. They're coded for his private trans file."

"You have any idea why?"

"Not in the slightest. But I will find out."

"I know," he said softly. "That's why I chose you. You're the best interfering bitch around."

"No, in the universe, Sullivan. Remember that." I headed for the corridor. "The best interfering bitch in the universe."

Sleep didn't come right away. I stared at Sully's jacket hanging on the wall. I didn't realize until I'd flopped down on the bed that part of my mind wondered if it would still be there. Or if he'd moved his clothes out, taken another cabin. Gotten out of more than just my mind.

Of course, he may have done just that and forgotten the jacket, left it behind in his haste. I could get up out of bed, rummage through his closet and the drawers. I could collect my data, find my answer.

But the answer I sought wouldn't be found in his closet. I knew that.

So I lay there and stared at his jacket until my eyelids felt too heavy to stay open.

I woke an hour before I was to start my shift. The spicy, pungent aroma of coffee greeted me. A hot mug was on my bedside table. Other than that, the cabin was empty.

Someone had brought me coffee. I didn't know if it

had been Sully or Ren until I picked up the mug. An angel of heart-stars card was propped up behind it.

He should've been off duty a few hours ago. But the coffee was hot. Maybe he'd moved his things to another cabin while I slept.

My hand hovered over the latch to his closet, then pulled back. I turned and padded to the shower. Some things I could wait to learn. And some things, I realized, maybe I didn't want to know.

The coffee was still warm when I came out. I gulped it down and, in between gulps, pulled on clean clothes.

"Captain's heading for the bridge." I waited, wanting to hear that typical Sully rejoinder, *Hell's ass. There goes our card game.*

But all I heard was Ren's soft: "Acknowledged."

It wasn't the same.

Sully accepted my thanks for the coffee with a soft, gentle gaze and a slight shrug. I didn't mention the card.

He didn't bring up our argument. But he and Ren had been playing cards. He only stayed on the bridge long enough to lose another two thousand credits, then left. He was keeping his distance from me. I didn't know if it was because he thought that was what I wanted, or if it was because that was what he wanted.

I didn't know why he'd left the heart-stars card. Maybe I should've mentioned it. Maybe I should be putting different colors into my rainbow.

Maybe, if I got up the courage, I'd ask Ren.

We were about two shifts from meetpoint. I went back to working the data but found nothing new. Ren went over it as well. We played with some theories about the confirmations sent to Thad's office, but Ren didn't have Sully's knowledge of Marker. He did, however, have some knowledge of Sully.

"He's stopped reading you. He's afraid to know what you feel."

I leaned wearily on the armrest. "He should have told me he's a telepath."

"He's been trying to. It's not easy for him."

I knew he'd been showing me things in small ways. I thought of how he'd echoed my thoughts when we were on Moabar, his comment about boot camp, his taunt about sibling rivalry with Thad. His ability to know when I was thinking of that night in Port Chalo. But there were other times when he'd seemed unaware of what I was thinking at all. Selectivity, Ren had told me in his quarters on Moabar Station.

"Peeking," I said to Ren. "He's been peeking into my thoughts off and on."

"And mine, as long as I've known him. But it's not something I fear as you do."

I'd picked up on the way Ren gave answers before Sully voiced questions. I'd ignored that, or rather, didn't want to face what that might mean. It didn't fit easily into one of my databoxes. "I'm not afraid—"

His slight tilt of his head stopped me. Empath. Who could sense emotions but not their reasons.

"Okay. I have fears. But I'm not afraid of him. I don't view him as some sort of soul-stealing demon." Like the hideous creature in the painting in Drogue's monastery.

"Then what are your fears, Chasidah?"

"Mistakes I can make—that I've already made—because I can't ask questions, find out what he's thinking, feeling. That's the advantage he has with me that I don't with him." That's how he knew I was attracted to him, wanted to comfort him after we'd learned Captain Milo had been killed. That's how he knew when I was ready to make love to him the first time. "All I can do is guess.

He ought to try it sometime. Feel what it's like to be un-sure of why someone's with you."

"He knows that now. He's stopped reading your res-onances since the incident with the *Morgan Loviti*. He's cut himself off from that part of himself, as much as he can. I've told him I don't agree. But he said that's the only way you won't be afraid of him. But it's also teach-ing him, I think, what uncertainty feels like." Ren flipped off his straps. "Just don't make it too harsh a les-son for him, Chasidah. Because he learned, long ago, what it feels like to be hurt."

Ren went off duty with a promise to come back be-fore my shift ended.

Then it was just me and my ship and the starfield in front of me. No more bogies. *Thank you, Philip*. I picked up the usual traffic in the freighter lanes on the scanners, ran the usual systems checks. And I wondered what Thad was doing watching certain incomings at Marker. That was a grunt's job. Not second in com-mand in the shipyards.

I wondered what Thad would say if he knew I was sleeping with a mind-fucker, human variety. Yet another disgrace Chaz has brought to the Bergren name, prob-ably.

Marrying Philip was the only correct decision I'd ever made, according to Thad. Divorcing Philip was proof that I was just like my mother. She'd divorced my father when I was two. Thad was four. The court split us. Lars got Thad, put him into a crèche on Baris Seven. Amaris got me, put me in a playpen in the corner of her office on Marker.

Amaris was career Fleet but had always been non-traditional. She would've liked Ren. She definitely would've liked Sully. She wasn't a woman who scared easily.

I hoped Philip and Thad were right. I hoped I was just like my mother.

Intraship trilled. Ren's voice. "I am heading for the bridge. Can I bring you tea, coffee?"

"You're early. I have two hours to go yet."

"I'm awake. Tired of soaking. And I enjoy doing my meditations on the quiet of the bridge, where I can feel the stars."

"All right, I know when I'm not wanted. Come take watch. And thanks, but no. No tea or coffee. I had dinner an hour ago."

Ren and a mug of tea arrived a few minutes later. I vacated my chair and watched as he settled in it. That was something else that would make Thad's lip curl. A Stolorth raised by Takas in the command sling of an Imperial P40.

Ren set his tea down, angled his head, reading me. "You are more peaceful, happier now, Chasidah."

My rainbows were improving. "I was just thinking about how much you *don't* remind me of my brother."

"I would imagine I'm very different from Thaddeus."

"Praise the stars for that, Ren." I patted his shoulder, let my hand rest long enough to absorb a much-needed warmth, and left the bridge.

My cabin was empty, the lights dimmed as I'd left them. The bed was neatly made, quite possibly just as I'd left it. I didn't know if Sully had been in, napped, or moved out altogether. I was about to open his closet, find an answer maybe it was time I faced, when I noticed the message light flashing on my deskscreen.

I sat and fingered a new angel of heart-stars card propped against it while I read.

Chasidah. Angel. I have lost those words that used to come so easily to me. They have all fled, shamed to be in my company. I'm left now with only a few simple ones. They are inadequate. They cannot begin to convey all that I feel. But they are all I have.

Chasidah. Angel. I am sorry. I am sorry. I am sorry.

Chasidah. Angel. The grievous wrong isn't as much in the questions you couldn't ask, but in the only real truth that I could tell, and did not.

Chasidah. Angel. I love you beyond all measure. That is the only real truth.

I stared at the screen, elbows on my desk, my hands cupped over my mouth.

He was right. He'd never told me he loved me. In the past two weeks he'd told me I was wicked, I was beautiful, I was wild, I was delightful. I was his obsession, his fantasy, his best interfering bitch.

His angel.

He'd caressed me, coddled me, and held me. He'd made me warm, hot, crazy, passionate, and delirious. He'd made me feel safe, respected, honored.

He made me his lover. He made me his friend.

And he'd tried to tell me, if only I'd been listening, that he was more than an empath. But I didn't want to know.

Just as Philip knew, when he married me, I was career Fleet. He knew I abhorred the crèches. But he'd rejected that when it became inconvenient. Rejected me, hurt me.

Sully hadn't hurt me. He'd shared his anger and pain and fear with me in a fashion far more intimate than I was used to. Perhaps even inappropriately. But he hadn't hurt me, hadn't stripped my mind, altered it.

I didn't know if he could have done anything that heinous. He was human, not Stolorth, not a hideous soul-stealing demon with the mythical power of "unholy light." But I suspected he could have taken command of the *Meritorious* away from me before I opened the vidlink to Philip. With a touch. With a thought. I'd heard stories of things like that happening during the war. But he hadn't. Angry and afraid, he'd waited, trusting that I'd do nothing to hurt him.

I sat and thought about that. I picked up the card again.

A dangerous man, Gabriel Ross Sullivan. An undeniably handsome bastard. But I couldn't imagine life without that wicked, wicked Sully grin. Risks and all.

I found him in the small ready room, sitting in semidarkness. A mug of tea was in front of him, still full, but no steam rose. No fragrance wafted in the air.

I moved the mug when I sat on the edge of the table. It was cold. So was his hand when he took mine. No warmth, not even a flutter danced up my arm. It was as if everything that Gabriel Sullivan was was gone.

Except for the dark, haunted look in his eyes. Which was something we had to discuss, something I had to face, before we could go any further.

"You're a telepath. Like a *Ragkiril*."

"Yes."

"This is what you didn't want me to know."

He nodded. "I don't want you to be afraid."

"Then you should've told me, not just gone ripping apart my memories—"

"I lost control. That's never happened to me before." His voice was rough. His shoulders hunched tiredly. "At least, not in a very long time. But I was ... reading such anger, such fear in you. I knew there wasn't time for questions. I reacted stupidly. Didn't even realize what I'd done until I was there. I'm sorry. It won't happen again."

"You've apologized. I accept that."

He sat up a little straighter, hopeful. His fingers curled more tightly into mine.

"I also think you could've done more than just view my mental scrapbook. But you didn't. I appreciate your trust in me, that I had a workable plan. Even if it made you angry."

"I was angry because I found out Guthrie was your husband. That you loved him. I thought then that you wanted to go with him, on the *Loviti*. I never knew you were divorced until you told me later." His mouth tightened. "I'm still not sure the divorce was something you wanted."

"I wanted Philip's options less." I offered my other hand, squeezed his fingers reassuringly. No way to send warm tingles now. "Remember Port Chalo?"

A small smile played across his mouth, then faded. "I waited for you to come back. I scared you away then too."

"I scared me away. The transmit waiting for me back on board was the finalization of my divorce. Believe me, I wanted nothing more than to go back to that bar and have you kiss me senseless. But I also didn't want to wake in the morning and find out I'd been just another drunken fling. I couldn't have faced that. Or myself. Or you."

"I wasn't drunk. You should've come back."

I slid to my feet, tugged on his hands. "I'm here now."

He drew me against him as he stood. "I'd still like to try kissing you senseless."

"My cabin or yours?"

He hesitated. "I hope mine is still yours."

"It is."

He started unbuttoning my shirt in the corridor, tossed his own on the couch as the cabin door closed behind us. I kicked off my boots and climbed into the middle of the bed.

He pulled me down next to him. His arms closed tightly, almost desperately, around my back, over my hair that I'd unbound. I splayed my hand against his spine, my nose nuzzled in his chest. I could feel his heart pounding.

But nothing more. Just the weight of his arms, the pressure of his mouth against my face as he brushed my cheek, my lips, my chin with gently fervent kisses.

And I felt my own very deep ache.

But nothing more.

He was staying out of my mind, out of my senses. Totally. Because of my fears, and his. Because I'd ordered him to.

A good captain knows when to rescind an order.

I placed my lips almost against his. "Sully. It's okay. I love you too."

There was a small intake of breath, then a question as he let the breath out again. "You're sure?"

"Yes."

Warmth cascaded, surging. Warmth, cresting into heat. Warmth, cleansing, curing, healing. Melting pain, melting aches. Spreading, flowing, gentling, caressing, lifting, cradling. Needing.

Kneading. Stroking, skin, lips, fingers. Touch.

Clothes. Come. Off.

Heat, skin slicking, soft, hard, wanting, giving, claiming.

Ecstasy.

Warmth. Surrounding. Cradling. Gentling. Holding.

Hands clasping.

Mine. Mine.

Love.

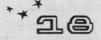

She had been built for opulence. Sully had stripped her and outfitted her for war, for speed. For stealth.

The *Boru Karn* hailed us ten hours into meetpoint. She slipped past my long-range, then tickled my short-range sensors only because, I knew, she was convinced she was safe. She sent a four-person tender out to pick up Ren and our meager belongings first. Sully and I secured the *Meritorious*, prepped her for tow.

An Imperial P40, towed by a luxury yacht. Unthinkable. Sully laughed at my silent bristling, tugging at my braid. "Snob," he challenged as we waited in the loading bay for the tender to return.

I turned, retort ready. He sucked it out of my mouth with a long kiss.

The bay sealed behind the tender, force-field lights dancing in a bright blue circle. Our boots echoed on the hard floor as we strode out to meet it. The airlock uncycled, slid sideways. The small ship had no ramp, just a short step folding down. A man waited in the airlock, arms crossed over his chest, a clear expression of curiosity on his face, which was the same color as Brother Clement's. The color of deep Imperial ale.

I knew the face. Marsh Ganton. About my age, maybe younger, maybe older. It was hard to tell with a nose that looked like it had been broken a few times and a scar that raked across his left eyebrow. His dark curly hair was clipped short. The arms crossing his chest were decidedly muscular. He offered his hand and I shook it as I mounted the stair.

"Captain Bergren."

"Hello, Marsh."

He nodded to Sully, and I was surprised to see how much shorter Marsh was. He'd looked bigger on the *Meritorious*'s viewscreen, probably because of his build.

"We're set," Sully said, resting one hand on Marsh's shoulder. The other held my elbow. "Strap in, Chazzy-girl."

It was a short trip back to the *Karn*, who waited, undoubtedly, with her weapons hot, sensors at max. She wasn't a ship to take chances.

She was already moving, sublights thrumming, when we exited into the tender bay. There was a loud hum, then a slight jolt. I recognized it as the tow field, locking on to my P40.

Unthinkable two years ago.

Salvation now.

Ren met us just aft of the bridge, visibly relaxed. His mouth curved into an easy grin. "This is finally a good day."

Sully arched an eyebrow. "Thought we'd never make it, did you?"

"I had some small concerns from time to time."

"Salved your worries with my losses, however."

"That helped."

God, how much did Sully owe him now? I'd lost count. But I knew Ren hadn't.

The sublights steadied. Marsh stepped by me and shot me a quick glance. "They're still playing cards?"

"Incessantly."

His gaze switched from Sully to Ren and back to me.

"Don't ask," I told him. "Last I remember it was over four million."

"Four million, seven thousand, five hundred twenty-five," Ren said. "Not that I am keeping track."

Sully hustled me forward. "To the bridge, please. To the bridge."

The *Karn*'s bridge was set up just like the *Meritorious*'s. Captain's command sling and helm were in the center. Communications on the left, weapons, engineering on the right. My brief perusal took in the familiar configurations, technical superiority. And another face I recognized.

Gregor.

I didn't know his last name. Fleet intelligence could never come up with one. But I remembered the face, the lanky form. Sully's pilot, always in the shadows, waiting for Sully's orders. He vacated the captain's chair as we came up behind him and greeted Sully with a brisk handshake, a nod. "About time, you son of a bitch."

"We ran into a few delays." Sully clasped Gregor's shoulder. They were almost of equal height. But Gregor was at least ten years older, wiry. His hair and eyes were a light muddy brown.

"Hope you fucked 'em good," Gregor said. His gaze fell on me as Sully withdrew his hand. "Well, well. Chaz Bergren. Pride of the Sixth Fleet." He said it with a smile. A cold smile.

"Gregor." I offered my hand, pretended I didn't see the hardness in his eyes. His resistance to my presence

wasn't unexpected. But I had no intention of acknowledging it. I could conduct myself like an officer, even if
he couldn't.

He shook it quickly, released it. "Looks like we did
what we came here to do. So far." Another narrow-eyed
glance focused briefly on me. Then he turned back to
Sully. "Want me to get Verno up on the bridge? Marsh
can show Bergren her quarters. Then you and I—"

"Chaz stays with me. My quarters." Sully's voice was
calm but held a tone that brooked no argument.

A slow, knowing smile from Gregor. Oily. "Sure,
Sully. You're the boss. Whatever you say."

Obsidian eyes narrowed slightly. "I want to unpack
some things, find that datapad we've been working on.
Chaz and I will meet you, Ren, and Marsh," he added
with a nod to the shorter man waiting, and watching, by
the comm station, "in the ready room. Get Verno to sit
helm. Fifteen minutes."

"I don't want to be an issue between you and Gregor." I
waited until the door to Sully's quarters closed behind
me before I spoke what was on my mind.

Sully picked up my duffel—pilfered from a locker on
the *Meritorious*—and hoisted it next to his on the bed. It
was a wide bed, in the middle of a bedroom larger than
we had on my ship. Two closet doors on my left flanked
a large framed star chart. Behind us, a salon in pale
grays and blues, with a long couch, two soft chairs, and
a low table. Commissary panels were set behind a high
counter with two padded stools. This had once been an
opulent ship.

"You're not. You won't be." He opened the duffel,
pulled out Kingswell's datapad, put it on the bed as I
came up behind him. He turned and placed his fingers
under my chin. His eyes were dark, infinite. "Hear me

well. One word. Mine. I give no quarter in that. Gregor's opinions will change, or be silenced."

Gregor had no idea what such a threat might mean. But I thought I did and, even after nearly three weeks, still wasn't comfortable with the power behind the threat. The very dark side of Gabriel Ross Sullivan. A side that made me uneasy the few times I'd seen it.

"I can fight my own fights very well, thank you very much." I let some arrogance resound in my words. "I just don't want it to come to that. We have an unwritten rule in Fleet: you don't have to like someone to work with them. That's all I'm asking for here."

The fingers that held my chin folded. He brushed his knuckles slowly up my jaw. "Gregor despises Fleet and all its rules. He understands none of them, my angel. But if you wish to make your point," he hesitated, eyes glinting, "make sure he sees this in your hand." He raised my arm so that the Grizni bracelet was between us. "He understands this."

"Last option," I told him. "Better plan is to remember we're all on the same side here."

His fingers slid into mine and he pulled me against him, bringing my hand to his lips. "Taming the beast?" he asked softly.

No. Just a ghost.

It was a good, working ready room, well laid out, with a round table in the center meant to defuse any power struggles. Its location was just aft of the bridge, but with direct access to it. The room held the spicy smell of coffee. Marsh and Ren waited, mugs in the recessed holders in front of them. Marsh stood, offered me a cup when I came in, but I waved him away, with thanks. I got my own, and one for Sully. And knew a second statement had been made.

Marsh was on my side, for the moment. Or rather, Marsh was acknowledging he hadn't forgotten that Sully was in command. He'd watched the exchange between Sully and Gregor on the bridge very carefully.

Sully put the datapad in front of him, linked it to the *Karn*'s system, brought up the data on a hologrid suspended over the middle of the table. Twice during these movements he glanced toward the door. Gregor was late.

His next glance was to Ren, across the table from us. It was a casual one, but I knew what it was. Ren had been listening to Marsh explaining the data on the grid, but his slight nod was meant for Sully.

We waited.

Sully reached for intraship just as the door to the corridor slid open. Gregor, whistling, strolled in. "Hey, don't start the party without me."

He spun one of the chairs as he strode by, then sat down on the other side of Sully, grinning.

We started the party, played with the data taken from the *Meritorious* for over two hours as Sully led us through the list, integrating new information the *Karn* had brought—ships incoming to Marker. More manifests.

Something was going on. Someone was building an elaborate medical facility on a ship, or using a ship to do so. That was clear from everything I saw, though nothing could definitely indicate it was a gen-lab. It could've just as easily been an auxiliary hospital ship, if we were at war. But we weren't. Yet.

I keyed all the manifest codes I knew into the *Karn*'s computers from memory. Even some older ones, because Thad would know them. More confirmations had been sent to Thad's office.

Gregor latched on to that bit of information right

away. "One hell of a family, the Bergrens, wouldn't you say? Fleet goes way back in their blood. Hard to believe you could just shrug that off." He pointed his lightpen at me. "Course, being sent to Moabar would make anyone believe you could. Found her right quick, didn't you, Sully? Convenient, don't you think?"

I already had my hand firmly on Sully's arm. Heat pulsed, simmered. He knew I could feel it and no doubt kept it tamped down. It wasn't aimed at me.

Let me handle this, I wanted to tell him. But the only link he shared with me was his empathic one. His intrusion into my mind when we'd face the *Loviti* had never been repeated. At times like this it would be convenient to be a telepath. I squeezed his arm instead. I didn't get to be a patrol captain by not knowing how to handle an ego, or a pissing contest.

I took my hand away and leaned on the table. I wanted to make sure Gregor knew I spoke for myself, by myself. Sully owned the *Karn,* owned the allegiances of Gregor and Marsh. And the rest of his crew I'd yet to meet. But I'd always fought my own battles.

"You're raising valid points, Gregor. I might do the same, if I were in your position. A Fleet officer who used to burn your tail with regularity suddenly sitting on the *Karn.* The ghost ship no one could find, not even me."

I smiled, let my mixed compliment settle in. "You may well have reasons to question my motives. I've faced that before, no doubt will again. So let me tell you how this is going to be handled. You have a problem with me, you tell me. Up front, out in the open. And I'll answer, up front. Out in the open. Agreed?"

He held up both hands, a startled expression on his face. "Hey, whoa, Captain Bergren. You touchy or something? I don't mean anything by what I say. We all know that, right?" He reached over, slapped Marsh on the shoulder. "I'm just talking, thinking out loud. I think it's just wonderful that Fleet's finest is here, helping us." He gave me a wide, innocent grin.

"I'm delighted to hear that, Gregor." I reached as if to clasp my hands together, but touched my bracelet instead. The Grizni sprang into my outstretched hand. I folded it back around my wrist again as if nothing had happened.

His gaze locked on it, then rose to my face.

I nodded slightly, gave him a small half smile. "But if you ever should have any questions..." I let my words drift off. My point, in more ways than one, had been made.

Discussion picked up again. Gregor slipped into the mode of everyone's friend. Marsh seemed not to notice. Sully relaxed. I had the feeling it was the role Gregor normally played. Only the appearance of Captain Chaz Bergren had made him slip out of it for a moment.

I understood why he saw me as a threat. I was a Fleet officer, trained as a pilot, a captain. But I wasn't about to take over his position, or this ship. Logic should have told him such a move on my part would be foolish. I was outnumbered here on the *Karn*. There were others on board besides the five of us in the ready room; I'd heard voices and footsteps when I was in Sully's cabin. And someone named Verno, from Gregor's earlier comment, sat on the bridge.

Did he think Sully would prefer my advice over his own? He had to know Sully better than I did. This was far from his first ready-room meeting, and I had no doubt Gregor was one of the advisers Sully had mentioned on Moabar.

Clearly, Sully had ignored Gregor's advice and gone looking for me. But so had Ren. If Gregor felt anyone was going to usurp whatever position he held with Sully, it should be Ren.

I decided to stop trying to figure out Gregor. I had no time. Gabriel Sullivan kept me more than busy in that regard.

Assignments were made informally. My area was Marker and incoming manifests. Sully assigned Ren, Marsh, and Gregor other trails to follow. Our research would overlap, in some areas duplicate. But we'd see each other daily, if not hourly. Corrections could be made.

Ren left, to soak. Marsh drifted out. Only Gregor remained as Sully tabbed off the hologrid and I put the coffee mugs in the small sani-rack.

The door to the corridor slid open. A short, squat, dark-haired woman bustled in, her wide face almost split with a grin. She looked as if she could be Marsh's older sister. Or aunt. "Sully!"

Sully turned, stepping toward her. "Dorsie, you sexy wench. Give me a hug."

She was already doing so, patting him on the backside as well, I noticed. She had on dark spacer fatigues like I did and a wide overblouse. A laser pistol in a holster peeked out when she raised her arms and grabbed for Sully's shoulders. She shook him affectionately. "You're late. You had me worried."

"For a good cause, I assure you." He reached toward me. I took his hand. "Chaz, this is Dorsie, the best goddamned ship's cook in the Empire. Dorsie, this is Chaz. Captain Chaz Bergren. The most beautiful goddamned interfering bitch," he winked at me, "in the universe."

I shook Dorsie's hand and returned her infectious grin.

"Yeah, I know you, Captain Bergren. Went on many a raid with Sully here, years back. Same ones as you, except on the other side." She laughed. "Told him we just ought to start inviting you to dinner. You were there every time we turned around, anyhow."

"Dorsie." Sully regarded her in mock sternness.

"Yeah, yeah, I know. I blabber. Shut up, Dorsie, he says. You're breaking my concentration. I can't play cards when you—" She tilted her face up to him. "What d'you owe him now?"

Sully shrugged. "Not that much, really."

She snorted. "Liar. I'll go find Ren. He'll tell me."

"He's soaking," Sully said as she turned for the door. "Probably naked."

Dorsie stopped, winked. "Better hurry, then. That's a sight worth seeing. Dinner's up in an hour," she called over her shoulder as she strode through the doorway. "Good to meet you, Chaz."

I smiled at Sully as the door closed. "She's a gem."

"Yeah, she's a charmer, isn't she?" Gregor came around the other side of the table but stopped by the door. "And just think, Chaz. There were at least a half dozen times you came close to killing her."

He stepped through the door quickly, disappeared into the corridor.

I hung on to Sully's arm as he lunged for the door. "Sully, wait! Let him go. Let him get it out of his system. That's all it is."

He stopped so abruptly I stumbled against him. He was breathing hard. Heat pulsed into me from where my hand grasped his arm.

The door, sensing us, started to open. He slapped at the override. It closed. He stared hard at the gray metal of the door. He didn't like this, probably never had to deal with it before.

Life as a mercenary, a pirate, was different than in the military. His leadership was clear, unequivocal, and of his own making. I knew what it was like to fight an enemy climbing the ranks from within.

"I'm not here to win any popularity contests," I told him. "I'm here to find out what's going on at Marker. To stop the breeding of the jukors. As long as he has the same goal in mind, it doesn't matter what he thinks of me."

His breathing slowed, but his jaw was still tense. "He's not here to think. He's here to fly my ship."

"But doesn't he also act as one of your advisers? The ones you told me were against your going to Moabar?" I needed him to start seeing the human factors involved, the jealousies, the jockeying for position that was part of everyday life in Fleet.

"We discussed options, risks. Just as we did now. But my say is final. Absolute. Always has been." He shook his head. The hard, dangerous glitter in his eyes was fading. Anger was dissipating, at least for a moment. "Gregor knows you know Marker like none of us ever could."

"Maybe he resents that. Maybe he wanted to be the one to save the universe. Maybe, like you told me, he just hates anything to do with Fleet. You have to realize," I continued, "that what he said is true. You and I came close to blowing each other out of the space lanes a couple of times."

"Never," he said. "You may have thought so, but in actuality, never. Now Guthrie..." He stared at the door for a moment, as if he could see Philip's face there. "I had him in my sights more than once. If I'd known he was your husband—your ex-husband," he stressed, looking at me again, "I would have. Gladly."

"You might have done me a favor, then. But not in the way you think. The court would've had a lot harder time convicting the widow of the legendary Captain

Guthrie." That had been the basis of Philip's offer of re-marriage: the power, the reputation behind his name.

He leaned against the doorjamb, clasped my hand in his. "Then I'd have to track you down...where? In a posh club on Baris Prime? Or the casinos in Garno? A ghost from Hell trying to seduce the young, beautiful widow."

I laughed. "I'd still be on the bridge of the *Meritorious*. The clubs and casinos were Philip's life, not mine. And as for seduction..." I gave him a haughty look. "Is that what you were trying to do, dragging me to a monastery, ferrying me to station in an old lugger, damned near destroying my ship in a cold jump?"

He grinned his wicked Sully grin. "That's because I am unique, my angel. Never forget that. No one else in the universe will ever love you quite the way I do."

He palmed the door back to auto. "But you forgot," he said as it opened, "the jukor. Amazing the lengths a man will go to in order to get a woman to run into his arms."

"I didn't run. You pushed me."

"A minor point. No, this way. Ren's cabin's down here. I feel a run of luck coming on."

"Stars have mercy."

Ren's quarters were a smaller version of Sully's, again reminding me this had once been a luxury yacht. There was a salon and dining area, and a separate bedroom off to the left. Like Sully's, the bedroom had two large closets. But where Sully's had the large star chart, Ren's had a mirror. There were none in Sully's cabin, I realized. But that was the only difference. The furniture, the color scheme, were identical: blues and pale grays predominated. A deck of cards sat in the middle of the square dining table, waiting.

"One game." Sully eased into the chair opposite Ren. "That's all I have time for. I've been playing with a theory. I think I know what I'm doing wrong."

Ren picked up the cards, feathered them. "Losing?" he asked, his mouth twitching with a suppressed grin.

Sully snorted. "Deal, you swindler."

The viewport in the dining alcove had a bench seat. I sat, bemused, glad to be away from Gregor's presence. I'd been on board six hours. Despite Ren's proclamation, I wasn't sure if this had been, finally, a good day.

One hand was dealt, played. Two. Sully lost the first but won the second. He was positively gleeful. Third hand, Sully lost. A dismissive flick of his fingers. "Lapse in concentration."

Fourth hand. Ren's cabin door chimed. He tilted his head, sensing. "Enter."

I sat up straight as a Taka ducked through the doorway. "Ren, I wanted to—" His gravelly voice stopped abruptly as his gaze fell on Sully, then me. "Pardon. Pardon. Didn't know. Sully-sir, glad you're back."

I looked at Sully. Ren. The Taka. Sully waved him in. "Come in, Verno. Ren, you want to do the introductions? It'll give me time to plot my next move."

Verno. A Taka. Suddenly I remembered where I'd heard the name before: Drogue, on Chalford's *Lucky Seven.*

"This is Captain Chasidah Bergren, Verno. Chasidah, this is Verno, my brother."

Brother Verno the brother? No. Verno. Ren's Takan brother. Verno ambled over behind Ren's chair, extending his hand as I stood. Takan fur was soft and coarse at the same time. His large hand enveloped mine. "Good to meet you, Captain. Blessings of the hour."

"Blessings," I replied back automatically, still somewhat in shock. "Verno...I'm sorry. Ren never said he had a brother." But he had repeatedly talked of his Takan mother, his Takan family.

Verno's laugh was a crackling rumble. If I'd been down in engineering, I'd be looking for a sudden fracture in the sublight thruster grid. "Little brother. Little brother the brother. This is the best joke, no?"

"Then you are a monk?" First a Stolorth brother and now a Takan one. The Englarian church was experiencing some changes. I wondered if anyone in Non-Human Cultures knew about that.

"Took full vows two years ago."

"Damned fine navigator too. The church's gain was almost my loss," Sully added, peering uneasily at his cards.

Almost, because Verno was still here. "You're not assigned to a monastery?"

The furred face tilted in an almost exact mirror image of Ren's. "Assigned to a mission, Captain Chasidah. Assigned to a mission."

A mission to right the wrongs being done to his people. I understood.

He patted Ren's shoulder. "I wanted to tell you Dorsie's making *srorfralak* pie."

"A Takan vegetable pie," Ren explained, fanning his cards on the tabletop.

"Hell's ass."

"Very delicious," Verno added over Sully's outburst as he stepped for the door. "Letting Ren win again? Kind of you, Sully-sir. Blessings all. Blessings. Captain?" He gave me a nod as he ducked under the open doorway.

I sat back down on the bench seat and stared at the door as it slid closed. A Taka. A Stolorth. A human cook who packed a laser pistol under her apron and baked *srorfralak* pie. Sully had one hell of a crew.

"Damn it all!"

"Tomorrow's always another game, Sully. Shall we escort Chasidah to dinner?"

Sully held out his hand to me. "That must be my problem. Lack of adequate nutrition."

I took his hand, felt him slip something into my palm. I pulled my fingers away as we followed Ren through the doorway.

A card. Angel of heart-stars. Grinning, I tucked it into my pants pocket.

We were two days into transit to the Baris–Calth border when the lights in the ready room flickered, died, and came on again, at half power. I shoved myself to my feet, quickly, Sully rising beside me. An alarm whooped discordantly in the corridor. He bolted through the doorway connecting the ready room to the bridge. I was right on his heels.

"Verno!"

The Taka sat on duty in the command sling, long fingers working the console rapidly. "Main-computer failure, Sully-sir. Auxiliary generators online. Tow's holding. Shields down—"

"Shit!" Sully lunged for the engineering station, brought up his screens. Raked his straps over his chest.

"—power's out to weapons, long-range. Enviro secure. Engines dropping at one-quarter sublight."

I took the helm in front of Verno, strapped in, verified course heading, speed. Automatically put manual on standby, in case we lost autoguidance. Which only kept us going where we were going. It didn't do one damned thing to help us get there safely. Without scanners, weapons, shields, we were as vulnerable as a newborn birdling fallen unseen from the nest.

And as blind.

I heard boot steps thumping in the corridor behind the bridge.

"What the fuck's going on?"

Gregor.

"Systems cascade failure," Sully barked back. "I see it but I can't halt it yet."

Hands grabbed my shoulder, roughly. I jerked backward.

"Move, Bergren!"

I flicked off my straps and vacated the seat, but only because we were in trouble, big trouble.

Gregor slid in, swearing, hands moving over the screens. "Helm secure," he announced.

I'd secured the helm before he got there. I let it go, slid into the seat next to Sully, strapped in again. Damn. Primaries were collapsing, function codes unraveling. Sully was half a breath behind the decline, throwing everything to manual. I took the verifications away from him smoothly at his nod and freed him up to continue the chase. I'd do the cleanup recoding behind him.

Behind me, Verno and Gregor switched places. Gregor was first pilot. He belonged in the command sling. Belatedly I realized he should have headed there when he came on the bridge. But he'd headed for helm, probably because that's where I'd been.

More footsteps thudded, then Ren's soft voice came from the comm station behind me. He had his headset on and worked intraship, coordinating with Dorsie and Marsh. And a man named Aubry I'd met only briefly, a mainteance tech who worked the shift opposite Sully's and mine.

Everyone was awake. Everyone was at a station, a console, doing something.

And the *Boru Karn*, defenseless, streaked through the big wide darkness.

Everything was out there. Fleet cruisers, patrol ships. Commercial freighters. Transport yachts. Barges. Beacons. We were deep in Calth between Port January, Starport 10, and the Walker Colonies. Without sensors, without shields, we could collide with debris or an Imperial destroyer. The only difference would be how quickly the hull ruptured.

"Get Dorsie on visual bogey check." Sully was thinking the same thing I was.

"Sublights still not responding," Gregor said.

A yellow light in front of me blinked rapidly, turned to red. "Who's opening the shuttle bay doors?"

Sully glanced quickly at my console, then back to his. "Damn it! Systems are self-activating. Overrides aren't holding."

They weren't. It was as if half the ship had no power and the other half had twice as much. I tabbed to another screen. "We've got power spikes in the secondary grid."

"Rekeying damper fields," Sully said. "Stand by."

I heard Gregor grunt out an acknowledgment, then, "Tractor field's engaged!"

Shit! The *Meritorious*. No longer held at a safe, static distance but being yanked toward us, reeled in by a tow field turned tractor. A Lancer-Class P40 coming hard, right up our tail.

"Override and disengage!" Sully ordered.

"Keying manual override, Sully-sir! Attempting to disengage."

Attempting wasn't going to do it. We needed that field link broken now. And we needed engines, fast.

"Evasive action!" Sully opened intraship. "Aubry, get me those sublights—move us!" The *Boru Karn* heeled to starboard, slowly. I could hear, feel aux thrusters misfiring.

"Ten minutes to impact, closing." Gregor's voice was terse.

Sublights shimmied, grabbed for power the auxes couldn't feed them in time.

"Eight minutes."

We were still in her path. At least, most of us, as Sully

had once taunted me. But most of us would be plenty enough for a hull breach on impact.

"Seven minutes. Closing."

We couldn't even fire lasers, shove her off course, push her away from us. My sweet little P40.

But I could destroy her.

I half-swiveled. "Ren! I need a hot trans link to the *Meritorious,* now!"

I caught Sully's desperate glance as I turned back. "Autodestruct. I can remotely activate her autodestruct."

"Do it." No hesitation.

I picked up the link from Ren on my screen and opened a transmit line. At the same time, I talked to Sully. "Shields. Forget sublights. We're going to need shields."

A P40 under autodestruct just might take us with her. But she was going to ram us, either way.

"Working on it."

"Working on it too, Sully-sir," Verno echoed. Only Gregor was quiet.

I worked on it, woke up my ship's slumbering systems, thrown into hibernation for tow. But a Fleet ship never truly slumbered. Even though the Boundary Wars had ended years ago, all Fleet vessels carried the same fail-safes. If boarded, abandon ship to the pods. Then blow the invaders out of the space lanes via a code-secure hot link.

My link went hot. The *Meritorious* answered, queried. *Who are you?*

I responded, fed her authorizations, verifications.

Then the link fluttered. So did overhead lights.

Sully jerked around. "Damn it, Gregor, sit on those generators!"

"Recalibrating now."

My link fluttered back on.

Meritorious.   Bergren,   Chasidah.   AuthCode 71995–RQ. VeriCode R1 Q5 3789 X4X4.

Verified. Acknowledged.

Initiate Autodestruct. Initiate Autodestruct. Delete reconfirmation. VeriCode R1 Q5 3789 X4X4.

"Shields?" I asked Sully. It was decision time. "A Level Two destruct is partial. A Level One, total. A Two may skew her into us. Or away from us. A One may damage us, without shields." Or destroy us.

Words, clipped and harsh, flew back and forth between Gregor and Verno, behind me.

"Level Two. I can't guarantee shields." His tone was grim. His dark gaze was steady but bleak. "Brace!" he called out to the bridge.

I heard Ren repeat it on intraship.

"Wise choice," I said softly, completing my code. Sending it. Sealing our fates.

"Chasidah. Angel." The words hung softly in the air as warmth, a sad, sweet, aching warmth, flowed over me.

Then I was jerked, hard, against my straps, the air sucked out of my lungs.

Chasidah.

I stopped floating and hovered. It felt as if I were hanging, limply, in a tingly space. Gray fuzzy soft. It felt familiar. Solid. My feet touched down. Gray fuzzy soft. But solid.

Chasidah. Angel.

Sully? I heard—no, sensed—his voice. Behind me. Must turn around.

No. Stay still. Don't . . . don't turn.

Gray fuzzy soft. Warm.

Something touched my shoulders.

Heat. Air!

I sucked in a gulping breath, my eyes opening wide. Sucked in another. Sully grasped my shoulders, steadying me. Sully in the darkness. What happened to gray fuzzy soft? Light, red-tinged. Red-tinged.

I know this, my brain told me.

Red-tinged. Emergency lighting.

"Sully! Status." I gasped out the words, grabbed his arm. His face was a mixture of shadows. A long dark streak cut down one side. I touched it. Wet. Sticky. "You're bleeding."

"It's nothing." He knelt in front of my seat. I was still at engineering, but my straps had unhooked. "Breathe once more for me, Chaz. That's right. Deep breath. Once more."

I sucked in air that was bitter, stale. Let it out. "Status," I croaked again.

"Minor hull damage, no breach. We're in emergency shutdown, but we should be able to get things online."

I nodded and tried to pull away from him, my thoughts now on the ship, making her secure, getting us moving.

I stood, wobbling. He was none too steady either. He leaned on the back of his chair as I turned. The bridge was quiet. Shadows were red-black. A large shadow...

I moved, heart pounding. Past Gregor, hanging loosely against his harness, but still breathing, one hand twitching. Past Verno, slumped, but still breathing. To Ren. Not at communications but crumpled against the rear bulkhead of the bridge. He wasn't moving.

My exclamation of denial stuck in a throat closed tight with fear. I reached for Ren, but Sully's hand on my arm held me back. He knelt down. I crouched beside him, then sprang up again. I knew what I had to find. Med-kit. Med-kit and a handbeam, somewhere. I found the panel, popped the latch, grabbed the kit. Flipped on the handbeam, crouched down again, med-kit open at my feet. I plucked out the medistat. Its screen blinked on, the unit humming softly.

Sully, beside me, ran his hands over Ren's body. His breath rasped.

Ren's didn't.

I shoved the medistat toward him. "Here, use—"

"No. No." He pushed it away. His hands framed Ren's face, moved down to the neck and gill slits. "Fluid shock."

Data scrolled across the screen as the medistat reset for Stolorth physiology. Fluid shock. Lungs stopped. Heart stopped. Life signs flat.

God.

I felt cold all over. The medistat slid to the floor. My mind grabbed another word from my emergency med training. Hypospray. I reached for the kit. Have to find a stim, generic. Then a hydrating solution. Get him down to sick bay, hook him up.

I found the stim, primed it. "Sully, here—"

"Hush. Chasidah, hush." His voice was hoarse, distant. His hands still framed Ren's face. And, inexplicably, gill slits lifted.

Then a pulse blipped across the medistat screen on the decking by my knees. Blipped again. Heartbeat. *Blip*. Heartbeat. *Blip*. Life. Where there had been no life.

I sat very, very still.

Sully put one hand on Ren's mouth, one on his chest. Sully breathed. Ren's chest lifted.

I moved my eyes toward Sully. Only my eyes, as I was afraid to move anything else. Something was happening—had happened. I didn't know what it was, only that I had no means of understanding it, no nice neat databoxes where it would fit. So I watched.

His obsidian eyes were open, staring at Ren. His fingers touched Ren's eyelids, lightly.

Ren's eyes were silver. Open. Clear, unclouded. He looked at Sully.

Ren breathed.

Sully breathed.

I breathed and my heart pounded, hard.

The suppleness was back in Ren's skin. His fingers twitched slightly, then relaxed. I could see his pulse, strong and regular, in his throat.

Another breath. Two. Three. Five.

Sully sat slowly back on his heels, his palms braced against his thighs. He was breathing hard, his shoulders stiff as if with pain. His obsidian gaze no longer focused on Ren, but at a distant, infinite point that existed far beyond the bulkhead before him. Then he dropped his gaze, back rounded, and seemed to stare at his hands planted against his legs. His eyes closed. His breath rasped, shuddering.

I was afraid to touch him. No. I wanted to touch him, but didn't know if I should. I was afraid I'd do something wrong. Whatever had happened was because of Sully. If he needed to be alone, if he needed . . .

One hand, palm up, was held out toward me.

I grasped it. His fingers closed tightly around mine, squeezing, holding on.

Small warmth now, soft flutters. They curled up my arm, through my body.

"Breathe. Chasidah. Breathe." A barely audible plea.

I took a deep breath, let it out. Another. He clung to my hand. The warmth traveled back and forth between us. Into me, out of me. In through me. Out through me.

Softer. Softer.

He angled his face toward me in the red-tinged darkness. Blood dripped down the side of his forehead. But there was a strength in him again. His fingers relaxed around mine. Slowly he straightened in his crouch.

My gaze darted to Ren, lying peacefully on the floor, eyes closed, chest rising and falling naturally. "He'll be okay?" My voice wavered.

He nodded.

"You?"

Another nod.

"Sully..." I reached for him. He clasped my hands, drew me against him, surrounding me with his body as if I needed comforting, not him. He held my hands against his chest, his face against my forehead, his breathing still deep and labored.

A thousand questions raced through my mind, but now was not the time.

Something ruffled through the air, like enviro shifting to a second cycle. Then there was a loud groan behind us. A cough.

Gregor.

Sully pulled away, fumbled for the medistat, and pushed it into my hand. "Go. Keep him busy. Need a minute yet."

I remembered my question to Ren. Who knows? Who knows about the mind talents of Gabriel Ross Sullivan? Not Gregor. Not Marsh.

I rose quickly and headed for Gregor, medistat open, keyed for human readings. It showed minor internal bruising in his chest, but that was all.

"Gregor. Sit still." I ran the unit across his body one more time.

Muddy brown eyes met mine. "Bitch," he said, softly. Very softly. A venomous sound.

"You've got some pretty good bruises there. Probably does hurt like a bitch." I deliberately misunderstood.

I went back for the med-kit I'd left on the floor. Sully lifted Verno upright. The Taka coughed.

I handed him the medistat when I returned to Gregor's side. As I primed another stim I thought for a moment how pleasant a double dose of trank might make my life for a while.

And kept it at just that. An amusing thought. "This'll help."

Gregor's hand shot to my wrist, squeezed. "No fucking way. Not from—"

A hand came down hard against Gregor's shoulder, shoving him back against the seat. It pinned Gregor there, fingers digging into the pilot's collarbone while he sucked for air, his eyes wide and frantic. Gregor's hand fluttered from my wrist, trembling, jerking spasmodically.

"I can, and will, break this." Sully's voice was flat, dark. Final. "Your choice."

Gregor's eyes blinked. Once. Twice. Sully plucked the hypospray from my fingers and shoved it against Gregor's arm. It released its contents with a barely perceptible hiss.

Sully took his hand away as if he'd touched something loathsome.

Gregor's eyes fluttered open, his mouth slightly slack. He stared at Sully but wouldn't look at me.

"Don't push your luck," Sully told him.

Gregor closed his eyes again and let his head fall back against the padding.

Verno wobbled upright behind me, his legs still shaky. "Ren?" He peered toward the corner.

I grabbed Verno's long arm. "Lean on me. I'll walk you over there."

I felt like a child next to a giant. If he fell he'd take us both down in a furry heap, but what support I gave him seemed to be enough. He lowered himself to the floor next to Ren, then took the webbed, six-fingered hand in his large one and patted it.

Ren's eyelids fluttered, his eyes clouded again. "Brother. Blessings." His voice was misty rain, pattering on warm stones.

"Brother. Blessings. I feel the need to pray."
"So do I."

The bridge became a flurry of activity. Dorsie, Aubry, and Marsh were in better shape. Deeper in the ship, they'd been less exposed than we were on the bridge. Plus, main enviro had stayed on. Only the bridge had gone, momentarily, airless.

It was supposed to happen the other way around. Bridge enviro was supposed to be the most secure, sealing itself under red-alert conditions. Bridge enviro had its own generator. Its own filters. It was supposed to be infallible.

Supposed to be.

I stood at helm, watched as each screen came back on. They would stay on now. We ran through a final systems check. I touched databoxes, initializing systems, programs, functions. Sublights hummed at idle.

Sully was in the command sling, mirroring my movements, mirroring Verno's at engineering. Ren was in sick bay, soaking.

Gregor was in his quarters.

"He has some things to think about," Sully had said.

Sulk over, more likely. Or seethe.

I understood what Sully did, why he did it. Physical force was the only thing Gregor understood. Gregor's insidious challenges to me challenged Sully. A man like Gabriel Ross Sullivan wouldn't tolerate that for long.

He'd heard Gregor call me a bitch. What he'd felt emanating from Gregor I could only imagine. We hadn't had time, or the privacy, to discuss it. Or to discuss what he'd done to Ren. For Ren.

Ren was dead, had been dead for several minutes when I'd flicked on the medistat. I'd been in Fleet too long not to know what the unit told me. Ren was dead.

Now Ren was alive.

Sully had touched him, breathed for him. Sully had touched him, beat his heart for him. Sully had touched him, healed him.

I had a thousand questions to add to the other thousand I already had from three weeks of Gabriel Ross Sullivan in my life. They grew like his losses in his card games with Ren. Double or nothing. I kept getting doubles. I stuffed them all into another one of my mental duro-hard containers and shoved them away, for now. There might be a time I'd want to bring them out, lay them before him. Ask.

But not now. Stars have mercy, I loved him. And questions hurt him. Answers hurt him. I'd felt his anguish, his fear, when one would pop into my mind, unbidden. I'd turn, forgetting the one thing that was very, very hard for Sullivan to face. And that was himself.

I remembered the feel of his voice in my mind, *No. Stay still. Don't . . . don't turn.*

Fear. He'd been behind me, somewhere in gray fuzzy soft. *Don't turn. Don't look. Don't look at me.*

What would I have seen if I had?

Right now, I looked through the main viewports. They framed something once beautiful in her own functional way. Something that had saved my life countless times. Something that had bestowed a title, a purpose to the name of Chasidah Bergren. And had continued on bravely, forever holding a piece of me in her memory when the court had stripped that same title and purpose away.

As long as she worked the lanes, as long as she streamed through the neverwhen, so did Captain Chaz Bergren. I always felt that even if I died, my codes, my programs, would live on in her.

I never thought she'd be the one to die first. And in such ugliness.

The shattered hull of the *Meritorious* hung lopsided against the starfield. The Level 2 autodestruct had gutted most of her starboard side, peeled back her hull plating. Her Imperial insignia was blackened. Her bridge, shattered. All that was left of her name were the first four letters: MERI.

Meri.

Good-bye, Meri, my sweet little P40. I'm so sorry. So very, very sorry.

"Weapons online." Verno's voice was gravelly, sounding normal again.

"Targeting. Locked." Sully shifted in the sling behind me. Then, softly, "Chaz?"

I didn't turn, just shook my head and raised my hand to push away his offer. I knew what had to be done. Why it had to be done. Nothing for the Empire to trace. Nothing for them to question. I just couldn't be the one to do it.

Fifteen. Fifteen lives. And now Meri's.

She was only a ship. My first and only command.

My sweet, sweet little P40.

A short, harsh sigh came from Sully. Then a word. "Fire."

Lasers streaked out from the *Boru Karn*. The *Meritorious* exploded, disintegrated into a thousand wheeling stars. Then she faded away.

We were about ten hours from the B–C border. But we were twenty-six from an inexplicable systems failure. And a total recovery. Providential, Ren had said. Everything had come back on, flawlessly, as if it had never happened.

Sublights thrummed at max, Sully-style. That meant max plus twenty to the rest of civilized space.

We'd all slept, exhausted, aching, then reconvened in the ready room with lots of coffee. Ten hours to the B–C border. Problems behind us. Troubles forgotten.

Gregor sat across from me, cheerful and jubilant. And noticeably apologetic. "Was real furred, wasn't I? Went babbling a few nasty words. Sure you know I didn't mean them. Sure you, being a Fleetie and all, must have heard them a hundred times over." He offered a wide grin and slapped the side of his head with his hand, skewing his thinning brown hair. "Still rattling around in there. Can't you hear it?"

Verno's laugh rattled a few viewports in the next quadrant. Ren's gaze brushed over Sully's, then mine. Marsh was on the bridge, listening on intraship. Dorsie and Aubry were sleeping, off duty.

"Chest healing better?" I was the picture of concern.

"Still some tightness, soreness." Gregor stretched, winced.

God, get me a theater. Any stage will do.

"Dorsie's got a cure for that," Verno said. "Her special tea."

With honeylace. She'd brewed a mug for Sully and Ren. I didn't need it. I had Gabriel Sullivan's bedtime stories.

Sully keyed a touchpad. The hologrid rose. Not with Marker manifests, ship movements. But with the system primaries for the *Boru Karn*. He'd captured them in the midst of disintegration, had the forethought to save the file.

We studied it now. It was a horrific mess and it seemed to hold no answers. No clues. Except one.

Sabotage.

"You brought her in for regular maintenance when I

left for Moabar." Sully jerked his chin toward Gregor. "Who worked on her?"

"Me. Aubry. The tech crew at Dock Five. Our usuals. No one touched her unless Aubry or I was there."

Sully watched him. If Gregor was lying, he was dead.

"I saw the repair logs." Sully picked up his lightpen, tabbed down the side of the panel. A second grid flashed up. "Nothing here," he pointed to the logs, "explains this." He pointed to the crazed primaries.

There was a long moment of studious silence.

"That's true, Sully-sir."

"How about a worm?" Marsh's voice came over intraship. He had a smaller version of both grids on his bridge monitors.

"Basically impossible," Sully said, "on my ship."

Sully was no pilot. But he was one damned fine engineer, and an even better systems tech.

"Impossible from outside." Gregor leaned back in his chair. "But how about right here?"

"Here? Gregor, you're saying one of us did this?" Verno pointed a long finger to the grid.

Gregor shrugged. "I'm saying Sully's right. He's got this ship rigged tighter than a whore's—pardon, Captain Bergren. He's got this ship locked down tight where our systems are concerned. It'd have to be someone who could get in from inside. Like, I don't know, the terminal in Sully's quarters." His gaze swept over me, quickly, then moved on. "Or on the bridge or maybe in here...."

"That's traceable," Sully snapped. "I already checked for it. Nothing showed up."

"Someone was real good, it might not." Gregor spun his lightpen on the tabletop but didn't look at Sully.

Sully stared at him, hard, for a long time. "We'll keep working on it," he said finally.

He moved his lightpen. The grid changed. "This is the latest we've been able to snag on Marker. We've got four days left till we hit the A–B. I want to move on the shipyards no later then ten days after that."

"We'll be ready, Sully-sir. We'll be ready."

An hour, maybe less, to the B–C.

Sully sat at the small dining table in our cabin, elbows bent, mouth resting on his folded hands. He stared at the mug of hot tea before him as if he could find answers in the curls of rising steam.

At least, that's what it looked like to me. The door slid closed behind me. I unhooked the holster from around my waist and tossed it, along with the laser pistol snugged into it, on the couch as I walked by. We were on the *Boru Karn* but I went armed, everywhere, on the ship now. We all did.

Sabotage. It hung heavy in the air. Even Dorsie's fragrant galley seemed a bit less for it.

Sully had just come from a private talk with Gregor. I wondered, but didn't ask, if Gregor had met Sully's hidden half, his talents, yet.

Intraship trilled on his deskcomp. He didn't turn. I answered it. "Bergren."

"Captain Chasidah. We've just crossed into Baris. Tell Sully-sir, if you will."

"Acknowledged. Thanks, Verno." I clicked it off.

He was looking at me when I turned away from the desk. "Sit." I could hear *please* implied. I could also hear the tiredness in his voice.

I sat next to him and took a sip of his tea. One of us might as well.

"It's not him," he said.

Gregor wasn't responsible for the near-destruction of the *Karn*'s primaries. The near-destruction of the *Boru Karn* itself.

"I didn't think so," I told him. "The man may be annoying, but not stupid. Or suicidal." Gregor would have died if we had.

"He wants very much for me to believe you're responsible."

"At least he's consistent." I became Gregor's nemesis the moment I'd set my boots on the *Karn*'s decking.

"He maintains that the worm had to have been entered by someone on this ship." He stared past me, past the tea I nudged back in front of him. "He asked if I checked the datapad you took from the *Meritorious*."

"Kingswell's pad? It's in the ready room. Want me to—"

"It's here. Now. I checked it." His tone went flat.

I was suddenly aware of my heart beating a bit harder in my chest than I wanted it to. "And?"

He nodded, slowly. "I found it."

A chill ran through me. "A worm program?"

"Traces of it. They usually don't leave a trail, you know. But there are always residues, skews. I found those."

"Who put it there?" I'd cleared Kingswell's datapad, dumped everything except what we needed to know about Fleet itself and about Marker. Could I have missed something coded to send a worm if the pad was used without authorization? But that would only destroy the pad, not invade another computer system. "Couldn't have been Kingswell. The man didn't have that kind of knowledge."

"Gregor and I discussed that. He maintains, and correctly so, that you do."

I sat back against my chair, sharply. Closed my eyes. For a minute I was back in the courtroom, in full dress uniform, and about to be stripped of my rank and command. I'd listened to everything, all the testimony, all the proof. And saw truth in none of it. Only lies, intricately, beautifully, professionally crafted. But I could disprove none of them.

Captain Bergren is the only one who had the ability to override that command.

Correctly so.

I opened my eyes. "I've left the datapad in the ready room enough times that anyone on board had access to it. I can't tell you what anyone else may have done"—I still didn't want to believe anyone on board would have tried to kill us—"but I didn't create a worm. I didn't load it into this ship."

"I know." He offered me his hand. I took it, warmth cascading through me. "But neither did Gregor. Neither did I. We're the only three who'd know how. And I'm not even sure at this juncture where the worm originated. Even Gregor agrees that the damage could have come from the fail-safes collapsing as the worm attacked our systems and, through them, the datapad. Though that probability is less likely."

He squeezed my fingers, gave me a brief, troubled smile. "I can't stop thinking about Milo. Someone told the stripers about the *Diligent Keeper.* Leaked that information. Or sold it. Milo's crew didn't know why he was on Moabar Station. Ren and I booked passage through the church. It was all legitimate. Only Milo knew why I was there. And, like Gregor, he's not—he wasn't—suicidal."

I knew all this. We'd discussed it and noted the warnings. But maybe we hadn't paid enough attention to what we saw. "Who on the *Karn* knew you were using the *Diligent*?"

"Everyone. Marsh, Gregor, Dorsie, Aubry, Verno. Milo met us at Dock Five, in the rafts."

I knew Dock Five. It was an abandoned mining raft converted to a way station at the A–B. Barely legal, but as long as its dockmaster regularly paid the Empire its share of the port charges, Fleet had no reason to shut it down.

"Drogue?" The round-faced monk had been nothing but helpful. But I had to ask. I was gathering data now. Facts.

Sully nodded. "He knew we came in on Milo's ship. He knew I came to retrieve you. But I worked too closely with him. Ren did, even more so. If he were lying, setting us up, we would've known." He hesitated. "Sensed something."

Just as Sully knew that Gregor was telling the truth. And that I was. Unless . . .

I curled my fingers tighter through his, tried to send rainbows along with my question. Because I knew he hated these kinds of questions. "Is there anyone who could block the truth from you, or Ren, if you were deliberately reading them?"

From my conversations with Ren I'd learned that reading an emotional resonance didn't necessarily reveal the reason behind the emotion. I didn't know if Sully had read his crew telepathically, going into their minds the way he had mine when we faced the *Loviti*.

His gaze went back to his tea. Cold now, steam no longer rose and curled, like gray fuzzy soft.

"On this ship? No," he said after a moment. "But elsewhere? Most are on Stol. But we'd see the block."

Like a DO NOT ENTER sign? "But what if you didn't see a block? What if you saw a false memory of innocence?"

His free hand angled out toward me, fingers splayed. His expression was thoughtful. "Memories are linked. Intertwined. False ones, or lies, float. Or have very weak foundations. I don't know how to explain this—"

"You're doing fine."

"Then understand that Ren might not see one, but I would. There's always the accompanying fear. Even if it's small. It's distinctive."

"What if the memory weren't false, or blocked, but erased?" Like Kingswell and Tessa.

A long sigh. "Same thing. A gap where it shouldn't be."

"But what if that mind assumed the gap belonged?" I thought of Dock Five. Seedy bars, nighthouses, honey-lace dens. "A conversation over a couple of beers, shots of honeylace on the side. Maybe a pipe of *rafthkra*. Or two. One hell of a hangover in the morning. One hell of a gap in the mind."

Obsidian eyes darkened, deeply troubled.

"Sully, we're not talking about a hauler full of synth-emeralds here. Or a smuggler's load of *rafthkra* or Tre-larian brandy. We're talking about gen-labs. And jukors. We're talking about something that could only be done with the backing of someone very powerful in the Em-pire. Someone powerful enough to keep it a secret. Prew maybe be a pompous dandy of an emperor, but he's not evil. This is evil. There's a very real power behind it."

"You're saying I'm facing another *Ragkiril*." His voice was quiet. "One who may have had access to someone on this ship."

Ragkiril. Another *Ragkiril.* Besides the one staring uncomfortably at me.

He'd never admitted that before. Only *telepath,* and then no further explanations on that. I knew we'd somehow taken a big step and kept my response as unemotional, as factual as possible, even though my heart and mind buzzed with questions. "I imagine Stol has a few cities full of them. The Empire's used them before."

"You're wrong." He clasped his hands against his mouth. Then pressed them, briefly, against his lowered forehead. His shoulders were stiff and tense, as if a weight lay against them. He turned back to me. "*Ragkir,*" he said. "A minor distinction, and one the Empire seems unwilling to comprehend. All Stolorths, and a few humans, have empathic abilities, from the basic ability to read emotional resonances to the deeper *Ragkir* mind talents. But *Ragkiril* ... well, there aren't cities full. The Stolorths would like us to think so. The Empire obliges them by thinking so, because it helps them fuel their prejudices. But since you're probing for facts, Chaz, I'll hand you one. There *aren't* cities full of *Ragkiril.* Those that I've met in my lifetime could fit in this cabin. Those I've read of, studied, could fit in this ship. And we'd all still have plenty of room."

I sat, stunned, fascinated. And a little frightened. But not so much as to halt my questions. My need to understand him was stronger. "And this minor distinction?"

"Basically, a *Ragkir* can do a *zral.* Erase memories. Affect what a mind knows, sees. A *Ragkiril* can do not only a *zral,* but a *zragkor.* He can kill the mind. And, depending upon other factors, training, he also can heal."

Ren. Sully, breathing for him. This was my explanation. Sully was a *Ragkiril,* trained to heal, perhaps by the Englarians in the same way they'd trained Ren. But they could also kill, he'd said. His confirmation was chilling and one that made me distinctly uncomfortable. I'd heard rumors of that. That was why the Empire hated *Ragkirils*, banning and damning any mind talents save for the most benign.

But those had been Stolorth *Ragkirils*. Not human. Surely the human mind talents weren't as lethal?

"Still think it was wise to come after me?" He tried to smile, failed.

I thought of him sending life back into Ren's body. "Yes."

He let out a breath I hadn't realize he'd been holding. "Sully—"

He raised his hand. "No. I can only do so much confessing in one day. Bear with me. This is more than I ever intended for you to know. If it weren't for what's happened, it would still be something we wouldn't discuss until later. Like, ten years from now."

"Glad to know you intend to keep me around for a while."

Finally, he offered me a smile back. "A few lifetimes, at least."

It would probably take me at least that long to figure him out, to finally get all the facts I needed about Gabriel Ross Sullivan. It seemed with every bit of information I learned, additional questions would surface. Like *Ragkir* and *Ragkiril*. And how the son of one of the wealthiest men in the Empire had come to learn his mind could touch another's, could heal. There was so much I didn't know about Sully, and what I did I barely understood. I pushed my uneasiness aside. I knew he'd sense it.

"Let's deal with the trouble in this lifetime. I think we may have made the serious mistake of underestimating the enemy. Someone told the stripers about Milo. And someone launched a worm into your ship's systems. And someone, in case you forgot," I added, resting my hand on his arm, letting his warmth tumble into me, "sent a jukor to try to stop us from ever reaching the monastery. Someone knows who we are, where we've been, what we're doing."

"And where we're going," he added quietly, his brief smile now gone. "Someone will be waiting for us at Marker."

Sully left to talk to Ren. I imagined that the discussion, while serious, would no doubt include a few hands of cards. It was his way of dealing with tension, or maybe his way of blocking out the emotions swirling around the ship that he didn't want to feel.

I flipped open Kingswell's datapad on the table—my own way of dealing with tension. Sully's admission had raised questions I wasn't ready to dwell on. Other problems were easier.

Sully had told me where he'd found the traces of the worm program. I wanted to look at them in case, as I told him, the program was a parting gift from the Imperial Fleet. Just because Kingswell couldn't create such a program didn't mean his crew had been equally untalented.

I was better trained to recognize Fleet worms than Sully was. But I didn't recognize these. At least, not the small residues, aborted snips of code that were all that was left. The program not only tried to destroy the *Karn*'s systems, it had destroyed itself, eradicating its identity.

Like a *zral*. Or a *zragkor*.

No wonder Sully understood these programs so well.

Only a few *Ragkiril*, he'd said. And by oblique admission, placed himself in their ranks. One of the few human ones. And the possibility, with the situation on Marker, we would face another.

Questions, a thousand questions. Again, my mind reminded me that with every one Sully answered for me, another ten popped up.

Let's deal with Marker, my brain said. *At least there, shipping manifests leave nice, linear trails that can be plugged into grids.*

I pulled up my work data, still intact in spite of the damage, and paged through to where I'd left off before we'd transferred to the *Karn*. I started reading, trying to pick up my train of thought. My note-mark flashed. Right. The stuff on Crossley. I'd never transferred my personal notes to Sully's hologrid in the ready room. We'd gone over everything else that day, but not my questions on Crossley.

I opened the note, reread the data. Crossley Burke. Not the vid-game people. At least, not anymore. Unless they were breeding jukors to add a touch of realism to their sims. Wouldn't get a lot of repeat customers if they were.

I was headed for Sully's deskcomp to see what the *Karn* held on Crossley Burke when the cabin door slid open. Sully, looking more relaxed than when he left but none too happy.

I took a wild guess. "How much?"

He hesitated only half a second. "Oh. Four million, one hundred thousand. And change. Or so."

"You have a lot on your mind. You can't expect your game to improve right now." I frankly didn't think his game would ever improve, but there are times when you have to make certain encouraging noises.

He looked positively affronted. "I am improving! I didn't lose half as much as I normally do."

He stripped off his laser pistol, threw it on the couch

next to mine, then sat, arms draped along the back of the cushions. "Still working?"

I settled into the desk chair, tabbed up the screen. "Ran across some notes I made a few days ago. I'm looking for a reference for anything to do with a firm, or a name, of Crossley Burke."

"This has to do with Marker?" He stood suddenly and was at the desk in two long strides. "Marker? This has—"

"Give me a chance to answer. Yes, this has to do with Marker. Either funding, or a concept group that—"

"Crossley Burke. You're sure it's Crossley?" He leaned his palms on the desk and stared at me.

"It's not Crossley. They used to make vid games."

"Show me the reference."

I knew he didn't mean the vid games. He followed me to the dining-room table, his hands fisted. I pulled up the data and pointed to it.

He sat and stared at my small screen. "Hell's ass. God damned son of a bitch."

"Sully—"

"Goddamned bastard. I should've known."

"Sully."

He ran a hand over his face. "Crossley Burke. Hayden Crossley Burke."

That sounded like a person. "Who's Hayden Crossley Burke?"

His eyes narrowed. "Someone I should've killed long ago, when I had the chance. Hayden Crossley Burke's my cousin."

22

I could see the resemblance. Hayden Crossley Burke, cousin of Gabriel Ross Sullivan, who was the son of Winthrop Burke Sullivan. They were men of similar height and build, and looked to be about the same age.

The news vidclip playing on the ready room's holo-grid, and on Marsh's bridge screen, had been shot last year at a charity ball on Garno. Hayden moved easily through a crowd bedecked in formal attire and glittering gems. The vidcam wasn't focused on him but on the parade of last year's vid stars silhouetted against the ever-familiar forms of old money and power, like Darius Tage, Lady Ailionora Petroski, or one of the Bell-Javieros. We'd see Hayden in the background, shaking hands, chatting, then lose him. Another few minutes, the camera would swing around to highlight another long-legged beauty revealing an amazing amount of cleavage, and there was Hayden. Shaking hands, chatting. Smiling.

"He's older," Sully said. "Four, five years."

Similar jawline, straight nose, dark hair. But Cousin

Hayden's eyes were light. And while Sully's smile was often playful, Hayden's was polished. Professional.

"Looks like he shits money," Gregor said.

For once, he and I were in total agreement.

Sully tabbed off the vid, perched on the edge of the round table, and crossed his arms. His expression was one of a man contemplating something unpleasant. I didn't know if it was Hayden himself or what Hayden funded. Or the very real fact that Hayden was in a position to do these things because Sully had refused to be a Sullivan. Hayden was not only the heir to the Crossley Burke fortune, but had control of the Sullivan moneys as well.

Sully outlined the wealth at Hayden's disposal and the contacts that came with that wealth, with no mention that it could have been his. He confirmed my suspicion that Crossley Burke, the megacorporation, had grown from the small vid-game firm I remembered. Diversified. Acquired. But most often in the background, quietly. Hayden and his father, Morley Burke, had negotiated a number of lucrative government contracts over the years. Sully admitted he hadn't paid much attention to them. Finding out what those contracts were was now a priority.

"You ever meet the guy?" Gregor was across from me, next to Aubry. He flicked the end of his lightpen at the blank hologrid as if Hayden's image was still there. "At Marker," he added. "Ever see him there?"

Gregor had avoided me since Sully's talk with him, no longer challenging me directly. But that tone of dislike still hung under his words when he spoke.

I shook my head. "Not that I remember." And I would have. Hayden was an attractive man.

"Not even talking to your brother?" Gregor persisted.

Ren exchanged glances, and I could only imagine what else, with Sully.

"I don't remember Thad ever mentioning his name either. But we didn't talk a lot, even before the trial. If we did, it was usually about Willym." Argued about Willym. I'd almost convinced Suzette to take him out of the crèche. Then I'd been arrested.

"Willym?"

"My brother. Half brother."

Gregor's eyes narrowed. "Where's he work on Marker?"

"Nowhere. He's nine years old."

Gregor snorted. "Your father must be—"

"You have a point with all this?" Sully's voice was hard.

Gregor shrugged and toyed with his lightpen. "Sure would be more useful if she could say, yeah, I saw Burke at Marker. On this or that date. Or, yeah, my brother told me about this party he went to with Burke."

"Thad's not the party type. And they're not even remotely in the same social circles." But Philip was. Shame I couldn't ask what he knew about Hayden. "The only reason he'd talk to Hayden Burke at all would be for shipyard business. And we don't have any proof right now that Thad has."

Ren leaned toward me, silencing any further comment from Gregor. "Verno and I were discussing the reasons your brother's office might receive confirmation of incoming ships privately. He asked that I mention it." Verno was off duty, sleeping at Sully's orders after one too many long shifts. "It could be that he suspects someone is misusing the shipyards. He may not know about the labs we suspect are being created, but be as suspicious as we are."

I'd thought of that. That would be very like Thad.

Fleet first. Always by the book. Even more than me. His mother had worn army boots too.

"If he is, he might help us." Aubry had a high, thin voice for a man of his bulk. He spent his off-duty time working out in the ship's small gym with Marsh.

"I wouldn't trust him," Sully said. "At this point."

"I agree." But I would, oddly, trust Philip. I just didn't know how Sully would react to that if I suggested it.

We passed another beacon shortly after Verno came on duty, three hours later. The *Karn* efficiently and secretively grabbed the news banks, traffic, and in-system advisories.

I brought up the data on Sully's deskscreen as I got ready for bed. The Farosians had staged a protest outside the government center on Aldan Prime. There'd been a major depot fire in Port January, losses in the millions. Two women, raped, brutally murdered in Crescent City in the Walker Colonies. Odd, engraved disks found at both crime scenes. . . .

While jukors were born and Takas died.

And other Takas killed.

Sully sat behind me on the edge of our bed and brushed out my hair. I was wearing my worry colors, he told me.

"I should learn not to watch the news before bed." I wished I could read his moods as he did mine. Wished I could tell when he was open, willing to talk. "What color is worry?"

His hands stilled, then lifted my hair. He ran the brush underneath. "Muddy colors. Like dirty water in a stream."

"Anger?"

"Reddish."

"Fear?"

"Yellow. The correlations are fairly commonsense."

"Does healing have a color? When Ren was injured on the bridge, you—"

"That's different." This time the brush did stop. I heard it clatter against the nightstand. It was a sharp sound, like the tone in Sully's voice. Then his arms wrapped around my waist, his face against my neck. Warmth fluttered, trickled.

"That's different," he repeated, softer this time. "But it's nothing that would ever hurt you. I'd never hurt you."

I covered his arms with my own. "I know." With a twinge of reluctance, I opened my mental cold storage, shoved that question back inside. I didn't want to hurt him either.

Sully and I'd discussed course changes before, but the next morning was the first time he ever had me initiate one. That had usually been Gregor's prerogative. I had no desire to step on toes in that regard.

"Dock Five. You're sure?" I leaned on the arm pad in the pilot's chair. Marsh and Aubry were due to come on in an hour. It was just Sully, Ren, and myself on the bridge. Just as it would be only Sully, Ren, and myself going on to Marker.

He'd said that too, just before he told me he wanted to head for Dock Five.

"We have to refuel, pick up supplies," he said.

I could name ten other depots that would do that just as well and told him so.

"But the *Karn* didn't stop at any of those before I left for Moabar. It was at Dock Five. We have to look around there before we proceed further." He motioned to Ren sitting at helm in front of me, his back to the console. "I told Ren about your theory. That another," he glanced quickly at the closed bridge hatchway, "*Ragkiril* may be involved. That might explain how the information about Milo was obtained."

"My only difficulty with that possibility," Ren said, "is that I cannot see one of my people, or anyone with *Ragkiril* talents, encouraging the breeding of jukors."

"I'll name reasons why someone might." I raised one hand, held up a finger with each item. "Greed, money, blackmail, power. Need more?"

Ren shook his head. "Of course, we're not immune to that. But not with jukors as a goal." He glanced at Sully. "You didn't explain this to her?"

My explanations, I wanted to tell Ren, were still coming in very small doses.

Sully took a deep breath, let it out slowly. "Not... completely."

I didn't like that tone. Part of me said, *What now?* And part of me said, *Oh, shit.* I didn't know whether to laugh or brace myself.

I must have braced myself, because Sully and Ren spoke out almost simultaneously.

"No, it's nothing—"

"Not to worry—"

"Explain. Please."

"To put it briefly," Sully said, after a short staring contest with Ren, "jukors can't be affected by mind talents. It becomes, then, strictly a physical battle. And few things are physically a match for a jukor."

"A modified Norlack did pretty damned well," I reminded him.

"The jukor's only vulnerable area is that small spot of its throat. You have one coming at you, you might take it down. You have ten, you have no chance. One of them will get you."

"So? Humans face the same type of threat from them. Why would that preclude a Stolorth, a *Ragkiril,* from working for a jukor-breeding project?"

"Because it takes away the advantage a *Ragkiril* has. That's why jukors were bred after the Boundary Wars. Not for security purposes, as the government claimed. But to make sure Stolorths, or anyone with *Ragkiril* talents, wouldn't challenge the Empire."

"It was unnecessary." Ren's voice held a note of sadness. "We have no interest in acquiring more worlds, like the Empire. Our very passivity makes the Empire distrust us. That and, of course, the Empire's experience with our *Ragkirils* when we did try to assist in the war. When our founders realized that, they thought it best that the Empire not understand the different levels and degrees of mind talents. That, it seems, was even a worse thing to do. Now we are all viewed as a latent threat."

Ren was right. I'd grown up with everything he told me. The fears, the prejudice, the condemnation of telepaths. The Empire, greedy and bloated, categorizing all others in the same way, assigning others their own motives.

I also saw why a *Ragkiril* might not work on a project to breed jukors. But I didn't discount it totally. "So we go back to Dock Five."

Sully nodded. "Pick up the trail, if there is one. See who's been watching us. And who's paying them to watch us."

"Crossley Burke."

A wry smile. "That would be ironic, wouldn't it? If Cousin Hayden does prove I'm still alive, he stands a good chance of losing his inheritance. All that Sullivan money."

"I thought your father disowned you."

"Oh, he did. But Hayden's not legal heir. He's assisting by right of next of kin, as I'm theoretically dead. But since my body was never recovered, you know the regs; it hasn't been seven years. If he proves I'm alive, then he's also proved he has no right to the money."

I looked at Ren. "I'd start keeping real good records of those card games if I were you."

Ren smiled.

Sully didn't come back to the cabin right away when our shift ended. Had some thoughts he wanted to play with on the hologrid in the ready room, he said.

I left him there. I had some thoughts of my own, circling, hovering, unwanted. No, not unwanted. Just unanswered. Tea, not coffee, sounded soothing. I was on my second cup when Sully came back to the cabin.

"Find anything more?" I'd kicked off my boots and was reclining on the couch.

He shook his head. "Bits and pieces. It's frustrating."

"I fully sympathize." My bits and pieces had hovered through two cups of tea. Empath. Telepath. *Ragkir.* *Ragkiril.* Stolorth. Human. Sully. I scooted my feet over on the cushions so he could sit.

He plopped down, covering his mouth with his hand for a moment. Then he splayed his fingers toward me. "I know. I also know my saying you have nothing to be afraid of sometimes isn't sufficient."

Damn. Even though I'd pushed my thoughts away— or thought I had—when he walked through the open door, he'd sensed them. Or saw the worry colors in my rainbow.

"I'm not afraid of you, Sully." It wasn't fear I felt most often when confronted with what Sully could do. It was frustration over lack of facts to work with. "I'm afraid of doing something wrong. Because I don't understand what it means to be a *Ragkiril*. Why you were chosen, or if it's something you chose—"

He flashed me an anguished look, his back stiffening. "Believe me, I'd never choose this." His voice was bitter.

"So it chose you?"

"It?"

I couldn't tell if he was angry or amused. "I don't understand. You're human, not Stolorth." I knew every inch of him. He was definitely human. "I thought your abilities might have come from a symbiote implant or genetic enhancement." Both had been outlawed after the Boundary Wars, but there were always places where money could buy anything. Especially if you were already an outlaw like Gabriel Ross Sullivan. Given his chosen line of work with smugglers, arms runners, and *rafthkra* dealers, some mind-reading skills could go a long way in keeping him alive.

But he'd not chosen the talent. He'd just admitted that. There was a deeper story here, one I didn't at all understand. One that clearly haunted him.

He leaned his elbows on his knees, hands clasped between them. Struggled. I could see it in the lines around his eyes, the tension in his mouth. I was about to tell him forget it, I don't want to know, I can't bear to see you suffer like this, when he answered.

"It's a random genetic mutation. It can happen about every four or five generations in humans."

"It runs in your family—"

"No. No one else." He spoke haltingly. "That I know of."

"Then how did you know—"

"At first I didn't. Things just . . . happened. Thoughts. Sounds. Pictures from someone else's mind. I didn't know how or why." His voice was harsh. "All I know is

I woke up one morning and looked in the mirror, and I was terrified, because I saw—"

He stopped abruptly and stared at his clenched hands. Not at me. He hadn't looked at me for several minutes. He closed his eyes, took a deep breath. "Because I saw," he continued, his voice forcibly calm, "what I am."

I remembered Ren's explanation of what I termed rainbows. There was nothing scary about rainbows. "Is being able to see your own resonance, these colors around your body, so frightening?"

He said nothing for a very long minute. "It can be."

If you weren't expecting it, I supposed. If you were . . . "You were a child," I guessed. That might very well be terrifying to see colors dancing all over your body.

He nodded.

"How old were you?" I asked softly. I thought I was beginning to understand a little more about him, a child alone with a terrible secret.

"Twelve."

Not that young, but at the precarious point between child and teenager. Puberty? Did puberty trigger the change from limited human mind to *Ragkiril*? "Is that usually when it—"

He shoved himself to his feet, headed for the door to the corridor. My heart plummeted. I wanted to call back all my questions, apologize, tell him it didn't matter.

He stopped, shoulders hunched, hands jammed in his pockets. Then he turned and walked back to the couch, but sat instead on the low table in front of me. I swung my legs off the cushions. He took my hands in his. "Sorry. For a moment I was that twelve-year-old again, looking in the mirror."

That explained something I'd not paid much attention to before. There were no mirrors in Sully's cabin.

Only a small one over the sink in the bathroom. Where there usually was one between closets, he'd hung an old star chart, framed.

He brought my fingers to his mouth. "Can we talk about something else?"

I smiled. "Sure. How much do you owe Ren now?"

23

I hadn't been to Dock Five in almost three years. The place hadn't changed. Except maybe to get a little more seedy, a little more raucous, a little more peppered with divergent humans and humanoids. Freighter crew, tanker crew, and barge workers all mixed in with shop-keepers, bartenders, and miners in transit. There were men and women of all shapes, sizes, and ages, but very few children. Just the odd pickpocket or some rafter's brat running loose while his parental unit slumbered, deep in hangover heaven.

Dock Five was an ugly structure, long, somewhat cylindrical. Six levels at its narrowest, ten at its widest, each level crisscrossed with corridors. Gravity only worked at its core. In the outlying areas, beyond the core, it was all free-float, zero-g boots required.

Sixty bays total, thirty a side, most around the center core. That's where the shops were, the bars, the night-houses, the *rafthkra* dens. Tool shops, ships' supplies hugged the outer core.

So did the *Boru Karn*. We waited an hour for the

berth to clear. Center core was more heavily trafficked, making an unscheduled emergency departure more hazardous. The *Karn* was always prepared for one of those.

We were listed in dock manifests as the *Lofty Echo*. Sully had a random list of names, words, and threw them together on a whim. This week, the *Lofty Echo*. Next month, the *Iron Sun*. It didn't matter. He had clearances and docs for them all.

We traipsed toward the core in plain spacer fatigues, myself in dark blue, Sully in his usual black. No ship patches. Weapons discreetly under jackets. My Grizni, as always, wrapped securely around my wrist.

Verno and Dorsie followed us down Blue Level. Dorsie had a list of supplies. She and Verno broke off as we came to Blue Corridor 6. There was a warehouse on BC 6 she dealt with regularly and trusted their prices. We'd meet up later in a pub on BC 12.

Gregor, Aubry, and Ren stayed on board, but only Gregor and Ren were on duty. Gregor because he was first pilot. Ren because there were sighted Stolorths on Dock Five. Being caught on an open dock was something he couldn't risk.

The office for the repair techs Sully used was on Green, one level down. The lifts were crowded. We took the nonworking escalator stairs. I didn't know if they'd broken again or hadn't been fixed since I was last there.

"Never fixed," Sully told me, then added a questioning glance. "Fleet doesn't dock here."

"I was on vacation."

"Here?"

"With a friend." I gave him a bland look and tried to throw *it's old business and not worth bringing up* into my rainbow.

He caught it, but it didn't stop him. "Not another husband."

I punched his arm. "One's more than enough, thank you."

"A friend in the freighter business?"

"Yes. Now what's the name of that office we're looking for?"

He chuckled. It'd been a while since I heard his deep, rumbling laugh. It sounded wonderful.

A young woman raised her gaze from her screen as we entered. She was pretty, with bright gold hair clipped back with a colorful assortment of pins. She sat behind a low counter that divided the room. Two men in coveralls were in the other corner of the office, studying an enlarged schematic on a hologrid. They turned.

Sully raised his hand. "Pops. When you get a minute, we need to talk to you."

The taller, bald-headed man nodded, splayed his hand in the air. "Five minutes?"

"Sure."

"I'll keep him busy, Pops." The woman rounded the counter, walked toward us. She was tall and slender, with tight leggings under a thin, clingy tunic.

"Well, hello, Ross. I didn't know you were on dock." She glanced at me, smiled, then returned her focus to Sully. Or Ross, the name he told me he used here.

"Business is good, Ilsa?"

"Can't complain. No, wait. Maybe I will. It's been more than six months since you even stopped in to say hello to me." She pouted prettily. "Doesn't Gregor ever give you my messages?"

"He has."

I felt Sully's hand at the small of my back. Ilsa's gaze flicked to the movement of his arm.

Ah. Ex-girlfriend meets current girlfriend. I didn't enjoy these kinds of meetings. Eventually it led to the almost subliminal stare-down, the message: *you've got him now. I'll get him back.*

Ilsa didn't waste time. She appraised me thoroughly. I could almost hear her thinking: *cute, but not beautiful.* "Known Ross long?" she asked me.

"Since the wedding," Sully put in before I could answer.

I almost choked.

Ilsa did. "Wedding?" She recovered. "You met at a wedding recently?"

"No," I said.

"Of course not," Sully said right after that. "Chaz and I got married recently. But I've known you how long, my angel?" He brushed a stray tendril of hair from my face, his dark eyes twinkling but smoky with desire. "Almost six years?"

My God, why were all the handsome ones always such bastards? But I was grinning. This was so Sully. This was so much the Sully I hadn't seen since the problem with Kingswell. Since the problems with the *Karn.*

Six years was about right. I just couldn't remember if it was synth-emeralds or silacksian crystals that had brought us together.

I was saved from answering by the appearance of the bald man. Ilsa's father, I guessed, from the resemblance around the eyes and mouth.

"You're looking well, Ross."

"You too, Pops." Sully took the offered hand, then motioned to me. "This is my wife, Chaz."

Pops exhibited none of Ilsa's surprise. " 'Bout damned time. And a lovely one you are. Chaz? Good to meet you." His large hand enveloped mine. "You in the business?"

I thought of all the things I knew Sully, as Sully, had done. I wondered what business Pops thought I was in.

"She's a pilot. Damned fine one," Sully said. "Good thing too. We had a bit of a problem with my ship."

Pops frowned. "Something my people worked on? I'd have a hard time believing that."

"So would I. Can we go somewhere and talk?"

Ilsa managed a rather frigid "congratulations" before we followed Pops to a back office and sat in spindly chairs permanently locked to the decking. Sully outlined the systems failure.

Pops rubbed his bald head while he listened, then brought up Sully's repair records. "Aubry or Gregor okayed everything. Just like normal. I can't see . . . Ross, I can't understand what happened." The news disturbed him deeply.

But if he was lying, only Sully could tell. I knew that's why we were here. He knew what those records showed, he'd listened to Gregor and Aubry's recounting. But he needed to talk to, to *read*, Pops. And read the three techs who'd worked on the *Karn*.

We had coffee while Pops called them in off their current jobs on the docks. Sully spoke briefly to them all. It was all he needed to clear them. We left without saying good-bye to Ilsa.

"Trying to make me jealous?" I teased as we climbed the uneven escalator stairs.

"Was I that obvious?" He paused a second. "Did it work?"

"I don't know. Depends if she and I are on the same list."

It took him a moment to place my comment. His list of confused women. The one I didn't want to be a part of.

"There is no list," he said as we reached the top of the stairs. He grabbed my arm, pulled me against him, kissed me. I revealed in his warmth as it fluttered invisibly over my skin.

"Shit!" A burly man in mining-company coveralls behind us almost knocked us down. "Go rent a room, will ya?"

I leaned against Sully's chest, chuckling, and let him drag me out of the way.

We were back on Blue Level. Pops and his techs had read clean. Just like Gregor and Aubry. "Who else had access to the ship?" I asked quietly as we walked past dingy storefronts, garish pubs.

"No one, officially. And if the boys were lonely, they'd go to one of the nighthouses. If they did bring a prosti back on board, they wouldn't let her out of their sight. That much I know. Besides, I asked Gregor that question."

"And Marsh, Aubry?"

He nodded.

"Dorsie?"

Another nod.

We stepped aside as a stout woman, her arms laden with boxes, walked unsteadily past us.

"Verno?"

"The Englarians have a small mission here. It was just before Peyhar's, you know."

That brought it back down to someone on board. I was the only new figure in the equation. "Kingswell's datapad had to have had some kind of delayed destruct program. Something I didn't see when I emptied it. I usually don't miss that kind of thing. Especially when it's Fleet."

"Unless someone put it there after you cleaned it."

I was surprised. "But you asked, you read..." I let my sentence trail off. I wasn't about to elaborate on his *Ragkiril* abilities in the middle of Blue Level.

"I did. But only resonances, looking for fear, evasiveness. I may have to ask again, more deeply this time. And I'll need Ren there, though they're not going to like it. I've never had to question my crew in any way that they were aware they were being probed, read."

"Do they trust Ren?" I'd noticed Marsh's attitude was friendly, but Gregor and Aubry rarely talked to him. Dorsie, however, was clearly fond of Ren.

"They tolerate him. Except for Dorsie, of course, who vacillates between wanting to adopt him and wanting to mate with him. Gregor and Aubry went flying out of their chairs like you did when I first brought Ren on board. I'm so used to having him around that I sometimes forget the effect he has on people."

A shop door slid open and two people exited into our path. We stopped, let them pass.

"How long have you known Ren?"

"Long time. Almost twenty years."

"You met him when he was ten?"

"Excellent math skills. And cute too. What a wife. I'm such a lucky guy." He gave me a Sully smirk. Then showed off his quick reflexes as he danced out of the way of my playful punch to his arm.

"I thought Ren lived with the Englarians. And his Takan family in the compound."

"He did."

"What were you doing there?"

He glanced down at me, a half smile on his lips. "Studying to be a monk."

My God. He almost *was* Brother Sudral. "Whatever made you want to become an Englarian monk?"

"It seemed appropriate. Shall we say, I stared at a painting of the revered Abbot Eng one day, and it spoke to me."

"And what did the painting tell you?"

He stopped and gazed upward at a blinking sign. *"Trouble's Brewing. We serve only the finest Imperial ales."*

This time my fist did connect with his arm.

He laughed. "Come on. Let's see if Dorsie left any money in my account."

The pub was crowded. "Where's Verno?" Sully asked as we sat. Dorsie must have grabbed one of the last available tables. Her ale arrived just as we deck-locked our chairs. We ordered a pitcher. "That is," Sully said as the 'droid server wheeled away, "if I have any money left."

"The way you play cards with Ren, you're worried about me?"

I knew Sully wasn't. Dorsie was an excellent supplies manager and a sharp-eyed guardian of her budget. I also wasn't far off in my initial appraisal of her. She was Marsh's aunt.

"Verno ran into a friend. He'll be here," Dorsie said. "How's Pops?"

"Not growing any new hair."

"He have answers?"

"Nothing we didn't know."

She nodded, looked at me. "Meet Ilsa?"

I nodded back. "Lovely young woman."

"Not sure what that means, Chaz. Did she or didn't she try to scratch your eyes out?"

I shot a glance to Sully. "No list, huh?"

"Honest. None. Not a one." He held his hands up.

"List?" Dorsie asked as the 'droid returned with the pitcher and two tall glasses.

"List of women. It was, um, a point of discussion between *Ross*," I said, stressing his current name, "and myself."

"Oh, Ilsa wanted to be on that list, real bad," Dorsie

said. She took another sip of ale. "Bet meeting Chaz here stopped that ambition."

"Meeting my wife here stopped that ambition," Sully said.

Dorsie's lips hovered for a moment over the rim of her glass. "Hell's fat ass. For a second there I thought you were serious. I thought you went and done it."

Sully grinned. "Ilsa thinks I did. But don't worry, Dorsie. You'll get one of the first invitations to the wedding when they go out."

Dorsie's look switched to me.

I shook my head, turned my hands outward. "I have no idea what he's talking about."

Sully placed his fingers under my chin. "Did I forget to ask you, my angel?" He brushed my mouth with a kiss just as Dorsie raised her hand in the air.

"Verno! Over here."

I pulled back from him and saw the tall Taka ducking under the low-hanging lights, saw heads turn. Saw a woman following behind him, in Englarian sand-gray robes, her face almost covered by her hood.

"Sully-sir! Sorry to be late." He put his hand on the woman's arm, guided her in front of him. "Sister Berri's been praying for you since you left. Knew you wouldn't mind if she came to see how the abbot has answered her prayers."

The woman's lips turned up slightly in a sweet smile that would make a saint jealous. "It's good to see you again. Truly, it is the blessings and providence of beloved Eng the Merciful that you are all safe." She bowed her head slightly, then raised her eyes to me. "You must be the brave Captain Chasidah I have heard so much about. Blessings of the hour, my sister."

Sister Berri Solaria. The inimitable Berri Solaria whom Drogue had spoken so highly of, teacher of orphans whose life I'd worn for two days on Moabar Station. She was, I realized, everything I'd always thought an Englarian nun would be. Just a lot younger.

Her voice was gentle, melodic, sweet. Her face was thin but delicate. She accepted the chair Verno held out for her, sat as if a cloud lowered her into it. She pushed her hood back. Her hair was a medium light brown, wound into a bun at the nape of her neck. Two wispy curls had escaped, trailed down the sides of her face.

She looked freshly scrubbed, innocent. Angelic, lacking only halo. I doubted she'd crossed her thirtieth birthday yet.

Sully rested his arm around the back of my chair, his fingers on my shoulder. "Sister Berri Solaria. Blessings of the hour. I didn't know you were so concerned about us."

"There's not a moment you have left my thoughts and prayers these past few weeks, I assure you, Mister Sullivan. Not one moment."

I felt Sully flinch and knew why: Sullivan. That was the name of a dead man, a ghost, and not to be used, even in places like Dock Five.

"Sister," he said, but she'd leaned forward, her voice rising as she did so.

"I know that your appearance here again is truly a sign from the beloved abbot." She fixed Sully with an imploring gaze. "You must permit me to assist you in this time of great peril. You must take me with you, to Marker!"

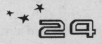

"Sister Solaria. Please. This is not the place to discuss things like that." Sully's voice was firm but kind. I relaxed because he did.

Verno angled his tall form into the seat next to Berri, put his large hand on her arm. He leaned toward her, his whispered words gravelly.

A pale pink rose on her cheeks. "Forgive me. Of course. In my fervor, I'm being indiscreet. I humbly ask your pardon."

"We'll discuss this later." Sully reached for the pitcher. "Grab the 'droid and get us another glass if you can, Dorsie."

Berri raised her index finger. "Oh, please, don't go to any trouble. Brother Verno and I will share."

Verno smiled. A Taka's smile was thin-lipped and showed lots of teeth, almost feral. Verno's was clearly the besotted version of that.

I realized how much I didn't know about Englarians. I based their use of *monk* or *sister* on the rather nebulous Celestialism most of the Empire followed. I vaguely thought that Englarian monks, like Celestial monks, were celibate. That was why Sully's admission he'd studied to take the cloth so surprised me. Celibacy and Sully didn't belong in the same sentence. But then, he'd only studied Englarian theology. Not actually become a monk.

And Ren . . . well, Ren was a Stolorth. I didn't know if they followed the same rules as human monks. I knew very little of their culture, their rituals, other than what the Empire fed us. Which was, it appeared, mostly erroneous.

But Ren, celibate? I thought of the body outlined by the tight shirt and slim fatigue pants. What a waste if he was.

Sully's voice was low in my ear. "That better be me you're thinking about."

Oh, shit. I jabbed him with my elbow. "I'm a married woman. Behave."

Dorsie asked Berri about Peyhar's.

"We do have a small celebration here on dock, for our brothers and sisters." She glanced up at Verno. "I'd hoped . . . well, I'd thought Brother Verno was staying for that. Then, next I heard, your ship had left. I—that is, we missed you, Brother."

Verno finally drew his gaze from Berri's. "I felt guided to accompany my ship. I hope you didn't mind, Sully-sir."

Sully-sir. Berri must have learned Sully's identity from Verno. Drogue had also known, I remembered. Evidently it wasn't a secret in the Englarian community.

"It's always a help to have you on board," Sully said.

Verno was almost tireless, like most Takas. Double shifts were his usual mode. I could have used him on the *Meritorious*. But Takas weren't permitted to serve in the Imperial Fleet, other than as security guards on starports. And there was no *Meritorious* for me to command any longer. I pushed away that small heartache.

We finished the pitcher, ordered another. Talked about life on the rim, about ore-miners and jumpjockeys, the main populace of Dock Five. About pubs that had been here forever, about pubs that lasted a week and closed. About a barge that had had a systems foul-up and rammed the dock instead of pulling away two weeks ago. For a moment that piqued my interest. But it turned out the pilot was more fouled up than the systems. Honeylace.

We finished the second pitcher and stood. Dorsie needed to head back, with supplies due in. Sister Berri touched my arm. "I would be honored to show you our small temple."

I caught Sully's slight nod. "I'd like that. Thank you."

"Drogue sends his blessings," Sully added as we emerged into the corridor.

"Guardian Drogue. A hardworking man, dedicated to the church. He's out at Moabar now, I hear. I didn't realize you knew him."

"We've been working supplies on the rim. But I met him, many years ago, at Calfedar."

"Calfedar. Ah, yes, he ran the Purity Project. Did you work on a supply ship in Dafir?"

"I trained under Drogue, as a novitiate."

"You aspired to take the robe?" Berri regarded him in undisguised surprise that mirrored my own earlier.

"Yes."

Sully's admission clearly startled Berri. She stopped walking, seemed to realize she shouldn't have, and quickened her steps. "Well. Praise the stars. Do you ever regret not taking the robe?"

"There have been times I regret renouncing it. Though not lately," he added.

This time I was shocked. I'd assumed by what he said earlier that he'd studied but never taken his vows. Never become a real pray-every-day member of the clergy.

"Close your mouth, Chaz." He grabbed my neck in an affectionate headlock, kissed the top of my head.

Berri appeared equally flustered, saying nothing until we stopped at the next bank of lifts. As usual, the lines were long. "Verno never told me you took the robe. Would you mind if I ask what name you took?"

"Sudral."

Berri's eyes brightened. "The name of the Immaculate Cloak. That which bound the winged demons, nullified their unholy light. Excellent choice. That shall be the subject of my meditation tonight. Thank you, Brother."

We stepped into the lift with Berri blessing everyone left and right.

The temple was about the size of the one on Moabar Station, but round rather than square. No services were under way. A few Takans—and several humans, I noted with surprise—sat silently, in meditation. Cloying incense that I remembered well drifted from two burners dangling from the ceiling.

The raised platform was curved, with the same backlit arch-and-stave on the wall behind it. A series of small paintings ran down the left wall. I followed Berri.

She stopped at the first painting, touched my elbow, whispered. "Here, of course, is the beloved abbot, in meditation to the stars. And this next one shows his first battle with a soul-stealer, in the sacred Valley of the Tunnels." A few more steps and a painting similar to the one in Drogue's monastery. The winged demon with the stave impaled in his back. This one's face was upturned, though, and had an uncanny resemblance to a screaming jukor.

"This last shows the purity process."

Another soul-stealer, kneeling, and the abbot's red cloak partially draped over his form, dimming the glow of the demon's unholy silver light. The long sword in the abbot's grip was just about to connect with the demon's neck.

"That looks like beheading."

"Of course." Berri's gaze was serene. "The only way to purify the vileness is to disconnect the creatures' filthy minds from their bodies while they are in their true form. The cloak, you see, constrains their shape-shifting powers. The holy sword, the boru karn, completes the process."

Sully was talking to Verno at the entrance to the temple. So he didn't hear Berri's words, didn't see me hesitate, lose my step, almost as she had earlier.

Boru karn. The abbot's holy sword of purity. Sudral. The abbot's holy cloak of purity.

And a poet mercenary pirate smuggler lover monk. Who was also a *Ragkiril*.

I didn't need any more questions right now. But they hovered again, beating their wings like little frenzied demons in my brain.

It wasn't the fifteen minutes of Berri's impassioned pleadings in the temple office that swayed Sully into agreeing she could come with us to Marker. It was the fact that she was going there anyway. Legitimately. Englarians were opening a temple in Marker to service the Takan shipyard workers.

"Providential," Verno said, grinning.

We could toss our plans for a surreptitious infiltration of the Fleet yards. We could walk in, unchallenged, bearing the arch-and-stave.

"I'm surprised Drogue didn't mention the new temple," Sully commented to her.

"Not surprising at all. The Marker temple has been my project now for almost two years. But it's in-system, under Guardian Lon. Moabar operates under our outsystem venue."

"Sister Berri's done much fund-raising," Verno added. "I'd always heard of the wonderful Sister Berri Solaria. But until we met six months ago, I didn't understand how very hard she's worked for this."

"The abbot guides me in his mercy, in all that I do," she said sedately. But she blushed.

Verno stayed behind to help Berri finish her duties. Sully wanted to spend a few more hours on dock, then head out. He never spent more than ten hours, he told me as we headed for the lifts, in any one stationary location, unless his ship was in for repairs. We'd already been on dock for six.

"Escalator?" he asked, seeing the lines.

I nodded. We turned. A cluster of female techs passed us by, but not without a few blatantly appreciative stares at Sully.

He grinned when I looked back at him. He'd seen the women, and me watching them.

"Sully . . ."

"Hmm?"

"How long were you a monk?"

A few more steps, and he was still grinning. "This surprises you, doesn't it?"

He knew damned well it did. He just wanted to hear me admit it. "I know you. Intimately. So yes." I paused. "How long?"

"Eight years, three months. Do you want weeks, days?" He asked the question over his shoulder, turning, because I'd stopped in the middle of the corridor.

"Eight years?"

"Eight years, three months." He thought for a moment. "Two weeks, four days? Or was it three weeks, four days?"

"If you're lying to me about this—"

"I never lie."

No. He just told me bits and pieces. "Why didn't you tell me before this?"

He stepped closer. "I'm not exactly comfortable with much of my past. I think you know that," he said softly. "Plus, I didn't think it was important."

"It's not." We started walking again. "It's just that I sometimes wonder if I'm ever going to figure you out."

"I hope not," he said with a wicked Sully grin. He took my hand and sent spirals of warmth up my arm.

We went to a pub up on Red Level. A long, narrow bar with, I was surprised to see, a Stolorth male behind it. He had bright, clear, silver eyes. In spite of everything I knew about Ren, about *Ragkirils,* a shudder went up my spine.

Sully motioned me to a bar stool, then took the one next to mine, unlatching it from the deck lock. He pulled his close, draping his arm over my shoulder.

"Two brown ales, Trel." He nodded to the bartender.

Like Ren, Trel's bluish hair was long, braided. But it was thin, his hairline receded. His lean features lacked Ren's elegance, and so appeared harsh.

"Ross Winthrop," Trel answered. "Didn't expect to see you so soon."

"Didn't expect to see me so soon, or didn't expect to see me alive?"

Trel glanced at me. Reading me, that much I was sure. I was in Fleet-captain mode, keeping my emotions flat. If he was a *Ragkir* or a *Ragkiril* I couldn't tell. Sully, I was sure, could. The fact that Trel called him "Ross

Winthrop" told me it was likely he was a basic empath or, at best, a *Ragkir*. Or else he'd know Sully lied about his identity.

The Stolorth shrugged at Sully's question and glanced at me again.

"My wife, Trel. Talk to her as you'd talk to me."

Trel raised one eyebrow. "Newly married?"

"Very."

Trel relaxed a bit, his mouth curving into a half smile. "She's still fighting that leash, Winthrop. You may not know that, but you know I can tell."

Sully's eyes widened in innocent distress. "Chaz. You told me you wanted to get married."

Trel had picked up on my inadvertent flinch when Sully called me his wife. I knew he was kidding, using it as a cover for a reason. But it still made me feel funny inside. "I did. I do. It's just that—"

"Bad first marriage." Sully gave Trel a knowing look. "At least, I hope that's what it is."

"I can find out for you." He held out his webbed hand toward me.

I jerked backward.

Trel seemed pleased. Not like Ren, who didn't want to hurt, didn't want to cause discomfort. Trel seemed to like the fact I was afraid of him.

"So why are you surprised to see me, old friend?" Sully moved back to the original conversation. "Who did I so piss off last time I was here that they threatened to come after me?"

"Besides Junior and the twelve thousand he lost to you in cards?"

Before I could stop them, the words were out of my mouth. "You won at cards?"

I was rewarded with another affronted look.

"Don't know your new husband too well, do you?"

Trel set a tall ale in front of me and one in front of Sully. "Took Junior for twelve thousand last time he was in. Took Junior and Scaper for twenty a few months before that. And those are only the big games that I know about."

"Amazing," I said.

"Thank you, my angel." His finger traced small circles on my shoulder. "So Junior said he was going to hunt me down?"

"Not that I heard."

"Then who's asking questions about me?"

Trel ran his wide hand over his head. "Running a little low on supplies these days."

Sully pulled out his thin comm pad from the front pocket of his jacket, tapped it on. "Your man signed for a playbox two hours ago. You might want to check your back room. We'll wait. Ale's cold."

Trel straightened, nodded, and left.

Playbox. Smuggler's term for a couple of containers of honeylace. "He knows Newlin?" I asked quietly but with obvious sarcasm. I'd just participated in an illegal drug sale with my new husband.

"No. But I'm sure they could be good friends."

I leaned toward him as if seeking a kiss. "*Ragkir?*" I breathed the word against his lips.

He kissed me, shaking his head in a small negative movement, then pulled back slightly. "Base-level empath. Not to worry. I've got you covered." He tickled my shoulder with his fingers again.

Trel came back, looking satisfied. Then his smile faded. He leaned his elbows on the bar, brought his face close to Sully's. "Someone's been asking about you. Not by name. Description. And not in here. But I've heard."

"Describe him."

"Human. Shorter than you. Light hair, eyes. Beard.

Looks like a hundred other jumpjockeys on dock except he tries to act quiet, stupid. And he's not. He's a fighter. Wears his shirts extra big, to cover the muscles. He can move real fast when he wants to. I watched him for a while. He was talking to Ilsa."

"Who else did he talk to?"

"Junior told him nothing. Don't know who else."

"How long ago?"

Trel thought. "I didn't notice him until Junior said something, and that was the day after your ship left last time. But when I saw him, that's when I remembered seeing him with Ilsa. And you were still here, because that's the night you took Junior for the twelve thousand."

"He was here while I was? While my ship was still in dock?"

Trel nodded. "At Pops's you were, right?"

"He stayed two, three days, after the *Echo* left?"

But Sully and Ren, I knew, left on Milo's ship. While the man hunting Sully watched the *Boru Karn*. While Pops's daughter, Ilsa, who wanted to be on Sully's list of women, had access to the *Boru Karn,* as one of Pops's employees. Would Marsh or Gregor question her appearance at the docks? Would they stop her if she tried to get on board, perhaps even offer her a tour of the ship, of their cabins? Or had she been a guest in Sully's cabin before and knew her way around?

Did she have the skills to initiate a worm program? Or did she even need to get on board? She had access to any parts going into the *Karn.* She had access to the ship's schematics in her father's databases. She would have been on board before Kingswell's pad was, but she could have tinkered with the hologrid in the ready room. . . .

Sully's firm grip on my arm halted my thoughts. Shit.

Trel was an empath. I'd momentarily forgotten that. I tamped down my speculations and sipped my ale. Sully wrapped up the conversation. I accepted Trel's congratulations like the blushing bride I was supposed to be and walked out, still snugged against him.

"Sorry," I said softly. "Sorry. Sorry." I was a Fleet officer. I knew better. But there were no regs against speculating in Fleet. "Once I grabbed what he was saying, I couldn't stop analyzing it."

He stepped out of the flow of traffic to wrap his arms around me. "Your mind is like a little whirlwind, do you know that? Everything gets sucked in, sorted, flung around, resorted, categorized."

"Sorry."

"Don't be. It was...fascinating." He paused. "You're not angry with me?"

Why would I—Because he'd been in my mind. Reading my thoughts. Watching me sort them, fling them around. Doing what I'd told him not to. But then I had rescinded that order. "No. You had to do that, because of Trel, is that right?"

"You don't know how to block your thoughts, your emotions. Trel's abilities, as long as he's not touching you, are about on the level of Ren's. I had to put up a temporary wall."

I looked up at his infinitely dark eyes. "I didn't even know."

"Couldn't tell?"

"No."

"Neither could Tessa."

A worry, one I still held on to. Young Tessa. Her mind in shreds, Philip had said.

Philip had lied. Or else someone had lied to Philip.

I closed my eyes, releasing the worry from my mental duro-hard, letting it go. Then wondered again why I thought Sully had told me nothing about himself. He had, he'd been telling me volumes. I just didn't know how to listen. "Thank you," I said softly.

"You're welcome, angel. Now, let's get moving. I've got to talk to Gregor and Marsh again. Ask them some direct questions in a manner they're not going to like. About Ilsa. And Lazlo."

"Lazlo?"

"Lazlo. A quiet but not stupid man with a beard. And a muscular build he doesn't want anyone to notice. My cousin Hayden's personal bodyguard."

25

I met Ren in the corridor as he left the ready room, his usual peaceful demeanor clearly troubled. He looked rumpled, his braid unraveling as if he'd been running his fingers through his hair. He'd been in there with Sully and Marsh, then Aubry and then Gregor, for almost two hours.

I'd been in the bridge hatchway a half hour earlier when Gregor barged out of the room and strode angrily down the corridor, his "goddamned filthy mind-fucker" litany echoing as he headed for his cabin.

His comment, I knew, had been aimed at Ren. No one knew Sully was the one doing the probing.

I touched Ren's arm. "Want me to get you a mug of hot tea?"

"Please. It would be much appreciated."

I brought it to his cabin. He was in one of the padded chairs next to the couch, elbows on his knees, hands clasped. I put the tea on the low table in front of him and went in search of his comb.

He sipped it as I perched on the arm of his chair,

untied his braid, and began combing it out. Slowly, his shoulders relaxed, his breathing became less shallow, constricted.

"Since everyone left the room still alive, I gather none of them helped Ilsa, or this Lazlo, set a worm into the *Karn*."

Ren sighed. "Both Gregor and Aubry knew Ilsa came on board. Neither remembered seeing Lazlo with her. Neither says Ilsa was left alone long enough to do any harm, but she was on the bridge. She did bring some grid boards. And as she'd been on this ship before . . ."

My hands hesitated only slightly, but he caught it.

"Not that way, Chasidah. She has never been Sully's lover, though not for lack of effort on her part. But she knows Marsh from when he worked on another ship."

"Thanks." I gave him a grin he couldn't see and tugged on his braid the way Sully often tugged on mine.

"Anyway, as Pops's daughter, her intentions, her allegiances, were never in question."

"Until now."

"Until now."

"Did she program a worm?"

"I don't know. Sully doesn't know. The grid board she brought was heavily damaged during the systems failure."

"Is Sully going to talk to her?"

"Lazlo's appearance interests him more. Whatever Ilsa did, if anything, was more than likely at Lazlo's instigation. It's Lazlo, or really Burke, we must be concerned about. Ilsa was simply a means, a method. It's also quite possible she's not even aware she did anything wrong."

I knew that. Someone posing as a parts supplier could have presented her with a new and improved grid. Or optic feed. Or sensor link. And she'd put it on the *Karn*.

At that point, she was still trying to get into Sully's bed. Not be a mourner at his funeral.

I finished his braid, retied the thin leather band at the bottom. "Better?"

He reached back, ran his hand down its smooth length. "Much."

"And you? I think you're wearing your worry colors."

He leaned back against the cushion and looked up at me with his clouded silver eyes. I didn't think Gregor had been the only one emitting anger, perhaps even hatred, at being probed empathically. Ren had felt it, taken it all, directed at himself. For Sully's sake.

"Things will be a bit tense for a while. They all felt safe, thought my blindness protected them. Now they feel their privacy is compromised." He hesitated. "Gregor is threatening to leave, to stay on Dock Five."

"Leave?" Gregor knew that Gabriel Ross Sullivan was alive, posing as Ross Winthrop. Gregor knew that Chaz Bergren was no longer on Moabar. And that we were headed for Marker, with the intention of destroying a portion of the Imperial Fleet shipyards.

Gregor definitely knew too much.

"Wasn't there any way you could have accomplished the same results, reading them, without their knowledge?" I hadn't felt Sully slip into my mind, my thoughts, at all in Trel's bar.

"Sully'd already done that, the first time he talked to them. But for a deep mind probe, physical contact is sometimes necessary. More so because Sully couldn't touch them without giving away what he is. The contact had to come through me, my hand on their arm. For that reason, too, it was still an inaccurate link."

"No one caught the fact that you were touching Sully too?" I would have. I saw it in Sully's cabin back at the

Moabar Temple. I just didn't know I was seeing them link at that time.

"I wasn't touching Sully. Ours was purely a mind link."

"You just said a deeper probe needs physical contact. How could Sully read without touching you?"

Ren hesitated. "Sully is a very high-level *Ragkiril*. He can work through another's mental link if a *ky'an*—that is, a permissive bond—has been established. Physical contact enhances that but it's not required."

I knew there were *Ragkir* and *Ragkiril*. And thought that was all there was. "There are additional levels of *Ragkiril*?"

"In both *Ragkir* and *Ragkiril*, yes. Sully told me he explained the differences to you."

"It's not sinking in, I guess. I do know some *Ragkirils* can heal."

"For which I am forever grateful." Ren smiled wistfully. "I have yet so much to learn, so much to experience. I wasn't ready to leave this existence yet." He tilted his face. His voice became softer, rain trickling over *maiisar* blossoms, ruffled by the breezes. "I would miss Sully. And I would miss you, Chasidah. You have become very precious to me."

I kissed him lightly on the forehead. "If Dorsie doesn't adopt you, I will."

He smiled, almost shyly, flustered. Very un-Ren. "So, to continue with your lesson, yes, there are different levels. Both with *Ragkir* and *Ragkiril*. Sully, being a high-level *Ragkiril*, can work outside certain physical parameters."

I thought for a moment. And that thought contained five angels of heart-stars cards. "Can a high-level *Ragkiril* manipulate matter?"

"What has he said when you've asked him this question?"

"I haven't asked. It just occurred to me." It also occurred to me that Ren's question was, in itself, an affirmative. Or else he would've simply said "no." Almost mind-boggling. Matter manipulation. That would explain his wins in cards on Dock Five. And his losses to Ren, who would catch such "tricks." "You know how he feels about questions, Ren. There are times he's willing to talk. There are times, I think, it's just too painful."

"The pain comes from a fear of rejection. I think you know this."

"Mistakes can be made through ignorance, lack of information," I countered.

"He knows this too. I can't find that balance for you. That's something you and Sully must find for yourselves."

I crossed my arms over my chest. "How can I adopt you, act like your mother, when most of the time you sound so much wiser than I do?"

"I am more than honored just to be considered your friend. Besides, it would pain me to know that you and Dorsie would be fighting over me."

A grin. A half smirk. I recognized it. Ren had his own Sully grin.

I punched him playfully on the shoulder as I stood to leave. "You've been hanging around Sullivan too much, you know that?"

Sully wasn't in our cabin or the ready room. When I asked Marsh, on duty on the bridge, where Sully was, he only shrugged. His eyes wouldn't meet mine.

"Did he go back on dock?"

Marsh glanced at the console. The *Karn* was running

through the usual predeparture systems checks, with two hours to go. "He didn't key out at the airlock, no."

I started to turn, hesitated. "Marsh, Ren's okay. Don't judge him like that."

Something hard flitted across Marsh's features. "Sure."

"I've been through it too—a mind scan. You know Sully wouldn't have asked him to do it if it weren't absolutely necessary."

"It wasn't necessary. Not with me. Dorsie and I've been with him for too long. That's the only reason I'm still sitting here. For Sully. Not for that mind-fucker."

I remembered that prejudice. I used to have it. It seemed like another lifetime ago.

I went down a deck. Aubry was in engineering, alone. The gym was empty. Crew cabins came after that, but I didn't bother checking them. I could hear voices—loud, angry—coming from Dorsie's galley.

"It was none of his fucking business, Sully. I told you. You want to know something, you ask. You don't like my answer, you tell me to hit the docks. That's the only way I've ever worked."

"You know it was necessary."

"I know you suddenly changed the rules. And I don't like these new ones."

I hesitated in the doorway. Gregor straddled a chair, his wide hands gripping the back. He was in profile to me and didn't see me. But Dorsie, next to him, did, though she didn't acknowledge my presence. She sat, arms across her chest, her face sullen. Her gaze traveled disinterestedly over me.

Sully stood on the other side of the table, hands shoved into his pockets. His mouth was a tight line. "No one walks off this ship right now. I can't risk it."

"And I can't risk having my brains fried by some

mind-fucker because maybe he doesn't like the way I answer a question. Maybe he doesn't like the way I scratch
my ass." Gregor jabbed a finger at Sully. "I saw these
fuckers during the war. I worked interrogation security.
I know what they do!"

Gregor suddenly turned, saw me. "You didn't turn
him loose on her, did you?"

"He did." I stepped into the mess hall, spoke before
Sully could.

Gregor's eyes glittered with anger. "I didn't see you
get called in for a private chat with our favorite
Stolorth."

"Chaz went through a mind scan right after it happened." Sully took a step closer to the table. "That's
how I knew she didn't program a worm into the datapad."

"You found one there!" Gregor challenged.

"I found traces of what a worm could do. Which
could be the residue of the program causing the sabotage. Or it could be the pad taking the same damage we
did since it was hooked into the hologrid when the
Karn's systems went down."

I remember Sully stating it was a possibility, though a
remote one. The damage could've come from an upload
or a download.

"Further"—Sully leaned his palms flat against the
table—"Chaz wasn't on board when this ship was at
Pops's for repair. Chaz didn't know Ilsa. And she sure as
hell doesn't know Lazlo."

Gregor's eyes narrowed. "Some mind-fucker tell you
that?"

Sully nodded slowly. "Some mind-fucker told me
that." He straightened and shoved his hands back into
his pockets.

I headed for the table on Sully's left while he argued

with Gregor. There was undisguised loathing on Gregor's face. Gregor hated Ren. And didn't realize that, by doing so, he also condemned Sully.

"This is what it comes down to," Gregor said heatedly. "You said you want me to stay. Fine. But only if that mind-fucker leaves."

"Ren stays. You stay. There are no options here."

Gregor studied Sully as if measuring him up. Perhaps remembering the hand that had pinned him to the pilot's chair. "Then I want him locked in the brig. Aubry agrees with me. So does Marsh."

"Unacceptable."

I recognized that word, that tone. Sully was losing patience.

"Then I walk. We all walk."

His mouth tight, Sully asked, "Dorsie?"

I couldn't believe Dorsie would back Gregor. She was friends with Ren, teased him. But she'd been silent since I arrived. I hadn't heard her voice in the corridor. And she hadn't seemed pleased to see me when I'd walked in.

If Dorsie left, Ren would be hurt. Terribly hurt.

"You told us he couldn't do those things." Her voice was strained.

"The fact that he can—this is more important than everything else he is?" Sully's voice softened. I knew he wasn't only asking about Ren. "Because of something he can't change about himself, something he was born to be, you condemn him?"

Dorsie knotted her hands together, her gaze on the movement of her fingers.

"Dorsie," I said. "Sully asked Ren for his help in this. It wasn't as if Ren just decided one day to go rummaging around in your thoughts. Or Gregor's. Or mine."

"But he could have," Gregor put in bitterly. "He could have. Anytime in the past. Anytime he wants to.

That's what he is, a mind-fucker. You're Fleet, Bergren. You know what they can do."

The Grizni flashed into my hand. I angled it at Gregor. "I could also have killed you anytime in the past few weeks. Anytime in the past few hours. That's part of what I am. But it's not the only thing I am."

I slapped the Grizni back around my wrist and looked at Dorsie again. "Is anyone here ready to let go of their childish fears and think about the larger issues? The Empire is breeding jukors again. And someone is trying to kill us because we want to stop that. That scares me one hell of a lot more than a blind empath."

"It's going to take some getting used to," Dorsie said uncertainly, after a moment. "But I'm willing to try."

Gregor slammed his hand on the back of his chair, shoved himself to his feet. "Fools, all of you." He glared at Dorsie, at me, then finally at Sully. "You don't know what they can do. I do. Destroying minds is nothing. They can melt your skin right off your body. Without touching you. They can take this, this chair." He wrenched it from the deck lock. "Make it into a laser rifle. Kill you with it. Or worse. Into a nightmare, some image they pull from your mind. Torture you with it."

He pushed it aside, roughly. It fell sideways, clanged against the decking. "And they can also," he said, as silence descended, "change what they look like. I've seen what they really look like." This last he aimed at Dorsie, then spun on his heels, stalked for the door.

He stopped just short of the corridor and turned. "You know those jukors you're so anxious to kill? Ugly things, aren't they?" He threw one more hard look at Dorsie. "Not at all like your blue-haired pretty boy." He paused. "Or are they?"

He strode down the corridor, his boot steps as hard and jarring as his words.

Dorsie's brow furrowed. Troubled. Worried. Frightened. I wanted to tell her that Gregor had exaggerated, misusing the old legends about soul-stealers, mythical shape-shifters, but Sully spoke first.

"Ren's not some kind of demon." Sully's voice was kind yet firm. "He can't—"

Intraship trilled, echoing in the corridor. The sound halted Sully's words.

Dorsie stood, reached for the comm panel on the counter behind her. "Galley. Dorsie." Her voice was flat, lacking its usual buoyancy.

"He's there?" It was Marsh, looking for Sully.

"Yes."

"Tell him Verno's on board. With that Sister woman."

"Acknowledged," Sully said, loud enough for Marsh to hear him.

"We've got clearance coming through, fifteen minutes. Any changes?"

I knew he meant more than just departure instructions. He wanted to know if anyone was leaving the crew. Or being confined to the brig.

"Confirm our slot, Marsh. Fifteen minutes. I'll be on the bridge in five."

26

Sully. Worried and troubled, anger simmering just below the surface. Sully. Afraid.

I didn't have a grain of empathic ability in my body, but I knew Sully, knew the dark, haunted look in his eyes as he glanced at me, then headed for the door. I hesitated only long enough to reach for Dorsie, squeeze the hand she held out to me. I wished I knew how to send those warm, comforting spirals Ren could. Sully could.

I sprinted for the corridor and caught up with him at the stairs. When I slipped my hand into his, his skin was cold.

"Hold up for a few minutes. Marsh knows the routine. Verno will be there."

He took his foot off the stair tread and leaned wearily against the stairwell wall. He was distant, nothing coming through his touch but a deep chill. A defensive mechanism. He was shutting himself off from all the emotions churning through the ship.

"They're staying," I told him. "Forget about anything else that was said."

"I can't."

"You have to. Gregor's always going to find something—"

"Not Gregor. Dorsie. She was ready to walk out."

"She was afraid."

"Of Ren. She was the only one who would even talk to him when I brought him on board. She was the only one who'd sit at a table with him. Share a meal, a drink with him. Laugh with him. Be his friend." He shoved himself away from the wall. "I just destroyed that. He doesn't know yet, but he'll sense it. Her rejection is going to scar him deeply."

"I'm sure he's faced that before," I said softly.

His eyes were hard, infinite. "She's not rejecting him because of what he is. She's rejecting him because of me. Because of what I am." His voice suddenly rasped. "How can I call myself his friend and permit that?"

Intraship trilled again in the corridors. "Ten minutes to push-back, Sully-sir."

"Fuck." Sully yanked his hand from mine and pounded up the stairs.

Aux thrusters fired, angling us. The *Boru Karn* slid away from Dock Five, sublights on idle but ready, bridge crew at stations but quiet, thinking, fearing, wishing, hoping...

Not Ren. Ren was in his quarters until things calmed down. Not Gregor, even though he was first pilot. Marsh sat his shift for now. Sully sat nowhere, not at engineering, not at any one place on the bridge, but walked, pacing, making small, meaningless adjustments on the boards.

Verno sat at helm, grinning, singing an Englarian hymn off key in his gravelly voice. All was well with his world. Sister Berri Solaria was on board, ensconced in the other bedroom in Dorsie's suite.

I sat at communications, flirted with departure control as if nothing was wrong, as if Sully wasn't mired in his own personal Hell, a ghost who suddenly realized his very transparency placed those who stood behind him at risk.

We hit outer beacon, downloaded the news banks, the advisories, the gossip. Everything that had happened in the past thirty minutes since we'd left Dock Five.

Verno keyed in the course change and headed for the inner lanes. For Marker.

Three days. Three days until we could save the universe from the virulent infection of jukors. Three days to try to work some healing miracles on board.

Sully. Ren. Nothing was dearer to me right now. Not even my own life.

Sully left the bridge when we hit the lanes. Work to do, he announced, on the hologrid in the ready room. I tried to catch his glance. His gaze swept over me, then turned away. I knew he needed some time alone. I gave it to him.

Aubry wandered in early. I let him take communications and went down to the galley again. I didn't know what to say to Dorsie. But I did want to tell her I'd been afraid of Ren once too. That I'd learned to see beyond that.

She was stacking supplies in a back room and straightened when I came in.

"Got a minute?" I motioned to the tables in the mess hall.

Her fists clenched, not in anger, I could tell, but indecision. She didn't know if she was ready to talk about this. Yet.

"It'll make you feel better," I told her.

I told her more: how I'd bolted out of my chair at the monastery, uncoiled my dagger when I saw Ren. How I'd watched him on the *Lucky Seven*. How he'd diverted the MOC officer's attention on station. How he'd gone to the dock to find out what happened to Milo. And how his calm presence pervaded it all. I told her I'd slept in a cot in Ren's cabin, knowing he was an empath, knowing he could read me. And that he'd read my sadness, early in the morning. Tried to ease my pain. Tried to assuage my fears. And tenderly, gently, ever-so-cautiously touched my face because he wanted to see a human woman.

When I'd fought with Sully, Ren had brought me tea, not questions or recriminations. When I'd rejected Sully—though I didn't tell her why—Ren made me understand the pain my rejection had caused. And Ren had sent me rainbows. That I did explain. His touch could send rainbows. Warm ones, loving ones, accepting ones.

She opened her hands to stare at her palms. "Once or twice, maybe. I remember that. But I didn't understand what it was."

"He has a gift. Gregor may call it a curse, but he doesn't know what he's talking about. I know Ren. It's a gift. He cares very much for your friendship, Dorsie."

"Gregor said he—they—look like jukors. They can change what they look like."

"I've spent most of my life in Fleet and have never seen anything proving shape-shifters exist. If they did, believe me, someone in Fleet would know. And we'd have been trained to deal with that."

She sat, shaking her head, then finally brought her gaze to meet mine. "Thank you. You've given me something to think about." She stood. "I've got to finish inventory."

Sister Berri was just coming through her cabin doorway when I passed by. Dorsie's suite, as well Verno's and the one Marsh and Aubry shared, were on this deck. Sully's cabin, Ren's, and Gregor's, as first pilot, were one deck up, behind the bridge.

Berri looked flushed, excited.

"All settled in?" I asked her.

"Praise the stars, yes. Such luxury. My own bathroom. I shall feel quite spoiled."

"If you need anything, let me or Dorsie know. You know where the galley is?" I realized, with all the turmoil and Berri's late entry, she might not have been given a tour.

She shook her head, confirming my supposition. "I'm sure I can find my way."

"It's not far." I pointed down the corridor. "Dorsie's there, working inventory. She might like some help."

"That's what I'm here for." Berri thrust her small chin higher. "Then perhaps later she might like to join me in prayer."

Some quiet, peaceful contemplation might do Dorsie a great deal of good.

I couldn't find Sully anywhere. Not in the ready room, not in our cabin. Not on the bridge. I called Ren on intraship.

"I've not seen him, Chasidah. Have you tried the gym?"

Not there either. Not in the galley, where I could hear Berri's melodic voice and Dorsie's sultry tones mixing.

I checked the tender bay, storage holds, engineering twice. Finally I went back to our cabin; worried, but not overly so. He'd been pacing earlier. He might well still be doing that now, and we were simply like two planets on opposite orbits.

We'd been off shift for several hours. I waited, not wanting to go to bed without him. I fought the desire to call for him on open intraship. It wasn't anyone else's business that the infallible Gabriel Ross Sullivan needed some time alone. I just didn't understand why he needed that time away from me.

That finally worried me enough to call Ren again. "Did I wake you?"

"Not at all. Just finishing meditations."

"Sorry." I paused. I'd hoped to hear he was finishing up a card game instead. "Sully's not here, Ren. I haven't seen him in a couple hours."

"A moment." I heard Ren sigh and remembered what he'd said. He could link with Sully—or rather, Sully, being stronger, could link with him. I waited.

"He's blocking me."

Because he didn't want Ren to know what Gregor had said. What Dorsie felt. "Do you know where he is?"

"No. Only that his pattern is strong. He may be working some things through."

"It's just that . . . well, never mind. Thanks."

"Blessings, Chasidah."

I clicked off intraship, then headed for the bedroom. I had to be on duty in five hours. I threw on my nightshirt and crawled into bed, leaving the light on the desk in the main room glowing on half power. I couldn't sleep. I stared at the red numbers on the clock in the dimmed cabin lighting.

The cabin door slid open, spearing the dim room with a shaft of bright light. Sully leaned against the doorjamb, then slowly walked in. He stopped at the chair, one hand on its back, steadying himself. Then stepped toward the couch. He collapsed onto it just as my feet hit the floor.

"Sully!"

He was angled into the corner, his legs splayed wide. He dragged one leg up, dropped his foot onto the low table with a thud as I kneeled next to him on the cushions.

"Chazzy-girl." He reached for me, his arm landing heavily on my shoulder.

I leaned forward, kissed him. And tasted the cloying sweetness of honeylace. "You're furred, Sully."

"Oh, very. Very, very."

I let out a sigh and touched his face. Chilled. Like his hand on my shoulder. "You okay?"

"Me? Sure."

I took his other hand and tried to rub some warmth into his skin. He felt clammy. His face was very pale.

"You're going to feel like shit when you wake up, you know."

He arched an eyebrow. "Never do."

I remembered him sitting in the common room of the temple, the morning after Peyhar's. His disheveled appearance then could dispute that.

"Where've you been? I was worried."

"Looking in a mirror."

I didn't know if he meant that literally or figuratively, though I knew he disliked mirrors. "Watching yourself get furred?"

"Something like that." His fingers skimmed my cheek. His touch was still very cold.

"I think you need a hot shower. Then some sleep."

"Later."

"Sully, you're like ice." I framed his face. Icy and sweating. This was more than just an emotional shutdown. Was he having a reaction to the honeylace? Did someone put something in the honeylace? Poison?

There was a med-kit in the bathroom. I rose but his hand caught my wrist, pulled me back down. "It'll pass. It's . . . nothing."

"I disagree. You're cold, sweating—"

"Respiration shallow, heartbeat erratic. It will pass." He was still half leaning, half sprawling on the couch, but his grip on my wrist was strong and firm. He seemed to realize that. His fingers loosened. "Get some sleep, my angel."

"Not without you."

"I won't be very good company. I'm certainly not a very good friend."

"Sully, don't do this."

He watched me through half-closed eyes. "I can't change what I am, Chasidah."

"I know," I said softly. "I don't want you to."

"Foolish child." His voice suddenly rasped. He pulled me onto his chest, wrapping his arms around my back. His mouth pressed against my forehead.

But it was a long while before I felt any warmth coming from his body.

When I woke, I was in bed, alone. I sat up quickly. Sully was gone. I had an hour before duty shift. I showered, dressed, and plaited my hair in a sloppy braid.

I went down one deck to the galley. Dorsie was making a fruit salad. I nibbled, then asked if she'd seen Sully.

"Had some tea with Verno earlier," she said.

"You doing okay with Sister Berri?"

"Sweet kid. No problem."

"Talked to Ren yet?"

Dorsie took her gaze from me to inspect a bright-apple. "I'll probably run into him later, if he comes in for tea."

I nodded, left. Didn't want to push it. Some things have to come about in their own time.

Verno was exiting the ready room when I walked up. "Will do, Sully-sir. Oh, blessings of the hour, Captain Chasidah."

I stepped in behind him. The hologrid was up, Sully seated in front of it. I could see the data on Crossley Burke and a list of shipping manifests. Sully watched me enter but said nothing.

I sat on the edge of the table in front of him. He was clean shaven, his dark eyes clear. Not a whisper of a hangover. "Headache?"

"Never. I told you."

"That's disgusting. Everyone should have to suffer a little." As soon as I said it, I knew it was the wrong choice of words.

His smile was thin. "I suffer in other ways."

"I talked to Dorsie yesterday. Just about Ren. I think things may be okay in that regard."

"Aubry's refusing to work with him."

"So let Gregor and Aubry work the same shift."

"I thought of that. I also don't know if I trust them in control of this ship while the rest of us are off duty, or sleeping." He picked up a lightpen from the table, held it between his fingers.

"You're saying they don't care what's happening at Marker?" Aubry had been very vocal in his hatred of the jukors.

"I think my mishandling of the interviews recently has eclipsed that."

"You did what had to be done."

"That's Fleet talking. Interrogations are Fleet methods. Not mine. Gregor was right. In the past, if I didn't like what someone said or did, they hit the docks."

"The situation here's a bit more serious than a disagreement over how to hijack a shipment of synthemeralds."

"All the more reason I know I've made an error. I now have a crew who may choose to ignore my orders. Marsh is undecided, but Aubry's been working on him. They want Ren off this ship or in the brig. I can't do that. I won't do that."

"You're talking three of them against five of us, six if you count Berri."

"You're assuming Dorsie will side with us, with Ren."

"I am."

"That still only gives us three who can actually run this ship: you, me, and, to some extent, Verno. Ren's capabilities are limited. Verno's job is navigation and only that. He doesn't know the systems, isn't certified as a pilot. Dorsie can cook but wouldn't know a hyperdrive if it bit her. I imagine the same's true of Berri. She can pray and bless us, but she can't work a shift."

"You sound like you're thinking of returning to Dock Five, letting Gregor go."

"I won't put Ren in the brig. It would give credence to what Gregor's been saying." His voice rose, became hard. "I won't have him persecuted for something he isn't."

"Then make it clear to them. Ren is not a danger. If you have to, admit the Empire's been ignoring the distinction between a *Ragkir* and a *Ragkiril* all along. The mind talents Gregor heard about during the war were *Ragkiril* talents, isn't that right?"

He hesitated for a moment, then nodded.

"People like facts. If you don't give them the facts,

they'll start looking for them elsewhere. And they'll make mistakes, like believing what Gregor says is also the truth about Ren. That's not Fleet methodology. It's just common sense."

He leaned back in the chair, lightpen twirling absently between his fingers. He glanced at the closed door. "I can't prove to them that Ren's not a *Ragkiril* without proving that I am. Ren alone couldn't have pulled the information from their minds."

"If they can accept Ren, why can't they accept you?" I asked softly.

He slanted me a glance, as if he couldn't believe I'd asked that question.

"I did," I persisted.

"A fact that continually amazes me, my angel. But things are tense enough on board because of what we'll face at Marker. Knowing there's not only an empath but a *Ragkiril* on this ship may well be more than any of them, Dorsie included, wants to deal with."

"This is what happens when you withhold information from people, Sully."

"Reminding me of that doesn't solve the problem."

The door to the ready room slid open. Berri Solaria stood almost frozen in the doorway, her eyes wide, her hood sitting awkwardly on her head.

Then she charged in, fists clenched against her chest until she came within inches of Sully and myself. "Filthy, venomous soul-stealer! Accursed demon!" She pointed at Sully accusingly. "Mister Sullivan, you have a hideous Stolorth on board this ship!"

27

I was on my feet immediately. I grabbed the irate woman by the shoulders, forcing her into a chair. "Calm down, Sister, calm down!"

She wrenched in my grasp. "I saw him! In the dining hall, about to attack Dorsie. I screamed prayers of exorcism to protect her purity. He fled! Vile monster." She turned to Sully, ignoring my hand, hard, on her shoulder. "Brother Sudral. You must assist me. We can hunt him down."

Sully stood next to me, unmoving. I didn't remember him getting up. He stared at Berri, reading her, I guessed. Feeling her hatred for Ren. For himself.

"Ren's part of my crew," he said after a moment.

"Brother, your name is that of the holy robe used to restrain these creatures. Your ship, the *Boru Karn*, the sword of purity. You know the dark evil that exists inside of them—"

"Ren has none of it." Sully's voice was flat. "He's blind."

She straightened. "Blind? You're sure?"

"He was raised on Calfedar."

"In the Purity Project?"

"He was a student of mine for several years."

Some of her fervor dissipated. "He's been cleansed, then. I see." She knotted her fingers together. "I was not aware. That is tolerable. Providing, of course, he conducts himself properly."

Something in Berri's tone, in the arrogant tilt of her chin, made me want to slap her. More than once. This was Ren she was talking about. An Englarian, like herself. The man Verno called his brother.

Obviously, Sully wasn't the only one with a tendency to omit the facts. Verno had never told her about Ren either.

"You have nothing to fear from Ren," Sully said.

"I have no fear of their evil. As Abbot Eng dispersed the dark ghosts of Hell, so can I. Just as you have, since you've subjugated him."

I waited for Sully to say something, to explain that Ren was his friend. But his silence said more, his mouth taut, a muscle pulsing in his jaw. Finally he spoke, in a voice as deathly quiet as footsteps on a grave. "Have you performed your meditations yet, Sister? If not, permit me to suggest two for you. The Four Tiers of Tolerance. And the Seven Steps to Holy Humility. Now if you'll excuse us, Captain Bergren and I have important matters to discuss."

He turned his back on her and stared at the data on the hologrid.

Berri rose slowly. "Do not consort with demons," she said tightly as she stepped toward the door. "Or their very foulness will become yours."

I leaned against the table after the door closed behind her, feeling drained yet angry. Sully still stared at the hologrid. It was a few minutes before he turned around. "We have a problem."

I nodded. "Verno never told her about Ren."

"You're not going to add that I taught him well?"

"As you said earlier, that isn't the solution. But you know more than I do. How big of a problem is she?" When he frowned slightly, I continued. "You were reading her, weren't you?"

"I don't normally do that. With her, it's difficult enough just to deal with her emotions, her resonances. They"—he ran his hand through his hair in an exasperated motion—"they can sound, feel as loud as screams. Louder." He let out a harsh sigh. "She's very intense. And she's also very devout."

"So's Drogue, and Ren's his friend."

"Drogue's a different sect. Now. He once was a part of the original Englarians, the Purity Englarians, like I was. Guardian Lon heads that. Most of the inner-system churches follow Lon's interpretations. Drogue's part of the Reformed Englarian movement. There's more tolerance of nonhumans, more acceptance. A push for unity, not for domination."

"But the Englarians have always cared for the Takas."

"Listen to what you said. They cared for them. As if the Takas were incapable of caring for themselves. Drogue doesn't see it that way. Lon does. Both sects still build schools, clinics, temples. But the reasons they do so are slightly different."

"Ren was raised by these people. How could they save his life and hate him?"

"They saved his life because he's blind. He's been purified of the mind talents they feel are demonic in origin."

"This is what Berri believes?"

"She's a Purity Englarian. I didn't realize they were part of the temple on Dock Five. That was a Reformed temple, last I knew. But I honestly haven't been paying much attention to church politics lately."

"Will she still help us get access to Marker?"

A smile twisted on his lips. "Not if she finds out what I am."

I couldn't see the horrible demon Berri would think he was. So wrongly thought Ren was. "Maybe you ought to go check on Ren."

"You must be a mind reader." He stopped just long enough to stroke my face with his finger, then strode for the door.

I called Verno off the bridge. He'd heard none of Berri's encounter with Ren. And realized now he never told her the brother he often talked about was a Stolorth. He didn't know the temple on Dock Five was Purity Englarian.

"I've only been there a few times. Sister Berri performed many of the ritual blessing of the ships, would invite crew to services. She'd distribute prayer vids or hymns for meditations. That's how I know her."

He was upset, chastened. "I must speak to Ren. And Sully-sir."

"Sully went to talk to Ren. But anything you can say to help Berri see Ren is a valued, wonderful person would be a big help."

"Oh, praise the stars! Of course." He went back to the bridge, quietly. And there was no more singing off key of Englarian hymns.

Dorsie was my next destination. She was at her desk in the small office off the galley. "She showed me pictures on her bookpad last night. I remember those stories about shape-shifters who controlled this evil light. That stuff scared me when I was small. I thought they were myths, but she says they're true. Then this morning, those names she called him. I remembered those too. Soul-stealer. Winged Hellspawn."

"Ren doesn't have wings." I gave her a soft smile. "He couldn't hide them under that thermal shirt he wears."

"You can't always see them, that's what Sister Berri told me. They grow them from that light they use to kill people. She says they're shape-shifters. Like Gregor said."

I leaned my palms on her desk. "Dorsie. Ren is harmless. He reads empathic emotional resonances. It's like seeing a rainbow around your body. That's the only thing he can do. I swear to you."

"I want to believe that, Chaz. But if there are shape-shifters, and if they look like jukors—"

"If Ren were a shape-shifting jukor, I'd help Berri kill him." I didn't know how to make myself any plainer. I couldn't believe Dorsie thought those old scare tales were true.

"Ren couldn't shape-shift if he wanted to," said a voice tiredly behind me. Sully leaned against Dorsie's office doorway. "He's not going to sprout wings. But he's also not going to demand you be his friend. That's something you're going to have to offer yourself."

Dorsie nodded, then straightened a stack of datatabs on her desk, not meeting my gaze. "Yeah, you're right. Thanks."

I followed Sully out. "How's Ren?"

He shoved his hands in his pockets, struggled with his emotions. I knew the animosity directed at Ren disturbed him deeply. Finally, he let out a short, frustrated sigh. "Upset but trying to be his usual placid self. He'd heard, like we all had, only good things about Sister

Berri Solaria. No one warned us she was a religious fanatic."

"She isn't, to her own people."

"Agreed." He headed for engineering. Aubry's desk was empty. "I had Verno call him up to the bridge to recalibrate something minor," he said when I glanced toward Aubry's station. "I have to recalibrate something major."

Primary codes. Sully was changing the *Karn*'s primaries.

"What happened?"

He glanced up from the console. "I saw Gregor talking to Berri Solaria."

There were three ways to access the *Karn*'s primaries. From the bridge, from engineering, and from the console in Sully's cabin. He wasn't taking any chances. He'd already been to the bridge.

We went back to his cabin, recoded the primaries for the third and final time. Sully and I now were the only ones who could initiate a course change, send any outgoing transmits, take the ship through a jumpgate. Gregor was no doubt going to react to the latter. But as we had only one jumpgate between here and Marker, it wasn't an argument we'd have to repeat.

"Verno told me he didn't know Berri long enough to talk in detail about families. He met her at services, ship blessings. They discussed music or meditation methods."

Sully keyed in a request for a mug of tea, then paced in front of the couch. "It was Ren's idea to use Verno to help get answers from the Taka, who wouldn't always talk to either of us. Drogue approved. But Verno's a monk. He's not trained, he's not used to how I work. He wasn't even supposed to be here this run."

I remembered Berri saying she'd expected Verno to be at Peyhar's with her. "Maybe once he speaks to her, she'll calm down."

He sipped his tea. "She just has to get us through the shipyard main terminal. That's all I'm asking. After that, she can go perform purity rites on every damned dock in the yards for all I care."

"We've only got six more hours to jump. And thirty-six after that to Marker. We'll make it."

I took the *Karn* into jump. The ship, as expected, performed beautifully. Her crew, less so.

Gregor was off the bridge. Sully admitted the only reason he was even on board was because once Sully, Ren, and myself went into the shipyards, someone still had to pilot the ship, come back, and get us at meet-point. It was too risky to leave the *Karn* at Marker Terminal. Which meant codes would have to be amended, again. Which meant we had to trust Gregor to come back and get us.

To avoid further incidents, Ren voluntarily confined himself to his cabin.

I had yet to notice Dorsie visit him. I avoided Berri. Her sweetness now seemed simpering; her innocence, arrogant. But Gregor and Aubry didn't seem to feel that. She flirted quite openly with them, I noted with surprise. In a sweet and innocent way, of course. Yet she had very little to do with Verno. He was tainted, probably, by his friendship with Ren.

Her attitude toward Sully vacillated. She persisted in calling him Brother Sudral, as if she needed to remind him what he'd once been. She seemed to want him to ally himself with her. Renounce his worldly ways. She said her meditations clearly showed her that she was on a holy mission. And that Sully, and the jukors at Marker, were a part of that. But she was also dismissive of him. He was, after all, no longer one of her lofty peers.

We came out of jump no happier than when we went in. Except for Berri Solaria, handing out blessings.

Thirty-two hours to Marker.

It was bedtime, but both of us were too keyed up to be tired. We'd left Verno and Marsh on the bridge, then retired to our cabin because if we didn't get some sleep we'd be in no shape to face whatever waited for us at Marker. Sully was restless, pacing the cabin, fiddling with a stack of chart disks. I handed him my hairbrush as a means to distract him. He accepted it, kneeling behind me in the middle of the bed as he brushed out my hair.

"Are Englarian clergy celibate?"

The brush slowed and I heard something that was a cross between a sigh and a wry chuckle of laughter. After what had happened in the past few hours, his chuckle was a welcome sound. "Still thinking about that?"

"Don't you know?"

"I only peek when necessary and when I have your permission."

"Then maybe I'm not asking about you. Berri's been getting rather friendly with Gregor."

"Jealous?"

I flailed my arm behind me and somehow managed to cuff him on the shoulder.

"Settle down, you wicked woman. I think she's looking to convert him. Bedding him would mean breaking her vows."

"Then celibacy is a part of the vows?"

A few long strokes of the brush preceded his answer. "Yes."

Surprise rippled through me and I knew he felt it. I wanted to make sure he felt it. Little by little, I tried to use more nonverbal means to communicate with him. Let him know, in my own way, that I was comfortable with the hidden part of Gabriel Ross Sullivan. Hoping maybe if I was, he would be.

"And, yes, they were part of mine too," he added, to my unasked question.

"Why?" Sully was a naturally sensual person. A touch person, always with a hand on my arm or at my waist. Celibacy seemed totally uncharacteristic. "Don't tell me it was because some painting told you to be."

"Okay. I won't." He ran his fingers through my hair. "Sully . . ."

"My parents have an estate in Sylvadae."

As did a handful of other exorbitantly wealthy people, like the emperor. "So?"

"It was staffed by Takas."

"Englarians?"

"They'd take me to services."

"Your parents didn't mind?"

"My parents weren't around." There was a derisive note in his voice.

I'd seen holovids of some of the mansions in Sylvadae. And pictured, for the first time, a young boy all alone. Going to Englarian services, hearing about demonic mind talents and unholy lights. And waking up one morning to find rainbows coursing over his body.

I clasped the hand that absently toyed with my hair and held it tightly. I sent love, approval. Not pity. "Did you join the church as a gesture to the Takas who looked after you?"

"Partly. I think I felt that since they cared about me, their beliefs must be the right ones. Even though they didn't know what I was."

"A *Ragkiril*." He hated the word. I felt something go cold in him whenever I said it. It was that which damned him. What Berri called the darkness inside him. I still couldn't understand why.

"I took it as a sign. A cure. If I were devout enough, the abbot would remove this curse from me."

I brought his arm around my waist and leaned against him. "Then where would I be? Unhappily married to Philip? Dying on Moabar? Horrified with myself, because I'd killed Kingswell and Tessa Paxton? And maybe worst of all, I would've watched Ren die of fluid shock and been unable to do anything."

He rested his face against the top of my head but said nothing. Then suddenly he sent something through me I'd never felt from him before. A growing, out-flowing sense of respite, a thawing, a cleansing. Like starlight, bursting through a clouded night sky.

"Should I list more?" I asked softly.

Yes. For the first time since the *Loviti* incident, his voice was in my mind. Gentle. Shamed. Needy. But strong, full of a sincerity and pride. A pride that needed the knowledge that he had done the right thing. Especially after all the hatred he'd felt aimed at Ren. And because of Ren, at himself.

"Where would I be without you to love me? To make me crazy because you send these fireworks through me with your thoughts? Other women must have told you—"

"Just you. No one else."

"You never . . ."

"Not sharing my emotions, touching someone's, no." He hesitated. *You have all of me. All that I am is yours.*

His voice in my mind was as clear as if he'd spoken out loud. It didn't frighten me. I understood what he told me and why he was telling me this way. Not just

Sully's body, but his mind. More than that. His trust. And my trust, in that I didn't fear what he was. That I loved him with all that he was.

That he loved me enough to trust me with all that he was.

Like a ship sliding toward the edge of a jumpgate, we'd cautiously approached this point where love and trust and faith merged. We could only pass through it together. That was his offer. All of him. For all of me.

"You can have all of me too. Every last whirlwind in there, if you want it."

He pushed my hair to one side, nuzzled his face into my shoulder. Breathed. Sent warm rushes in and over me. Tingles. Heat. But still he held back something.

I want. Desperately I want this with you, Chasidah. Angel. But this is a very deep link. You must be sure.

"I am."

We have time. Just knowing you're willing is enough for me.

"But not for me. I want all of you."

He groaned softly. His hands stroked, caressed, explored me outwardly while warmth began to build, pulse. I pushed him down on the bed and stroked him in return. My mouth caressed a fire on his body.

His mind sent me his passion, mixed it with my own. Blended it, hard fire with sweet fire. I felt something stronger than the warmth that always flowed through my veins at his touch.

It felt molten. Yet it was incredibly delicate, like the whisper of a flame. It traced and retraced every inch of my body as if he knew me, yet didn't.

Because he didn't. This wasn't Sully the mercenary. This was Gabriel Ross Sullivan, touching with gentle fervency the edges of my mind with his own as we made love. Then slowly, going deeper, claiming everything I was as his own. It was as if his breath was mine, the beating of his heart was mine.

I relaxed into his strength, his power. And I invited him in.

Not yet, Chasidah-angel.

He rolled on top of me, all hard male, heated skin. That made me shift my focus outward, to the physical. I could smell the soap from his shower, clean and slightly salty, like the taste of him.

I wrapped my legs around him, took his mouth as he entered me, but it was slow. Very slow. Long, hard, and deliriously slow.

I arched against him. Waves of heat built, threatened to crash. He held me, poised, almost breathless . . .

Then body sensations and mind sensations merged, collided with a rush of incredible pleasure. I was soaring. Felt him soaring, rising. Felt as if a thousand wings beat against my skin, inside my skin, inside my heart.

I felt his passion crest as if it were my own. It was my own, flowing into his. Flowing from him. For a moment I glimpsed my own face as if through his eyes, my hair drifting like a cloud around me, down my arms, over his. Behind us and around us, gray fuzzy soft everywhere.

And then gray fuzzy soft exploded into bright silver stars, a thousand, a million. I closed my eyes and still they danced through my lids, sparkling. We plunged through them, clinging to each other. Spiraling upward.

The spiraling slowed. A warm wind rushed over me, past me, around me. Gentling me. Caressing me. I'd felt that wind before, but couldn't quite remember where.

I heard a sound, a soft hush, softer than our breathing. I'd heard that soft hush before, but couldn't quite remember when.

The wind caressed me again. Flowed down across my body. Moved up.

I had to know. My eyelids fluttered open. The darkness of Sully's infinite eyes was all I saw.

"Hush, Chasidah." He kissed my eyelids closed. "Don't . . . don't look. Just let me love you."

Warmth again. Caressing me. Surrounding me. Floating with me, rocking me gently. I felt safe. Loved. Incredibly complete. Both of us.

All that I am is yours.

I woke with Sully, warm, behind me. I turned, curled my fists into his chest, and nuzzled my head under his chin.

"Coffee?" he asked.

"Is it that time already?"

"You saw the clock when you turned over." He laughed quietly.

"Damn." I sighed theatrically, aware of his gentle presence in my mind. And that he'd seen the clock's red numbers through my eyes. "Yeah. Coffee."

Sully and I met Dorsie in the corridor between Gregor's cabin and Ren's. She had a pot of coffee in her hand. I hoped it was a good sign.

"How's Ren?"

"Haven't seen him yet. Marsh asked me to bring this to the bridge." She flashed a tight smile and moved past us.

I turned to watch her go. Sully's hand on my shoulder sent warmth seeping through in small waves. "You tried. I did too. There's not much more we can do."

The anguish in his eyes mirrored my own.

Eighteen hours.

Marker Shipyards was actually five starports of varying sizes on the fringe of the Aldanthian Drifts, a rich asteroid field that was the source for both metals and fuels. It was surrounded by security beacons and backed up by Fleet security patrols. The beacons would scan you, then warn you.

The security patrols would target you and, if you were lucky, just shoot your engines out so you could live to be interrogated.

Marker-1 was the largest starport, a cylindrical core out from which jutted the larger repair hangars and new-ship bays like thick, ungainly branches on a tree. Marker-2 was smaller, an administrative and residential facility a short shuttle hop from M-1. Commander Thad Bergren lived and worked in M-2. So did more than three hundred other people, both military and civilian. Marker-3 and -4 were secondary residential and repair facilities for smaller ships and less-prestigious workers. Techs, dockworkers, and Takas were usually housed in M-3.

M-5, also called Marker Outer Terminal, hung on the edge. Not dissimilar to Dock Five, it was long, like a mining raft. Three beacons guided us in. They were friendlier than the beacons surrounding the rest of the shipyards.

But then, we also squawked the right entry codes. Winthrop's *Gallant Explorer,* in service to the Englarian Church.

I watched the news vids we'd snagged from the latest beacon while we waited for dock space to clear. The *Karn,* now the *Explorer,* was a small ship compared to the commercial liners and freighters also queuing for space. We were also, therefore, low priority.

Welcome to Imperial News Watch. Top stories for in-system viewers.

Another mysterious rape and murder in a spaceport in Baris. And another mysterious disk left on the woman's body.

I flipped off the vid, glanced at the Englarian robes draped over the bed. Brother Sudral and Sister Chadra would accompany Sister Berri through security. Sully was in engineering, making sure this time my forged medical files were up to date.

I brought up the schematics on Marker-2. I knew the place by heart; I'd grown up there. But there had been some changes in the past few years. Changes I didn't know about, even when I'd visited Thad. Changes that had built private research labs with Crossley Burke money in a section of M-2 that used to be nothing but storage holds.

It had taken us two weeks of sifting every bit of data we could get, but that's where we believed the primary jukor labs were.

We didn't even want to think about the secondary

one yet—the one we believed was on a ship, movable, but not yet completed.

We had to start with what we did know. If we were lucky, we'd find evidence filling in the gaps about what we didn't know.

I reviewed the files Sully had tagged. There might not be another chance after this. My first selection was the vidclip of Hayden Burke at the party. Lazlo was there, in one frame, briefly. Sully had tagged it but I wanted to look for the man on my own, make sure I could pick his face out of a crowd.

I slowed the vid down, scanned it. It was easy to pick out Hayden, even with his back turned. I searched for Lazlo, not seeing him at first. Then I did.

But something else caught my eye, just before that.

Something that flitted through my mind with the briefest recognition, the kind you can't directly identify but only feel. Not so much the recognition of a face, but of a stance, an arrogant tilt of a chin. A woman talking to Hayden, leaning on his arm, her face upturned. Seduction was all but written on her forehead. She was beautiful, her features highlighted by elaborate makeup, her long honey-blond hair curling at her shoulders. Her slender figure draped in a dress of a rich, shimmery blue fabric.

I was wrong. She didn't look familiar at all. Maybe it was because her hair color reminded me of Ilsa's. But that was the only thing that did.

I went back, picked up Lazlo in the vid, and studied him. The vid shifted and I lost him in the crowd, then picked him up again a few minutes later. This time, the blonde in the rich blue dress was just stepping past him, her hand briefly on his shoulder. Her back was to the camera; I couldn't see her face but I recognized the dress as well as the elegance of her movements.

A friend of Hayden's or a friend of Lazlo's? Or neither, just another female trolling for a good time that night?

I dismissed her. I'd located Lazlo again, on my own. That's all that mattered.

Sully came in, followed by Ren. Ren's hair was still wet—a final soak that would have to hold him until Gregor came back in. Both men were in black. I wore a black shirt but dark green pants. But no holsters, no weapons. We couldn't get those through the gate scanner. They were hidden in our luggage, shielded in a special compartment.

"Everything set with Gregor and Marsh?"

Sully nodded. "He's cooled off a bit, probably because he's in command again and has the codes."

"And because neither Ren nor I will be on board."

Sully tugged on my braid as he walked by, his gaze on the screen. I had the news running again.

"Another?" he asked. Then before I could answer, "Verno's leaving to go with Sister Berri."

I glanced at Ren, then back at Sully. "Why?"

"He belongs back in the monastery," Ren said. "It's where he feels most comfortable. Plus he wants to work with his people, teach them that murder isn't the answer. He'll still be a good contact for us if there are any other reports of gen-labs using Takas."

"You'll miss him." With Verno gone, and Dorsie distancing herself from him, Ren now had only Sully and myself.

"I never expected him to stay. This is not his path, as it is mine."

Gentle acceptance and understanding. Just like my brother Thad. Ha!

Sully clicked off the screen. "We'll be docking in fifteen minutes. Go put on your robes, my friends, and try like hell to look pious."

Sister Berri Solaria reached up and adjusted my hood before I could back away from her touch. "There, that's better. We must at all times be aware that our outward appearance mirrors our humbleness and our mission to serve selflessly." She yanked on my robe. "It would help if you'd at least try, Captain Bergren."

Supercilious bitch. I heard Sully's voice clearly in my mind as he brushed by me, his hand briefly clasping my shoulder. I had to bite my lip to keep from laughing. I caught his half smile when he stopped by the airlock with Ren and Verno. He felt my laughter just as clearly as I heard his words. Could hear them, ever since we'd made love and I willingly granted him entry into my thoughts.

It still startled me slightly when his thoughts accompanied his touch. Though the few thoughts he'd sent to me since then, like the one just now, were all light in tone. Gentle. Teasing. Still testing. I could feel that. Still cautious. Still making sure, as he'd asked me outside Trel's bar, that I wasn't angry. Afraid.

I wasn't. I knew him. No gill slits, no webbings, and, as I'd told Dorsie, no wings framed in unholy light. Terribly human, terribly male, wonderfully—

The *Karn* jerked. Marker Terminal's gateway impacted against us, locking on to our hull.

I took a deep breath, patted my ID secured at the belt at my waist, and, when I caught his dark gaze, nodded to Sully.

Showtime.

Verno handed his ID to the Taka guard at the bottom of the gateway. "Blessings of the hour, Brother."

"Blessings to you. Brother Verno?" Their conversation was a gravelly, growly exchange of voices.

I still had trouble reading nuances of tone when Takas spoke. They always sounded angry, annoyed. But then, Ren and Sully were probably scanning, reading. If there were troubles brewing, I'd know.

Verno extended his hand toward Berri. "Sister Berri Solaria. We're here to open the new temple."

"Missed Peyhar's. Would have liked that." The guard took Berri's ID, scanned it through. Took mine, Sully's, Ren's. Studied Ren for a few seconds more than I liked. But he let us pass.

"Next Peyhar's!" he called after us. "Good celebration then."

"Praise the stars." Verno waved back.

We walked into Marker Terminal's main corridor. My heart started beating again.

Fleet personnel were everywhere. I kept my head tilted down. The chance I'd run into someone from Thad's office was slim, but it existed. We followed Berri and Verno to the luggage and cargo ramps. Berri moved confidently through the corridors and cross-corridors, heading for a bank of lifts. She'd been here before.

We threaded through the crowds down one level to baggage. I worked on calming myself. They'd let us through. Our luggage was tagged as church property. No reason to expect it contained weapons. Explosives. Poison gas.

Everything was shielded in special compartments. Sully knew what he was doing. He couldn't have worked as a smuggler for all those years if he didn't.

We passed through a second set of security gates before we entered the luggage ramp area. About a half dozen people milled about, all human, except for two tall forms I was startled to realize were Stolorths. The only Stolorths I remembered seeing on Marker belonged to a diplomatic delegation. They'd been well-guarded, and I'd seen them only from a distance. These wore freighter uniforms, their ship's patch unfamiliar to me. They were deep in conversation, didn't look our way, didn't seem to notice the humans staring nervously, purposely giving them a wide berth. Ren had turned and kept his back to them. Berri glared at them openly, her lips pursed, but said nothing.

The Stolorths wandered off with an antigrav pallet wobbling behind them.

I took a deep breath.

Berri became cheerful again, blessing everyone left and right as she headed for a stack of boxes and duffel cases. The small electronic sign underneath read GLNT EXPLR.

Verno grabbed a pallet, activated it, and began to load the boxes stenciled with the arch-and-stave on all sides. Supplies for the new temple. Sully loaded a second pallet, smaller, with our duffels, arch-and-stave tags dangling.

A Takan guard glanced at our IDs again, waved us through.

Praise the stars.

A shuttle would take us to M-2, Berri and Verno to M-3. There'd be no further security checks. We were cleared, as safe as if we'd been through Berri's purity process. She and Verno stepped into line for the M-3 shuttle. I realized maybe I didn't dislike her as much as I thought. She was, if nothing else, true to what she believed. Even Sully said he sensed no duplicity in her. She was deeply fervent—perhaps misguidedly so in my opinion—and committed to her work with the Takas. Maybe someday she'd revise her opinions on Stolorths and *Ragkirils*. She and the rest of the Empire.

I extended my hand to her. "Blessings of the hour, Sister Berri. And thank you." I meant it.

Her smile was angel-soft. "I see the holy sword of the abbot behind you as you proceed." She nodded to Sully.

Verno hugged Ren, one of the odder sights I'd ever seen. An eight-foot-tall Taka embracing a six-and-a-half-foot-tall Stolorth.

Praise the stars.

We passed a news-bank holovid on our way to the M-2 shuttle. The 'caster's bronze-skinned face turned, as if following us, as we walked by. "And in sports news, zero-g racquetball competitions heated up in Port January yesterday when . . ."

"I'll take the pallet to the baggage ramp," Sully said as the gate came into view. "You stay with Ren. Watch for unfriendlies."

That meant anything from other Stolorths to Marker stripers to Lazlo. I requested three tickets from the 'droid attendant. Next shuttle was due in fifteen minutes, a second five minutes after that. M-2 was a popular destination. If we didn't make the first shuttle, we'd be first in line for the next.

Sully came back and we retreated into a quiet corner not far from the gate, blessing anyone who looked our way but not deliberately making eye contact. Most didn't. This was Marker. Everyone was in too much of a hurry, with projects and duty schedules on their minds.

I leaned back against the wall. Eleven minutes. Sully snugged his hand against the small of my back. His fingers made small circles, sent warmth. He and Ren talked zero-g racquetball. Port January had a good team, but there was no way they could beat out Garno's.

"Would you be willing to place a wager on that?" Ren asked softly.

I fought an urge to roll my eyes and focused instead on two young men and a woman in Fleet dress uniforms taking shuttle tickets from the 'droid attendant. They were laughing, relaxed. Just back from liberty, I guessed. The man ruffled the woman's curls and she turned around.

My heart stopped, my breath caught in my throat. I recognized her.

Tessa. Looking straight at me. Twenty, maybe twenty-five feet separated us. I could see her clearly and knew beyond a shadow of a doubt that she could see me. Her laughter faded to be replaced by a soft, knowing smile.

Shit.

Chasidah. Nothing to fear.

Nothing to fear? She and one of the men walked toward us, toward me. I fought the urge to run, knowing that would only make things worse.

Sully pulled his hand away from me and bowed slightly as she approached. "How may we assist you?"

"I don't mean to trouble you, Brothers. Sister." She nodded to me and didn't appear to be the least bit disturbed by my heart hammering loudly in my chest. "But Dylan and I just got married. Would you mind blessing our rings?"

She and her husband held out their hands, their matching rings glistening in the bright overhead lights.

Sully took their hands in his. "Guardian of love, Guardian of wisdom and mercy, hear now my plea..."

I bowed my head, trembling, listened to the deep, soothing tones of his voice. The absolute sincerity in his voice. He meant every word. He asked for blessings upon the love and peace Tessa had found. And because she had, so, finally, could Gabriel Ross Sullivan. Poet, monk, mercenary, *Ragkiril.*

I prayed a prayer of my own, one that had no words. And realized that maybe, sometimes, miracles do happen.

"... for the love that resides now in your hearts, forever. Praise the stars."

"Praise the stars," Tessa repeated softly. Sully raised his head, smiled.

"Blessings, thank you," Dylan said as he hooked his arm through Tessa's. He led her back to their friend waiting near the gate.

Sully met my gaze, still smiling.

"Thank you," I whispered. The words caught in my throat. Tears prickled gently at the back of my eyes.

Chasidah. My angel. Nothing to fear.

29

It was a half hour to M-2 on a crowded shuttle, though Tessa and her new husband weren't with us. We exited quickly upon docking and retrieved our pallet five minutes later. I walked purposefully, knowing exactly where I was going.

This was Marker-2. I'd lived here with my mother for fifteen years, until she'd died. Then stayed three years after that, until I'd entered the academy.

M-2, like M-1, was a cylinder but more squat, with three wide access rings splitting it irregularly and two series of smaller gate rings on Level 2 and Level 8. Access rings and gate rings served as landing pads for small shuttles and cargo tenders. Fleet offices filled Levels 1 through 11. We'd docked on 13, in the middle of the commercial levels. Shops, pubs, private offices flanked both sides of the curved corridor. I found the bank of lifts I wanted, crowded the three of us and the pallet into the narrow lift. No room for anyone else. We headed down.

Below the commercial levels was residential, both

Fleet and private, though private was kept separate in a small section of Level 17.

We descended past that, heading for Level 27. Storage, auxiliary offices, maintenance. And, if we were correct, one level from a fully operating gen-lab.

But we couldn't head there yet. Not dressed as Englarians, in full view of everyone scurrying through M-2's corridors. No one must be able to connect the destruction of the gen-labs with the church. Not simply out of concern for Englarians, but because we still needed our identities in order to get back to the *Karn*, unquestioned and alive.

Our request under a fictitious name for rental of storage space on M-2 had provided us with knowledge of bays and offices that were empty. We chose one down a side corridor that on the schematics would be out of the way of most pedestrian traffic. I remembered it being so as well.

There isn't much else to do when you're sixteen, an orphan—unless you count the father you never see—and the only respite you get from the overbearing guardian the court appointed to watch over you is a game of hide and seek. I'd easily slip the lock on my mother's apartment after Proctor Fernanda would leave. As far as she was concerned, after dinner her duties for the day were concluded. Then I'd just as easily slip into the throngs of stationers going somewhere, going anywhere, for the night.

There were six of us—Fleet orphans and castoffs, like me—the year I turned seventeen. We'd steal bottles of ale from unsuspecting 'droid waiters' carts and head downlevel, savoring our freedom as we sipped our ale. Sooner or later someone would break out a deck of cards. We'd drink, laugh, and gamble. Sometimes there was even a little kiss and grope. And sometimes there was a flask of honeylace, a pipe of *rafthkra*. Not for me. Amaris was dead but she wasn't gone. She'd made me promise her. *Always have fun in life. But never, ever be stupid. Only fools have no fears or refuse to see the danger in front of them.*

I had a friend die from an overdose of *rafthkra*. And I'd heard stories of people who drank too much honeylace and thought they'd grown wings, like soul-stealing shape-shifters, and tried to fly.

I had fears, well-grounded fears. I was no fool.

I walked down Level 27's corridor with Sully, Ren, and all these memories by my side. Knowing exactly when the groups of stationers would thin, as they did. Knowing exactly when more offices were closed, or vacant, which they were. I saw the signs of decay, of neglect. And now and then an empty ale bottle tucked between the handrail and the corridor's inner wall.

If the neck pointed up, tonight's party was on. Down, party was off.

"Really?" Sully seemed impressed when I pointed it out. Ren laughed softly, a bubbling stream, as frothy as ale.

Green 8. A short corridor, dead-ending at station core. A core that was a large maintenance shaft, holding lifts and pipes and clusters of cables. Crisscrossed with scaffolding, thin metal ladders. Emergency exits. Narrow tool bays.

I knew all that too. Another world, when you're seventeen. Behind the scenes, behind the walls and bulkheadings. Private, dark, mysterious, dangerous.

I knew that the moment I stepped into it, two words would sound in my mind: *welcome home.*

Ren and I stood together, heads bowed, our bodies shielding Sully as he played with the lock pad by the door. Our pallet was skewed, one end resting on the decking, the other wobbling in midair. To anyone passing by, we were two luckless monks, praying while waiting for a repair tech.

Three people did. We nodded, smiled, blessed them. Yes, unfortunate how no one made a reliable pallet anymore. Blessings of the hour.

"Got it!" A hushed, gleeful exclamation sounded behind us.

We stepped quickly into the dark, windowless room. The door slid closed, relocking with a muted click. The next click was the lights. One overhead. The others were burned out.

"They wanted three hundred twenty-five credits a month for this dump?" Sully put his hands on his hips, surveyed the room.

"Bathroom works. Shower, no tub," I announced.

Ren nodded. "That's sufficient, if we're delayed."

I hoped we wouldn't be. We had eight hours until our first meetpoint with the *Karn,* arriving as the *Iron Sun,* back at Marker Terminal. If we weren't there, Gregor had instructions to return at the twelve-hour mark, under another ship name. Our third and final meetpoint at the terminal was at twenty-four hours from when we disembarked.

There was no fourth meetpoint. After that, we'd be on our own. Or dead.

We pulled off the robes, opened the duffels, pulled out weapons and explosives. I sat on the floor and began assembling the small charges laced with poison gases.

"Let that wait." Sully knelt next to me, a dark and powerful figure in black fatigue pants and black high-necked thermal shirt. Black holster straps hugged his shoulders; the Carver snugged against his left side. "Our first priority's to confirm location."

He found the small datapad, flipped it on, and brought up M-2's schematics. We were in Green 8, Level 27. The gen-labs were on Level 28, M-2's lowest level, with a small access ring running around its perimeter. The labs were in a converted storage area either on Level 28-Blue, directly across from Green, or Level 28-Yellow, between Green and Blue.

Sully snatched his jacket from where he'd dropped it on the floor. "I want to find that lab, make that first meetpoint, and get the hell out of here."

I put down the casing and arched an eyebrow. "Late for a hot date?"

"No. A wedding." He winked, then pulled me to my feet. "What's your guess, Ren? Level 28-Blue or -Yellow?"

"Blue," Ren said, without hesitation.

"Fine. I'll take Yellow. Double or nothing?"

"Agreed. Double or nothing."

"You're witness to this, Chaz."

"I'm witness to this, Sully."

I looked at Ren. "How much does he—No. Forget it. I don't want to know."

Sully slapped me affectionately on my rump. He handed me my dark green jacket. "Let's go."

He unlocked the door to the corridor. There was an access panel a few feet away at the corridor's end. I had it unlatched, sliding sideways in a matter of seconds, feeling sixteen years old again. Slightly giddy. And more than a bit frightened.

I squatted down, squeezed through with Sully immediately behind me, sliding the panel closed.

Abrupt darkness closed around me. I crouched, unmoving, aware of the open grating under my boots, aware of the low railing at my side. Aware of the open core beyond, a drop of hundreds of feet to the bottom

filled with the hard, jutting forms of generators and re-
cycs and other machinery that kept M-2 alive.

Aware of Sully behind me, one hand on my shoulder.
I waited for my eyes to adjust to the red-tinged dimness.

Shadows sharpened and became less muddy. Everything was painted in shades of gray and black and dark
red. A constant clanking of lift mechanisms far to our
right and left echoed hollowly. Thin stripes of light
showed the location of lift corridor doors. And there
were other noises. Water rushing through pipes, the occasional squeal of metal stressing.

I turned, still hunkered down, put my back against
the wall and took a deep breath of the cold, sharp air.
Sully moved as I did. We did nothing, said nothing for a
moment. Just so I could hear it clearly.

Welcome home.

I felt, more than saw, his wicked Sully grin. "Downlevel?" he whispered.

"Downlevel."

We soft-footed, carefully, quickly. It was always possible to run into a maintenance tech or three. But, as I'd
told Sully and Ren while we were on the *Karn,* they were
typically noisy. They had a right to be in the core.
Stealth was unnecessary for them.

The double red light on the wall ahead signaled a ladder. I headed for it, stopped just short of it, and touched
Sully's arm. "The double lights," I whispered. "Down or
up, they—"

His hand clamped over my mouth just as a sharp
clang sounded, followed by several short clanks. A light
flashed above us as an accessway opened. We flattened
ourselves against the wall.

A woman's voice sounded harsh, tired. "Goddamned
breaker feeds. Think they'd invent one that'd last more
than two goddamned weeks."

Another voice, unintelligible but male, filtered in from the corridor.

"Yeah, yeah, budget. Well, screw budget," she answered. There was more clanking, then a hissing sound and a loud clank.

Then darkness.

I let out my breath in a long rush. "Sully—"

"Hush, Chasidah." Fingers against my lips. *Listen.*

I listened.

Let me link with you. There is safety in this. No sounds from us as we move, but no lapse in information either.

I started to open my mouth to speak but caught my action. *You can do this without touching me?* I knew he could with Ren, but I wasn't Stolorth or *Ragkiril.* Then I remembered his angry probe spearing my thoughts when we'd encountered the *Morgan Loviti.*

I can, yes. He hesitated for a moment and I damned the uncertainty he no doubt had sensed in my mind. *Will you be comfortable with this?*

Yes. No problems. After all, he'd also been in my mind when we made love.

Okay. I felt his smile, his warmth. *Got it.*

I reached for the ladder. Stopped and put my fingers instead on his arm. *Sully?*

Yes, Chasidah.

All my thoughts? When we made love, I was focused on him. But I belatedly realized now that our current situation might lend itself to some rather undiplomatic thoughts on my part from time to time. I'd be in the captain mode, not lover mode. I didn't want him hurt by the kind of things he'd uncovered when we'd met up with Philip's ship.

Except for emergencies, your touch or mine is the signal.

I climbed down first, Sully following. Reached Level 28's grated, narrow platform. Swung off the ladder, grabbed the handholds, scooted sideways.

Touch. *Blue's across the way,* I told him. *Yellow's closer.*

Double or nothing?

Oh, shut up.

It took us five minutes to go a quarter of the way around the core, almost to the single bank of lifts between Yellow and Blue. There were no more interruptions, no more flashes of light. Only the clank and clatter and hiss of a station at work.

I stopped at the third access panel, its handle painted yellow, as the one we'd entered through was painted green. It was difficult to see in the dim lighting, but then, maintenance techs all had handbeams. We did too, but not to use right now. Not unless we had to.

Touch. *Midpoint here,* I told him. We had to exit the access, unseen, and cross the corridor. Blend into any stationers passing by, our jackets covering our weapons.

He fingered the access lock. *Ready?*

I nodded. He pulled it back an inch. I listened, held up one hand when I heard footsteps, forgetting I could send my thoughts. The footsteps faded.

Touch. I remembered this time. *Okay.*

He slid the access hatch sideways. We slipped through, straightening quickly as if we just stepped from an office, not the core.

The corridor was quiet, though I could hear voices far behind us. Sully draped one arm over my shoulder, pinning my braid down. I reached back and flipped it out. He snugged me closer. Just two freighter crew on break, catching a little body-heat time.

Windowless metal doors studded the bulkhead on

our left. Some had names. *In-System Datatronics. Namkhai Sound and Vid. Storage Bay 6-Yellow.*

We were looking for Storage Bay 10-Yellow.

A man in a blue lab coat walked quickly by, head down, eyes on the datapad in his hand. I turned casually as he passed to read the letters on the back of his coat. *In-System Datatronics.*

What did I expect, Jukor Gen-Labs?

Probably won't say Crossley Burke either.

Quit peeking!

Gentle laughter filtered through his link with me. *Sorry.*

Sorry, my ass.

We can discuss that as well, if you like. But later.

I elbowed him. So much for a subtle touch signaling my thoughts.

But I knew what he was doing. My heart pounded. I'd crossed nervous when we'd left our appropriated office. I was into scared that could head easily into panic, Fleet training or no. He was trying to keep me relaxed, trying to keep me from focusing on the fact that I had to face a jukor again.

Only fools, as Amaris had taught me, had no fears. And jukors—winged Hell-spawned demons that were immune even to the mind talents of a *Ragkiril*—ranked right up there on the top of my fear list.

Storage Bay 9.

We slowed. I could see a wide set of doors about ten feet ahead of us on the left. I sniffed. Nothing. We came closer. I sniffed again. Jukors had a rank, rotting smell. Though how someone wouldn't notice, and inquire, had probably already been considered by Cousin Hayden and friends. They'd have to have put powerful air recyclers in place.

Storage Bay 10. Doors were locked, in need of painting. But the dust on the decking was mottled, unlike the undisturbed coating of dust in front of Storage Bay 9.

Someone had walked through those doors recently.

Sully slowed, stopping a few feet past. Touch. *Wait.* One hand rested on my shoulder, the other in his pocket. He pulled out a handful of lightpens and dropped them on the floor. Then bent down to pick them up.

I stooped to help.

His eyes were infinite, dark. He stared over my shoulder as I picked up the pens, one by one. I pressed them into his hand. He accepted them, automatically, his focus beyond the wall behind us. And beyond my comprehension. Then he pulled me to my feet and pushed us onward.

Touch. *No.*

No? Disappointment mixed with relief. *That means Blue 17.*

Great. There goes my shot at double or nothing.

The arm draped over my shoulder seemed to weigh a little heavier this time.

We crossed into Blue. Our target was another storage bay. This one was numbered 17.

More offices, more repair shops. Many more doors with no names. Several storage lockers and bays. We almost collided with two stripers exiting from one, a pallet between them loaded with boxes labeled TOILET PAPER.

I scooted sideways as soon as I saw the uniforms. *Shit!*

Prophetic, that.

Oh, shut up.

Yes, my angel.

The stripers didn't even look twice at us. Marker Shipyards had always prided itself on its security. If you were on M-2, then you'd been cleared and belonged here.

Storage Bay 15, 16. Then 17, only a few steps away. I was prepared for the routine this time: pens scattering to the floor and both of us bending down. Sully turned. His eyes seemed incredibly dark, incredibly distant. I tried sniffing but smelled only dust this close to the decking. But here too the dust was blotchy.

Sully straightened, slowly, took the pens I offered, pocketing them absently. His arm clasped tightly around my shoulders, moving me on. We walked.

Sully?

No answer. His eyes were still dark, no difference between pupil and iris but all obsidian.

We kept walking.

Sully?

A minute.

My heart started pounding. I waited and felt as if my throat wanted to close up.

He pulled me into a side corridor and pushed my back against the wall, his body covering mine. I could feel him breathing hard, almost rasping now. I raised my hands to his shoulders. To anyone passing by, we were lovers, catching that serious body-heat time.

He closed his eyes, his lips resting against my forehead. Then his finger touched my mouth. *Chasidah?*

I nodded, waited, listened. Heard one word.

Yes.

A shudder spasmed through me.

Yes. Jukors. Not twenty feet from where we stood. Jukors.

Up until that moment, part of me prayed we were wrong. The holo of the mangled body of the Takan woman had been faked. Or the result of something else.

But it wasn't. Sully's hard *yes* was final. Through that one word, I could feel he was as shaken as I was. He didn't want to believe it either.

We stood for a few seconds longer, then quickly broke apart. We knew where they were. We needed to get back to the schematics, find a way to get in there. We headed for the closest core access, slipped in. Now it was best to be seen as little as possible in the corridors. Best someone not recognize us, having seen us before.

We found the first ladder, went uplevel. We were still in Blue when we reached Level 27.

Touch. *This way.* I took him through Red, looping around the main lift shafts jutting out, with narrow walkways between the three banks. No walls here on the back side of the lifts, though, just a high railing on one side, a lower railing on the other. It opened to a wide chasm of darkness below.

I had a reason. Touch. *Emergency shut off for the main lifts, here. If stripers are called, shut down the lifts. Won't stop them, but will slow them down. They never think to use the core.*

A lift whizzed by us, wind whipping our clothing, my hair, momentarily blocking the thin stripe of light from the corridor. I grabbed the railing but Sully stood still, perfectly balanced as if the forced rush of air bothered him not at all. He nodded.

We moved on.

Green. I counted access panels and found ours. We knelt down. Sully touched the access lock, touched me. *Ready?*

An inch of light cracked into our darkness. I listened, then nodded. *Clear.*

We moved quickly, the access panel sliding closed just as the office door opened. Ren ushered us in.

Coincidence? Then I remembered. Sully had a link with Ren too.

I stood in the middle of the room and wrapped my arms around my chest. Small explosive charges were in a neat stack, like ten tiny party favors, at my feet. All were keyed for remote activation. All were short-range and shouldn't pierce the station's hull. But should, very effectively, dismantle anything inside a closed storage bay. The poison gas released before that would kill any living creature within twenty-five feet in seconds. We had to get into the lab, plant the charges, and seal enviro to keep the gas from leaking out. And we had to leave, alive.

I stood, hugging myself, listening to Sully confirm to

Ren that Hell indeed lived on Level 28-Blue of Marker-2.

"Two breeding pair." Sully positioned himself as if he faced the lab, showing me, telling Ren. "Here, on the right. Narrow, deep cages. A trough of some kind, fluid or liquid, not water." He etched a line in the air with his hand.

"Takas?" Ren asked.

"One female. She's . . . she's in the advanced stages of pregnancy." He wiped one hand over his face, visibly distressed. "The infant has already started to consume her. She's in constant agony. She's—" He glanced at me, his gaze almost pleading. "I'll need time to put her down. Peacefully."

I nodded. "You'll have it." As if I had any control of what would happen when we got in there.

I glanced at my watch. Six hours. We had six hours to meetpoint. No, five. We couldn't assume we'd catch the first shuttle. We had to allow a half hour, an hour to get back to Marker Terminal.

And pray no one followed us or tried to stop us.

I uncrossed my arms and lowered myself onto the floor next to the datapad. It clicked softly as I flipped it open. "Storage Bay 17-Blue, Level 28. Outer location means we can't access it through the core. But it's a bay. That means higher ceilings and a larger clearance area above that for overhead access to equipment. And if it was ever used for ship repair . . ." I tabbed through the schematics, brought up Level 28 only. "Shit. No maintenance pits underneath. We have to find an enviro hatch, come in through the overhead. Trickier. Weight will be a problem. It will be crawling all the way. That's going to slow us down."

"Only going in," Sully said wryly. He sat on the floor next to me. Ren was next to him.

Going in really was our only problem. Going out we'd use the main bay doors. Quickly.

"Guards? Med-techs?" Ren asked.

"One lab tech, human, male," Sully answered. "In a private office, on the left. I'll take him out, get the Taka. You two handle the charges."

I paged through the schematics while he spoke, hoping to find some easier way in, like a tandem bay. Some of them were built that way, with false walls, movable for expansion. But not Storage Bay 17-Blue.

"We'll need the files in that office too. Whatever you can grab."

"Agreed." Sully peered over my shoulder. "Did you find an enviro hatch?"

"Closest one's at the 24 mark. We'll have to backtrack." I kept paging. It looked like the only way. I took my fingers off the touchpad and rested them on my knees. Asked what I had to know but didn't want to know. "When?"

"My first instinct is to go back there now. But I don't think that's the best plan. It's better if we do it as close as we can to meetpoint. We'll release the gas as soon as we seal the lab doors. That should take care of the jukors. I'll key the explosives when we're in the shuttle. I don't want to wait too long in the terminal. Once those charges blow, they're going to be looking for us. I guarantee the lab's wired for alarms. We have to realize we could get caught at the terminal. They might not let Gregor bring the *Karn* in."

"Eventually they have to." I just hoped it was before Ren's forty-eight hours were up. "So when?"

"We're five hours from meetpoint, given transit time. I say at the two-hour mark, we move. Agreed?" Sully's gaze switched from me to Ren. We both nodded.

"Okay." He brushed my hair back from my face,

then ran his hand down my braid. "Now, no worries until then. We go in with clear minds."

"And empty pockets?" I asked as his hand snuck inside his jacket.

He brought out his deck of cards with a wicked, wicked Sully grin on his lips. "I've got to recoup that double or nothing. Besides, I have a new theory."

I turned back to the datapad. Sully and his card theories could be painful to watch.

"Shall I deal?" Ren asked.

"Only if you keep your hands in sight at all times. And pull up those sleeves."

"Certainly. Glad to oblige."

God. We were sitting in Marker-2 with enough explosives to take out a gen-lab—a gen-lab breeding jukors—and the most pressing issue was a game of cards.

But I couldn't help myself. I watched the first two hands. I counted the angel of heart-stars cards, holding every one in memory as a good omen. We needed all the good omens, and all the good blessings, we could get.

What was it Berri Solaria said as she left us? Something about the abbot's holy sword guiding our way. Appropriate image. The sword often stuck out of the backs of the demons in the Englarian paintings. But all I had was my little dagger. Not jukor-proof, that.

I paged through the datapad and opened the Crossley Burke file again. The firm maintained a small office here on 2, uplevel, where the real estate got expensive. Shame we couldn't get into that as well. I was in the mood to find out just what kind of contributions Burke made to charity. I could still picture him in his finery, oozing through that party....

The image of the sultry woman in blue flashed through my mind again. Superimposed, this time, with another image.

My hands hovered over the touchpad.

It couldn't be. I had to be wrong.

I pulled up the vid, much smaller now on the datapad screen. Hit ENLARGE, ENLARGE, ENLARGE. Refocused. Brought her in, brought her face in, the arrogant tilt of a chin, the thin delicate features. I wasn't distracted by the elaborate makeup highlighting her features this time. I recognized a smile as pure as an angel's. Or as wicked as a devil from Hell.

Berri Solaria. With her hair down around her shoulders, not back in a bun as I'd always seen it. And it was several shades lighter. Her makeup was skillfully applied. I stared at the entrancingly beautiful Sister Berri Solaria. Leaning on Hayden Burke's arm.

"Sully!" I barked out his name. My hands shook. I pointed to the screen. "It's her. She knows him. She knows Hayden and Lazlo."

"Who, Chaz? What—" He leaned toward me, the smile dying from his face. Cards fluttered through his fingers. His eyes snapped to infinite black. I felt something move through the room, like a hot, angry wind.

"Bitch!" He knelt in front of the pad and grabbed for Ren. Webbed fingers clasped his and the blind Stolorth saw.

"By the stars. No." Agony laced Ren's words.

"Look." I segued quickly to the image of her with Lazlo. Her back was to the camera, but her hand was clearly on his shoulder. It was the same glossy honey-colored hair and rich blue dress.

Sully shot to his feet. Cards scattered, fluttering. "We move. We move now. The bitch works for Hayden. She knows we're here. What we're doing. Which means, so does he."

I felt the holy sword of Abbot Eng pierce right through the middle of my back.

I grabbed his arm. "They'll have guards—"

"They didn't an hour ago." He checked the Carver, adjusted the straps of his shoulder holster quickly. "She may not have reached him yet. Or she may not know our schedule."

"What does she know?" Ren was calm, the voice of reason.

"Whatever Verno's told her," Sully shot back. He was angry, sparing no one.

"Verno didn't know we knew the location of the lab," I said, pulling on my jacket. "Slow down. Five minutes isn't going to make a difference now."

Sully hesitated, his mouth a thin line. But he listened.

"Verno didn't know we had the labs located on Level 28. Berri only knows we took the shuttle to M-2."

"No," Ren said. "She left first, for M-3. And none of us mentioned M-2 around her."

"But Verno knew we were headed for M-2," Sully argued. "She knows we're here to take out the labs."

"Then it's a fifty–fifty split," I said. "She knows we're in Marker-2, looking for the lab. She doesn't know we know where it is."

"She said she wanted the labs destroyed as well," Ren said. "Or was she lying? I never sensed a falseness."

"I never heard her say she wanted the lab destroyed." Sully's voice was flat. "All she ever said was she wanted in on our mission. She called it her 'holy mission.' We all just assumed..." He clenched his fist, took a deep breath. "We assumed too goddamned much. I should have seen, I should have known her coming to us was too easy. Too much coincidence. But, God! I wanted the easy way in, after all we'd been through. After losing Milo."

"Is it possible," Ren asked, "her concern, and Hayden's, is not the lab but control of the Sullivan fortune?"

I remembered Sully's comment about him—not Hayden—being the real heir. It was an enormous amount of money to have at one's control. I could understand why a man like Hayden Burke would kill for it.

"Hayden knows you're alive," I told Sully. "That's not an assumption. That's a fact."

Sully nodded. "All the more reason we move and move now. Should have moved," he said, shoving the charges into the inside pockets of his jacket, "when we confirmed the lab."

"They'll watch for us at the terminal." Ren had a handful of charges. "She knows the *Boru Karn*."

The holy sword of purity.

Sully nodded. "We may need another way out of the shipyards. I only hope Gregor's smart enough not to let himself get taken."

I only hoped we'd live long enough to find out if he was.

I put the rest of the charges in my pocket, packed up the datapad, scooped up the cards. Sully handed me the robes. I shoved them in the duffel.

"We bring the bag into the core, leave it near an access panel. If we can get back to it, fine. If not"—he held up a charge—"this will be inside. It'll blow when the labs do. I don't give a damn who it takes with it either."

He picked up the duffel and slung it over his shoulder. "Let's go."

We moved though dim, red-tinged darkness, through the clank and clang, through the hiss, through the high whine of some unknown mechanism far below. Ren, between us, followed our thermals.

We downleveled and hit 28-Green. Ten minutes to

walk halfway around the core. We couldn't hurry. The walkway was narrow. Hurrying could kill you.

Exiting at Blue, we left the duffel behind, just inside the access hatch. Ren's silvery-blue braid swung as he walked. No hiding he was Stolorth at this point. Fortunately, there were others in the shipyards.

Past Bay 17. Sully shuddered slightly, sensing the jukors, sensing the dying Taka, the winged beast in her belly clawing, tearing its way out.

There may not be time to put her down peacefully. Quickly might be all we could give her. One shot, center mass.

And a prayer.

There were people in the corridor. Instinctively I noticed them, categorized them, but only as threat or nonthreat. No stripers and none that had uniforms like private security guards. There were a few techs in lab coats, maybe one in overalls. I couldn't tell if they were male. Or female. I didn't care.

A single doorway loomed. Enviro 24. That held an accessway to the air handlers and recyc filters, as well as whatever else maintenance and station designers wanted to stuff in the overheads.

I noticed someone coming, a woman, a pallet trailing behind her. We slowed, as if stopping for conversation, but no words came. None of us could think of anything to say. But we couldn't just stand awkwardly in front of the doorway, mute. And we didn't have time to waste by moving on, backtracking.

I looked at Ren, trying to force words out of my brain, when Sully grabbed me and kissed me hard.

I could hear Ren laugh, softly, hear the woman's footsteps, the low hum of the antigrav pallet getting louder. And I could feel Sully. Heat cascaded through me, swirling, cresting.

I wrapped my arms around his neck, thrust my fingers into his short thick hair just as my tongue thrust into his mouth. It met his own as we tasted—no, devoured each other.

An hour from now we could be dead. I might never kiss him again.

No! The word shot into my mind, sweet, pleading and aching. *I will not lose you.*

I heard a woman's light chuckle.

"I think this means she said yes," Ren told her.

I leaned my face against Sully's chest, breathless.

"Tell 'em the honeymoon comes after the wedding." Her footsteps faded quickly, more quickly than she came.

I forgot. She was talking to a Stolorth. Don't be impolite. But don't tarry.

I looked up at Sully. "Good thinking."

He answered with a sad smile, but no words. The poet had run out of words, again.

"Any more?" he asked Ren.

"No."

Sully pulled out a thin tool, touched the lock on the door, and watched the lights dance. Click. It slid open.

"Go."

We surged into a small room cramped with ductways and squat filters. Cables snaked overhead, disappearing through a large hole in the ceiling. Metal bars hung down from one side.

Sully reached up and pulled down a telescoping ladder.

I went up first.

It was hands and knees crawling on a narrow rampway that creaked under our weight. I found that placing my hands, and knees, on the outer edges kept sound to a minimum. When the creaking stopped behind me, I knew Sully and Ren had done the same.

It wasn't as dark as the core. Light filtered in from the overheads in the corridor on our left, blocked only by the thick bulkheads that spanned to the outer hull of the station. Narrow passageways had been cut into each one, with recessed hatches that sealed in case of a hull breach. We had to pass through seven to reach the gen-lab.

I counted down in my mind. Six. Five. Four. Three. Two.

I stopped, waiting until Sully and Ren were closer behind me. When I glanced back over my shoulder, I caught Sully's nod, answered it.

His voice sounded, clearly, unexpectedly in my mind. It wasn't preceded by a touch. *Chasidah. We link. You. Me. Ren.*

I borrowed his favorite phrase. *Got it.*

Got it too. Ren was now in my mind, through the link with Sully.

I went forward, slowly, barely breathing. I could smell the fetid odor of the jukors. Huge enviro boosters were off to my left, blocking much of the light from the corridor. But it didn't matter. Because the light from the lab filtered up through the breaks in the ceiling panels.

I moved another few inches, listening.

Then I heard it. A wheezing. Something crackling. Like the sound tissue paper would make if it were made of glass.

I crept forward on my knees in my odd, wide gait, looking for a break in the ceiling, looking for a way we could get down into the labs, as quickly as possible.

Some ductwork had tilted, leaving a hole as big around as my fist. It wasn't far from the rampway. I leaned to my left, held my breath. The stench was stronger. I looked down.

The long, grotesque face of a jukor stared back. Mucus dripped from its snout. And its red eyes gleamed back at me like the fires of the damned in the depths of Hell.

I jerked back. Sully's arm on my shoulder was the only thing that kept my head from slamming into the hard metal ceiling. He pulled me sideways, against him. I was breathing hard, bile rising in my throat.

Easy, Chasidah. Calm. Ren's presence floated through me.

I tried to focus on Sully, my eyes blinking rapidly. God. God. But what I saw looked nothing like anything any God had ever made. Ever could've made. I'd never seen one that close, that clearly before. The ones in the transport ship I'd escorted had been crated. The one on Moabar had attacked at night. The forest had been shadowed. Its hideousness less distinct.

I heard the crackling noise again. Wings moved below me. That was followed by a wheezing, snuffling sound. The jukor was scenting for me.

It knows we're here, Sully. A sick feeling rolled through me again. Then immediately something cool, like clear water. Ren.

It senses something, Sully answered. *It doesn't know*

what. That's okay. It senses people passing in the corridor all the time.

A parade out there might be a nice distraction. Know any way we could rig one?

Another gentle nudge from Ren.

My breathing slowed.

Our greatest threat, Sully said, *is from the lab tech. Still just one. Male. In the office. He's most likely armed. One of us needs to crawl out there, take him out from above.*

Sully pointed toward the far corner. Out there meant no rampway. Out there meant using the ductways themselves, and the narrow crossbeams they rested on.

Out there meant the lightest of us all. Me. One more kill to add to Captain Chasidah Bergren's list of the dead.

This was the first one I knew I wouldn't mind.

I sat back on my heels, checked my functional, reliable Stinger, reholstered it. Sully's and Ren's voices flitted through my mind. There was an airlock on the exterior wall. Evidently the lab used it and the access ring beyond it. That was why no one else in Marker had reported any knowledge of the lab. All they had to do was clear the beacons—which for someone of Hayden Burke's wealth and power wasn't difficult to do—and then gain entry to Marker-2 from their own private loading bay.

That bay also had two ladders flanking the wall. They led to the manual overrides here, in the overhead. I considered suggesting opening the airlock, disabling the force field, letting the lab, jukors, and solitary tech get sucked out into the blackness of space.

Nice thought, but we might not get behind the

airtights in time. Plus, we need the files in that office, Sully said, being practical. *You're okay with this?*

Yes. It wasn't as if I'd never killed another sentient being before.

I kneeled on the rampway, then pushed myself onto the ductwork. It creaked, buckled slightly. Shit. I adjusted my weight, using my palms to test each section as I moved, slid, crawled.

Below me, jukors crackled, hissed, wheezed. I could also hear a low, keening cry. The Taka, in intense pain and dying. It tore at me.

I crossed over the main section of the lab, a wide area. Through infrequent breaks in the ceiling I could see monitors, a bed with restraints, and other medical equipment. I was aware of Sully and Ren, felt their presence, heard their voices. Both distinctly different.

I was almost to the lab's office. I placed my hands on the next section of ductwork and felt it give, rapidly. I pulled back, hunching over. The ductwork rested on a narrow platform. I could fit one boot, but not two. But I had no choice. I stepped down, my back cramping, my knees hurting, my heels hanging over the edge. If I fell backward, I'd crash through the lab ceiling. If the tech was armed, I'd be dead before I hit the floor.

I held my breath, worked on calming my heart thumping against my ribs. Then I moved. Slowly.

A crossbeam. Finally. The edge of the office. Then another large air booster and filter, for the office alone. The lab tech would spend most of his time in there because, even with the boosters filtering the main lab, the stench was nauseating. I sidled over to the booster. The duct was snug, no gaps. It took me five minutes to peel back the tape, to open a hole to where I could see into the office below.

Sounds drifted up. The trill of an intercom. I heard the tech answer, his name garbled. The caller, on speaker, was clearer.

"HQ just notified us of a possible intruder. Code Red status immediately. Secure all doors."

Berri had finally reached Hayden.

I felt Sully's agreement with my assessment. There was no time left now.

I lay the short barrel of the Stinger against the small opening, targeted the top of the lab tech's head. Fired.

He slumped backward in his chair, his head lolling to one side.

Go! I told Sully. *Go!*

I ripped the rest of the duct away, put my boot through the ceiling tile, once, then again. It buckled, resisted, then finally collapsed, falling onto the desk below.

I grabbed the support beam under the unit, swung myself down. My boots dangled a good ten feet from the desk—more than that from the floor.

I let go and tried to remember to bend my knees as I hit the desk. For all my training, I skidded sideways, flailing, and ended up tumbling against the tech's lifeless body.

Sully pulled me upright. "Good work. I activated the airtight seals. I need to break into these files, grab what I can. Go help Ren."

I charged through the office door.

The stench hit me immediately. That and the frenzied flapping of the jukors—four of them—in their cages. Ren had one hand on a long table near the center, placing charges underneath. He was feeling his way. Tables had no thermals.

I reached into my jacket and grabbed two explosives, then placed them on either side of the door. Two more I put near the Taka's cage. Her eyes were wide with fear. She tried to prop herself up on her cot, her large belly protruding grotesquely through the thin shift covering her. It was filthy, stained. It occurred to me then that I had no idea how large jukors were when they were born. But I doubted even a Taka child would make her look so.

I reached through the bars and offered my hand. She stood awkwardly, took three unsteady steps toward me then sank down to her knees. She clasped my hand, tears rolling down her face. I could see her body spasm.

"It will all be over soon." I couldn't think what else to tell her.

She drew her hand back, lay her long, furred fingers on her belly. "Kill this. Kill me. Please." Dark gold blood trickled from her mouth as she spoke.

I nodded, choking back my tears.

Something trilled behind me. The lab tech's intercom and someone demanding he respond.

I felt Sully's frustration, anguish. *No more time. We have to get out of here.*

The Taka—

Chasidah, there's no time. I'm sorry.

Sully!

A moment's hesitation was laced with despair. *Fuck.*

He strode quickly from the office, Carver aimed at the lock on her cage. It disintegrated as he moved. She tried to stand. He waved her down. "No, sister. It's better if you . . . just stay there."

He knelt beside her, taking her large hand in his. The

Taka's face twisted in fear for a moment, but then Sully's voice seemed to make that fade.

"Guardian of light, guardian of wisdom, of love... sister, you don't know me, but you do. Sleep will come now, peace will come. But you must trust me. You must listen to me."

She nodded.

"You will feel me in your mind—"

She jerked her hand, but Sully hung on.

"Sister, it will not hurt. The pain will be gone in a moment."

She laid her hand against her belly. "Kill this."

He nodded. "I will."

She closed her eyes. "Do it. Blessing be with you."

"And with you, sister. Listen to me, listen to my voice..."

Ren's hand on my shoulder startled me. "We need to wait by the door. They've probably sent a security team."

I turned for the wide doors and didn't look at the jukors, flapping wildly, slamming themselves against the cage. I didn't look at Sully behind me, silent now. I drew out my laser pistol, checked the charge, held it up. Ren did the same by touch. We flanked the doors.

"Anyone out there?"

Ren tilted his head, sensing, listening. Suddenly the jukors screamed, a high, shrill, piercing noise. Instinctively I turned, but Ren grabbed my shoulder. "Chasidah! Wait. Don't turn."

I remembered Sully's voice. *No, don't turn...don't turn.* "Ren?"

"The jukor infant." He said the words hurriedly. "The Taka's passing expelled it. Let Sully do what he has to."

I closed my eyes, felt my stomach clench. The whine

of Sully's Carver was followed by another piercing scream, a frantic beating of wings. The air seemed alive, stinking. Then Ren's grip eased.

"It's over."

I saw pain etched on his face and heard heavy footsteps behind me. Sully.

"Get the doors." His voice rasped. "Let's get the hell out of here."

I hit the palm pad. The doors irised open. Sully was at my back, Carver out. I wanted to turn, to look at his face, to touch him, but to do that would mean to see the bodies of the Taka and the jukor infant. I didn't want to remember that. I knew if I saw it, I'd never forget it.

I stepped into the doorway, braced my back against the jamb, and checked the corridor for movement. Ren did the same, seeing without seeing.

"Clear," I said.

"Clear," he said.

We moved out, our pistols tucked just out of sight under our arms. The corridor was empty, for now. HQ had sent a Code Red to the lab. I could only guess what else was on its way.

"I'll release the gas when we hit the core." Sully had the transmitter in his pocket. We walked quickly back toward the accessway, toward the duffel and the robes that would grant us innocuous identities again.

Suddenly, I heard noises. Footsteps, running, thudding.

How many? Ren asked.

We slowed, our pistols coming out.

Seven. Eight. Sully stopped. His left hand snaked to his pocket and pulled out the transmitter. There was a barely noticeable flick of his thumb. I heard muted thumps behind me in rapid succession. "They're at our access point."

"Blow it," I told him, meaning our duffel, with the charge. It might distract them, give us time to find another way out.

Another flick, a breath, and then a muffled explosion.

"This way." He grabbed my arm.

We turned and ran past the lab, silent now, past the short corridor on our right with no core-access panel. The next was farther down, around the corridor's curve, past more locked doors, vacant storerooms. We were still in Blue.

"Option." I huffed as we ran. "Secondary lift bank in Yellow. We could—"

Four men, armed, appeared around the curve in the corridor in front of us. Not stripers. They were private security, with unknown emblems on their shirts. And pistols in their hands, drawn, targeting.

"Down!" Sully shoved me against the corridor wall.

Laser fire spit through the air.

I landed on my backside, swung my arm, fired. Sully was behind me. Ren was in the middle of the corridor, prone, laser pistol in his hand, answering with fire of his own.

The men jumped sideways, hugged the interior edges of the corridor as we did, utilizing the curve.

Ren! Now! Sully leaned out, sprayed the corridor with fire, covering Ren as he scrambled toward us. He slammed against the wall in front of me.

"You okay?" I asked him.

Yes. Praise the stars.

Laser fire erupted behind us. Sully swung around, the Carver's high-pitched whine like staccato.

Shit. Where in hell are the stripers? These aren't—

Burke's. Sully answered in my mind, following my thoughts as he fired. *Star-over-X emblem. Crossley Burke.*

So where in hell are the stripers?

Probably putting out a fire somewhere. Diversionary tactics. It's what I'd have done.

The four to my right popped out again, fired. Shit. I swung around, targeted, missed.

The others were coming closer. Eight of them, Sully had said.

We were trapped. There was no doorway behind us, no short corridor. Across was a vacant storage locker, but that would go nowhere. Even if we could decode the lock in time, it would simply serve as a coffin. Only the gradual curve of the corridor kept us alive.

"Sullivan!" A woman's voice called out. I identified it as Sully did. Berri Solaria.

I wanted her to step into view around the corridor's curve. Badly.

"Sullivan!" she called again.

"Blessings of the hour, Sister." A wicked smile flitted across his mouth. "How may I assist you?"

"Step out. Drop your weapons. You won't be harmed."

I couldn't see her, but at least the four behind us stopped firing.

"Please tell Cousin Hayden I regret I can't do that."

"Fool! If your life means nothing to you, then how about the woman? And your demon-spawned friend?"

"Bargaining with me, Berri?"

"Those of us who know our holy mission are always prepared to show mercy."

"A holy mission that breeds jukors?" Sully glanced up and down the corridor as he spoke, assessing, planning. I knew he was reading her, reading those in her group. Whatever link I had with him and Ren had gone quiet. He was buying time, talking to her, but I had no idea why.

"A holy mission to cleanse the Empire of the filth of soul-stealers. Surely you understand that!"

"Some of my best friends are soul-stealers," he yelled back to her.

"Bastard!" she shouted. "Infidel!"

Ren touched my arm. *Chasidah.*

I glanced at him. Glanced past him, past the four men flattened against the corridor walls. And I saw something move, something large and shadowy, behind them. I saw the distinct outline of a Norlack, pointing.

Verno. With a rifle that most eight-foot-tall Takas normally didn't need.

Praise the stars.

Four short bursts and Sully was suddenly pushing, shoving. "Go! Go!"

I ran backward, firing, spraying cover. Sully did the same.

Berri's people fired back, but there were four less now, and we had an open passageway.

I could hear Berri screaming behind us. Something about Lazlo. Call Lazlo. Reinforcements. More of their people, more weapons.

"Here!" Sully darted down the inner corridor with core access. *Lifts. Cut them off.*

Reinforcements would be slow in coming without the lifts.

He slid the panel back. We tumbled through into the darkness.

I grasped Verno's arm. "How—"

"I knew. When she hated Ren, I knew."

That was all we had time to say. Voices, loud and angry, trumpeted in from the corridor.

"Red's that way!" Lights flickered as the main lifts moved up and down. I pushed past Sully and skittered down the rampway just as the access panel slid open again. Berri's people, following us.

Sully turned and fired. "Split up!" Ren and Verno were on the other side. "Lift controls. Shut them down!"

They headed toward Yellow. We pounded toward Red.

32

I moved by memory, by touch, not by sight, other than what was illuminated by the flickering glimmer of lights that signaled the main lift bank. Three lifts jutted out into the core, narrow rampways between them. The emergency control panel was set in the middle. Shut them down. Had to shut them down. Then it was only us against Berri and her seven followers. And I knew the core.

Up. We could go up. The darkness and the lattice-work of ramps and ladders offered many more possibilities than the open corridors. We could exit, hit the corridors, then enter the core again. Move up.

Somehow I felt if we got to the commercial sector we'd make it. That's where the shuttle bays were, back to the terminal. That's where the shops were on the promenade. More people. Stripers.

I heard Sully breathing hard behind me, felt his light contact with Ren. Ren was at an advantage but a disadvantage. The darkness didn't hamper him. The narrowness of the rampways, and the fact he couldn't sense them, did.

Watch Verno, watch Verno. Sully sent caution wrapped in encouragement. He sent to Ren what the panel would look like, what to do to disable the secondary lift bank. Only one lift there. Not the three we had.

The station rumbled slightly, jarring me sideways. A small tremor, but I knew what it was. Sully had set off the explosives in the lab. A final parting gesture.

We crossed into Red, Berri's people grunting, careening behind us. They weren't used to the core, as I was. They fired occasionally, but off the mark.

We didn't return fire. It would only give away our location.

The core groaned, clanked, pinged as if to protect us. Machinery squealed on, whined off. I ignored the sounds, well used to them. I doubted Berri and her people were.

"Sullivan!" Berri's voice echoed. "You can't escape. Your ship's marked. We'll take her."

I hoped Gregor was smarter than that. I might not like the man, but I never thought he was stupid. At least not stupid enough to let the *Karn* be taken. Dorsie was on board. I still had hopes for her and Ren.

We got to the main lifts before Verno and Ren reached the secondary. A lift whizzed by, buffeting us with a sharp wind, plunging us into darkness. Then we were in the light leaking in from the corridor, silhouetted. Laser fire burst through the air. I ducked down as Sully did, his hand on my arm.

Chasidah!

I'm okay. I'm trained for this, remember? And I was. I was back in Fleet mode again. Moving. Focused. Singular.

He squeezed my arm. *I'm going to try for the panel. Cover me.*

I swung the Stinger out in a two-handed grip, locked

on where I'd last heard Berri's voice, moved up from that. Fired. A harsh groan, a half scream. Not a kill. But it gave them something to think about. And, I knew, it also gave them a need to search for a med-kit.

I saw and heard more movement. Berri's people had split up too. Some followed us. Some followed Verno and Ren.

Shit. I should've gone with Verno, and Sully with Ren. But things had happened too fast. It didn't break that way. Just like cards when dealt. Only this time, they were more in Sully's favor than Ren's.

The lifts behind me shuddered and groaned just as Sully's *Got it!* echoed in my thoughts. Nothing behind us but endless thin stripes of light. Nothing in front of us but the gaping maw of the core.

And Verno and Ren just now reaching the secondary lifts, with Berri's people closer, firing again. As unfamiliar with the core as they were, they could move faster than Verno and Ren. The closest exit into the corridor was still ten, twenty feet farther in front of them. They'd never make it. They'd—

The light of the lift behind them approached, slowly. Their silhouettes disappeared.

I threw images and words, and prayed Ren would understand. *On the lift. Top. It's stopping. Handholds. Clear space. Ride up!*

I felt Sully grab my thoughts. His hand clamped hard on my shoulder as he rose halfway. His other lifted the Carver, laying down cover fire, drawing attention to us. Not Verno and Ren.

Two tall figures scrambled onto the stopped car that was innocently, conveniently disgorging its passengers from the other side into the corridor. Passengers who had no idea a life-and-death struggle waged behind them.

Kneel! Handholds on the floor! Grab them! I'd ridden lift cars hundreds of time as a teenager. A game of betcha-can't, betcha-I-can.

The lift moved, surging upward, two forms hunched at its top. I felt Ren's slight trickle of amazement. Water moving upstream.

Berri's people fired but Ren and Verno rose, moving too quickly. Safe. Gone.

That left only Sully and myself.

Berri and her armed associates knew that too. Sully was who she and Hayden Burke were really after. Lots of money rested behind that wicked, wicked Sully smile.

I wondered if Berri realized how expendable she was as well. Hayden Crossley Burke didn't strike me as someone willing to share, his charitable works notwithstanding.

My thoughts exactly, angel.

Sully!

Where to? This is your backyard.

Up. I sent images of the crowded corridors on Levels 12 to 15. Shops, bars, hotels. We could play a serious game of hide and seek, aided by stripers whose presence would be an impediment to Berri's armed thugs. Sully's ability to link with Ren guaranteed we'd find him again.

Up it is. We broke in a low run toward Green. Boot steps resounded toward us and behind us, hoping to converge on us before we hit a ladder.

They didn't. We did, upleveling to 27, then 26. I was sucking air, my lungs burning. Level 26 dead-ended. We had to go left to pick up the next ladder, our pursuers close on our heels.

I searched for the double red light, saw it, lunged for it, my hands hitting the cold metal of the ladder. Pulled, pulled, pulled, hearing Sully breathing hard behind me.

Laser fire burned around us. I zagged, zigged on

instinct. Through it all, I blessed my boot-camp instructor, Maguire. Regretted the day I'd ever called her an ignorant slut. She'd taught me well.

Level 25, 24. We hit another dead end, the uplevel ladder far to our right this time. We had to cross over the now-dead main-lift banks in Red. We'd be open, exposed on both sides, with angry, armed religious fanatics on a holy mission right behind us.

I jogged to the right, stumbling on an uneven section of rampway. Sully caught me under the armpits and pushed me on. His brief touch was warm, reassuring, but contained a flare of need, desperation, encouragement.

"We'll make it," I gasped.

Don't talk. Save your air. Think.

Got it.

Suddenly there was more movement on the rampways, more boot sounds, more shouts. I'd caught a flash of light moments before, but hadn't put it together. An access had opened. Berri's reinforcements had arrived on Level 24.

Three. Only three.

But it was three too many, too close to Sully and myself, momentarily stopped at the lift banks, with stripes of light from the closed corridor doors glowing dimly behind us. Laser fire arced again. I spun, crouching, and fired.

I wasn't so lucky this time. No groans responded, no med-kit seemed to be required.

Sully fired in the other direction. Berri's people were between us and any ladders uplevel. We'd killed the lifts. We couldn't use them, like Ren and Verno. We'd be too exposed in the time it would take to reactivate them. Plus, there was no guarantee one would stop so we could climb on.

I stayed in my crouch, watching our three new

players approach. They were our best chance. Only three. Still six on the other side, gaining rapidly. We had to get by these three. Had to get to the next ladder—

Chasidah.

What?

Two things. First, trust me. Second, under no circumstances scream.

What?

Sully rose up quickly beside me, pulling me with him. *Arms around my neck, now.*

What?

Do it!

He yanked me against him. My arms coiled automatically over his shoulders. Instinctively, I tightened my grip on my gun. He raised his boot to the railing. I didn't like this position. There was nowhere to go but down. And down, in the middle of the core, was a deadly location.

"Sully—"

"Sullivan!" Berri was close. The rampway vibrated as feet pounded in approach.

He grasped me, tight, hard, locking my body against his as he pushed off from the rampway, pushed *away* from the rampway. We dropped backward into the center of the core, where there was nothing but darkness, but emptiness, but falling—

Don't scream.

My God. He was committing suicide and taking me with him.

I buried my face against his shoulder but didn't scream. It didn't matter. Terror washed through me. Terror and wind rushing, gravity grabbing, bodies plummeting . . .

Up.

We were going—inexplicably—up.

Wind rushed against my face as I raised it, wet with tears.

Wind, and a hushed sound.

I knew the sound. I'd heard it every time I'd imagined that nebulous haze of gray fuzzy soft. We were in gray fuzzy soft now. It was brighter than I remembered, almost blinding. But no, brighter only along Sully's shoulders, his arm . . . through slitted eyes I could see one arm raised, light streaming from it, flowing outward. It seemed to cone around us like the glow surrounding the winged demons in the Englarian paintings. Unholy light, a fatal silvery translucence . . .

Impossible. That would mean Sully was—

My thoughts halted abruptly as I felt a jolt. His boots hit something solid. My boots found purchase on the rampway. I snatched my arms away, feeling frightened and confused. More frightened than when I thought we were going to die.

I lurched backward, slamming against the wall. My knees were suddenly rubbery and refusing to cooperate. My breath came in long, hard gasps. My eyes focused on the silvery, illumined form standing before me.

Light flared, settled, like a long cape. A hazy surge of energy—

Don't look. Those were the words he'd always said to me in gray fuzzy soft. Sully's hands, touching me, caressing me. Sully, making love to me. But don't look. Don't look at what's touching you. At what's making love to you.

But that had been in my mind. My imagination. I'd never seen light glowing from a human before. Only in the Englarian paintings. And those demons were anything but human.

My knees gave way. I collapsed onto the gridded rampway with a thud. My gun slid under my bent legs.

Chasidah.

I cringed and sucked in a sob. He was in my mind. He'd been in my body. And I didn't even know what he was. Oh, God.

The light faded as he knelt down slowly, a rustle of fabric. My fingers coiled through the latticed gridwork, hard. Painful. I hung on to the flooring for no rational reason, other than I could.

"Chasidah." He said my name out loud this time. It was Sully's voice. But in the dark, his face was in dim outline. I didn't know if it was Sully's form or the scaly demon from the painting. "We have to find Ren. Verno."

You go find them. I'll stay here. It's nice. Quiet. Dark.

I can't do that. Warmth flowed, trying to reach me, trying to tell me things words could not. *Angel, it's not what it seems.*

My gaze flashed to his face, even though I didn't want it to. And I saw Sully. Just Sully, now that he was close. But I didn't know what he'd looked like minutes before.

"What are you?" My voice broke, hoarse.

"Someone who loves you." He sounded almost as hoarse, but his words were soft. "Someone who can't change what he is. Someone who doesn't want to believe those two things are incompatible."

I stared at him, part of me intensely aware that we had to find Ren. Verno. Berri and Hayden's people still pursued us. We had to get off Marker alive. But all I could feel was a pain lacing through me, searing me. Pain of my own doing. I recognized it. I'd felt it before, with every step I'd taken with Gabriel Ross Sullivan.

Mercenary. No, not just mercenary. Empath. No, not just empath. *Ragkiril.* Memory-wipes. Mind-deaths. Then Gabriel Ross Sullivan, in my mind. Harsh. Intrusive. Unwanted.

Loving, reaching, caressing. Becoming part of me.

All the while, ask no questions, though I clearly remembered his question to me: *Can you accept me as I am, now, on faith? With what you know, and nothing more?*

Explain faith to me. Explain goddamned faith. Explain why I'm the one scared, hurting, alone. Ignorant. Every goddamned time. Explain that to me, damn you!

I waited for an answer, but heard nothing. At least, not from him.

But another voice, one I knew as Chasidah's but for a moment sounded almost like Amaris's, spoke to me. And it told me I was still alive. It told me that I was still alive because of the man—one of Abbot Eng's soul-stealers—kneeling before me.

There'd been no other way off that rampway. We were surrounded. It was either death, or up.

I was the one who'd chosen up. And he'd complied, somehow hurtling us to safety up through the core's deep shadows, where Berri's people would never think to look for us. If they'd seen us jump, if they'd looked anywhere, it would have been down.

Who would have thought to look up? Soul-stealers were mythical. Imaginary.

I struggled to my feet and tried to focus. I grabbed my Fleet-issue personality out of cold storage, slammed it on. Human, *Ragkiril,* or demon—whatever Sully was was less important at the moment than our survival. Jukors were born and Takas were dying. My fears seemed petty in comparison. "Where are we?" My voice shook but sounded definitely stronger.

Sully rose with me. "Level 13. You felt it would be safer with the shops, people."

"Did I? What the fuck do I know." I pushed away

from the wall, remembering to holster my Stinger, and stumbled toward the closest exit I could find.

I kept my distance from the man walking alongside me as we threaded our way through stationers coming and going, eating, drinking, and laughing on Level 13's Red-Sector promenade.

What the hell did they know?

We passed a news kiosk, the 'caster's bland face following us. There were still no answers concerning the mysterious disks left at the scene of a recent rape and murder.

Something flitted through the edge of my mind. Ren's voice, through Sully's link with both of us. A series of thought-pictures skittered by: Berri peppering Verno with questions about Sully, then giving Verno a disk of hymns after a service. Verno innocently loading them into the entertainment system on the *Karn* while Sully and Ren headed to Moabar. Verno, explaining to Ren. Ren, sending to Sully. Sully's analysis, back to Ren. The worm program had to have been on those disks and coded to activate once Sully was back on board.

But whether Berri's actions were to ensure Hayden's acquisition of the Sullivan fortune or because she—and Hayden—knew Sully was tracking the jukor labs, Verno didn't know. And Sully could only second-guess. But it seemed likely that both were possible: whatever Hayden wanted to do with the jukors could only be helped by the additional funding the Sullivan fortune could provide.

"Where are they?"

"Two levels up in Yellow." He scanned the crowd as we walked. I could feel an edginess, a wariness in him. Just as I knew he felt mine. I had no doubt I was wearing fear and anger like a heavy coat around me.

"We meeting with them?" We'd have to backtrack to the main lift bank and then hope it was operative.

"I need to get to a secure terminal first." He tapped at his jacket pocket. "This goes to Drogue. He knows what to do with it."

Berri knew we'd try to return to the *Boru Karn*. Which meant we couldn't leave Marker that way. Which meant the data had to be sent now. Before Berri found us again.

"Up," I said, even though the last time I'd said that, my entire life shattered. "We need to go up. Level 2. Do you want to get Ren and Verno first?"

"They're safe where they are. It helps if they're watching the corridors."

Main lifts were functional again. I knew they would be. The lifts were easy to shut down. Equally as easy to start up, if no one's shooting at you.

I glanced at an M-2 clock as we waited. An hour past the end of the business day. That meant less people to see us, ask questions. That was good.

We squeezed into a lift already crowded with a maintenance tech and a large cleaning unit on a pallet. I hit the button for Level 2 and stepped back into the only available space in the corner. Sully's hands closed on my arms, hesitantly.

Chasidah. Heat and ice flowed through me, alternating. I shivered, crossed my arms over my chest and tried to dislodge his touch. Tried to keep my mental duro-hards from bursting open, flinging questions, fears, anger. All were more than I could face at the moment.

Level numbers pinged by: 8, 6, 5. The maintenance tech nodded disinterestedly at us as he exited, guiding his pallet into the corridor. No one else got on. The doors slid closed. I stepped out of Sully's grasp.

But not out of his emotional range. Pain. Pleading. Hope. He sent those to me. Shame followed. *Chasi—*

"Stop it." Speaking out loud kept my focus outside my feelings and what he was making me feel. "I can't deal with that, with you, right now."

Level 3, 2. The doors opened to an empty corridor. Admin offices had been closed for over an hour. I headed straight for the checkpoint, manned by a security 'droid. It scanned entry badges. I had none, only the emergency access code created over twenty years ago for use by the Admirals' High Council on Marker. My mother had been part of the tech team and had violated every rule and regulation in making me memorize it. *In case anyone ever tries to harm you,* she'd said. *In case I'm not around to protect you. Go uplevel, get to the people you know will.*

I put the code in again and held my breath. The force field hazed, dropped. Praise Amaris. Praise the stars.

And pray like hell Berri or Lazlo didn't have the same code I did.

We moved quickly down a long hallway, then turned left. I passed three doors before I came to the one with a nameplate that read COMMANDER T. BERGREN. I touched the palm pad with another code I knew by heart, stepped in, locking the door as Sully followed. An unexpected sense of relief washed over me. For the first time since we'd left the *Karn*, I felt safe.

The outer office was dimly lit. There was a long desk to the left and three chairs on the right. Everything was tidied for the night: neat, orderly, deskscreen dark. No sharp-eyed assistant to ask questions. No fellow officers dropping by for a chat who just might recognize Thad's little sister Chaz and ask more questions. Our timing was almost too good.

Straight ahead were the wide double doors to Thad's inner office. My code opened those as well.

Sully said nothing, sent nothing that I was aware of. I knew he had to be telling Ren where we were. He had to be formulating plans.

The illuminated display cabinet on Thad's back wall

cast a wide shaft of light across the carpet. The cabinet was crowded with Fleet plaques, award statues, mementos. I headed past it, past the elegant dark blue couch and plush chairs to my right, past the round conference table and hologrid on my left.

I slid into Thad's high-backed chair and half-swiveled it around. I tabbed up the deskscreen. The light over the desk automatically came on.

Sully handed the datatabs to me.

"Everything goes?" My voice was calm, flat. Captain Bergren in command.

He nodded, saying nothing, sending nothing. Like another time I remembered. *Stay out of my goddamned mind*, I'd said. He had. He was.

I slotted in the thin tabs and tried to ignore the small tendrils of pain and fear weaving around my heart. Instead, I concentrated on appending the data to a transit file. Then I realized I had no idea of the exact receipt address. "What's Drogue's—"

A series of numbers flashed through my mind, staying there as if it were my memory. Not his. So the link wasn't broken. Just silent, until I needed something.

I keyed in the address. "You want to add a message?" It would take at least five minutes for the three tabs to encode and append.

He nodded. I vacated the chair and headed for a low cabinet by the conference table, knowing it usually held spare power clips that would work in my Stinger. At least, it always had in the past. I might feel safer in my brother's office, but I knew it was at best temporary. We still had to get off station, out of Marker. Alive.

I tabbed on the conference-table lights, put a fresh clip in my laser pistol, then shoved another in my jacket pocket. Fleet didn't use Carvers but they did have a similar, high-power laser pistol. Thad had one clip that might work.

It will.

I turned from where I knelt in front of the cabinet. Was he reading resonances or my thoughts at random? I wasn't sure I wanted the latter.

It's safer if we keep contact.

Obviously true when we'd infiltrated the jukor lab, when we were running from Berri and Lazlo. When answers, decisions, information had to be quickly shared. But at the moment we sat in my brother's office behind two sets of locked doors. I wanted to listen to my own thoughts, to feel my own reactions. Without Sully's comments, and his pain, wearing at me.

Without him gathering information on me. While I'd never been permitted to gather any about him. Though now I knew why.

I handed him the spare clip. Anger slipped out before I could stop it. "You're not just a *Ragkiril,* are you? You should have warned me."

"I hoped, given enough time, it wouldn't matter." His voice was soft.

"Lies are lies, whether they're said now or ten years from now."

The computer beeped softly in the silence, segueing data into transmittable code.

"I never lied," he said finally.

That was true, only because he'd never permitted questions. I turned away, hugged my arms over my chest and went to stare at Thad's trophies. I tamped down my anger. But the pain, and the fear, refused to go away.

Why were all the handsome ones always such lying bastards?

The click and tap behind me told me Sully worked on his message. Not through a vidlink—too easily intercepted. What Drogue would receive would topple lives. Powerful lives.

Then maybe no more jukors would breed. And no more Takas would die.

And maybe Chaz Bergren would find herself at a stellar helm somewhere, on a freighter that worked the rim, whose owner asked few questions and cared less about documentation. There'd be the peace of jumpspace again. And the ever-present game of hide and seek with rim pirates. Like Sullivan. Pirate. Poet. Smuggler. Mercenary. Monk. *Ragkiril.* And...?

I broke the silence with a question. If he didn't want to answer, fine. But no one was going to stop me from asking them anymore. "Does Drogue know what you are?"

Sully took his fingers from the keypads. "To him, I'm just a mercenary with a conscience. In a way, my occupation was his idea."

"Drogue?"

"It was the Englarians who showed me how little the Empire did for those who weren't in their favor. Takas. Stolorths. A variety of colonies on the rim, where people routinely died of diseases cured a hundred years ago. It felt wrong for me to wear the robe, knowing what I am. But it wasn't wrong to continue to help the forgotten, the outcasts. Clinics and orphanages need funds to survive."

Ren had said the reasons behind Sully's piracy would surprise me. In spite of my anger at Sully's deception, he was right.

"Your family's money couldn't have accomplished the same goals legally?"

"I had no reason to think my father would be charitable."

The deskscreen flashed. Data encoded and ready to transmit.

"Will you go back to doing that, when this is finished?"

"When this is finished, Hayden won't be in control of the Sullivan moneys. I may not be the preferred heir, but I am the legal one."

I leaned against the cabinet as the ramifications sunk in. This was more than Takas and jukors. This was a wealth of almost unimaginable proportions. Gabriel Ross Sullivan would shortly become a very sought-after, very influential man.

Unless those seeking his influence learned he was a *Ragkiril* with the powers of a mythical demon. That was more than sufficient reason to hide behind lies. To have a Stolorth friend to take the blame, or credit, for what he did. Or maybe it wasn't just friendship. Maybe Ren saw the numbers too.

He tapped the deskscreen, sent the data. "You have good reason to be angry with me, but you've no right to dishonor Ren."

I straightened abruptly at his retort to my unspoken comments. "Damn you! Stop—"

Sully lunged to his feet, his hand grasping under his jacket for his laser pistol. Fear clamped my heart. For a few tense seconds I thought I'd finally pushed him too far. Then the wide double doors on my right slid sideways. I swiveled, grabbed my Stinger.

"What in hell do you—" Commander Thaddeus Bergren took a half step into his office and stared at the man standing behind his desk. "Sullivan? You're dead."

I lowered my laser pistol. "Hello, Thad."

He jerked his head toward me, his pale blue eyes widening. "Chaz!"

"Sit down." I motioned toward the conference table

and four chairs. And shot a glance at Sully, who still had his Carver trained on my brother.

He lowered it. *He's genuinely glad to see you.*

I hoped so. We needed him. I reholstered my laser pistol as I took the chair next to Thad's. My brother was out of uniform, dressed casually, evidently not returning to his office on business. I recognized the light blue sweater he wore. I'd given it to him for his birthday two years before. "Listen to me. A firm called Crossley Burke is running a gen-lab here on M-2. They're breeding jukors. We're not sure why—"

"I know."

A sick feeling grabbed my stomach. Thad knew. Was there nothing left of my life that wasn't twisted, full of lies? I looked at my perpetually virtuous older brother with disgust. "How could you get involved with that?"

He knotted his fingers together and stared at me for a moment. I was surprised by how much he resembled our father. Same angular face, pale blue eyes, sandy-red hair, now with glints of silver. But Lars's face had never showed the kind of turmoil on Thad's now.

"I got involved with that," he said quietly, "to keep you alive."

It took me a few heartbeats to process what he said. "Explain."

"I found out Burke was doing something with jukors. I began pulling manifests, incomings, thinking it was just some rich man's whim to increase his personal security force. Stupidly, I confronted him. He warned me that if I acted on it, you'd be the one to suffer. I didn't believe him. It sounded too implausible. Why would he take such a risk, just because he wanted some guard beasts for his estates?"

Thad shook his head, as if remembering something unpleasant. "Next I know, you're up on murder charges. Dereliction of duty. I never connected Burke with what happened until I got into a lift and Burke was there, with a bodyguard. A bearded guy with a laser pistol. He stopped the lift, told me you'd get the death sentence. But if I kept quiet, he'd see to it you were sent to Moabar. I knew it was Hell there, but at least you'd be alive. Maybe, in time, I could find a way to get you pardoned."

I didn't remember breathing. I didn't remember not breathing. I stared at him. "But you could've gone to the Admirals' Council. Hell, you could've gone to Darius Tage, had him talk to Prew!" If there was a name synonymous in the Empire with unflinching honor and ethics, it was First Barrister Darius Tage.

"Burke owns people high up in the Empire. I don't know who they are. This project of his isn't about guard beasts. It's much bigger, political. I have no proof, but my guess is he's looking to fund some kind of interquadrant war. I knew if I talked to the wrong person, Burke would come after you. Kill you."

I barely recognized my strong, always-in-control, authoritative brother. Hayden Burke had him by the one thing I never suspected mattered to Thad. Me.

My brother actually loved me. Pieces of my shattered life started to flow back together. "We need to get out of Marker. We took out the gen-lab on Level 28 an hour ago. We lost Burke's people in the core, but—"

"The fire alarm? That was you?"

"We used low-impact charges to destroy the lab."

"Not all of it." Sully sat on the desk. He picked up the databs. "That proof you didn't have is in here. It's on its way to people in Dafir, and on Moabar Station, who can use it. They can't be bought out or threatened. It may take time, but they will be believed."

Sully slipped the datatabs back into his jacket. "We

need a ship, Commander. The information is safe. We're not."

"I can get a maintenance tug to get you back to the terminal."

I shook my head. "Burke's people know about the ship that brought us here. They'll be watching for it, and us."

"You have any freighters heading out-system?" Sully asked.

"Not that I have immediate access to. Fleet ships are always going in and out, but I don't know who I can trust." Thad's mouth tightened into an angry line. Angry at the situation but probably angry at himself as well. *I don't know* was never one of his favorite expressions.

"Except . . ." Thad threw me a hesitant glance. "The *Morgan Loviti* came in a few hours ago."

The name shot through me with a jolt. "Philip's here?"

"I'm meeting him for a drink in . . ." He pulled up his sleeve, uncovering his watch. "I'm late. I stopped to pick up a new ship design I wanted to show him. Didn't know I'd find you." His gaze flicked to Sully, then back to me.

Sully holstered his Carver. "What makes you think he'd help us?"

"The Guthries have considerable power, are well-respected. Philip Guthrie is one of the most ethical people I know. His family publicly denounced the jukor project twenty years ago. I have no reason to believe he's changed either his mind or his morals."

"You're willing to risk Chasidah's life on that?"

"You probably don't know she was married to him. He still cares for her, very much."

I touched Thad's arm. "We ran into Philip about a

month ago, in Calth. He could've impounded the ship, sent me back to Moabar." I looked past him, at Sully. "He let us go."

"I'll meet him in the bar, talk to him."

"You can't guarantee what his intentions will be when he learns Chasidah's here. What we've done."

"Of course not, but—"

"I can. Bring him here."

Sully's unexpected offer surprised me.

My brother's eyes narrowed. "A man like Philip Guthrie doesn't respond well to questions at gunpoint, if that's your plan."

"If he's lying, if he's working for Burke, or if he has any intentions of returning Chasidah to Moabar, I'll know when I see him."

Thad frowned. "How—"

Sully shoved himself off the desktop. "Mind-probe. I'm a *Ragkiril*."

"Ridiculous. You're not a Stolorth."

"He can read Philip, scan him," I told Thad when my brother's startled gaze focused on me.

Thad rose slowly. "And if he is working with Burke?"

"Then I can make him forget he ever saw us."

A clear expression of distaste crossed Thad's features. But he made no comment. He stopped at the doorway to the outer office. "I'll be back in ten minutes."

Sully remained standing, quietly, after the doors closed behind my brother. I felt him link with Ren, saw the flash of thought-pictures. Not Berri or Lazlo, but there were people in the corridors, looking. Ren sensed their searching, but he had no visual link with Verno and couldn't provide detailed descriptions, other than *male humans, discreetly armed*.

I leaned my elbows on the table, resting my face in my hands. I was exhausted, emotionally and physically. I wasn't sure of how I felt about Philip's involvement but knew what Thad had said was true. Philip was ethical. To the point, perhaps, of being stodgy. His family had been vehement in their objections to the jukors bred during the war. And they'd never support an insurrection in the Empire, not one funded by Burke and carried out through the use of jukors.

The issue, of course, would be how he'd react to Sully. Pirate. Ghost. *Ragkiril*.

The chair next to me squeaked. Sully folded his hands on the tabletop.

I propped my chin on my fist. "He could refuse to help us on a matter of principle. Nothing to do with Burke."

"And miss the chance to play hero?"

I ignored his sarcasm and voiced a disturbing thought that had been hovering. One that touched on things Gregor had said back on the *Karn*. "Could you force him to help us?"

Sully took a deep breath. "If I say no, I'd be lying. If I tell you the truth, then I've added to your fears."

"If you can do things like that, why didn't you know Thad was coming into the office until he was at this door?"

"Strictly a priority error. I was focused on you. And keeping a light link with Ren. It's like picking a conversation out of a crowded room but not being able to hear all of them."

I leaned back, nodded. "But you could force Philip to help us?"

"I could make him believe that's what he wanted to do. But if we ran into three or four of his officers who dissented, there'd be problems."

"I heard Gregor tell Aubry he saw a *Ragkiril* strip the minds of four prisoners during the war."

"A *Ragkiril* can't. A *Kyi-Ragkiril* could."

"Explain."

Sully hesitated only a moment—out of habit, perhaps. Or perhaps listening to Ren tell him it was time to start answering my questions. "A *Kyi-Ragkiril* is one who draws power from an energy field called the *Kyi*. Those energies can be used, manipulated, shifted. The *Kyi*'s not that different from jumpspace. A neverwhen of sorts. You called it 'gray fuzzy soft' when you saw it. Others, centuries ago, labeled it an unholy light. Abbot Eng demonized it, falsely. The *Kyi* is light. Energy. It's no more holy, or unholy, than the person using it."

"You're a *Kyi-Ragkiril*."

"Yes." No hesitation this time.

"But you said you can't—"

"I didn't say I couldn't. I said if I had to control a number of people, there'd be problems. The larger the requirement of energy, the more visible it becomes. Telekinesis, aggregate thought control, serious physical healings—"

"When Ren was hurt, on the bridge, I didn't see any light."

There was a long, hard silence. His shoulders were stiff under his black jacket. "It was there."

"I was right next to you." Touching you, holding you. "I would've seen—"

"I changed what you saw. I had to. It was wrong. But there was too much at risk."

Ren had been dying. The *Karn* in shambles. The *Meritorious* almost totally destroyed. And Sully had been in my mind, just like in Trel's bar. But this time, not shielding the emotions I was sending. But altering what I saw, and I hadn't even known.

Part of me understood he had valid reasons for what he'd done. But another part of me, a part that was far too crowded with unwanted mental duro-hards, recoiled. Shocked. Angered. "You had no right!"

"None at all. I also had no choice."

"Next time, try honesty. It—"

Sully held his hand up, stopping my words. "Thad's back. With Guthrie."

Philip's resonant voice filled the outer office. "How about telling me what's so damned important you couldn't—"

He stopped in the open doorway. He was in his gray working-dress uniform. Dignified. Handsome. I watched emotions flicker through Philip's eyes as I worked on reorienting my own.

"Chaz!" He stepped toward me, hand out, then hesitated. "This is what the security stops are for. I should've known."

He raised his chin, his gaze on Sully, who wasn't safely in the recesses of my ship's bridge. As with Thad, recognition took a few moments. "I gather Hell was full."

"Still room for you, Guthrie."

Damn it, don't start. We need his help. I was angry but forced myself to bank my emotion. It was useless right now. I took a deep breath, offered my ex-husband a bland smile. "Why don't you sit on the couch. We'll tell you what's going on."

Philip moved easily, as if my showing up unexpectedly again, in the company of a dead smuggler, was part of his everyday schedule. He leaned back against the cushions, propped one leg on his knee. Thad sat at his desk.

"That was the *Meritorious,*" Philip said to me as I swiveled my chair around.

"I had reasons not to tell you."

I could see his mind opening and inspecting those mental Fleet-issue databoxes. He nodded to Sully. "I gather you helped my wife escape?"

"She's not your wife."

I shot a warning look at Sully, then turned to Philip. "We need a safe way off Marker. Will you help?"

Philip studied me for a moment before his gaze flashed to Sully. "I only want what's best for you, Chaz."

"That could mean a lot of things," Sully said, rising. His voice was soft, but there was an underlying forcefulness.

Philip met Sully's obsidian gaze squarely. "What's your interest here?"

"At the moment, you. Your intentions. Your allegiances."

"You question me?"

"We have to question." I put my captain's command voice behind my words. "We don't know if we can trust you."

"Why? What did you do?"

I chose my words carefully. "We destroyed a jukor lab. Here. Level 28-Blue."

"Impossible."

"That we destroyed the lab?" Sully asked.

Philip responded with a dismissive glance. He turned back to me. "Breeding jukors was banned years ago.

The labs were destroyed. All embryos, genetics, everything."

"A jukor attacked us on Moabar," I told him quietly. "The lab we destroyed a few hours ago had two pair, Philip. Two breeding pair. And a Taka female, serving as surrogate."

He stared at me, hard. "Who's doing this?"

"My cousin, Hayden Burke." Sully's voice was cold as he stepped toward Philip. "And, according to Commander Bergren, a number of very powerful people close to Prew. Are you one of them, Guthrie?"

Philip shot to his feet, anger twisting his face, his clenched fist moving. Sully caught his arm, held it firmly for a moment. Philip jerked his wrist out of Sully's grip. Anger vibrated across his face, radiated from his body. But he didn't move.

Sully's eyes were already infinite, dark. And locked on Philip's. He held his hand open at chest level, his fingers splayed slightly, but not touching Philip. A barely perceptible silvery energy rippled over his shoulders, down his arms. It flowed toward Philip, as if going through him and around him at the same time.

I held my breath.

Thad swore softly.

Then it was over. Philip blinked as if he had suddenly, and unexpectedly, awakened.

Sully turned to me as if nothing unusual had happened. "Son of a bitch hates Hayden as much as I do. We can trust him."

Philip's lips thinned, his expression hardening. "Mind-fucker!" His fist caught Sully on the side of the jaw, throwing him back against Thad's desk. I was already on my feet.

Sully lunged, pinning Philip onto the couch. I grabbed Sully's shoulders. "Stop it!"

Philip swung again. Sully jerked away before the blow could connect.

I tried to push Sully backward and grabbed Philip's arm with my other hand, pushing and tugging at the same time. My feet tangled with Philip's legs. I lost my balance and fell onto the low sofa table just as Sully surged forward.

Thad shoved by me, grabbing for Sully's arm. I blocked him, catching him in the stomach with my elbow. "I said, stop it! All of you."

I plowed in between Sully and Philip again, braced one arm against the back of the couch. Thad sank down on the low table, clutching his midsection, breathing hard.

Philip glared up at me. Behind me, Sully's breath rasped as he stood.

"We had to know," I told Philip. Another no-choice situation. Like on the bridge of the *Karn*. I pushed myself upright and faced Sully. His arms were clenched at his sides. His chest heaved. A reddish bruise had blossomed on his jaw. "Power down. Both of you," I said.

Philip sat up, raked his hands through his hair.

Thad was back on his feet. "She needs your help, Philip. I'm not any happier about dealing with . . . him than you are." He slanted a glance at Sully. "But Burke threatened to kill her before. He will now. Unless they stop him first."

Philip took a deep breath as if to center himself. "Tell the whole story, from the beginning."

I did. I told him how jukors were breeding and Takas were dying. And other Takas were taking revenge, raping and killing human females. How Berri Solaria was working with Lazlo and had uncovered Sully's plans through her friendship with the Takan monk Brother

Verno. Who had risked his life to save us, and a Stolorth, Brother Ren Ackravaro.

Sully spoke tersely, gave Philip facts, figures, what names he knew. He showed him the datatabs, their information now on the way to Guardian Drogue.

"I'll need a copy of that sent to the *Loviti*," Philip said.

Sully hesitated. "I'm not sure I trust official Imperial channels right now."

"For good reason." Philip's expression looked suddenly pinched. I had a feeling what he'd heard didn't surprise him as much as I thought it would. "And I'll make sure those official Imperial channels don't see it. But there are people, people I know, who need to."

He did know something. "Philip?"

He slanted a glance at me. "Later. I'll explain later. Thad?"

My brother sat behind his desk, stared at his hands, and told how Burke had threatened my life when he'd confronted him with the jukor data. He admitted that my ship's logs had been falsified, my trial manipulated. My sentence on Moabar was a warning to Thad to cooperate.

Philip exploded in anger. "Damn it, Thaddeus! I needed that information. Why didn't you tell me?"

"Burke owns people—"

"A Guthrie? Me?"

"My first priority was keeping her alive. I didn't have time to find out who I could trust."

"So you hired him?" Philip pointed dismissively at Sully, leaning against the edge of Thad's desk.

"Nobody hired anybody," Sully said tiredly.

Thad leaned back in his chair. "I thought he was dead. Like you did."

Philip regarded Sully as if he were some sort of

specimen. "*Ragkiril*. And a human one. A genetic rarity. But immortality isn't one of their attributes. Even if he is a *Kyi*."

Sully straightened slightly.

"Didn't think I'd know that, did you?" Philip appeared clearly satisfied with the impact of his words. "I know what you are, what your kind can do. My family researched *Ragkirils* during the war. *Ragkirils* and jukors. It sounds as if your cousin wants to make sure you stay dead this time."

"Few people know what I am. Hayden's not one of them. And yes," Sully continued as Philip started to speak again, "Chasidah knows."

"Only a *Kyi-Ragkiril* can read without touching a subject," Philip told me, as if to make sure I knew what Sully was. "Watch for a silvered haze. In bright light you can't always see it. It's an energy field he uses. And watch his eyes, the way they seem to go totally black. He's monitoring my thoughts, probably yours and your brother's as well. So don't think for a minute he doesn't know we're all afraid of him. We have good reason to be. He can do a lot more than just see what we're thinking."

"She knows," Sully repeated tightly.

I stepped forward. "We need off Marker. Will you help?"

"If it were just him, I'd tell him to find his own damned way off. But there are other issues here, issues you don't know about. So, yes, Chaz, I'll help." He motioned to Thad. "I'll need to use your deskscreen."

My brother vacated his chair and exchanged a brief, troubled glance with Philip.

"Ever seen the paintings in an Englarian temple?" Philip asked Thad as Sully shoved himself away from the desk.

I didn't bother to watch for my brother's affirmative nod. I felt Sully's annoyance, felt him keep his reactions in check. Philip's knowledge, and confidence, clearly bothered him. He took a seat at the conference table and swiveled away from Thad and Philip.

I was glad for once I couldn't read rainbows. A distinct edginess hung in the air. Considering what we faced, it was counterproductive. I decided to lead by example—a tried-and-true Fleet method.

I sat next to Sully. "What's Ren's status?"

"There's a worker bar on Level 14. Mostly Takas. They've been able to stay there for a while."

"Any chance of getting back to the *Karn*?" Sully and Philip on the same ship for any length of time wasn't going to be a workable situation. And it would take the *Loviti* a while to reach Dock Five, or Dafir.

He angled toward me, his hand opening as if reaching for me, then he closed his fingers into a fist. He stared at them. "Guthrie still thinks of you as his wife." His voice was quiet.

I glanced at Philip. His concentration was on the deskscreen and the conversation he was having with his ship.

"We don't have time for personal issues—not his, not yours, not mine."

His hand opened again. "You're not his wife, Chasidah."

"I know that," I said.

His eyes snapped briefly to infinite darkness. *Mine.* Then the harsh tone in my mind softened. *Chasidah-angel. Philip says to fear me. Do you have any idea how afraid I am of him?*

"My private shuttle will be at Access Bay 7-Blue in twenty minutes." Philip tabbed off the deskscreen and leaned back in Thad's chair. "We're going to run into the security stops. Do you and your friends uplevel have ID?"

Sully swiveled slowly around, leaving emptiness, longing, and warmth in my mind. His sensations hovered around my confusion.

"Ren and Verno have Englarian clearances on file. Get me any two cards," he said to Thad, standing behind Philip. "I'll get Chasidah and myself through from there."

Philip scowled openly, but Thad agreed. "I'll need my desk back."

Philip grabbed the back of the chair next to mine, sat. He leaned his elbows on his knees, clasped his hands together. He deliberately ignored Sully as Sully pushed himself out of his seat, and chose instead to study me for a long moment. "I want you to consider something. I have no idea what your plans are after we get out of Marker, but with this information on Burke I can go back to Tage's office. I told you when I intercepted you out in Calth that I hadn't abandoned you. I've been talking to Tage, a few others, to get you transferred. Now I know I can clear your name. A captaincy could be yours again. It will be, because I'm on the Admirals' Council now. The Chaz Bergren I've known most of my life would never turn that down. Not even to work as a pilot for a smuggler, a *Kyi-Ragkiril*, a rare human one at that, who might yet end up being one of the wealthiest men in the Empire."

"I've got two cards." Thad's voice cut between us.

Philip shoved himself to his feet. "Think about it."

Thad drew me into a very un-Thad-like hug as we got ready to leave his office. He would stay behind, run interference through his access into the security system, and work on the copies of the data Sully had left him.

He'd be in touch, through a private comm tran I could access.

I feared for his safety, knowing what we did of Hayden Burke.

My big brother was more concerned for mine. "Philip's appointment on the council should halt most questions." Unless Burke had people in places higher than a Guthrie could go. There weren't many. He squeezed my hands. "Be sure...of what you want to do," he said softly.

He glanced at Sully, a few feet away in the outer office.

"Trust Philip," he added.

I bussed his cheek. "Watch after Willym for me."

Sully checked his Carver, adjusting his jacket around the weapon. I did the same with my Stinger. He had both ID cards in his pocket. "Ren and Verno will meet us at the bay at 7-Blue." He touched my arm. *I need a constant link with you.*

Agreed. I pushed away my unease at Philip's warning about *Kyi-Ragkirils.* If there were problems, Sully, scanning, reading, would know before anyone else. I wanted that knowledge.

Two stripers in the corridor watched us approach— Philip and Sully, with me in between. They saluted. "Everything all right, Captain?"

"Optimal."

But we were still on Fleet property. The security checkpoints were in Marker's public areas. The stripers there might be less intimidated by the Guthrie reputation.

The security 'droid at the checkpoint we'd passed through earlier now had a human companion.

"Lieutenant Halpert. Do you need to see my ID again?"

"No, sir, Captain Guthrie. But we had reports of a problem. I'll need to check the others' IDs."

Sully gave Philip a barely perceptible nod as he fished in his jacket for the ID.

"We're on Admirals' Council business," Philip continued. "I don't want to be delayed through a misidentification. I need clearances sent from here through to 7-Blue."

"Very good, sir. I still need to log them in to do that."

Sully held the cards out to Halpert. "For my wife and myself."

I knew Philip heard, but his only reaction was to clasp his hands behind him, rock slightly back on his heels. A sign that meant he was holding his temper.

Halpert scanned the cards, frowned. "I'm sorry, but—"

Sully's hand grasped his shoulder in a casual manner. "A problem, Lieutenant? I think the system's just running a little slow right now."

"A little slow." Halpert took a deep breath. "Sometimes this happens."

Sully removed the cards from the slots. "We're clear to go."

"You're cleared."

A second barely perceptible nod. This time from Philip to Sully. An acknowledgment of what he knew Sully could do. Change what someone thought, what someone saw. Just as Gregor had said.

I toyed with questions while we walked. It was early evening, station time. Less work uniforms, more civilian clothing on the clusters of people passing by. But I wasn't thinking of Marker 2 at the moment.

Why didn't you do that when we got to Moabar Station? I remembered how my card had read out an error in Berri's medical files. Drogue, Ren, Sully, and I had all crowded around the scanner.

Takas get suspicious when touched by humans. I had to wait for the MOC officer to focus on the screen before I could "show" her the file was clear.

He'd brushed against her, I thought. Or touched her. Changed what she saw.

In the core, why didn't you make me forget what you did?

I felt a small twinge of pain. He was remembering my fear, as I was.

Besides the fact I'd have no explanation of how we'd arrived uplevel?

So it's not like a zral, or . . . I didn't want to say the other word.

It's more like a distraction. A sleight of hand. It has to be consistent with the situation. I don't like when I have to do that, Chasidah. It's a decision I make; it's something I do only when I have no other choice. When lives are threatened.

A group of people waiting at the lifts talked excitedly. I thought about Sully's answers as I watched the group. I had to watch all the stationers moving around us, toward us. Berri and Lazlo were out there. But so were others, others I wouldn't recognize. We had to get to Blue, halfway around from where we were in Green.

Two stripers on patrol nodded but said nothing. Sully flashed thought-pictures over his link to Ren. They were moving cautiously, Verno's short rifle concealed, wrapped in his jacket.

Philip slowed, his hand rising slightly. "General checkpoint ahead. You can read if there are problems from this distance, can't you?"

On the left side of the corridor were a portable scanner and three stripers, two female, one male. All human.

That was a good sign. No Takas who didn't want to be touched.

Sully's eyes darkened. Philip watched him. I wondered what his family's files on *Ragkirils,* on *Kyi-Ragkirils,* had told him. Enough that he'd known what Sully was after he'd scanned him. Enough to be angry at the intrusion. Enough to state we all had very good reasons to be afraid.

"They're bored," Sully said after a moment. We picked up our pace. "Nothing interesting's happened. If Halpert sent through our clearances from the Fleet checkpoint, we should be fine."

"If he hasn't, he'll find himself sitting a few rather unpleasant duty shifts." Philip squared his shoulders, held his ID out to the tall woman security officer, read the name off her tag. "Cortez. We're on Admirals' Council clearance. My ID should suffice."

Cortez scanned it and briefly studied us. She was an older woman. Her duty pins showed twenty-five years. I couldn't remember if I'd ever seen her on Marker before, but it wasn't unlikely.

"Captain Guthrie." She handed him back his card. "Jumptalk has it you're up for an admiralty. Congratulations."

"It won't be official until next week, but thank you." Philip flashed her a smile, full of Guthrie confidence and magnetism. She smiled back.

Hell, it'd worked on me for years. He ranked right up there on my list of charming bastards.

"Your associates are clear." She waved us through. The male striper leaned over, said something in her ear.

Cortez responded with a narrow-eyed glance. "That's Philip Guthrie, you idiot." She caught Philip's glance back to her. "Sorry, sir. We've been told to watch for Farosian terrorists."

"I'm aware of the advisory. Thank you for your co-operation." He leaned toward me as we walked. His fingers closed around my elbow for a few moments. "The advisory might be genuine, or something Burke's put in place, looking for you. He's evidently trying to drag the Farosians into this. His contact in Prew's circle either has a reason to shed suspicions on Blaine's people or else his imagination is severely limited. Every time something happens lately in the Empire, the Farosians are blamed."

"That's because I'm not around anymore," Sully said, his gaze straight ahead.

"You, however, were at one time responsible for a large number of problems. Including the one you're in now. Mind telling me how a *Kyi-Ragkiril* didn't know this Solaria woman worked for Burke?"

"Because she believes she's on a holy mission. That's all I read from her. The insane believe their lies to be truth. Her insanity fits nicely into her religious devotion."

The corridor curved slightly. In the center, a group of young Fleet personnel, all ensigns, talked animatedly, laughing. They saw Philip's captain's insignia and quieted for a moment.

Philip steered me around them, his hand grasping my arm again. "Do the Englarians know what you are?" he asked Sully.

"They know I'm doing everything I can to stop the gen-labs. Beyond that, they haven't asked and I don't volunteer."

Valid reasons. I remembered him saying that. *But isn't an omission a lie?*

If the truth is so unacceptable, what have I achieved by revealing it? And if it prevents them from working with me, then jukors breed and more Takas die.

I held my thoughts for several steps. Words like *risk, fear,* and *wisdom* surfaced after a moment, but they were my own words, not Sully's. I thought about what had happened on the *Karn.* Revealing he was a *Kyi-Ragkiril* would have jeopardized the mission at that point. Finally I nodded. *But sooner or later, you have to trust someone. Especially if you're asking her to trust you.*

I've learned that. Don't give up on me, angel-mine.

Don't give me any more half-truths.

None.

Warmth filtered through me, lay softly against those painful tendrils gripping my heart.

We were almost through Yellow, Blue sector not far away. One more checkpoint and then the shuttle bay. I fell into my little time game, the one I'd played when we'd headed for the *Diligent Keeper* on Moabar Station. Ten minutes to freedom. Five minutes to freedom. Then I remembered it hadn't brought me any luck. Though things this time did seem to be going better. However, I wasn't ready to dub it, in Ren's words, "a good day."

We crossed into Blue. Three stripers waited, again, at the checkpoint. One female, two male. Philip went through the routine, turning on his charm to the appropriate gender. Turned on his authority and Guthrie heritage to the one male striper who took a bit too long with our ID.

Sully walked casually toward the scanner, smiled his own rakish smile at the woman. Reading, scanning, his eyes already darkening. Ready.

But it wasn't needed. They let us pass.

The traffic in Blue sector was lighter. Dinnertime was over, people were back in their apartments or perched on a bar stool somewhere. The *Loviti* had a damned fine galley, as I remembered. I didn't know what I wanted more: dinner or a long, hot shower.

Or a captaincy again? Philip's words rolled through my mind.

"The next set of double doors are 7-Blue's," Philip said.

Where are Ren and Verno?

On their way. They opted for the freight lifts. Slower, but more Takan workers, less chance of Lazlo following them.

And Takas would defend their own.

Philip glanced at the pad as he keyed in his access code. "Shuttle's in early. Good. I'll feel one hell of a lot better once we're back on board." The doors slid open and he put his hand on my shoulder, guiding me through. "We'll get cleaned up. You and I should have dinner. We have to talk about a lot of things." His mouth tightened. "Something's happening in the Empire, Chaz. I don't like it."

"And Burke's behind it?" We were back to what he'd alluded to in Thad's office.

"He, alone, doesn't have that much power. That's why all this doesn't make sense. I have to talk to Tage again." He squeezed my shoulder. "Actually, Burke's move may be the proof I need."

If Philip had been talking to First Barrister Darius Tage, then this was serious. Very serious.

"Later," he said, again, when I looked up in question. "I'll explain later."

Sully followed us into the small airlock control room, open and unsealed now with a ship in the berth. Through the wide doorway the sleek form of an Imperial captain's pinnace appeared almost suspended in the center of the cavernous, dimly lit bay. Behind her, outer-door guidance lights formed a half halo, casting eerie shadows through the ladders and maintenance rampways on the left and right. Boxy cargo stages for loading and unloading dotted the floor. The ship's six wide landing struts and short rampway were darkened, telling me the pinnace had probably been in longer than we thought. I would've preferred a hot shuttle, with engines ready to go.

The corridor doors slid closed behind us. Philip leaned over the small ops panel, hit the intercom, opening the link to the bridge of the pinnace. "Tyler, Guthrie here."

I let out a short sigh and stared at the pinnace and wide shuttle bay, seeing neither. I might well drop from exhaustion before we got to the *Loviti*.

Sully's arm curved across on my shoulder. His breath ruffled against the top of my head. A rush of warmth curled through me. Demanding. Giving more.

"Tyler, this is Captain Guthrie."

I heard Philip's note of concern, but I couldn't move away from Sully. Or from the warmth, the now relentless spirals of pleasure. His hand moved to my face, touched the line of my jaw. He brushed his thumb across my lips. I saw myself, for a moment, reflected in a mirror. Wearing an Englarian nun's robe, my hair braided with a leather and silver beaded tie. And Sully, eyes smoldering, standing behind me, caressing my face.

Mine. All that I am is yours.

I never knew he'd said those words to me that night. I knew them from when we'd offered them to each other. Not in the monastery now called up in my memory. But in that place I called gray fuzzy soft. In the *Kyi*.

Mine. All that I am is yours.

Another memory washed over me. Sully's memory. *I saw a bulkhead before me; I felt only pain, fear, desolation. Then arms came around my waist, from behind*

me. Chasidah's arms. Holding me, sending acceptance,
forgiveness. For what I am. For what I had to do to
Kingswell, to Tessa Paxton.

She didn't understand, I hope to God she never un-
derstands what I do, what I am. To be damned by the
darkness that lives inside me.

To be saved by her love.

No more half-truths. No more omissions. Sully was
starting to show me all.

The abrupt sound of Philip's hand slapping against
the comm link jolted me. "Damn unit's off-line."

Sully's hand slid down my arm, leaving a hazy feeling
of warmth, love, trust.

"Problems?" Sully and I asked simultaneously.

"Comm link's not functioning, again. I'll go open the
ramp hatch manually." Philip strode through the wide
opening toward the pinnace.

Something clicked three times behind me. Ren? But
corridor doors click once on opening. Three clicks...I
spun around. The status lights on the door to the corridor went from green to red. Locked. Someone had auto-
locked the doors.

The red went to red-flash. Airtight lock. Outer-bay
doors were prepping to open, to let in the vacuum of
space.

Sucking any living thing in the bay out. Dead. Lifeless.

I grabbed Sully. "Airtight's active! Find overrides,
shut it down! Don't let those doors open!"

I didn't wait for his response. I tore out of the control
room, screaming Philip's name.

35

Laser fire spit through the air. Philip dropped to the ground. I dove, hit the decking hard, Stinger out.

He flattened himself next to me, swearing because he was unarmed. "There!"

I fired at the telltale red point of light, heard the high whine of another laser pistol behind me. Sully, angled against the edge of a door panel in the brightly lit control room.

"Airtight's on!" I sent a few more shots into the darkened bay. "Get back to the control room."

Philip's voice was a low rumble. "Room's not sealed. That won't help us."

He was right. The wide door panels, large enough to permit cargo access, were still locked open. The edges of the doors, the single row of chairs, and the small ops desk provided little cover.

"Looks like someone wanted to remove that option," he added. The rapid discharge of Sully's laser pistol whined behind us. "They must have gotten to Tyler too." His expression was grim. "Can we disable the outer doors?"

"Sully's headed there."

Laser fire sizzled a few feet from us. I answered with three shots back at the source. "How'd they find us?"

"My guess is this Lazlo had someone watching Thad's office. Probably followed us, realized my pinnace was in. Put two and two together, got here first."

Another barrage streaked in our direction. Much too close this time.

"Move!" Philip barked.

I sprang into a crouch, then bolted for a low ops console, Philip beside me.

"Been a while since we worked together like this." He was breathing hard.

I automatically scanned left and right. "You always were one for night training."

"It kept you close to me." His hand wrapped around my upper arm. "On three. Break for that back wall. Lots of cover there."

He squeezed my arm. "One. Two. Three."

We ran in a semicrouch. Laser fire followed but fell short. It stopped when we reached the side wall.

I saw outlines of the familiar ladders, panels, more ops consoles jutting out. Large storage containers offered the best protection. I sidled behind one. Philip snugged up against me. We were both breathing hard now.

Then suddenly a scream, a woman's voice, echoing in the bay.

"Sullivan! The unholy shall die!"

Philip's eyes went wide.

"Berri Solaria," I told him. Laser fire continued to whine through the bay. "Devout. And persistent."

My eyes adjusted to the dim light. There was a wide rampway grating overhead, ladders, more ops consoles. More containers. Berri's people couldn't cross the center of the bay without being seen. And they couldn't run along the outer doors, which were ringed by lights. But they could cross overhead on the maintenance rampways.

Philip's gaze followed my own. "We'd hear anyone coming across there. Could get a clear shot at them. I don't think they're that stupid."

It had been over five minutes since I'd run after Philip. He was right. Berri and her friends wanted us together in the center of the bay, walking to the ship, easy targets. Now we were in two different places. We needed to get back together, find a way out.

I turned. Philip's mouth came down hard on mine, his arms locking around me. He kissed me with an intensity I'd forgotten, with all our arguments, our anger and hurt feelings. He kissed me with an intensity of a man who'd known my body, intimately, for eight years. And knew exactly how I liked to be kissed.

Laser fire whined again. I jerked back, shaken.

"Chaz. I'm sorry." His voice rasped.

"Not here. Not now." I ignored my unsteady emotions, pushed myself quickly to the edge of the cage, and tried to make out shapes in the shadows. My ears strained for footsteps, the rustle of fabric. But except for Philip's harsh breathing and the pounding of my own heart, it was quiet again.

Too quiet.

Red target beams erupted into white streaks from the patches of darkness under the pinnace. I trained the Stinger on the lights. The underside of the ship flashed in more small bursts. I hit landing struts, scanner arrays. A cargo stage near the ship's stern sparked. But not our attackers. They must have moved under the pinnace when Philip and I had run for the far wall.

More laser fire came now from my right, from far

down the long bay wall, flaring against the pinnace's hull. Sully. I caught a flurry of thought-pictures. Ren and Verno pulling back into the lifts just as two Crossley Burke security jogged past. Reinforcements. Lazlo was bringing in reinforcements.

Tell Ren to call Thad's office. I sent Sully the link number and an emergency code.

He acknowledged, adding, *Tell Lover Boy to keep his goddamned hands off my wife.*

His label for me since Dock Five. To dissuade Ilsa, tease Dorsie. And now, no doubt, to irritate Philip.

Sully fired off another long burst toward the ship. *Panel's trashed. They're not going to open the bay doors. They want those datatabs first. Badly. We must have stumbled on something very important.*

Whatever it was, it was on its way to Drogue. *Who's with Berri?*

Lazlo. And another male, name's Talard. Feels like a professional shooter.

Three against three. I liked those odds.

Philip's pilot. Tyler. Can you sense—

On the pinnace? Yes. Unconscious but alive.

A small bit of good news.

We need a manual emergency hatch, he continued. *Or we're going to have to take the pinnace.*

I knew the core. *Shuttle bays aren't my specialty.*

Another burst of laser fire. An ops panel about fifteen feet in front of me sizzled, sparked. Sully hadn't answered my comment about shuttle bays. I hoped he was linked to Ren, that Ren had found Thad quickly. That—

Not yet. Chasidah. I felt a pause, wariness. *We need that exit hatch. Guthrie has to know the layout. But when he learns you're linked to me, he's going to . . . react.*

I frowned. *React?*

I love you. I'd never hurt you. Don't ever forget that. Sully?

Tell him what we know.

I stepped back behind the cage edge, suddenly afraid, but I didn't know why. "Philip. Listen to me. Tyler's alive but unconscious. He can't help us. Berri's out there with Lazlo and another professional assassin, Talard. Ren and Verno know what's going on. They're trying to reach Thad. But Burke has people in all the corridors now. We need to get out of here. I don't know shuttle bays. You do. We need a manual exit hatch."

Philip stood very still beside me. "How do you know all this?"

"I have a link with Sully."

"Telepathic." It wasn't a question. And he didn't give me time to respond. "How long?"

"What in hell does it matter? We have to—"

"How long!" His voice was rough. "Since I intercepted you in Calth?"

"Before that."

"Damn him!"

"It doesn't—"

"It does. Goddamned *Kyi-Ragkiril* filth. And he's hearing me, through you, he's hearing me. He's probably even telling you not to listen. He doesn't want you to know the truth."

"He's not—"

"He is. He has. I'll tell you what he's done. He touches you, constantly. Overwhelms your senses with intense pleasure. Then he makes you his lover. Has he taken you, has he mated with you in the *Kyi*?"

I was dimly aware of laser fire whining in the bay behind me. But I remembered clearly the hot passion, and spiraling upward in Sully's arms through gray fuzzy soft.

Philip took my silence as an implied admission.

"Bastard!" Contempt hardened his words. "He's made you his *ky'sara,* his bond-wife, slave. He controls you through the link. When he tires of you, he'll break it through a *zragkor.* Or he'll kill you. That's what a *Kyi-Ragkiril* is. That's what they do."

I stared at Philip, aware of my heart beating rapidly in my chest, aware that my breathing was just as rapid. Aware that there was nothing in my mind but silence. And pain.

I remembered what I'd been taught in Non-Human Cultures 101 about *zragkors.* About *Ragkirils.* Intense pleasure. And then you die.

"We need an exit hatch, Philip. Manually operated." My voice shook.

"Chaz." He touched my arm.

"If we don't get out of here, it won't matter. None of it. So tell me where there's a goddamned exit hatch!"

"There are two." His voice was calm. But his grasp on my arm tightened. He was fighting anger. I was fighting pain. "This Lazlo knew what he was doing, coming at us from the right side. Main emergency hatch is back there. The other's under the pinnace, in the maintenance pits. He's got that one now too."

"Then we have to take the pinnace, or the hatch below it. Sully says we can do it."

"Agreed. If I were armed, we could take them from three different directions."

I shoved the Stinger at him. "I've got my Grizni. If I can get close enough—"

No! Guthrie takes my Carver.

"Chaz?"

I held up my hand, stilling Philip's question. *Then you'd have nothing.*

Hell-spawned Ragkiril filth don't need anything, angel-mine.

Sully, stop it! In spite of my own wrenching emotions, the raw pain in his words tore at me.

A gentling flowed through me, like a wordless apology. *I'll be fine. I have a few tricks left. Give me a minute to move to your position. Tell Guthrie he's getting my Carver. But not my wife.*

I tried to lower my hand but Philip held on to it. "Give me the Stinger back. Sully's giving you his Carver."

He hesitated only a second before he handed me the laser pistol. "There are supposed to be ways to break a *ky'saran* link. I'll help you."

"I need to cover Sully. They might pick up his movements." I pushed myself to the edge of the cage again and locked my gaze on the pinnace. Locked my emotions in the biggest mental duro-hard in the universe. Soldered it shut.

Shadows were hazy in the grayness. Only the outer-door ring lights were bright. But they were shielded, angled to shine toward incoming ships. The bay received their residue and their reflection off the dull metal doors.

I heard a rustle of movement but didn't take my gaze off the pinnace. Sully swept against me, hot, hard, and sweaty. He dragged me into his arms. We stumbled back against the bulkhead, my face and my Stinger in his chest.

Philip's hand clamped my shoulder. "Let her go."

Sully's arms were locked tightly around my back. He was breathing hard, each breath pulsing warmth, tenderness, desire. Just like Philip said.

I splayed one hand on the front of his shirt, angled back. His arms relaxed. In the dim lighting, I could see his eyes were infinite, black, endless. And focused behind me.

"You know nothing of me, Guthrie." His voice was soft, but his words were clipped and hard. He reached between us for the Carver, held it out.

Philip checked the clip for power, blatantly distrustful.

I stepped away from both of them. "Where's Ren?"

"Going back up to Thad's office. Burke's people have this level fairly well locked up. I'll know more of what Thad can do when Ren and Verno get there."

"What do we do now?"

"The pinnace is my first choice," Philip said quickly. "Could blow the bay doors, if we have to."

Sully made a short motion with his hand. "Her ramp's very exposed. How long to uncycle her hatch lock?"

"Two minutes, if her codes haven't been scrambled."

"And if that won't work?" I asked. "Where does the exit hatch go?"

"Maintenance tunnel between levels. If I were this Lazlo, or Burke, I'd expect we'd try that. That might even be how they're bringing in reinforcements."

Sully tilted his head. I thought of Ren. "Not yet. Still just the three there."

"We have to draw them out, split them up. Get control of the pinnace before reinforcements arrive," Philip said.

"Berri will come after me, once she sees what I am. It's her mission."

I remembered her charging, wild-eyed, into the *Karn*'s ready room, screaming about demons. "She has a rifle."

"She won't try to kill me right away. Her type always

lectures you first. You two handle Lazlo and Talard. We'll make it."

"There are two cargo stages between here and the aft of the pinnace." Philip touched imaginary points in the air. "It's a bit of a zigzag, but it's cover. We can probably make that."

"I'll head for the bow. Draw Berri out that way."

Philip frowned. "They'll see you before you're halfway across the floor."

"I have no intention of using the floor."

"Sully—"

He placed his finger on my lips. "Hush, Chasidah."

Even in the dim light I could see a hazy energy ripple across his body like a rolling wave. Rising, merging. For a hundredth of a heartbeat I saw a ghost shadow behind him, stepping into him and out of him at the same time. It coalesced, a silvery glow flowing lightly over his skin.

He touched a finger to my lips, his eyes obsidian. He was neither a demon nor a jukor. Just Gabriel Ross Sullivan. A silver-hued *Kyi-Ragkiril* with infinite eyes.

He brushed his thumb over my mouth. *Chasidah-angel. Nothing to fear.*

Philip's shoulders were rigid. Sully glanced at him. "Your research is excellent but incomplete. You've explained *ky'sara*. You owe it to Chasidah to explain *ky'sal*. Or is that the truth you don't want her to know?"

Philip's voice was harsh. "I only know what you've done to her. I have no proof of any link—"

"An equal link." Sully stepped toward the edge of the cage, listened for a moment to things only he could hear in the shuttle bay. "If she is *ky'sara* to me and I am *ky'sal* to her, it's a link forged of love, not control. And that *zragkor* you threaten her with would kill me. Or isn't that in your family's research?"

"I don't know what her link is to you."

"But she does," Sully said softly. "All that I am is hers." He studied the rampway overhead. "Keep their focus on the ground for a few minutes, will you?"

Sully—

Nothing to fear.

36

I aimed for one of the starboard struts on the pinnace, pulled off a series of quick shots. Sparks arced outward. Behind me, there was a rush of air.

Philip targeted a console, hitting the monitor. It answered with a shattering sound, more sparks. His hand closed around my arm. "The first cargo stage is about thirty feet in front of me, to the left."

"I see it." A boxlike structure, low but wide.

"I'll move first. You follow. We'll go to the next stage, then the rear strut."

I listened to Philip's orders but scanned the dim shadows in front of me for Sully. Ops panels and cargo stages dotted the perimeter of the bay. Rampways lined the walls, crossed overhead. But none seemed to hold a shadow larger than usual.

A strong resonance that I recognized as Sully told me he was moving. Concerned. Focused. I held on to that in almost the same fashion as Philip held on to my arm. Lightly, but with a definite possessiveness.

"Chaz. On three."

I checked the power level on my Stinger. Nodded. Listened to the numbers.

We ran in a crouch, as softly as possible, weapons out. A surge of fluorescent green mist danced across the bow of the pinnace, drawing fire and an unintelligible curse from Berri.

"Energy fields," Philip whispered when we reached the cargo stage. "Only a *Kyi* can do that."

I hunkered down quickly, Philip leaning over me in the small area. We were far from safe. Their lasers could reach us here. Our shadows were stark in the lights from the docking ring. But I could see three forms more clearly under the pinnace as well.

"Options," Philip whispered in my ear.

I shook my head. "I can't get a clear shot from here."

"Not what I mean. Options, Chaz. I'll find a way. You don't have to stay with him."

"Shut up, Philip." I crouched down further, as if I could get away from his words. I kept my eyes on the shadows under the pinnace. Berri and a large shadow were having an argument.

Laser fire suddenly flared back in my direction. It sizzled against the ops panel we'd hidden behind earlier. Nothing was there that I could see. I wouldn't have answered their fire even if Philip hadn't clamped his hand on my arm.

"If he's got them shooting at ghosts, he's close. A *Kyi*'s range is twenty, twenty-five feet if he's strong, and this one is."

This one. Philip's dehumanizing word choice made me flinch.

"I confirmed that when I had him scan the stripers before," he continued.

Something in the shadows moved quickly around the

bow strut. In the sudden dark movement, a hazed shimmer...

Gabriel Ross Sullivan, stepping softly out of the shadows, head high. He walked toward the pinnace, one hand extended, a silvery glow pulsing around him.

My heart leaped to my throat, pounded. I locked my gun on the bow of the pinnace, ready to fire on the first red glow I saw.

"Sister Berri." Sully's voice was deep, seductive. "I know you've been looking for me. Come out and play."

"Defiler!" Berri screamed at him. Either Lazlo or Talard held her arm. She tried to jerk away.

"Now!" Philip said.

We're moving in, I told Sully. I ran softly, hunched over, never taking my eyes from Berri, Lazlo, and Talard.

We reached the second stage, pressed on to the rear strut, blending into the patches of darkness underneath the ship. Berri broke free. She pointed her rifle at Sully as if it were a holy sword. "*Ragkiril* filth!"

Lazlo appeared behind her. He clearly knew how to use the Carver in his hand. It was aimed at Sully.

"Hands out, Sullivan! No tricks." Lazlo wasn't sure what he was seeing. I could hear it in his voice.

I searched for the third shadow, found it hanging back, watching Sully. Not watching for us, to his right. Talard, probably as surprised as Lazlo was. I could take him out. Not with the laser pistol. Lazlo and Berri would hear the laser pistol. But my Grizni would be silent.

There was another strut and about fifty feet between Talard and myself. If I could get behind him, I wouldn't even need to be that close. I had a damned good throwing arm.

I made my decision. My own. No one controlling my

mind but Chaz Bergren. I touched Philip. "Talard's hanging back. I'm on him."

He tore his gaze away from Berri and Sully. "Chaz—"

"My own decision. My mind. You cover Sully." I skittered into the shadows.

"Where're your friends, Sullivan?" Lazlo pulled Berri back as she stepped forward, rifle raised in one hand.

"There are no others."

"We saw them—"

"You saw what I wished you to see."

I made the next strut just as a gray mist swirled up by Sully's side, took vaguely human form, dissolved. I was close enough to see Talard shift nervously in his stance.

"Then that makes it easy." Lazlo's arm jerked from the recoil as his laser pistol fired.

Sully surged up, silver light flaring out around him. Berri swung her rifle, shouting. Lazlo grabbed for her, dragged her to the floor as Philip's laser pistol whined. Lazlo rolled and fired overhead.

I couldn't see Sully. But he was alive. I could feel that. I clung to that.

Talard moved but so did I, darting, laser fire sizzling behind me.

Berri struggled against Lazlo, thrashed him with her fists. "He's mine! The demon's mine to kill!"

He hit her with the Carver, hard. Her face twisted in pain. He shoved her away from him. She sprawled awkwardly on the floor, her rifle skidding back toward the pinnace.

Chasidah! I felt a clear warning note from Sully. *Burke's people. Side emergency hatch.*

Shit. Reinforcements. I was too far away to warn Philip without revealing my position. I had to take Talard out now.

Talard half-turned to his right, searching for the red glow of Philip's target lock. I dropped to one knee, clasped the Grizni. It vibrated ready, uncoiling with a snap into my palm. My eyes narrowed, focused. I whipped my arm forward. The blade shot from my fingers. It struck the middle of his chest.

He fell backward. I ran, Stinger out, and reached him as life flickered out of his eyes. I pulled the Grizni out, slapped it, still dirty with blood, around my wrist. Time. We had no time.

I heard the muted groan of an emergency hatch from the far wall. I grabbed Talard's Carver, shoved it in the back of my pants.

Sully?

Behind you. The sound of boots thudded softly on the floor.

I spun around just as the hatch door clanged back against the bulkhead. Shadows streamed out. I lunged for Sully, shoved Talard's Carver into his waiting hand.

He pushed me to the floor. "Down! Get down!" He was trying to warn Philip, on the far side of the pinnace, heading for Lazlo.

The air above my head screamed, flared. I fired toward the hatch. Out of the corner of my eye I saw Philip dive to the floor.

Sully swung the Carver to the right, strafed the floor by the hatch.

Forms disappeared behind the containers and ops consoles.

"How many?"

Five. So far.

Where's Ren?

Dealing with Burke's people, close by.

Movement churned on my right. Philip rising, going

after Lazlo. Berri twisting on the decking, half-sobbing, half-screaming.

I shifted onto my elbows, tried to get a clear shot at Lazlo, partially hidden by a wide strut. I saw the profile of his Carver, saw the small glint of red, then his arm jerked up. Philip, kneeling, firing.

Lazlo's body arced backward. Berri screamed. Lasers streaked through the air. Flashes of light sizzled, burst around Philip, prone on the decking. Sully fired, covering him.

Berri turned over onto her stomach. Blood dripped down the side of her face. She crawled with a slithering movement, trying to reach the rifle.

Philip angled up. Two forms sprang from behind the cover of the wall cage.

Watch Berri! Sully fired. One form fell, the other jumped back.

I didn't have a clear shot at Berri. But I did at her rifle. I hit it on the stock, splintering it, just as she caught sight of me in the shadows.

"Demon's whore!" Her hair, matted with blood, fell in disarray about her face.

Three forms surged out of the darkness, firing, using the ops consoles and containers for cover.

Keep them busy.

Sully angled up, splayed his hand in a wide sweep along the floor while I laid down cover fire. A mist arose from nowhere, gelled into a boiling, writhing red mass. It surged toward a low cargo stage.

Berri's piercing voice carried clearly. "I curse you, spawn of Hell!"

A man jumped back toward the protection of the cargo stage. I heard Philip's laser pistol whine. The man spun, fell.

Then an answering whine, close, too close. I tore my

gaze from the boiling mist. Berri was on her knees, Lazlo's Carver in her hands. She fired again, laughing.

Philip was on the ground, his body jerking from the laser's impact.

A harsh cry rose in my throat. I fired, once, twice, again. All three, center mass. The Carver dropped from her hand and hit the floor a second before her body did.

One more attacker tried to flee Sully's red mist, found the white laser fire more lethal. That left two. Against two of us. Philip . . .

Sully? Ren, dying. Sully, breathing for him. I hurled that image, that plea, to the man lying prone next to me.

Her first shot grazed him. But her second got him in the chest. He hesitated. *I'll try. Cover me.*

I strafed the ops consoles and cargo stages. Sully ran under the pinnace toward Philip.

The two remaining attackers ducked down. I pushed myself to my feet, bolted after Sully. I could cover him best if I were in front of him. They'd have to shoot me first.

I crouched down, using the wide-based struts for cover as Lazlo and Berri had when they'd pinned us against the opposite wall. Burke's people were now farther to my left. There were a few blind spots, but they were small. If either moved from behind his cover, I'd get him.

One tried. I sent him scuttling back.

I could hear Philip's breath rasping a few feet behind me. I wanted to turn, I wanted to know what was happening, but I couldn't take my eyes off the two who were still alive and armed. Or the emergency hatchway, which could bring more of Burke's people. If that happened, we wouldn't survive.

Suddenly, something washed over me. Something

warm, familiar. I kept my gaze locked but let it speak to me, in its wordless way. Recognized it.

Ren. *Ren?*

An affirmative sensation. Close. So close that—

The corridor door exploded into the control room. I raked the cargo stages with a barrage of fire. Forms plunged through the wide opening, firing where I did. Boots pounded into the shuttle bay. Thad's voice shouted my name.

I spun around on my knees, not looking for my brother but to protect Sully. He had to be shielded from the squadrons of stripers pouring into the bay. From the Fleet Admin personnel at my brother's side. All those who would hate him, damn him, because he was a *Kyi-Ragkiril*—a demon from Englarian legends come to life.

He knelt beside Philip's form. The gray mist, the *Kyi*, clung to him and hovered over Philip. I quickly squatted across from him. Laser fire whined across the bay.

Philip's gaze flicked briefly to my face. Sully had one hand on his chest, covering a large, bloodstained area. The other rested lightly at the base of his throat.

"Sully. Ren and Thad are here. And half of Marker."

He nodded without looking at me.

"I don't think they've seen you yet. Stop—"

He shook his head. *I can't yet. Besides, he'd die.*

Fear and anguish surged through me, colliding at my heart. *They'll see you. Know what you are.*

Risks, Chasidah. Risks.

He'd said it in the temple on Moabar, just before he kissed me. All life's a risk. Ren had reminded him of that, just before I'd learned Sully was a *Ragkiril*. Risks.

He kept taking them. They kept hurting him. But he kept taking them.

"How can I help?" My voice was barely a whisper.

Infinite, obsidian eyes met mine, briefly. He took his

hand from Philip's throat, held it out. *Help me give him life. You can do that. You're ky'sara to me.*

I moved next to him, clasping his hand, putting my fingers at Philip's throat. I felt the *Kyi* flow through me, grow. Philip's pulse fluttered under my fingers.

Breathe, Chasidah.

I breathed.

Sully breathed.

Philip breathed.

Voices shouted, hard and angry. My brother's voice was one. "Chaz! What in the hell—"

I squeezed Sully's hand, raised my gaze. "Get a medtech, fast. Philip's been shot. And get someone on the pinnace. The pilot's in there, injured."

Thad barked the order at a uniformed woman behind him. She acknowledged. I heard other voices in harsh, hard whispers.

"My God. A soul-stealer's killed Captain Guthrie. We got to—"

Two large forms stepped forward. I knew their identities without raising my face. Ren. Verno. Warmth surrounded me, like a flow of water from a bubbling spring. Voices became quieter, backed away.

I breathed.

Sully breathed.

Philip breathed. His eyes slitted open again, focused on me.

I felt his questions, fear. "Thad's bringing the medtechs. You'll be fine."

Loud boots and the discordant hum of an antigrav stretcher came closer. Ren backed away and two new pairs of boots came into my field of vision. "Holy brother of God!" A blue-coated med-tech dropped to his knees across from me, ran the medistat over Philip's body. "Impossible! He's—"

"Alive." Sully's voice was raspy. "It's your job to keep him that way."

Two more blue-coats knelt down, scanning, probing, hooking Philip to their machines. They lifted him onto the stretcher.

Sully sat back on his heels, his shoulders hunched wearily.

I clasped my arms around his neck and buried my face into his shoulder. He drew me tightly against him, sent warm but slightly ragged spirals through me. But another emotion, one that wasn't his but was aimed at him, hovered on the edges.

Hatred. Fear. Revulsion. Med-techs, security guards, Thad's officers. Hatred emanated from them like a thick, acrid smoke.

This was Gabriel Sullivan's Hell. This was what he sensed every time he became what he was, what he had no choice but to be.

"Chaz!" Thad's voice, harsh. Thad's hand, yanking my arm. "News cams, reporters—"

Sully stood abruptly, jerking me to my feet with him. He grasped my wrists as my arms fell from around his neck, held them tightly. He was shaking, something trembling through him like a jumpdrive engine far out of synch.

Silvery energy shifted, moved, for the second time in one hour, fading slowly. And judging from the tightness around his eyes, painfully.

"Get us out of here," Sully said roughly.

Bright white lights suddenly flared to my left, blocking our exit to the corridor. Vidcam lenses glinted.

"The maintenance hatch, behind you," Thad said. "Get back to my office."

We ran.

It took us twenty minutes to carefully weave our way
back to Thad's office, Ren and Verno mirroring our
moves. Another fifteen before Thad joined us. Sully was
drained, unnaturally listless. Ren was close to his limit,
needing water. Both dismissed my and Verno's well-
meaning concern, but Ren accepted a wet towel Verno
brought out of the office lavatory and draped it around
his neck.

It was another two hours, and several more changes
of location on Marker, before we were transferred to the
safety of the *Morgan Loviti*. We were greeted tersely by
the ship's chief of security, an older woman I didn't
know. She reminded me of Dorsie. I wondered if the
jovial woman was still alive.

"Commander Bralford's in sick bay with the captain,"
she said, ushering us into the ready room behind the
bridge. "He suggested you might want to listen to this."
She flicked on the room's screen and left.

The public-relations executive for Crossley Burke
had issued a statement disavowing the corporation's

knowledge of, and involvement with, the "unfortunately but obviously mentally unstable Sister Berri Solaria, and their recently terminated security officer, Zabur Lazlo." I replayed the vidclip twice on the ready room's central screen. It was a beautifully crafted piece of obfuscation.

"His excuses are very believable. We may have underestimated him." Sully had his back to me and stared out the large viewport. His arms were crossed over his chest. I handed Ren a cup of tea from the replicator, then rounded the long table to stand next to Sully. Wordlessly, he declined the tea I offered him. He was obviously dismayed by Hayden Burke's aggressive response.

But I knew he was also unsettled by the reaction in the shuttle bay. Angered, and hurt, by those who saw him as a despicable demon, in spite of the fact he'd saved Philip's life, pushing himself, I realized, to the very limits of his human and *Ragkiril* strength to do so.

I wrapped my fingers around his arm, squeezed.

He sent warmth but no words. Still struggling.

"They'll change their song when the truth comes out, Sully-sir." With his long legs and arms, Verno overflowed the high-backed chair in much the same way as his continual optimism flowed over the strained tension in the room. Even learning Sully was a *Ragkiril* hadn't shaken that. Verno was a true blessing. "Captain Guthrie's position on the council will make all things right."

Sully didn't answer, but his mouth tightened at the mention of Philip's name. Philip knew far more about *Ragkirils* and *Kyi-Ragkirils* than Sully was comfortable with.

"You saved his life," I said softly, hoping he'd see that Philip was indebted to him. Surely my ex-husband would reconsider his prejudices. As Thad had pointed out earlier in his office, the Guthries were nothing if not a highly moral family.

Dark, infinite eyes turned from the starfield and studied me. "I did so because you asked."

"So? That—"

"You risked your life, and mine, to save him. If I were him, I'd take that as a very encouraging sign."

"He was my CO."

"He was also your husband."

Pain arced through me, but I didn't know if it was his or mine. "Sully—"

"Hush." He laid his finger on my lips. "I know. My confidence waxes and wanes like Sylvadae's summer moon when I'm tired."

The ready-room door slid open. Jodey Bralford, the *Loviti*'s first officer, stepped in.

His smile was genuine. Jodey and I had always gotten along. "Brother Ackravaro? We have a cabin with hydrospa ready for you. I apologize for the delay."

It hadn't been fifteen minutes since we'd come on board—perhaps ten since we'd been given clearance to depart Marker. With Philip in sick bay, Jodey was in command and, until we left Marker, had more serious things on his mind than a cabin with a tub. Ren's weakened condition wasn't yet life-threatening. Still, Jodey had always been the epitome of efficiency. Ten minutes was unacceptable to him.

Ren stood, a little unsteadily. Verno held out his hand. "I'll go with you."

Jodey was of stocky build, and only a few inches taller than I was. He glanced from the rising Taka to the tall Stolorth, no doubt thinking that Verno was in a better position to help, should Ren collapse. "Excellent idea."

"We'll be fine here," Sully said. The ready room had a

replicator, a lavatory, and a comfortable couch along the far wall. It suddenly looked very comfortable.

Jodey's eyes narrowed slightly. I'd no doubt he'd heard what had happened, what Sully was, but was too much the professional to express it openly. I caught the change in his expression only because I'd known him for several years.

"Actually, Captain Bergren, I've been asked to bring you to sick bay."

For a moment my heart froze, but then logic kicked in. If Philip had died, that's the first thing Jodey would have stated. And his demeanor wouldn't have been so outwardly calm. He was a professional, career military, as I was. But he was also one of Philip's close friends.

"I'll finish your tea while you're gone." Sully took the mug from my hand. He arched one eyebrow, winked at me. But it was a show, for Jodey's sake. I felt nothing from him, no warmth, no teasing caress.

Then: *Go see Guthrie. Remind him that he owes me. Remind him . . . that he doesn't own you.*

I touched his hand, then followed Jodey into the brightly lit corridor.

Philip's second in command said nothing until the lift doors closed in front of us. "It's good to see you safe, Chaz." He slanted me a glance. "We've been worried. I know some of what you've been through."

"Philip's awake and talking, is he?"

His affirmative nod didn't surprise me. Sully had restored much of Philip's strength. The *Loviti*'s sick bay probably wouldn't have all that much to repair.

"Philip's very concerned." All formality was dropped. It was just Jodey and me in a quietly humming lift. "He thought—*we* thought—you should let Doc Draper run a few tests."

As if being *ky'sara* to a *Ragkiril* was a disease.

"He can help you," Jodey continued, when I didn't reply.

"I've a few bumps and bruises, but nothing to bother Doc about, Jodey. Thanks, anyway." I flashed him a smile.

His answering one was tinged with sadness. And that bothered me. I guess it felt as if in allying myself with Sully, I'd lost Jodey Bralford's respect. And that was something I didn't want to happen. He'd been one of the few, besides my own crew, who'd voiced opposition to my arrest, who'd been emotionally supportive during the trial. He was one of the very few who'd bothered to keep contact with me afterward, while I was in prison, awaiting transfer to Moabar.

The doors opened. "On a different note," he said as we stepped into the corridor, "I have some good news." His voice was bright, but a shade too bright, as if he knew his opinions of Sully affected me. "I've been offered a captaincy."

"Jodey!" I ignored the fact that the corridor outside sick bay was dotted with *Loviti* crew. I threw my arms around his broad form and hugged him. "Congratulations!"

I was genuinely pleased for him. It was an honor that was long overdue.

"The *Nowicki* doesn't have the reputation the *Loviti* has, but she's a good ship." He motioned for me to precede him through sick bay's wide double doors and reassumed his first officer's demeanor as three med-techs turned, noting our arrival. "Captain Guthrie's in Trauma Room 3, Captain Bergren. If you'll come with me?"

Doc Draper briefly clasped my hand as we met up at the door to Philip's room. "Captain," he said.

"Come in, Chaz." Philip's voice, even weak, held a tone of command.

A biomesh regen unit covered part of his chest. His left arm was tattooed with med-broches. He held out his right hand. I clasped it. "Burke's denying all involvement," I said as I took the seat next to his bed.

"I'm glad to see you're alive, Philip." His mouth quirked into a teasing grin as he said the words I hadn't.

"I am glad to see you're alive," I repeated.

He squeezed my hand. "I saw Burke's delightful disclaimer. Not unexpected, considering who he is. And what he owns."

"And who he owns?"

"Thad intimated as much, yes. It's something I'll have Jodey check into, before he transfers. He told you, I take it?"

I grinned. "Couldn't happen to a nicer overly efficient man."

"He thinks highly of you. He's . . . worried. As I am."

"The reason you're worried is the reason you're still alive. Did you tell Jodey that too?"

"That's not the issue here."

"I think it's part of it."

"Good deeds don't change what he is, Chaz. What he's done to you. You don't fully understand—"

"I do."

"You don't. He's placed a filter around your mind."

"It must not be a very good one, because I'm hearing every word you say."

"Are you?" He shifted his hand, held my fingers more tightly. "Did you hear what I said to you in Thad's office? A captaincy could be yours. Jodey's leaving. My duties as admiral preclude the daily running of this ship. The *Loviti*, Chaz. I'm offering you the *Loviti*."

Captain of an Imperial destroyer. For a moment, for a

very brief moment, I felt the pull, the thrill of those words.

"Once I clear things with Tage, I'll have the authority to make that offer." Philip's voice interrupted my reverie.

"I appreciate whatever you can do with Barrister Tage. But your offer... no."

"Is that your answer, or his?"

"Mine!"

"It's not. I'll tell you how I know, Chaz. Don't pull away. Listen to me, because your life may depend on it. It's his answer, his desires, not yours. The look on your face when I made you the offer told me you wanted to accept. But then you tell me no. Why? Ask yourself why." He released my hand.

I sat back in my chair, suddenly angry, insulted by Philip's belief that I didn't know my own mind. Of course I did. "I'm flattered you'd consider me for a captaincy. But that doesn't mean I have to take it."

"If he weren't on this ship, you would."

"Philip, that's nonsense."

"Prove it." He reclaimed my hand, uncurling my fingers from the arm of the chair. "We'll meet up with his ship. Let him leave, with just the Stolorth and the Taka. Stay on the *Loviti* a week. Spend some time with Doc Draper. If after that you still want to be with him, I'll deliver you personally."

Something that felt like fear trickled through my senses. It was small, distant, barely discernible. But it was there. *Sully?*

"Chaz!" Philip yanked my arm. I blinked, shook my head. And for a moment had no idea where, or who, I was. Then it came back to me, flooding over me. Moabar, Sully, Ren. Gregor, Marsh. Berri Solaria.

Sully.

"Let me think about it," I said.

Philip said nothing until I'd almost reached the door. "One week, Chasidah Bergren. One week. Prove it. Not to me. To yourself."

Fear. I felt it more strongly.

Only fools boast they have no fears.

Sully turned from the viewport when I walked in. I wondered if he'd been standing there since I'd left to talk to Philip. It had been over forty minutes. Fifty, actually, because I hadn't gone straight back to the ready room from sick bay. I'd stood in a recessed section of the ship's corridor for ten minutes, just thinking, and listening to my mind think back.

"He offered me command of the *Loviti*." I rested my hand on the high-backed chair Verno had occupied earlier. "But then, you know that, don't you?"

"I felt something upset you."

"Then you also know he said you filter all thoughts coming into my mind."

"No." He looked tired, as tired as I felt. But he didn't look angry. And I wasn't sure if I was or not. And if I was, I wasn't sure at whom: Philip, for his accusations; Sully, for silently prying; or myself, torn between believing Philip and not caring that Sully pried.

"I felt something upset you," he repeated, more softly this time. "But I didn't listen in. And I don't, in spite of what Philip says, filter your thoughts. Or form opinions for you."

I sat in the chair I'd been swiveling. "But you have, in the past."

He closed his eyes briefly. "On the *Karn,* when Ren was dying?" he asked when he opened them. "Yes. And on Dock Five, to protect you from Trel. Circumstances left me no choice. But I told you on Dock Five, as soon as I could. To do otherwise would be repulsive to me. And as much an insult to myself as to you."

I nodded.

"So," he said, "did you accept his offer?"

The ready-room doors swooshed open as I started to answer. Jodey Bralford strode in, a datapad in his hand, a grim expression on his face.

"This just came in." He held up the datapad. "Phil— Captain Guthrie said you should see it." He darted a glance to Sully. It was the first time he'd looked at him since coming into the room. "Both of you."

"Trouble?" I swiveled, stood.

"Darius Tage, First *Barrister* Darius Tage, just released a statement." He stressed the man's title but he didn't have to. I knew the name. Everyone in the Empire knew the name of Prew's venerable senior adviser. And a longtime family friend of the Guthries. The man who could clear my name. Who might even be able to return to Sully his rightful inheritance.

Jodey shoved the datapad toward me. "Son of a bitch has come out in solid support of Hayden Burke."

"Tage?" I plopped back down in the chair, disbelief and dread churning through me.

"Cousin Hayden's pulling in favors." Sully's voice held a distinct sneer.

"So it seems," Jodey said. "You'd better read it."

Tage's statement quoted an independent investigation confirming rumors that the mercenary outlaw, Gabriel Ross Sullivan, had faked his own death two years prior. Sullivan was described as *dangerous and delusional,* and new information now revealed he was a *known honey-lace addict* with violent tendencies.

It was believed he was behind the recent terrorist activities on Marker, not only assisting the Farosians but in a personal vendetta against his cousin, Hayden Burke.

There was no mention that Sully might also be a *Kyi-Ragkiril.* It was possible Tage and Burke didn't know. Lazlo, Berri Solaria, and most of the other Crossley Burke operatives were dead or in custody. There was no one to inform Burke of his cousin's abilities.

But Burke owned people, possibly people still on Marker. He'd damned near owned my brother. It was also possible that Burke knew but was just waiting for the right time to reveal it.

"They'll be looking for you," Jodey said.

Sully arched one dark eyebrow. "Hayden's been looking for me for two years. He's found me only because I felt it was time."

"But Tage?" I turned toward Jodey. "Why would Darius Tage ally with Burke?"

"We don't know." Jodey sounded distinctly troubled. I knew he was speaking for Philip as well. "But maybe it's time to tell you what we do know." He paused. "Something very ugly is happening in the Empire. It's one of the reasons I accepted the command of the *Nowicki*. We need the right people in command of the Fleet."

Jodey's tone disturbed me almost as much as my frisson of fear had earlier. "What are you saying?"

He sighed, ran his hand through his short-cropped dark hair. "I'm saying that one of the first things Philip told me when I saw him in Marker's med-station a few hours ago, was: 'It's started.' "

"But he didn't know about Burke. When Thad told him—"

"We didn't know who. Or rather, we didn't know which of several 'whos' have been behind an undercurrent we've been aware of for some time. Burke was on the list, yes, but there were others we felt would make a move first."

Sully nodded, clearly understanding more than I did.

"What kind of move?" I thought of the usual political power struggles that had dotted the news vids over the years. Ego contests, in my opinion. Nothing like this, nothing like Jodey was intimating.

"It goes back to the Boundary Wars. Promises were

made about mining rights, trade rights, succession in power that would in effect remove much of the control from the councils. Some of those promises were kept. But some weren't."

That I had seen. It was something my mother often commented on. The councils had become ineffectual. It was something Sully had noted: the Rim Worlds were disproportionately rife with suffering.

"Burke's charged with enforcing those promises?" That didn't seem possible, not even for Hayden Burke.

"We don't have all the facts yet. Our sources," and he grimaced wryly, "keep mysteriously dying. But Burke's father was on one of the original committees." He shot a glance at Sully. "So was Winthrop Sullivan."

"I don't share my father's political allegiances."

But Hayden Burke did. And had the money to fund his beliefs. Starting with the jukor labs. Which both Crossley Burke's and Tage's statements referred to as *illegal weapons laboratories* created by Farosian supporter Zabur Lazlo. No mention of jukors. No *proof* of jukors, thanks to Sully's firebombs.

Only the data on its way to Drogue—data that my brother and Philip also had. But data could be altered, faked. I knew that firsthand from my trial. Odd that the very people who'd ruined my career would now use the same defense I'd tried to. I had a feeling they'd be much more successful than I had been.

"This list of yours." Sully pulled the datapad toward him but didn't look at it. "I take it Darius Tage wasn't on it."

Jodey shook his head slowly. "Not only was he not on it, he knew about it. He knew about our suspicions. He was one of the people we thought we could trust."

Silence followed Jodey's pronouncement. The ready room felt suddenly cold, as if wrapped in sheets of ice.

Tage had also been one of the people Philip had talked to about my transfer off Moabar. A sick feeling settled in my stomach.

Sully clenched his right hand into a tight fist. "How much does Tage know?"

"We thought he shared our goals. A more equal distribution of power, more control to the councils."

"How much does Tage know?" He leaned toward Jodey.

Jodey's mouth was a tight line. "Everything."

The only good piece of news came about an hour later. The *Boru Karn* responded to one of Sully's coded hails. At top speeds, she was less than an hour from us. Using the ready room's main screen, Sully briefly brought Marsh up to date. Gregor was off shift.

"We were tagged but we lost them," Marsh said. Two ships of unknown origin, bristling with weapons, had challenged the *Karn* but were unable to complete a capture. I remembered the feeling. Sully's ghost ship had a well-earned reputation.

Sully uploaded the data he'd taken from the jukor labs to the *Karn*'s banks, then we traded coordinates and set up a meetpoint.

Marsh signed off with "Good to know everyone's in one piece." I wished Sully's telepathy worked over long distances. It seemed to me that some of Marsh's antagonism was gone. But I knew I might just be reading more into a perfunctory phrase than was actually there because returning to the hostile environment we'd left on the *Karn* was more than I wanted to handle right now.

Jodey's broad face furrowed in worry as he stood by the ready-room door. "I'll inform navigation, code the course change myself. I have bridge crew stripped down to a minimum. There's too much at risk."

More than just my life, Sully's, Ren's, or Verno's. Everyone who'd helped us, if Tage was able to convince the Admirals' Council that Philip Guthrie and the *Morgan Loviti* had assisted Farosian terrorist Gabriel Ross Sullivan.

That was the only thing Jodey felt fairly sure Tage didn't know yet. They'd intended to contact the first barrister's office once we came on board, but Philip would have to be the one to do that, and he was in sick bay. The *Loviti*'s departure had been unremarkable, and—other than the fact that her captain and a pinnace pilot had been injured in a "shuttle-bay explosion"—without incident.

We could only guess at what Burke knew from his sources on Marker. Which meant Thad's life, too, was in danger.

"Your brother's a smart man, Captain Bergren." Jodey stopped in the opening doorway. "But you know Captain Guthrie and I will do all we can. There are still people we can trust."

Then Sully and I were alone for the first time since Jodey had burst in with news of Tage's defection. Or, perhaps, revelation of which side he'd been on all along.

"Did we accomplish anything, other than placing more innocent people in harm's way?" I asked after the doors closed.

"Guthrie's far from innocent. He knows how this game is played. He's tracked it probably as long as I have. Just from a different angle." He shook his head slightly, his mouth twisting as if the thought for some reason amused him. But not pleasantly so.

"But did we accomplish anything? There's a second lab somewhere."

"Not somewhere." He tapped the datatab in his

pocket. "We know where. Or rather, I know its most likely route."

I hadn't had the chance to study the information Sully found. Didn't know it was so specific. So workable. Hope blossomed. We *could* stop them. "A hospital ship?"

"Not yet completed. With the Marker lab gone, they'll put more energy into this. That's how we'll get them. And we will." He covered my hand with his own. A tiny warmth trickled through our contact, fluttered up my arm.

"Do we know who 'them' is, Sully?"

"Some, though most names I saw were coded. I was more interested in the data on the second lab. We already know Hayden's involved. But it might be worthwhile to compare lists with Guthrie. Though he might not like what he'd see on my—" He turned, the sound of the door sliding open stopping his words.

I turned too, expecting Jodey with confirmation of our position relative to the *Karn*. But it wasn't Jodey leaning in the doorway.

"Philip!"

He was in Fleet's generic brown workout sweats, the soft sweatshirt unzippered, revealing a thin medimesh hugged to his torso. I couldn't see the trail of med-broches on his arm covered by the long sleeve, but I suspected they were still there. His silver hair was mussed, his eyes shadowed. His mouth was a tight line, reflecting his physical pain.

"You shouldn't be out of sick bay!" I shoved myself to my feet, pulling my hand out from under Sully's, and reached for him.

"Doc Draper's already tried that line. It didn't work." But he accepted my hand. I helped him into the chair next to mine. He waved me back down into my seat.

"My first officer informs me we're less than forty-five from meetpoint with your ship, Sullivan. That doesn't give us a lot of time. You know about my error with Tage."

That was typical Philip. I highly doubted it was solely his error to trust Darius Tage. But I was surprised when Sully echoed that sentiment as well.

"It's one anyone would have made. He wasn't on my list either."

"I think Thad Bergren and I have sufficiently muddied the Marker incident so that it will reflect only what Burke's release stated: Farosian terrorists and an unstable Englarian nun attempted to sabotage Marker's core and were killed when trying to use a Fleet pinnace to escape. There's no record of your visit to Commander Bergren's office. No record of your transfer to my ship. It will take Tage a lot of work to prove you were on Marker."

Because Philip had been our escort. There was no record of us passing through the security checkpoints in the corridor, only people's memories. We could have easily been any two of the more than three hundred on board the *Loviti,* accompanying their captain back to the ship.

But that had never been my worry. "How many people saw Sully in the shuttle bay?" Besides Thad and two of his officers, I could remember seeing at least three med-techs and a half dozen or more security. The word *soul-stealer* echoed viciously in my thoughts.

"Enough. But there've been rumors of Stolorth support of the Farosians. That's most likely how it'll be remembered."

Sully leaned his forearms on the table. "Those same people saw Ren there," he added in agreement.

Philip nodded solemnly. "Now we have to talk about what will happen when your ship gets here."

Sully sat back slowly. "I take it you're not interested in the navigational mechanics of its arrival."

"Chaz stays with me."

"Philip—"

He held up one hand. "I'm asking you to let her go. I'm asking you because, first, the woman has her own mind and the right to use it. But second, I'm asking because you must know she's safer with me. Burke knows you're alive. He may even know what you are by now. Your family's wealth aside, that gives him two reasons to kill you."

"The first has always been sufficient. He's never managed to accomplish it."

"You're willing to risk her life on that?"

"Philip!"

He ignored me. "You can offer her nothing but heartache. You'll be fugitives. Welcomed only in places like Dock Five or the rim. My family has properties, places she'll be safe. She'll lack nothing."

I'd many times visited the Guthries' palatial estates. He was right. Every luxury was there. But I'd walked away from luxury before. Wealth was a very cold bed partner. Besides, too much had happened to Chasidah Bergren since Moabar. Hell, since she'd been in command of the *Meritorious*. Even if Sully and I had never been more than partners in a cause—jukors breeding, Takas dying, and now the Empire I'd committed my life to infested with a vile corruption—that cause would make Philip's silk sheets and expensive wines a mockery of everything I believed in, everything I was.

"He doesn't control me, Philip." My voice was soft, but I remembered that tone of command Fleet had insisted we adopt, and I used it. "I am going back to the *Karn*."

Warmth, hope, relief surged through me. Sully wasn't touching me, but it was as strong as if he was. I realized, suddenly, that he'd been totally absent from my thoughts, from my senses, save for that brief spike of fear when I'd talked to Philip in sick bay. And even then it had been withdrawn as quickly as it had appeared.

That's what had made me suddenly light-headed. Not that Sully was in my mind. But that he wasn't. I'd become used to his reassuring presence, and when it hadn't been there, I felt off balance.

There was no way I could accept captaincy of the *Loviti*, though I doubted Darius Tage would approve of that now. There was no way I could accept Philip's offer of protection, and all the luxuries as well. Because I'd lack the one thing I knew I could no longer live without. That wicked, wicked Sully smile.

And the man, the *Kyi-Ragkiril*, it belonged to.

"Chaz, listen to me." Philip's voice was strained.

"Listen to *me*, Philip. The time has passed where any one person's safety is more important than what we know has to be done. And you know this is me talking, not anyone else, because it's a failing you've said I've had all along. I will not suffer injustice quietly. We're faced with more than injustice, my friend." And, yes, I felt Philip was my friend, perhaps for the first time in a very long time. "We're faced with corruption, with a heinous misuse of power and with blatant murderers. And they're running the government we know as the Empire.

"I will not and cannot let that continue. And I won't be shuttled off to one of your estates, like some fragile but useless piece of sculpture. There are things I can do. There are things Sully and I *will* do." Destroying that second lab topped the list. "And we will do them best because we're not a part of that government. We're ghosts, Philip. They may think they see us, but they'll never truly be sure. Because we're ghosts."

Philip stared at me a long time, studying me, seeing again, perhaps, the young recruit he'd mentored in boot camp, the lieutenant he'd commanded on the *Loviti*. The woman he'd loved, married, and divorced. The woman he'd watched go to prison, who'd never once looked back, never once flinched.

And who had never backed away from what had to be done.

He rose slowly, unsteadily, the pain on his face more than physical. But when he turned toward Sully, his blue eyes narrowed.

"Anything happens to her, Sullivan, and I will tell Hayden Burke all I know about you. Hell, anything happens to my wife, and I'll help your cousin kill you."

He turned, lurched unsteadily for the door, then plowed doggedly out into the corridor.

39

"Thank you," Sully said softly, a heartbeat or two after the doors closed behind Philip. "For your faith in me."

I turned. I'd been staring at the closed doors, Philip's parting threat in my mind. His words hadn't seemed to bother Sully. He still leaned back in his chair, but his posture had changed from a defensive one—arms crossed over his chest when he'd been speaking to Philip—to a more relaxed one, with one elbow propped on the arm of his chair.

"You don't make it an easy task." I thought of all the half-truths, the almost-lies that Sully layered around himself as a protective wall. And I reclaimed his hand when he offered it because, if I expected him to be honest with me, then I had to be honest with him. For all that I loved him—and I did, beyond all measure, as he'd once told me—part of me was angry over his deceptions and his usurping of my choice when he'd made me *ky'sara* to him. I wouldn't have refused, but it would have been nice to have been asked. He needed to feel that, read that from me.

He did, holding my hand, watching my whirlwind thoughts. "I tried to explain that what I offered you, what I wanted with you, was a very deep link. To say more...to have said I'm not only a telepath but a genetic mutant who can manipulate energy fields...For very selfish reasons, Chaz, I couldn't. Not until I felt you knew me better. The legends of Eng's soul-stealers are still too prevalent in our culture."

And frightful, like the paintings in the Englarian temples. "They're not legends, are they?"

"My research has never turned up any *Kyi-Ragkirils* with scales or wings. But we can change what people perceive. That's probably where the shape-shifting stories come from." His eyes narrowed for a moment, thoughtfully. "I could almost be tempted to ask Guthrie for his information on us. But I don't think I'd like what he'd ask for in return."

"For the link you have with me to be broken? Would that really be fatal?"

He nodded solemnly. "To me, because I am *ky'sal* to you. Guthrie doesn't understand that. If his family gathered most of their data during the war, all they would have seen were mind links for the purpose of defense or interrogation." He rubbed his thumb over my fingers. "That's not a unique attribute. The hand that caresses can also kill."

"But fatal only to you?"

He sighed. "He told you there are ways to break a link. There are, though they're not without risk. But since I'd be an unwilling participant and since my focus would be on keeping you alive and not protecting myself...yes, fatal, but only to me."

"Then why—"

"Because, my angel, you are worth the risk to me."

"But the risk would be to both of us."

"Not if I died first."

I started to speak, stopped. This was something almost beyond my comprehension. A gentle warmth flowed through me. Sully, sensing my consternation, sending reassurance.

I promised you. I would never hurt you.

No, he wouldn't. He'd just make me wild, make me crazy, make me delirious with passion; make me angry, frustrated, and confused. He'd make love to me until the universe skewed on its axis. And he'd risk his life, if it came to that, to keep me alive.

But hurt me? No. I understood that now. I believed that now.

He slid his hand out from under mine. "Watch." His fingers curled into a loose fist, and only because I was looking for it did I see a faint spark of something silvery. He opened his hand slowly. A crisp angel of heart-stars card unfurled.

I took it. For the first time in several hours I saw the glimmer of a wicked Sully smile play across his lips. And saw something other than darkness in those infinite, obsidian eyes. There was a twinkle of starlight, an effervescent, silvery light. I knew what it was now.

All that I am is yours, ky'sara-*mine.*

Ky'sara. And to me, he is *ky'sal.* An almost unbreakable link. All that I am is his. All that he is is mine. A selfish, hedonistic desire to have in a time that was sure to get more troubled, more dangerous, more desperate. A time when jukors are born and Takas are dying. A time to fear.

Only fools boast they have no fears.

No. Only fools underestimate the power of love.

A former news reporter and retired private detective, Linnea Sinclair has managed to use all of her college degrees (journalism and criminology) but hasn't soothed the yearning in her soul to travel the galaxy. To that end, she's authored several science fiction and fantasy novels, including *Finders Keepers, Gabriel's Ghost,* and *An Accidental Goddess.* When not on duty with some intergalactic fleet, she can be found in Fort Lauderdale, Florida, with her husband and their two thoroughly spoiled cats. Fans can reach her through her Web site at *www.linneasinclair.com.*

Be sure not to miss

an accidental goddess

The next hot and exciting title from

Linnea Sinclair

Coming from Bantam Spectra in January 2006

Here's a special preview

an
accidental
goddess

On sale January 2006

It wasn't the first time Gillie had hazily regained consciousness flat on her back in sickbay, feeling stiff and out of sorts. And unable to account for a missing two or three hours. Pub-crawling did have its side effects.

But it was the first time she'd been unable to account for a missing two or three *hundred years*. Not even a week of pub-crawling could explain that.

Three hundred forty-two years, sixteen hours, Simon's voice stated clearly in her mind. *If you want to be absolutely accurate.*

She didn't. Her math skills had never been her strong point. And three hundred years was a close enough estimate to cause her stomach to do flip-flops in a way a bottle of Devil's Breath never had.

The possibility that she'd died flitted across her mind, though logically death wouldn't have thrown her inexplicably into the future. Even so, she thought it prudent to pull her Essence out of her physical Self and make a cursory examination of her own body on the diag-table. By all appearances, she was still short, blonde, and very much alive. The readout on the medi-stat confirmed the last part of her hastily conducted diagnosis. It detailed a few bumps and bruises as well as notations on a mild concussion, no doubt the source of her blistering headache.

A headache that wasn't the least bit helped by whatever heathen concoction was being pumped into her system through the round med-broche clamped to her wrist. Med-broches! Raheiran technology rarely used such invasive things. She longed to alter its feed rate but knew her mental tinkering would likely set off some alarm. She'd almost tripped a few when she'd awakened ten minutes ago, groggy and achy, then tried to spike into this sickbay's systems.

Impatience invariably leads to sloppy work, Simon had chastised.

Sloppy work, a bitch of a headache, and a reality that suddenly did not make sense.

How in the Seven Hells had she ended up three hundred years from her last conscious moment, flat on her back in some unknown space station's sickbay? With Simon in a similar state of disarray a few decks below.

The Fav'lhir.

Ah, yes. Small matter of a large warship intent on her destruction. Obviously, the Fav hadn't succeeded. Though something *had* happened.

They're vicious and powerful, Simon, but they don't have time-travel capabilities. Neither do we. Someone or something else pulled us here. Wherever "here" was. That much she ought to find out.

She stepped away from her diag-table and peeked around the corner of the small room. Felt foolish and could hear Simon's wry chuckle. No one could see her.

At least, no one other than Simon, who, from his tone, was very aware she'd pulled out of her Self to explore her surroundings. *Have a care, My Lady. You were injured.*

We've more serious things to consider than my few aches and pains. There were two other patients in the sickbay in much worse shape than she was. She didn't know them; there'd been no one on her ship when the Fav had attacked, other than Simon and herself. The girl on the diag-bed was too young to be part of the squadron she'd worked with in the Khalaran Fleet. Almost automatically, Gillie touched their Essences as she walked by. Then she sidestepped quickly—and unnecessarily—as a thin man in a blue lab coat hurried past and into the corridor.

She followed him and for the next fifteen minutes was thoroughly astounded, and more than a little disconcerted, by what she saw.

Wide corridors were filled with people in various modes of dress, from the utilitarian freighter-crew shipsuits to more exotic costumes with flowing skirts and elaborate fringed shawls. She heard all three Khalaran dialects and a few languages that were harder to identify. Rim world tongues, most likely, clipped and rapid in their sound.

She raised her eyebrows at the anti-grav pallets trailing behind a group of dockworkers, surprised by the pallets' advanced configuration. Raised her eyebrows further at the state-of-the-art holovid news kiosks and station diagrams near the lift banks. Those she studied carefully, listening to the chatter around her—tech talk about scanner arrays and enviro grids. That matched what she saw on the diagram suspended three-dimensionally out from the bulkhead.

The Khalaran Confederation, with her assistance, had just been developing the technology to create a deep-space station the likes of which she looked at now. At least, they had been a day ago.

Correction: three hundred and forty-two years ago.

Yet it wasn't this jump in technology that bothered her. Nor this space structure bristling with unexpected weapons and sensors and databanks. Nor her headache. Nor the stiffness in her left shoulder, the result of her sudden collision with the bulkhead when the Fav'lhir ship had exploded a little too close for comfort off her starboard side.

Even the unexplained missing three hundred and some-odd years failed to bother her. Or the fact that—in those three hundred and some-odd years—there'd been no other Raheiran advisors in this sector.

Given her people's minimal intervention policy, that was one of the few things that made sense.

No, none of those things bothered her at all.

What really bothered her was something she heard in the corridor chatter, something she viewed on the news kiosks and station diagrams. And finally, something she saw as she stood before the temple's double-doored entrance, shaking her head in disbelief.

What really bothered Gillaine Davré was that during her three-hundred-and-some-odd-year absence, the damned Khalar had gone on a shrine-building kick, and made her into a deity.

Simon? There's a temple with my name on it! But I'm not—

It appears they think you are, My Lady.

Oh, hell. Oh, damn. This wasn't a minor error in alien protocol: a wrong phrase, an inelegant gesture misinterpreted. This was a mistake. A big one that encompassed an entire culture. Gillie shuddered at the ramifications. *We have to get away from here. Now.*

Now is not possible, I fear.

When?

Three weeks, perhaps less. There's much damage to repair.

There'll be worse damage if they find out who I am!

Calm down, Gillaine Kiasidira. There's no reason they should. Just try to avoid contact with any crystal and, of course, any itinerant witches or sorcerers.

The Khalar aren't mageline.

Then we'll have no problems, will we? Just be your usual charming self for the next few weeks and no one will know a goddess walks among them.

I'm not a goddess!

Nor are you seriously injured. Therefore, if you don't return to your Self rather quickly that medical officer trying to wake you may start running tests you won't like.

Damn!

Rynan Makarian frowned at the irritatingly incomplete data on his desk screen and knew it was all his fault. It had been four months since he'd been given the command to establish a Fleet presence on Cirrus One and secure it for the Project. Station systems were still far from optimal. *Cirrus One* was far from optimal—the station had passed its prime well over eighty-five years ago.

"Give it to Mack. He'll fix it," someone in Fleet Defense and Logistics no doubt had said.

It wouldn't have been the first time it had been said, either. He knew his reputation for unerring efficiency preceded him. It had bestowed upon him the rank of Admiral in the Khalaran's newly organized Fifth Fleet at the unlikely age of forty-three. And bestowed upon him the derelict monstrosity known as Cirrus One, to rehab into a usable headquarters. And, eventually, serve as something even more important than that: as the primary terminus for the critical Rim Gate Project.

That project, more than Cirrus One, had drawn him off the bridge of the *Vedritor* and ensconced him behind a desk—a well-dented, slightly rusted desk—at forty-three.

But it was Cirrus One that took up the majority of his time. Yet time was the one thing he lacked. He had little more than a month in which to get his HQ fully operational and secure. Missing supplies, incomplete data, and delayed support staff notwithstanding.

He rested his elbows on that same battered desk and leaned his forehead against his fists. Damn. There was a wisdom in imperfection. He saw that clearly now. What was that adage Lady Kiasidira's priests used to comfort the misguided? *We are all in a continuing process of growth. There are no mistakes. Only lessons.*

Cirrus One was one hell of a lesson.

Had he allowed himself a few mistakes in his career, he might well still be on the bridge of the *Vedritor*. A mere senior captain, not an admiral with an impeccable reputation to solve the unsolvable. To rectify the—

His intercom trilled. He tapped the flashing icon and leaned back in his chair. "Makarian."

A familiar thin face wavered, solidified on the screen. Doc Janek, his chief medical officer. His blue lab coat bore the *Vedritor*'s insignia. Like many things Mack had requested, Fifth Fleet uniforms were still "in transit." As supply routes went, Cirrus One wasn't in the middle of nowhere. It was just the last exit before it.

"Admiral, you asked to be notified. Our visitor from that damaged freighter's awake."

Yet one more thing to plague his schedule with delays: an unauthorized ship with an unconscious pilot. An image flashed through Mack's mind: a pale-haired young woman in nondescript spacer grays lying awkwardly on the decking, just behind the pilot's chair. Emergency lighting had tinged the small bridge with glaring shades of red, casting eerie shadows over her small, still form. Another smuggler, he'd thought at that moment, whose ambitions had far exceeded her ship's weaponry.

He had a studied dislike for smugglers, yet had felt it would be a shame if this one died. He'd caught little more than her profile as the med-techs had lifted her onto an antigrav stretcher. But it had been enough for him to mentally tag her as beautiful, before he was even aware he'd done so.

That wasn't like him. It was unprofessional, judgmental. She was nothing more than a temporary annoyance.

But she was beautiful. It made the job of questioning her a bit less unpleasant.

"On my way." He slapped off the intercom, threw

one more frustrating glance at the inadequate, nonsensical data and strode from his office.

The sights and sounds of Cirrus One assaulted him immediately. He'd thought by now he'd be used to them. Had the sights and sounds been continually repetitive, he probably would be.

But there was always something new. Or rather, there was always *something*. His office was a few steps from the Main Atrium. Raucous laughter barked out from a level or two below, or possibly above, as Mack stepped into the open corridor. A man and a woman in the blue shipsuits of a starfreighter crew leaned against a wide metal pylon on his left. They were locked in a passionate embrace, oblivious to his presence. And oblivious to the snickers of a trio of adolescent boys in various stages of sartorial rebellion loping past, their long skirts catching between their gangly legs.

Mack shook his head, sent a mental plea to the Gods for understanding. And patience. He missed the orderly routine of the *Vedritor*.

There was a loud whoop, a high-pitched screech. His gaze automatically jerked to the right. A flash of bright yellow and blue hurtled quickly uplevel through the atrium's center.

His hand automatically tapped the intercom badge on his chest. "Makarian to Ops."

"Ops. Lieutenant Tobias."

"I thought we'd solved the parrot problem."

"I thought we had too, sir."

"I just left my office." He sidestepped a merchant whose balding head barely topped the bolts of cloth stacked in his arms. Evidently someone was getting hard-goods deliveries. Where in hell were those uniforms? "Main north, Tobias. Heading uplevel. The problem's not solved."

"Logged and noted, sir."

He tapped off his badge. Fleet crewmembers, whose

uniforms showed mixed insignias, nodded respectfully as he passed. Stationers and freighter crew, whose clothing and demeanor showed an unholy mixture of unknown origin, simply ignored him. Janek's sickbay was at D5-South—five levels down, opposite section of the ring. He headed for the stairs. Cirrus One's lifts had been known to ignore him, too.

The lanky CMO turned from the medi-stat panel when Mack stepped through the sliding doorway. "She's in Exam Four."

A second sliding door—this one ceased opening at the halfway point. Mack squeezed through sideways, after Janek.

The young woman on the diag-bed had her knees drawn up under the silver thermo-sheet, her arms wrapped around them. There was a flush of color on her cheeks, a slight curve on her lips. And an engaging, almost challenging tilt to her chin.

She was most definitely beautiful. But young. Couldn't be any more than twenty-five years old, though sickbay's analytics transed to him earlier had stated early thirties. Something more than her youthfulness didn't fit the smuggler's profile as he knew it. He couldn't pinpoint what it was but then, his mind seemed very reluctant to focus on business at the moment.

Janek moved to her bedside. She smiled, then her gaze found Mack.

"This is Admiral Makarian, commander of Fifth Fleet on Cirrus," his CMO was saying, but Mack only half listened. The other half of him was unprofessionally captivated by the color of the young woman's eyes.

Green, yet lavender. Her eyes widened slightly at his introduction. He assumed the cause of her surprise was his age—he was the youngest admiral in Fleet history to date—or his uniform. His shirt, like Janek's lab coat, still had the *Vedritor*'s insignia. The bars decorating his breast pocket showed only the three for senior captain.

His admiral's bars, like the requested uniforms, had also not yet materialized. Now he wished they had. For some reason, he wanted to look his best in front of her. He shook off his uncharacteristic self-consciousness. She was just a smuggler. She was—

"Gillaine Davré." She leaned forward, extended one hand. No salute. Therefore, she wasn't military, or even ex-military.

He took her hand, got a closer look at those eyes. They were an odd combination of green and lavender. Green with decidedly lavender flecks. His fingers tightened around hers. A man could lose his soul in eyes like those. The direction of his thoughts jolted him. Quickly, he cleared his throat, refocused. Put a firm tone in his voice. "Miselle Davré? Or is it captain?"

"Captain, technically. But mostly just Gillie."

He released her hand. She had a voice almost as intriguing as her eyes. Firm, yet with a sultry undercurrent. He imagined her laugh—

He had to stop imagining. He didn't imagine. He never imagined.

He stepped back, clasped his hands behind his waist. "My CMO tells me your injuries aren't serious. Your ship has significant damage, however."

The exam room's utilitarian overheads were harsh, bright, but their light played through her short, pale hair in a mixture of silver and gold like moonlight and starlight. There was an almost ethereal beauty about her. Mack felt as if he knew her, but from a dream.

He halted this additional imaginative mental wandering. "Your ship also has no sanctioned Confederation ID. I need to know, Captain, just who you are. What you're doing here."

"Recuperating in your sickbay is what I'm doing here, Admiral." The edge of her mouth quirked upwards slightly. "It's not as if Cirrus One was my intended destination."

Obviously, neither his rank nor his tone had managed to intimidate her. He tried to keep the frown off his face. She wasn't military. His infamous frown would be wasted on her. "Where were you headed?"

"The Ziami Quadrant."

"Ziami?" His frown was back. In a huntership as powerful as the *Vedritor,* that would be four months and two jumpgates. In a small freighter like hers, that could take eight months, maybe a year, if the ion storms kicked in around the Sultana Drifts again. What in hell would a young woman be doing in that Godsforsaken quadrant? Cirrus was bad enough.

"My family runs a depot in Ziami. When we trade here, we run our ships under a Khalaran Kemmon flag. I was headed home, running empty. I'd already archived my Confed clearances. However, if my ship's not too damaged, I should be able to pull them up for you."

That sounded reasonable. But Mack rarely accepted reasonable, especially in explanations without documentation that might concern one of the more volatile Khalaran states, such as one of the rim Kemmons. "Which Kemmon do you trade with?"

She shrugged. "Depends on the commodity and the destination."

"No, Captain. *This* run."

"Not the Fav."

"The Fav'lhir and their Kemmons haven't plagued us for over three hundred years, thank the Lady. That wasn't my question." Yet in a way, it was. He'd watched her face when she'd answered, noted the dislike when she'd said the name of the longtime enemy of the Khalar. Not that the emotion couldn't be a sham. But she didn't strike him as a Fav'lhir agent. Plus, he'd seen her ship. That definitely wasn't up to Fav standards.

"I had a transfer for a Kemmon-Drin tri-hauler," she

said after a long moment. "Then I had some personal business to take care of. I may have overstayed my clearances."

So that was it. He relaxed slightly, matching a fact to his suspicious feeling. Now he knew why she'd avoided answering his questions. Not quite a smuggler. A rim-trader, and that's what he was sure she was, could have any type of interesting "personal business," from a genuine love affair to an illegal trade in drugs and weapons. Or, more likely, rune stones. Life-crystals. Most of which were probably fakes but willingly snatched up in the market, as anything even remotely connected with the Tridivinian Gods, or Lady Kiasidira, always was.

"When do you intend to release her, Doc?"

"I want another scan of her concussion. An hour."

"Your ship's in a repair bay on D11-South, Captain." He tried to ignore the color of her eyes, the softness of her mouth as she leaned against the diag-bed's pillows. Straightening his shoulders, he reminded himself that he wasn't in sickbay to notice such things, but to get answers. "You can show me those Drin clearances in one hour."

She seemed about to say something, but then only nodded and smiled.

The exam room door opened completely this time. He took it as a signal that his departure was advisable, as well as an omen to try the lifts. Either way, he had to get out of her exam room before the decidedly unprofessional imagination he didn't have got the best of him.

Ops Command 2 was on Upper 6-North. Or rather, it was being slowly integrated back into its rightful section, as Mack viewed it, of Upper 6-North. Eventually, his office would be there as well. The previous administrators of Cirrus had firmly declared their priorities when they'd appropriated that square footage, as well as a large portion of Ops, and transformed the space into a casino gaming parlor. One of his first projects had been the reclamation of that space, back to more functional—at least in his opinion—utilization.

For now he could deal with his temporary office. Getting a real operations and command center running was more important. The Rim Gate Project would depend on them.

He headed for the left side of Ops' lowest level. A stocky red-haired woman monitoring enviro readouts glanced his way briefly, nodded. She was one of the station's civilian techies, in a wrinkled orange jumpsuit that showed no insignia. Another orange-jumpsuited man leaned over an engineering console beyond her. He was deep in argument with someone on station intercom.

Tobias was at the long communications console, his muscular frame shoved into a chair, his thick fingers moving quickly over the screen pads. Like Janek, Fitch Tobias was a former *Vedritor* officer. One of nine who'd volunteered to follow Rynan "Make It Right" Makarian to Cirrus One. Ten Fleet officers from the *Vedri* plus one hundred and seventy-five from other Fleet ships and postings comprised Mack's current staff, with Tobias as his second-in-command. One hundred eighty-five of his people versus five hundred and fifty—give or take a couple dozen illegals—longtime residents of Cirrus. And their parrots.

That his staff was outnumbered by an eclectic, somewhat eccentric civilian population was a fact Mack rarely forgot. But that wasn't his only problem. He rested one hip against the comm console, crossed his arms over his chest.

"Still working on the avian invaders, sir," Tobias said, without raising his close-shaved head.

"I'm not here about the parrots. I've been trying to make some sense out of this past week's PSLs." Especially the ones in the Runemist sector. That's where his patrols had found the intriguing Gillaine Davré. Who occupied his thoughts at the moment only because of her ship's location in Runemist, of course.

Tobias shoved his heel down on the chair's deck lock release. He pushed the chair to his right, slid down the track to the empty station at the secondary sensor screens. Fleet HQ on Cirrus had yet to officially open for business. Stations were understaffed. Everyone, including Mack, did double duty or more.

"This quadrant's known for unreliable Perimeter Sensor Logs. Sir," he said when Mack caught up with him.

"Agreed, Lieutenant. But this unreliable data was a bit too regular. Plus it came out of Runemist. If someone uncreative wanted to create sham unreliable data there, that's probably what it would look like."

"Like this, sir?" Tobias' screen flickered to life.

Mack leaned his palms on the edge of the console. "Like that."

The screens in Ops were better than the hastily constructed setup in his temporary office. They were on a direct link to the main data banks. His office, well ... the parrots soaring up and down the atrium core were probably a more effective means of data transport than what he worked with.

He saw now what had been missing from the data on his screen. And didn't like at all what he saw.

The toe of his boot found the deck lock tab at the base of Tobias's chair. He unlocked it. "Get me the *Vedri* on high priority scramble."

Tobias pushed the chair to his left, sailed back to communications. "Hailing."

"I'll take it on your screen when you've reached her."

It took ten minutes—he absently timed it on Ops' main clock—before Iona Cardiff's face flickered onto the screen. "*Vedritor*. Comm Officer Cardiff."

Cardiff was second shift. At least, she had been, four months ago. He didn't think the *Vedri*'s new captain, his former first officer, would have changed things that quickly.

He was right.

"Tranferring your call to Captain Adler's office right now, sir."

"Admiral. What can I do for you?" Steffan Adler was a short, wiry man a few years older than Mack. They'd served together for almost seven years. Adler had learned Rynan Makarian rarely made social calls. Mack could see Adler's hand poised over an open datapad, ready to take notes.

"I've got PSLs out of Runemist I don't like. We have three patrol ships posted in that sector. Need you to take a closer look."

"What do you think I might find?"

"Someone, or something, that shouldn't be there and is doing a barely passable job of covering their tracks."

"Smugglers?"

"That's my best guess. Patrol may have brought in one of their friends earlier. Says her name's Davré." Mack permitted his imagination to resurrect, briefly, Gillaine Davré's image. But only because he was discussing her in a professional manner.

"What was she running?"

"It appears she might have been running *from* someone. Her ship took considerable damage to the starboard side. She's sitting in sickbay right now."

"Is her ship in our files?"

"I won't know until I access her clearance. Her ship was in full shutdown when we towed her in, a few hours ago. We have no ID on it, or her. But she was found not far from my suspicious PSLs."

Adler glanced down at his console. "Receiving your data now, sir. We're on it. I'll report back as soon as we're in range."

The screen flickered to black, then filled with Cirrus One's logo.

There were fifteen minutes yet before Janek would release Davré from sickbay. Mack still had work to do before he met with her. He took Ops' internal stairway up to Ops Main and the primary scanner console.

Stationmaster Johnna Hebbs' dark scowl greeted him

as he unlocked an empty chair and slid it to an open scanner station. She leaned against the command sling, watching him with undisguised disdain. Amazing how this woman could be so beautiful yet so unattractive at the same time.

Hebbs was old guard, second in command when Stationmaster Quigley had controlled Cirrus One for the Cirrus Quadrant Port Authority. The Port Authority was a branch of the Khalaran Department of Commerce and not known for its enthusiasm for the Khalaran military. But in this instance, CQPA agreed with Fleet that Quigley, and his gambling operation, had to go. They insisted, however, that Mack retain Hebbs as stationmaster because she knew Cirrus. And because she was popular with stationers. The tall brunette was popular with *male* stationers, Mack had learned. Female stationers knew better than to cross her.

Mack acknowledged the stationmaster's tight nod with one of his own, then turned his attention to the console. He brought up the logs again. Frowned. Something was definitely going on in Runemist and at a time he could least afford interruptions. Three jumps out from the major space lanes, the Cirrus Quadrant was too remote for such unusual activity. The Runemist sector, with no habitable worlds and only a few derelict miners' rafts, even more so.

No one came through Runemist unless she had a damned good reason. She was either looking for trouble, or running from it.

The intriguing Captain Gillaine Davré had better be prepared with some very good answers to his questions, and documentation to back it all up. Or else Mack intended to make sure her troubles in Runemist would be the least of her problems.

After all, she'd just added to his.